THE BONDS THAT TIE

Forced Bonds

Also by J Bree

The Bonds That Tie Series

Broken Bonds
Savage Bonds
Blood Bonds
Forced Bonds
Tragic Bonds
Unbroken Bonds

The Mortal Fates Series

Novellas
The Scepter
The Sword
The Helm

The Trilogy
The Crown of Oaths and Curses
The Throne of Blood and Honor

THE BONDS THAT TIE

Forced
Bonds

J BREE

J BREE

J BREE

Prologue

GRYPHON

The taste of a lie is like nothing else on Earth.

Like ash on the tongue but more acrid, with the promise that if it were a smell, it would be pungent and putrid and every other disgusting adjective you can think of.

An unspoken truth is a very different beast.

It's not a taste or a smell. It's not something you can really put your finger on, not something I can see on someone just by looking at them.

It's a feeling, deep in my gut, that something is missing.

When I walk into the security room, I find Sawyer Benson sitting behind a computer in his underwear with a gouge above his eye and blood still running down his face.

Gray is standing behind him looking as though he walked out of a dust storm with the amount of dirt covering him. They both turn to look at me and, if I hadn't already picked up on the feeling, their faces give away everything.

A smirk stretches over my lips and I shrug at Sawyer. "There's no point trying to hide whatever it is. If you don't tell me, I'll hack into your brain and get it the harder, more painful way."

I say it as a joke, expecting him to roll his eyes and snap back at me with some sort of sarcastic joke, but his face only hardens as he gets defensive.

Something is really fucking wrong here.

He looks up at Gray and then back at me, his jaw flexing like he's grinding his teeth. When he answers, it's as though the words are being dragged out of him. "I'm showing you this because I know that my sister is both innocent and a victim. I know that you'll do the right thing here and think things through with your actual brain and not make rash decisions. Don't make me regret it, Shore."

He doesn't really need to say anything else because there's only one thing he could be talking about, but even as I take in his words, they don't make any fucking sense to me.

I glanced down at him, because it couldn't possibly be Sage. The traitor in our haven couldn't possibly be the soft-hearted, sad little Gifted girl that my Bonded clicked with the moment my TacTeam had dragged her home to us all. Then the footage starts playing, and there's no denying it.

She walks over to Dara Smythe and talks to her for a minute, distracting her enough that the Shield turns her back, and then she strikes, dragging the knife across the other girl's throat without the slightest bit of hesitation, even as the blood spurts and pours out of the wound.

The tension fills my chest cavity so quickly that my heart feels as though it's pumping acid through my veins.

My voice comes out lower than normal, raspier, like I'm dying of thirst and not just fucking horrified at what the hell is going on here. "Oli just left to go to her."

The silence that comes after my words is damning and my voice is nothing but rage this time around as I bark, "Show me where my Bonded is. Show me that she's alive and *here* and untouched. *Right now*, Benson, before I reach into your brain and ruin you."

Security room now, not a request, I send to North directly as I check in with Oli quickly. She's calm, happy, and doesn't feel any danger around her. Her bond would react if there were something wrong… wouldn't it?

Sawyer rolls his eyes at my threat and snaps back at me, "The medical examination rooms don't have cameras! That decision was made for a variety of reasons, including the fallout of that time that your Bonded was being carried around half-naked by you lot and Draven had a fucking coronary about there being footage of her. Can you imagine what would happen if we had a camera on her while she was getting an IUD in? Fuck, he'd actually explode and take the town out."

The desire to choke the sarcastic little fuck out is so strong that my arm lifts and my hand reaches out before I can stop myself, my bond flaring to life inside of me and becoming another problem to deal with. It might not behave like Oli's or either of the Dravens', but it's still strong enough to wipe him out without much input from me if it really thinks my Bonded is in danger.

It's starting to feel that way.

"This is not the time for your fucking lip—"

"I know it's not, it's called a coping mechanism! My fucking sister, the person I've known and loved the longest and would trust with anything in my life, just killed someone for what I'm pretty sure was the first time ever. I mean, the same girl who puked her guts up at the thought of dissecting a frog in science class just slit Dara's throat… Dara, the kid we used to steal champagne from our asshole parents with and get drunk off of three sips as middle school degenerates. None of this makes sense, Shore, and I'm *freaking the fuck out here.*"

Deep breath.

I check in, but North is still working his way towards us

and Oli is still cracking jokes, Gabe and Bassinger within arm's reach of her. That barely helps to keep the adrenaline pulsing through my veins under control, my entire body practically vibrating with the need to go after any threat to my Bonded or our family.

Even if that threat is someone we all trusted so much.

Gray leans forward and mutters something quietly to Sawyer, gesturing at areas on the screen, but I can't see anything there worth pointing out. I step forward to look there too, but the lines of coding on the screen mean nothing to me.

I give Sawyer a very pointed look and he grimaces at me. "There's nothing in the system to say we're being watched. There's nothing here to show there was a security breach on any level, except the Shield being... taken out."

"So, what you're saying is that your sister is the only sign of treachery here? And that she's currently in a room with my Bonded, who has no idea we've been betrayed by her, giving her the element of surprise that she just used to murder Dara?"

He hesitates.

He fucking hesitates.

Gray darts in front of him, as though the Telekenetic has a chance of stopping me when I murder his boyfriend-slash-fellow-Bond-Group-Member, and holds up his hands right as Sawyer snaps, "I'm not saying my sister would hurt your Bonded, but whoever the fuck is in her head right now, because there is *no other explanation* for this, might still be in there… waiting to get Oli alone. Get them apart and get Sage isolated until we can figure this out. I *will* figure this out."

Gray takes a deep breath as he sees the murderous rage on my face simmer down a little. Sawyer has just saved his own life.

He curses under his breath and leans in his chair to look past Gray at me. "North is here. Any chance you could stop him from setting his creatures on me? I'm not opening the door for him until you convince me."

I'm not convincing him of shit.

I lean past him to hit the button for the door, listening to him cuss me out under his breath. When North stalks in, I don't say a word to him, just gesture at the screen where the image of Sage's knife buried in Dara's throat is still up.

"Where the fuck is Oleander right now?"

The words aren't even fully out of his mouth before he's reaching out to her. *Where are you?*

I glance over at him, of course he wouldn't ask any questions of Sawyer in this moment. It doesn't matter that he's been the greatest asset to the Sanctuary outside of our own Bond Group, but everything has changed in the blink of an eye.

I can feel Oli's exasperation, and I cut in before she

does something unintentionally dangerous right now, *Oli, who is with you right now? Don't say anything out loud or react. You need to be discreet.*

Unease fills her, clearly thrumming down the connection to all of her Bonded. I can feel the ripple of irritation run through Bassinger, but he stays out of it for now, either sensing that shit is going down or just through dumb luck.

I'm in the medical center, exactly where North told me to be. I have Gabe and Atlas with me. Kieran, Sage, and Felix are too. I'm safe.

I share another look with North but he's already got his phone out, his fingers flying over the screen as he calls for backup here. "I'm getting her out of there now."

Sawyer starts to run his mouth at him and Gray gets between them both, but I'm too busy trying to discreetly get into Sage's brain from this distance without alerting her, or anyone who might be in there, to take much notice.

Tell me now. Whatever it is, tell me now.

If I tell her, she won't believe me. Fuck, if Sawyer had just told me, I wouldn't have believed him either.

But I can show her. The moment I do, I feel her shut down, the complete and total freakout that causes her to just empty her brain out the way her Neuro father taught her to. It's a blessing because only her Bonded will be able to tell that she's losing her shit right now.

Gray tugs Sawyer away from North and my eyes meet the Death Dealer's across the room, a million unsaid words crossing between us.

North's eyes flicker to black and then back to blue, a momentary slip of his control, and he says in a dangerous tone, "Nox is closest. I'm sending him to her now."

FORCED BONDS

OLI

My chest is on fire. My lungs are screaming for air and my heart is thumping inside my rib cage at a frenzied pace, but I can't force any semblance of calm into myself as I stare across the room at Atlas, his eyes hard but steady on mine.

I can't look at Sage right now, not with the sight of her killing Dara still clear in my head even though the image Gryphon had sent me has faded away. Atlas' eyes bore into mine, his own anger at the betrayal of my closest friend simmering just under the surface, but to say anything right now, with two of her Bonds here with us, is a nightmare sort of situation.

Things could escalate so freaking quickly.

Especially considering that Felix is healing up the scrapes and bruises all over me, so his hands are directly on my skin. Kieran is a highly trained TacTeam operative who has more training and skills than the three of us combined… plus there's the small fact that he's a Transporter and could just disappear with her the moment we say anything.

There's a small part of me that wants him to, that wants him to get her the hell out of here before the consequences of her actions catch up with her because, well, she's my best friend. Does that make me a terrible person?

Maybe, but the small voice in the back of my mind definitely crosses that line for me, whispering that my bond could take care of all of this for us.

I don't want it to though, and… strangely, it's quiet in my gut, as though the feast of the Charge's soul was enough to put it into a short slumber.

Does that mean I'm safe in this room right now and this is all just some huge misunderstanding? Or does it mean that I've finally got a blind spot, a small mistake that my bond has made to let a Resistance spy close to us all?

My head feels as though it's about to explode with all of the unknowns and betrayals. Why did it have to be *Sage,* of all people?

Felix's voice snaps me out of my spiraling thoughts. "Oli, your heart rate is insane right now. Take a breath. Is this a panic attack because your bond came out or something else? Gabe, grab her some water, and, Atlas, you might want to get your shirt off to start a transfer. She needs *something*."

My eyes snap back over to them both, but neither of them move at Felix's commands or attempt to answer him.

Gabe stares at me and I blink back at him, hoping he can read enough of my face to keep his cool here and not question any of the crazy that's happening right now.

I've told him what's going on, just stay calm. We're on our way.

I swallow at the tense sound of Gryphon's voice in my mind, but I can't find the words to send anything back to him. I can't figure out how to address any of this without breaking the fuck down.

Sage can't be a spy.

She just fucking can't.

"You look really sick, Oli, should we... get you back to your place to rest?" Sage says in her same sweet and caring tone that I'm now doubting and reading into like she's a criminal mastermind, because *what the actual fuck* is going on here?

I clear my throat and say, my voice sounding all sorts of messed up, "It's— I'm fine. I think it's my bond acting up, nothing I can't handle."

Sage gives me a concerned look back, empathy and warmth flooding out of her in my direction like it always does, and my chest tightens even more. Kieran frowns at me and glances at my Bonds, and the lines around his mouth only deepen. He knows something is up but before he can call us out on it, the cavalry arrives.

Thank fuck.

I feel him before I see it.

My eyes flick down to the tendrils of smoke streaming in from under the door, but I look away quickly, hoping no one else notices it.

Of course, Felix does.

His hands slip away from me as he stands, moving towards Sage. He only makes it a single step before the smoke floods the space, a tendril curling around his ankles and stopping him from any further movement. He lets out a yelping sound, like he was thinking coherent words but the fear of the nightmare smoke dried up his rational thoughts, but it's too late. The smoke wraps around Kieran and Sage, pulling them both apart and rendering them completely immobile. Kieran is frowning but not resisting, his eyes snapping around the room at us all and taking note of the way that the smoke is targeting his Bond Group alone.

When he turns to me, I look away, not wanting him to see my own reaction to what is happening here.

Sage, who is clearly panicking and making my heart hurt even more in my chest with her wide eyes and shaking voice says, "Oli, what the hell is this? What is going on?

Why is North—"

The door opens and Nox steps through, one of his creatures at his feet in its savage Doberman form, its sharp and deadly teeth exposed as it snarls at the entire room, and drawls in his most acidic and dangerous tone, "Not North, though he's on his way with a lot of questions for you, Benson. You might want to start working out your answers, and quickly, because betraying us all in full view of the security cameras wasn't the brightest thing you've ever done."

"What the fuck is that supposed to mean, Draven?" Felix snaps, still struggling against the smoke, but Kieran just stares at him with cold eyes.

"Let me go. I'm going to North now."

Nox scoffs at him and steps across the room, circling Sage as more of his creatures take form amongst the smoke and fall into line around him. Brutus rumbles under my ear, not as a warning, but as a comfort to me so I know he's still there and ready to step in if I need it. I have no doubt he will, not a single fleeting doubt has ever filled me about his loyalty to me, and I raise a hand up to pet him, even as it shakes just a little.

I can't look at Sage right now.

I'll either break down or start screaming.

Nox takes another step into the center of the room, the smoke thickening until my eyes have to shift to see clearly through it. He answers Kieran, "I just said he's on his way and that none of you are going anywhere. If I had things my way, you'd all be locked up until Gryph can sift through every little second of your lives and find out whether it's just Benson, or if you're all in on this. I thought more of you than this, Black, but nothing here will really surprise me. Not even you betraying us all—"

Sage makes a noise like she's struggling for air, but it's more of an outraged sort of thing, and I still can't force myself to look her way yet.

Kieran makes his own sound of outrage and strains against the ropes of smoke, even though they don't budge. "Betraying you? What the fuck is that supposed to mean? Just because you have your own little bullshit mission here, trying to psych out your Bond because you're absolutely fucked—"

Oh, I don't like that.

Neither does my bond, waking up finally to the absolute mess we're in, but when I poke at it, expecting a whispered threat or *something*, it's silent. Wary and watchful, but silent.

I mean, I know that we have our problems, a whole fucking pile of problems. But they're our problems to deal with. Someday. Maybe.

They're not up for public discussion.

Atlas' voice is sharp as it cuts through the haze and

through Kieran's tirade. "She murdered our Shield. Sawyer just showed the evidence of it to North and Gryphon. This isn't some inside job, Black. This is us keeping everyone in the Sanctuary safe, not just our friends and family. If her brother was the one to start this, then there's absolutely nothing you can say to Draven about this being a witch hunt. Besides, look at what this is doing to Oli... If you believe nothing else, do you think I'd be standing here and letting him do this to her if I hadn't just seen Sage *murder* that woman myself?"

There's a stunned sort of silence, and then I startle at the booming sounds of doors being slammed open and dozens of sets of boots stomping through the medical center, signaling that the cavalry has finally arrived. I take my first real, deep breath and then another one.

Still, Sage doesn't try to defend herself or speak a word.

Is she just too scared to try? Does she know that Gryphon is listening through me, his gift flooding me and watching everything that's happening here and waiting for a sign that maybe she is a willing participant in... all of this?

Or is she waiting for me, her best friend and most loyal confidant, to defend her and get her the hell out of this mess like I always have?

I want to be sick.

North and Gryphon step into the room, a group of Tac personnel behind them, and I move over to them instinctively, seeking out my Bonded to get me through this cluster-fuck of a situation. North catches my face in his hands and tilts my head back until he's staring into the black voids of my eyes. Whatever he sees there, he doesn't like, and his mouth hardens even more.

He leans forward just a little, his brother's smoke still obscuring us both from everyone else's view as he murmurs to me quietly, "Go home and get some rest. I'll take care of this. Stay with Atlas and Gabe and just leave it to me to handle, Bonded."

"Oli?" Sage says, her voice trembling a little. Even though it hurts me, I finally look up at her and, thanks to my void-like eyes, I can see her clear as day.

She looks terrified.

The words tumble out of me as I scramble out of the door, "I'll be back, Sage. Just... just answer all of their questions. We'll figure it out."

It only occurs to me as Gabe and Atlas each flank either side of me that Nox had put himself between the other Bond Group and I.

As we step out together in the afternoon sun, I feel the

flutters of anxiety deep in my stomach. The destruction from the Resistance soldiers is everywhere around us. Cars are overturned, craters are in the once freshly paved roads, and debris littering the ground everywhere.

I try not to get upset looking at everything that North and his family have worked so hard for us all to have that's now been destroyed for nothing but the Resistance's whims and sadistic games. It's all so fucking pointless, and the ripples of irritation tug at my bond in my chest that has gone back into its dormant and resting state, as though I actually want the cantankerous bitch to wake up.

I still can't figure out why it's sleeping.

Atlas wraps an arm around my shoulders to tuck me into his side closely while Gabe takes my other hand.

"Everything is going to be okay, Sweetness," Atlas murmurs into my hair as we start off, but I don't have anything to say back to that.

I know that we're going to survive it. I know that North and Gryphon are going to go into full damage control mode and fix the leaks that caused today to happen. But as I blink away tears, I can't help but feel as though things are *not* going to be okay.

Sage was the person who kept me going here when everyone hated me. She'd loved me and accepted me from the moment we'd sat together in the dining hall, without question. Our mutual 'outsider' labels and social shunning had been the draw, but it was the sassy and strong heart of her that won me over.

If I lose her, I won't be okay.

The panicked flutter in my chest starts up again, stealing my breath. It's as though we're once again moments away from our Bond Group being torn apart. The little bit of peace I've found here in the Sanctuary is gone with one swipe from the Resistance. They've just taken a swing at us and, through Sage, I have taken a direct hit.

She's my best goddamn friend, and if she's been a spy this whole time… I can't even process that. I don't even want to try.

I can't find the words to say this to either of them though, not without causing them both to go on some sort of killing spree in my honor. I swallow roughly around the lump in my throat and duck my head in an attempt to block out the carnage as we make our way over to the house.

All I want is a hot shower and a bed to hide in for the rest of the day, *any* bed really, I'm not fussy. We fall into an uncomfortable silence, but it's clear they can both tell I'm upset. Gabe's hand is tense in mine, and Atlas continues to pull me closer into his body as we walk, as though he will somehow be able to absorb all of my worries and fears if he can get close enough. I can't find the words to comfort either of them.

When we make our way past North's offices and the

dining hall, Gabe squeezes my hand gently before pulling us all to a stop. I keep my eyes down and he squeezes my hand again to get my attention.

"Look around, Bond. Everything really is going to be okay here."

I glance up and look in the direction that he's pointing to find a long line of TacTeam operatives and civilians surrounding the front steps of the dining hall.

Everyone is helping out to move away the debris and rubble that is blocking the path and the doors, while the chef and kitchen staff are standing out front with trestle tables, all of them covered with enough food to feed an army.

There's a group of children standing around laughing and giggling with disposable containers of something hot and delicious looking in their hands, munching away on crusty bread and chatting amongst themselves.

All of the adults around them are covered in dirt and dust, but have smiles on their faces where the kids can see them. Whenever the children look away, you can see their parents grimacing and looking concerned at the state of things, but they're all coming together to set things right.

Gabe holds my hand up to press a kiss to the back of it and murmurs quietly, "This place was never going to stay a secret for long, but I still think it's worth it. I still think keeping these people safe is worth it, Bond. We're exactly where we need to be. We're all safe here because of you."

I swallow again, my voice still trapped somewhere in my chest, but this time, I don't feel as if I'm being choked with guilt and terrible emotions.

As we head back off towards the house, Atlas offers to grab me something to eat as we pass the amazing smells from the dining hall, but I decline. I can't think about food right now, not with the memory of my bond munching on a soul in my gut still so fresh.

My stomach churns at the mere thought of it.

It's only as we're walking back up the stairs that I remember our water contamination issues and the fact that I'm still not allowed to take a shower. Tears fill my eyes again but I hastily swipe them away. I'm not going to work this hard to have my shit together only to lose it now over some goddamn hot water.

Gabe notices anyway and runs his thumb over mine, a silent show of support, and I give him a grimacing sort of smile back.

When Atlas finally gets his keys to work and swings open the front door, we find Sawyer and Gray sitting at the table together, waiting for us.

My heart drops to the floor.

Sawyer rolls his eyes at me and pokes a finger in my direction. "Don't look at me like that, Fallows. I'm here to fix this fucking mess, because we both know my sister didn't kill someone in cold blood."

My spine crumples and I slouch towards the table, throwing my arm out dramatically because, dammit, if now isn't the time to get dramatic, then I don't know when is. "If I hadn't seen it with my own eyes, I wouldn't have ever believed it either, Sawyer. But... How the hell are we going to explain it? I can't... fuck, what the hell are we going to do? I can't even blame North, Gryphon, or even Nox for being so forceful about this because... Dara was *murdered*. Someone needs to be held accountable, and if it's not Sage, then we need to figure out who it really is and we need to do it now."

He rolls his eyes at me all over again and pulls his laptop closer to himself, flicking a look at my Bonds, who are both watching us warily from the door like they're waiting for a moment to jump in and pry us away from each other.

I'm not worried about Sawyer.

I'm his best chance at getting Sage out of this and we both know it. I have no freaking clue how we're going to do it. There's a burning sort of guilt inside of me at the fact that I'm still not absolutely sure that she's innocent here, because I watched the knife slice through Dara's throat. But there's no way I'm not going to investigate every second of Sage's last movements until I'm sure either way.

She's my best friend, dammit!

I walk over to slump into one of the other chairs at the table, picking the opposite side just so I don't completely mess with my Bonds' overprotective natures. The last thing this situation needs is one of them going off. My bond is still silent in my chest in its weird dormant state. It is thoroughly freaking me out, but also that might not be such a bad thing right now.

Sawyer starts clicking away at his keyboard and speaks without bothering to look away from the screen. "Clearly, we need to figure out who it is, and not just because the fucking asshole needs to die for involving my sister in it. Dara was a huge loss, both personally and strategically, but there's a lot of other assets living inside these walls. Did you know that Unser is here now too? If he gets his throat slit while he's sleeping or something, then we're *fucked*. Not to mention Councilman Hannity and his family. Oh, and then, I don't know, your *entire* freaking Bond Group of overachievers and void-eye savages. If someone got the jump on you, then we'd have serious fucking problems."

Atlas scoffs and walks over to pull out the chair next to mine, perching on the edge of it with a kinetic sort of energy still thrumming through him, as though he's preparing himself to dive at either one of them if they look like a threat to me. Gabe is less concerned, probably thanks to knowing Sawyer and Gray his entire life, and he slumps in the other seat next to me so that I'm flanked entirely by overprotective Bonds.

Sawyer glances up at the two of them and pulls a face at whatever attitude he's facing from them, then flicks me a much more sedate face. "Whatever is going on here, the water contamination was the first incident. Sage has already been ruled out of that, right? Why don't we start there and work our way over to the... murder," Gray says, all sorts of reasonable and level-headed and zero sass, which makes him a better planner here than the rest of us about a million times over.

I nod and rub a hand over my face, tugging Atlas' jacket from my shoulders and setting it over my legs. "Okay, so... we start at the beginning. Where were we all this morning when Dara was murdered?"

E verything comes back to Riley and Giovanna.

Sawyer tracks every last second of our morning, even when Atlas wants to murder him for all of the snide comments he makes about the two of us spending the night together out in that cave. That now feels as though it was a million years ago, but we find nothing out of the ordinary.

Sage woke up in her bed super early, said goodbye to each of her Bonded as she went on her routine morning run, and then made her way over to one of the wall security outlooks.

Then she killed our Shield.

There's nothing else there for us to pull apart, no one approached her or injected her with some mind altering substance. She woke up and... chose murder?

"It has to lead back to Giovanna. She's the one who is into mind control and fucking us all in the ass with a fucking cactus for the Resistance. We've let that situation stew for too long, and now they're using the only in they have with us," Sawyer rants, his fingers a little more frantic as they fly across the keyboard than they normally are.

Gabe pulls a face and leans back in his seat, still frustrated at how little we've figured out in the time we've been stuck here. "Could Giovanna really do that? Do you think she has enough power to go through Riley to Sage, even though they're not Bonded? That's... a lot of power. A lot more than I ever thought that manipulative bitch ever had."

I glance at Sawyer but he doesn't look away from his screen. "She's always masked how much power she has because she was using so much by messing around in Riley's head. I'm not ruling it out. Someone needs to go after her, rescue Riley, and drag her back here until we can rule it out. If it's not her... I'll keep digging."

Atlas side-eyes me like he's sizing me up and figuring out exactly how I'm going to react before he adds in, "And what are we going to do if it turns out that Sage is a turncoat? I don't want to believe it either, but someone needs to say it."

I shift in my seat uncomfortably, mostly because it's

been the one thing circling in my head this entire time, and the guilt might just eat me alive.

Sawyer, ever the unpredictable sass-master, shrugs and snaps, "If she's evil, then I guess she'll be dealt with. I'll also need to hand myself in for being the most gullible and blind dickhead in the entire Gifted Community for not seeing it, so you'll lose us both in one fell swoop. Oli, make sure you take care of Gray for me."

Gray shoots Sawyer a dry look, like he's a little insulted, but Sawyer just grins back at him. It's not a proper grin, a little tense around the edges and it definitely doesn't reach his eyes, but I can appreciate his effort to fake it until we get out of this mess.

I take a deep breath and blow it out slowly. "Okay, so we just need to convince North and Gryphon that moving in on Riley and Giovanna is the only priority moving forward so that it happens right now, at the latest. That can't be that impossible, right?"

Gabe grimaces next to me, pulling a face, and Sawyer smirks at me. "What do you mean 'we'?"

And that's how I find myself heading back over to North's office.

It's not the easiest thing to do, but I managed to convince Atlas and Gabe to let me walk over there by myself. I'm sure they only do it because Atlas is in my head the entire time talking to me and joking with me. Plus, with Brutus and August padding along silently next to me, there's not really much they can say about my level of protection.

No one would ever attempt to approach the shadows, especially not immediately after the carnage they'd just wrought all around us. Even knowing they'd done it to defend us and drive out the Resistance from the Sanctuary, I'm sure the other Gifted are practically shitting themselves over my precious babies as we walk the streets together.

The offices are only a few hundred yards away, but the walk over is good to clear my head a little from the conversation with Sawyer and Gray. The streets are still bustling with people clearing away the debris or heading to the dining hall for something to eat. It's good to see that they're all resilient enough to get on with life once they've been given the all clear. I try to memorize the faces around me, to remember the people who have a backbone around here, but there's too many.

I smile softly to myself and take a second to pause, tipping my head back and letting the warmth of the sun overhead soak into my skin. There's a tiny whisper of a breeze that flutters my hair just a little, but it barely touches against the bright rays falling over my face and neck.

I take a deep breath, then another one for good luck.

Everything feels like a mess and completely overwhelming, but there's also a part of me deep down inside that *relishes* the opportunity to finally do something in this fight.

Being stuck on the sidelines, coddled and protected as though I am some precious, breakable possession of my Bonds, has been incredibly frustrating. Especially with my own bond whispering dark and blood-soaked plans at every opportunity. I already know I'm the greatest weapon that our side has.

Now I just need to convince North and Gryphon of that.

Brutus butts his head against the back of my legs in a play for attention, so I crouch down a little to scratch him behind his ears. August had come to a heel a step in front of me when I'd stopped, always putting himself between me and any potential threats. Both of his ears are standing straight up at sharp points and as he looks around, I'm struck with the thought that it's not often that I'm reminded that they aren't actually puppies but that they are shadows made from my own Bonds. The stillness in him is an echo of the deadly calm in North.

It's eerie and comforting at the same time.

You should hurry up and get to the office, Atlas sends directly to me, and before I can answer him, mostly with snark and attitude, North's words trickle into my mind.

I can see her from where I am, Bassinger. She's perfectly safe, for now. If she needs a minute alone, then now is the best time for it.

I duck my head to hide my grin, burying my nose into Brutus' soft fur and taking one last deep breath, and then get back to walking down the rest of the path to the offices.

Everyone I come across gives me a wide berth as I pass them, not at all surprising, with a few mumbles and glances of fear. But there's a lot more smiles and quiet acknowledgments than there were before, mostly from the Lower Tier families and, God, do I hate the way that sounds even more now.

They were all far more competent in the fighting than the Upper families. Gabe had told me about the people he'd helped hide in the school, about the Shields who had worked together to offer their families and community what protection they could... I will never have respect for the others who just cowered and ran, all while holding ten times more power than the others who chose to stay.

Never.

I smile and wave back to them all trying to look docile and not at all like the killing machine that they've all just witnessed me being, but I don't attempt to approach any of them or stop to have a chat. I don't want to push it. And honestly, I need to get this conversation with North and Gryphon out of the way.

I don't think it is going to go well.

There are three TacTeam personnel standing guard at the office doors, but none of them attempt to stop me or speak to me as I walk past them with the shadow pups. Again, not surprising, and I'm sure if North had spotted me out of his window or on some big security camera of his, then he'd have warned them of my arrival.

Actually, I'm sure Gabe called ahead.

I stupidly left my key pass behind at the house, but one of the personnel is nice enough to swipe his to get me into the elevator up to North's office. When I thank him with a smile, he gives me a curt nod back, one hand resting over the butt of his gun subconsciously as though even knowing we're both on the same side he can't help but reach for it in comfort. I won't hold it against him.

It seems strange to me that the elevator has music. Such a normal and boring thing to have while the world around us burns.

"That's a little dramatic, Bonded. There's barely any scorch marks out there," Gryphon drawls as the elevator doors open, his hands reaching in to grab a hold of me and drag me out into his arms. It feels a little desperate, a little bit too eager for my calm and sure TacTeam Bonded, but I accept it without a word.

It's been a shit day.

"If you haven't already figured out that I'm a little dramatic in the *supposed* privacy of my own head, then that sounds like a you problem," I grumble under my breath, but my arms are just as tight around him as his are around me.

I take a moment to let myself soak up some of his strength, leaning on the solid weight of him as he just lets me melt into him without a word of complaint. He's been my safe place since he showed up at my shitty dorm room and manhandled me into the bed to take away my horrible period pains, even when I couldn't accept it or admit to it.

I need him desperately.

It's also as though seeing the images of Sage's *supposed* betrayal and all of the bullshit that had come after that fucked-up moment has sapped the last of my energy away from me.

It's a strange feeling, because the entire time my bond was in control and using so much of my gift, I didn't feel as though I was using up my gift or running out of power. I *never* feel as though my gift is going to run out. But usually, when my bond slips away and I find myself back in control, I have no energy left, as though I have run an ultra-marathon.

This time has been different.

Whether it was because of my other Bonds and the way I had been passing energy on to them, or if it was the Gifted soul that my bond consumed, it was only after hearing about Sage that the bone-deep exhaustion took over. I'm pretty sure that's been more of a defense mechanism than something that is really affecting me physically.

I give myself a full minute of squeezing Gryphon back as hard as he's clutching me before I move to pull away, stepping back and taking a look around.

North's offices look far more untidy than I have ever seen any of his spaces look before. The couch is still half made up from where Nox tends to sleep on it, blankets and pillows and his ever-present pile of books stacked there, waiting for his return. There are files and boxes of paperwork littering the floors everywhere and a computerized white board has been set up behind his desk, blinking away with all sorts of information.

My eyes finally land on North himself, looking older than he had just a few hours before, the toll of the day weighing heavily on his shoulders. The first stirrings of my bond start up in my chest. I don't like to see him under such pressure. I can't stand to see the ways that it's affecting him to be at the helm of this community and be responsible for so many lives.

How he's still standing is beyond me.

"We've moved Sage into one of the more comfortable cells in the underground bunker here," Gryphon murmurs quietly, and I glance back to him with a curt nod.

It's now or never, I guess. "I'm here to talk with you both about her. I can't believe that she did this... I *won't* believe she did it."

Gryphon shares a look with North over my head. And

even though his mouth is downturned, he nods slowly. "We don't think she's a spy either, Bonded, but there are only a few explanations that we can think of."

North cuts in, his tone soaked with frustration and exhaustion, "And we can't risk leaving her in the general population until we know exactly what happened and how to stop it from happening again. I need you to promise me, Oleander, that you're not going to attempt to get her out. This isn't about your friendship. This is about keeping people safe. I need to know that you are going to work with us on this."

For the tiniest of moments I want to be insulted, but I have to remind myself that I have walked into a burning building for that girl and they both know it, so instead I look Gryphon dead in the eyes and say with complete honesty and surety, knowing that he will be able to feel it through my words, "I am going to find out what happened. I am going to save my friend. I am not going to risk anyone's lives unnecessarily while I do so."

There's a small pause and if I didn't already know that my complete honesty was a turn on for Gryphon, the heat that fills his eyes would be a dead giveaway. He doesn't make a move to act on it though, now isn't really the time, instead he just nods to me slowly and lets out a breath.

Nothing else really matters though. I've never been so serious in my entire life as I am when I say those words.

Sage would never turn her back on me, and I'm not going to turn my back on her now.

Whatever it takes, I'm clearing her name.

"Riley and Giovanna are staying at Daniella's lake house, about an hour away from Draven. Riley's headaches and nosebleeds have been happening more frequently, so they decided to spend some time out there for him to rest and recover," North says, tapping at the screen on his tablet. The computerized board starts to show a GPS map and photo images of a traditional style lake house that looks as though it costs at least a couple million dollars.

Gryphon had been called out for some issues that had cropped up in the town clean-up. North had taken one good look at me before insisting that I sit with him to go over my plans.

The room is dark around us, the curtains drawn so that all of our focus can be on the information lit up on the screen. I'd teased North about the board when I'd first seen it. It had seemed like such an unnecessary luxury when the Sanctuary was still only half built, but I can see the appeal of it now. With a few simple taps, he can send anything up there for us to look over together and discuss. Maybe this whole 'richer-than-sin' thing isn't so bad.

I wiggle a little in his arms, settling further into his chest and enjoying the way his arm tightens around my waist like he's trying to get me even closer as well. Hell, I think I'd burrow into his skin at this point, just so I could make sure no one could ever keep us apart.

My eyes stay glued to the board though, the information up there is both concerning and vital to figuring this all out. There are timetables and delivery schedules, appointments they have booked and daily routines. Giovanna is *definitely* that type of psycho who takes a morning run, willingly and on her own volition, every day at six a.m.. Everything we could ever need to show up there and kidnap them both is up there.

It had been my idea to be in his lap, mostly because I needed him close to me, but also a small part of me is hoping that it'll soften him up enough to let me do what I need to here.

"I want to forbid you from going. I want to insist on keeping you here in this room with me and send Gryphon out to do this for us all," North murmurs to me, as if he's reading my mind.

I tip my head back onto his shoulder a little to whisper back, "But? There has to be a but here, Bonded."

He chuckles quietly, his legs widening a little so that my body settles even lower onto his lap until I can feel his dick hardening under my ass. "*But*… my bond wants you to do it. My possessive, jealous, murderous, and malevolent bond who has writhed in fury over the very mention of you being in harm's way is telling me to let you go there. Why exactly do you think that is?"

The grin that tugs over my lips is an easy one with a little flirty edge to it. I rock just a little against the hard line of his cock, a purposeful tease. "Because he trusts me? He knows exactly what I'm capable of? Maybe he loves me more than you do."

The words are out before I even really think them through. Before I can curse myself out or try to take them back, North tosses the tablet onto his desk and manhandles me until he has me turned around in his lap, now straddling him and facing him dead on as one of his hands cups my jaw and forces me to look directly at him.

"Impossible. There's no one, not my bond or any of the other Bonds you're tied to, who loves you more than I do, Oleander. I will argue that point until I die, vehemently and with great pride. You're the reason my heart beats, and even if I don't deserve you, I'll go to my grave doing everything I can to be the man you do deserve. I know I've done a shitty job of it so far, but I'll prove myself to you."

I swallow roughly and nod slowly, leaning forward just a little to press our lips together softly. "You're already doing a great job proving it. I love you too. *All* of you; your bond and your shadows too. None of that stuff scares me or worries me. I'm proud to call you mine… even if we're both terrifying monsters."

He scoffs at my teasing and leans forward to give me a proper kiss this time. "Your bond is the only reason I'm agreeing to your little trip outside of these walls. I know I can trust it to not hesitate."

I deepen the kiss, ready to lose myself in him and maybe escape from the chaos in my head for a minute. Then his computer chimes and he groans against my lips, a frustrated sound that has nothing to do with the searing heat of his dick straining through his pants.

I pull away and duck down to press my nose into the crook of his neck, breathing him in for a minute. "I'm guessing that's not one we can just ignore? Are there *any* we can ignore?"

He presses a kiss into my hair and then wraps his arms around my thighs, standing up and taking me with him as he moves back over to his computer. I don't attempt to fight it; I already know he's strong enough to haul me around. If he's happy to lug me around while I cling to him like my life depends on it, then I'll let him.

I might not be able to fully explain how off-center this has all made me, but I think my actions are clear enough.

I don't bother trying to look at what North is doing. I don't really want to know about what bullshit the council and Top Tier families are up to right now, so I keep my face tucked into his shoulder.

"Sometimes it's very clear to me that being a monster and using our gifts without so much restraint would make life a lot easier," he mutters, and I huff out a laugh.

"I've already offered to kill your enemies. That's still on the table if you need it."

He scoffs back, one hand absently rubbing down my back in an action that I'm sure is just as much a comfort to him as it is to me. "And while I'm grateful, I also know that neither of us could stomach the thought of killing non-Gifted people just because they're ignorant fucking idiots."

Non-Gifted?

I lean away from him to catch his eye. There's a tension in him that wasn't there before. "Why would you be worrying about them? I know you do charity work in their community, but why would that have you dealing with idiots?"

His lips are in a hard line and his eyes stay glued to the screen behind me for a second longer before he finally meets my eye. "The Resistance amping up and making a mess of things has caught their attention. Now there's a lot of... unpleasant publicity about the Gifted community circulating. I'm now being subpoenaed because a particular group of non-Gifted have banded together and are taking legal action against the council."

Unease trickles back into my gut and he spots it straight

away, one of his hands moving to cup my chin. "Don't worry about it, Bonded. It's a pain in my ass, and the worst timing, but there's nothing for you to worry about. I will sort it out and keep you safe. Nothing is ever going to separate us again, any of us. I swear it."

FORCED BONDS

J BREE

ATLAS

O nce I know for sure that Ollie is safely at North's offices, I let Gabe know that I am heading out for the day. I'm not one to check in and report where I'm going to be but, thanks to current circumstances, I don't need anyone questioning my loyalty or my allegiance.

Sage being the one to kill the Shield wasn't just a shock to me, it was a threat. If Oli's best friend could be one of the people betraying us, then there isn't much doubt in my mind that they could point the finger in my direction too, thanks to my family's allegiances.

"Do you really think it's a good idea to go and see your sister?" Gabe says, his phone in his hand and his eyes on the screen as he questions me, as though he's so nonchalant about the answer. But I know that couldn't be farther from the truth.

I have no idea who he could possibly be texting, it's not like he has any friends really outside of the Bond Group. A ripple of frustration creeps down my spine and I have to shake my head to clear it.

I force my tone to be calm and even as I reply, "I was avoiding speaking to Aurelia because she's my sister, and I don't really want to listen to my family's indoctrination bullshit coming out of her mouth. But… if there's anything that she might know about this, then it's my responsibility to find out. If Oli can face everything head on, even when it's breaking her fucking heart to do it, then so can I."

Gabe glances over to me and nods slowly. If I really look hard enough, I think I can see some respect in his eyes. I never really cared about what the other Bonds think of me though, so I don't care to look too hard for it.

So without another word, I grab my jacket, the same one that I'd slung over Oli's shoulders a few hours ago, her sweet scent still clinging to it, and then I head back out to track down Shore. I need to get a pass to see one of the Transporters to go back to Draven and see my sister at the council offices there.

I already know that he will insist on sending someone with me to watch my every move and report back on me, but that isn't something that bothers me anymore. Now that I'm sure we're all on the same side when it comes to Oli, nothing else matters to me. Whatever little tests and boundaries and bullshit they set for me, I'll deal with it all if it means she's safe here and has a whole lot of eyes on her at all times.

The fact that they'll all spend the rest of our lives doubting me and waiting for me to turn on them should probably bother me more than it does, but Oli's complete trust and faith in me is all I really need. The fact that she chose to bond with me even after she found out about my family's ties to the Resistance and their involvement in her capture and time in the camps? There's no doubt in my mind that Oleander Fallows is the perfect Bonded for me, made for me to devote my life to and worship until my dying breath.

I'm still furious that our time together had been cut short thanks to the attack, finding out about the Shield's death, Sage's possible betrayal, and now trying to figure out what the hell is really going on around here. Knowing that she's going to sleep in someone else's bed tonight is incredibly frustrating, especially since North had kept her in his rooms for days after they'd Bonded. Not that I'm pissed at Oli, none of this is her doing. Having five Bonds to split her time with would be fucking hard in the best of circumstances.

The poor girl has to deal with five alpha males with

huge egos, overprotective tendencies, and impossible safety standards... not to mention Nox fucking Draven's issues here.

The streets are still looking as though the Resistance came here on a mission just to destroy as much as they could which, honestly, might be the case. There's a reason their camps are all made out of temporary structures; cheaper, easy to replace, and everyone who lives amongst the tents are entirely disposable to the higher families of the East Coast.

Even Silas Davies.

Sure, he's powerful. Really fucking powerful. The type that makes warning bells sound in your head the moment you step into a room with him, but he's not at the top of the food chain. Someday, I'll talk to Oli about him... about where he sits, about who he's Bonded to, about all of his weaknesses and the ways that the higher families keep him in line.

Someday, when her best friend isn't in question and she's not completely fucking fried by the fact that maybe we've all been flirting with the goddamn enemy here.

I find Shore in the small town square area with a group of TacTeam personnel surrounding him. Black isn't there, thank God, and I would have a lot to say if he had been given an out just because of his high position within Shore's team. Rockelle is there though, and when he spots me coming, a sly smirk stretches across his smug, mouthy-asshole face.

When he opens his mouth, Shore cuts him off before he can let out any of the bullshit brewing in his brain. "Focus, Rockelle, we're not here to talk shit. We're here to get this mess cleaned up and the holes in the security fixed before nightfall. Get your head on straight before I get you removed from rounds and put on probation."

Rockelle doesn't let the threat to his job affect him in the slightest. Instead, he jerks his head in my direction and snarks back, "Oh, my head is where it needs to be, but I doubt yours will be for much longer. No doubt there'll be an exception for your Bond Group bullshit though, won't there?"

If I were a Rockelle's superior, I would have knocked him on his ass for that disrespect. Sure enough, the look that Shore gives him would make a much stronger man's balls shrivel away to fucking pebbles.

His voice is light in a very obviously fake way as he says, "I'll see you at the training rooms tomorrow morning, first shift. I've needed a new training partner. Good of you to offer."

The guys surrounding them both start to snicker and murmur to each other and finally Rockelle looks as though he's regretting opening his stupid fucking mouth.

His mouth is downturned and his tone is rueful as he

gripes, "I'm not in the first rounds. I was assigned the third so that I can check over new recruits—"

Shore cuts him off. "And now I'm reassigning you to the first rounds. If you have any complaints, feel free to go and raise them with my superior."

Rockelle pulls a face and turns away from him, muttering under his breath, "You don't have one."

Shore turns to face Rockelle fully and the way he moves is deceiving. You'd guess he was a Shifter or some other physically Gifted with the sheer presence he has when he's pissed off, but then I guess the level of Neuro he is isn't something to be taken lightly.

My father would sell his soul to have access to the inner thoughts of others like that.

Shore's voice drips with derision as he says, "Exactly. No one cares about your opinion on how things are done around here. You've gotten away with too much because of your counselor daddy, but that ends here. Shut your mouth and get back to work. All of you."

The group disperses quickly, none of the other personnel have a single thing to say back to their commanding officer. Shore stays with his back to me until he's sure they're all heading off to where he's assigned them. Rockelle practically *runs* away from us both.

I scoff at the sight of it which catches Shore's attention. He finally looks over his shoulder to acknowledge me, his face hard. The scar on his face is darker with the exhaustion he's clearly feeling. It makes him look older and angrier, but I'm sure the weight of the day is heavy on his shoulders.

He and Draven both carry the brunt of it all to keep the Bond Group, and more importantly, *Oli*, safe.

"What can I do for you, Bassinger? I thought we already assigned you cleanup duties."

I shrug. "I've given them to Ardern. We thought it would be smarter if I went to speak to my sister, to see if we could figure this shit with Benson out a little faster."

That gets his attention.

He turns on his heel to face me fully and says, "You want to speak to her? That was one of your hard lines. You really think she's going to know something?"

I let out a frustrated breath and try not to just shrug at him again. This feels like another interrogation, and I have to remind myself that he's doing all of this for Oli. We're *all* doing it for Oli.

Except that fuck, Nox.

"I think it's an avenue we haven't tried yet. I'd be a selfish dick if I didn't at least give it a go."

It's the truth and he knows it with a thousand percent accuracy, so in under a minute he's told Draven we're leaving and has a Transporter there to move us out. Things happen quickly when you're Gryphon Shore, apparently.

Shore claps one hand onto the Transporter's shoulder

with a firm nod, his mouth downturned as he widens his stance a little in preparation. All of his movements are small signs that he finds this as hard as Oli does, only he's had years of training and experience to keep his stomach in line now.

She relies on his Neuro abilities to settle hers for her.

The Transporter stares at me like he'd rather pick up dog shit with his bare hands than touch me to do the job and he murmurs to Shore, "Are you positive that he's not in on the attack? You know what they say about Bassingers."

Shore stares at me and replies, "Do your job, Godden. I don't answer to you, and neither does Atlas."

It's the first time he's used my first name, and I know that it's a very strategic move. I'm not a Bassinger to them anymore, at least not publicly, and they've all made their choice to side with me.

Now I just need to pull my weight and prove that I'm worth the risk to everyone, not just to my Bonded.

The Council offices are like a ghost town.

The last time we were here, they had been quiet, but there were still a few employees milling around and other council members here. Those were the ones who had refused to come to the Sanctuary and instead stayed in Draven in their gilded mansions as easy prey to the Resistance. I see their unwillingness to go through the vetting process as a clear indicator of their treachery. I'm sure Gryphon and North feel the same way.

The Transporter steps away as soon as our feet hit solid ground as though he's worried about being near me, or maybe it's being so close to Gryphon and his vicious mood that has the guy worried.

It doesn't worry me. Gryphon simply barks out an order to keep careful watch while we're gone, then we're stepping away to head to the elevator. There's only one in the building that goes down to the containment area, and it's here in the underground parking. I've already mentioned to North that it's a security risk for us to always be transported to the same spot. He'd agreed with me, but nothing has changed yet, so I'm careful as I look around, watching out for some sign that we're about to be ambushed.

Gryphon is less concerned, and when I meet his eyes, he taps a single finger to his temple, a reminder that he can now 'hear' when people are around.

Right.

The moment the elevator doors shut behind us, he turns to me and then says quietly, "I will need to be present for the conversations with your sister. It's standard procedure for me to monitor and assess whether or not she's telling the truth. It's also protocol to have a TacTeam member there with you in case she attempts to harm you or escape in any way, so don't take it the wrong way."

I nod and shrug at him. "I was expecting you to be there anyway, and it's handy to know whether or not she's lying. I... think I can tell, but I'm also aware that I'm too close to her and can't be completely impartial about this. I wish I could be. I want nothing more than to just be done with her but... it's different. It's different with her than it is with my parents."

He nods and looks away from me, offering me what little privacy with my thoughts that he can. "Of course it is. You were raised together. You know exactly how they brainwashed her, so you're struggling because... some of this isn't necessarily her fault. The problem is that life isn't fair. She's an adult who made decisions that she has to face up to now. You made different ones."

I scoff and mutter, "For Oli. If it weren't for her then—"

"Don't go there. You'll just drive yourself insane. You can front all you want about not giving a shit about any of this, but I saw your face when you saw those kids who'd been killed. You're not a villain, no matter how much you might wish you could turn your humanity off."

When the elevator doors open to the long hallway of cells, I find that the majority of them are now empty. The last time we were here, every single cell had at least two Resistance members in them, so either a lot of processing has happened... or there was a raid here that I was unaware of.

I turn and give Gryphon a look and he gives me a dry grin back. "We've been very busy. There's no point in feeding all of these people and wasting our finite resources on them just for the pleasure of their company down here. There's only so much information any of them can give us."

I feel a small seed of dread in the pit of my stomach at the thought of them *finishing* with my sister in the same way and putting her down, but I also know that she has probably been given more leeway in this place than she deserves, thanks to me.

I'm not sure what the fuck I'm going to do about it either. She has made this bed for herself and now has to lie in it. She has to face the consequences of her own actions. It's just the guilt that's nagging at me. The guilt that will eat me alive if I let it.

Would I be the same as her if I hadn't seen that file on my mother's computer and the footage of my Bonded being tortured?

There's every chance I would be sitting in one of these cells, waiting to die or to rot away, because once upon a time, I'd lapped up every last bit of my parents' propaganda and indoctrination.

It's sickening to even think about.

Gryphon steps ahead of me to unlock my sister's cell and move her into the interrogation room. She doesn't fight him or attempt to use her Gift in any way, which is strange to begin with, but when he steps out into the hallway with her and her face turns up to mine, I see the white ring of light around her iris that is Gryphon's Gift hard at work. He's hacked into her brain to ensure her complete and utter obedience while he's interacting with her, which is both incredibly smart and a little terrifying.

He's a much bigger weapon in this fight than I've ever given him credit for.

She looks thinner and more haggard than I have ever seen her before. I already know that North wouldn't torture her through starvation or that form of deprivation, but clearly her time in captivity is not treating her very well.

Not to say that they're above treating prisoners the way that they deserve, but being my sister has clearly afforded her more allowances than the other prisoners ever received.

Gryphon adjusts the grip he has on her wrists and then marches her into the interrogation room. She complies with his every order without a word. It's not until he has her restraints secured to the chain running up from the concrete flooring and her ass in the hot seat that the white ring in her eyes disappears.

He moves around to the other side of the table as I watch her blink back into herself.

The sneer on her mouth when she finally looks up to see Gryphon standing there is instant. Every inch of her is radiating that ingrained loathing that we were raised to have for *these people*, the ones who are so far beneath us that they're practically a different species.

Her voice is thready and cracks when she speaks. "I don't know why you keep coming here to see me. There's nothing left in my brain that you haven't sifted through already, nothing there that hasn't been picked over, so either kill me or leave me to rot away in peace."

Gryphon nods slowly to her and then jerks his head towards the open door where I'm standing. I'm obscured from her view but watching her every move through the double-sided glass. "I brought someone here to see you. I thought maybe you would want to speak to someone familiar instead of me for a change."

For a small moment, I can see the tiniest shred of hope in her. "You've captured Jericho? He came for me?"

There's a pang in my chest at that. The one Bonded she has that actually loved her, the only one who treated her as though he truly loved her, of course she'd be hoping to see him before her inevitable death here in captivity.

"Your brother, actually," Gryphon says, and the hope in her eyes dies out.

She doesn't look happy about it or even relieved, which is strange because she saw me at the camps and must have already guessed about my ties to the Dravens. I would have thought she would want to use me to get out of here.

I'm not offended by her dismissal though, and I slip through the doorway easily, taking up the seat across the table from her. Gryphon looks between the two of us and then steps out of the room, shutting the door firmly behind him.

I didn't need him to tell me that he was going to be watching us both through the double-sided mirror.

"What have you gotten yourself into, little brother?" Aurelia says, shaking her head as her lank and filthy blonde locks fall around her face.

I make sure I keep my eyes on hers, never wavering so that she knows that there's no shame in me as I reply, "I found my Bonded. I'm a part of the Draven Bond Group. I went into those camps where we found you with every intention of helping to find and destroy every last Resistance member that I could find."

She blinks at me and then nods slowly. "Did Mom tell you? Or did you find out by yourself? You should take the girl and run, Atlas. You should do what Jericho and I should have done a decade ago, and just get out of here before they get to you."

Jericho.

She's still only worried about him, no mention of the others.

When I say this to her, she just shakes her head back to me, her voice breaking as she admits, "I don't want the rest of them. I don't want to go home to Father. I want to see Jericho one last time, and then I want to die, Atlas. I want to fucking die here."

My stomach turns. Gryphon had told me that she had been a shell of a woman in his interrogations but… I was never expecting this. "Aurelia, how can you say that? How can you—"

She cuts me off, her voice shrill and panicked, "If I get out, then I'll have to go back to them all. I don't want to! I went to the camps to die. I went there to be done with all of this, Atlas. I just want to be done."

She starts to sob, and it takes everything in me to stop myself from walking around and pulling her into a hug because she's just… broken. Desperate. So far into her own misery that she's completely given up.

"Aurelia, what's been happening? Give me something, anything, and I'll try to find Jericho for you."

I might be lying to her, I'll go to hell for saying it, but she chokes on a sob and sputters back, "We're better off dead, Atlas. What they have planned for us all… we're better off *dead*."

OLI

I stay with North in his office until long after dark. Instead of watching him work or distracting him in some deliciously tempting way, I get myself set up with one of his many spare laptops. I work my way through the information that Sawyer is slowly feeding me. Sawyer is keen to see if I recognize anyone or if there is anything about the Resistance that raises flags with me, and I'm more than happy to help out however I can.

It's slow and frustrating work, mostly because there isn't much that I find, but it's still better than sitting around doing nothing, and I'm the first to admit that I need the distraction.

There's a nervous energy radiating through me now

that I know that I will be leaving the Sanctuary tomorrow to hunt down and recover Giovanna and Riley. I'm not worried about being hurt or captured, my bond has grown and come into its own so much in the last few weeks that I'm not really scared of anything like that happening anymore, but it's more the fear of failure that is freaking me the hell out.

Sage's life depends on this.

I'm not stupid, I know that proving her innocence without a shred of doubt is the only thing that I can do right now to save her life. If there's even the smallest chance that she's involved with the Resistance, then she'll be locked up forever.

If they don't just kill her instead.

Neither of those things are options here.

I also don't want to disappoint my Bonds or prove myself to be a liability to any of them. I want them to all know that I can protect myself and any of them if the time comes. Even after clearing out the Resistance from the Sanctuary this morning, I still feel as though I have a long way to go.

Maybe I have some weird-ass praise fetish or something, who knows?

I keep the live video footage of Sage's cell playing in the corner of my screen the entire time I'm working, just to make absolutely sure that she's safe there. Just because

I can trust my Bonds and my friends with my life and hers, doesn't mean I can trust everyone. There are a lot of TacTeam personnel, council members, and other members of the community living here. While I have no doubt that security will be tight, stranger things have clearly been happening around here. I'll be damned if I let anything happen to her on my watch.

When North finally calls it a night and closes his computer down, shutting his laptop with a quiet snap, he groans and leans back in his chair until his back makes a satisfying crunching noise.

I startle back into myself and glance over at him, blinking owlishly as my eyes adjust away from the harsh lights of the screen. I hadn't really noticed how much time was passing while I was working. When I glance out towards the window and see that it's dark outside, it's a little bit of a shock to me.

I open my mouth to make some smart comment about it when my stomach growls, and North shoots a scowl my way.

"Why didn't you say something sooner? We could have headed home an hour ago, or more," he grumps, and I roll my eyes in his direction.

"I wasn't hungry before. I didn't really even notice that it was dark. Besides, I'm sure it's been much longer since you've eaten anything. I'm not so delicate that I can't handle a late dinner."

He huffs at me quietly and then stands, packing his laptop away in its bag and then slinging it over his shoulder. It seems like such a mundane and normal thing to do that I almost want to laugh at him. He looks like the calm and collected businessman that I'm sure he wishes he could be. Instead, he is the stressed and overworked councilman making too many big decisions for the entire community. He's too good at it for his own damn good.

I shut my own laptop and move to put it away in his desk, back where he'd pulled it out from. He catches my hand as I shut the drawer and pulls me into his body, wrapping me up until I'm pressed tightly against his chest.

"We can stop at the dining hall and grab something to eat on the way back."

I shake my head, my nose rubbing against his chest as I do. "I don't really want to be around everyone right now and be the spectacle for the entire community like I was this morning. I'm sure everybody's heard about Sage, and I don't want to be fake right now."

One of his hands runs down my spine in a soothing gesture and he murmurs back to me, "You don't even have to make nice. That's my job. You just have to stay alive, happy, stress-free, and, most importantly, *mine*."

Possessive Bonded.

"I'm sure it would make your life easier if I was at

least civil to them all though. Can we— is there food at home? I'm sure I could throw together something for myself... and you, if you're willing to eat normal food like a sandwich or eggs or something."

He scoffs at me and moves me around to tuck me under his arm, leading me over to the elevator and getting us both in there without much help from me. "I can do one better and make us dinner myself.

The streets are quiet as we make our way back to the house. The dining hall is the only real sign of life with its lights on and a small crowd of people still waiting to get in.

North raises a hand to wave at someone who calls out to us, but I duck my head and tuck myself into his side a little closer. I wasn't lying when I said I didn't want to make nice. Today started off as a nightmare and only got worse as time went on.

North doesn't attempt to speak to me or drag me into a conversation, which I'm thankful for. I don't really have it in me right now. And when we get back to the house, he lets us both in and doesn't bitch me out when I kick my shoes off and leave them on top of Atlas'. It's a little fight I'm having with my other Bonded, mostly because we both know it's getting on everyone else's nerves and it's sometimes nice to piss people off in such a low-stakes way.

It's sad how petty we've been forced to become for our

own enjoyment.

The house is empty and dark, so I move through it and start turning on lights ahead of North to try to breathe some life into the place. It still doesn't feel like anything more than a house, a temporary dwelling. We're all living out of suitcases and boxes and that makes it hard to feel settled. When the others are all out, it makes it even harder to pretend everything is normal and okay here.

North pulls his coat off and tucks his laptop into his room securely as I duck into Atlas and Gabe's room to check if either of them left any signs of where they are or what they're doing, but there's nothing. I send Gabe a quick text message to check in with him and use my mind connection with Atlas to do the same. He gets back to me immediately. *I'm at the council offices with Gryphon, questioning my sister. We're heading back soon, Sweetness.*

I wince and send back, *Be safe. I'm sorry you had to do that.*

He doesn't answer in words, only with a feeling of warmth and love that makes me want to crumble to my knees in the hallway and just sob like a child.

North walks up behind me and takes my arms into his warm hands, rubbing slightly as he murmurs, "The water contamination issues have been fixed. Go have a hot shower and climb into my bed, Bonded. I'll bring your dinner in there for you."

And that's why I love this man.

The shower is basically a lifesaving measure.

I spend too long in there, long enough that by the time I shut the water off and climb out of the very utilitarian stall, I can smell the delicious aroma of dinner wafting in through the door. It helps me to rush my way through pulling my clothes on. By clothes, I mean a pair of boxer briefs I'd stolen from Atlas weeks ago and left behind here for myself and one of Gryphon's old training shirts. It's a little obscene, thanks to the giant armholes that expose a good deal of my chest, but I'm sure North won't be complaining. It'll be a good little way of showing my appreciation for the food, though I'll probably need to eat quickly before he decides that I'm dessert.

When I get the door open, North already has plates piled with food on them set up on the small tables at either side of his bed. He's standing there with his shirt open, his chest and gorgeously tanned abs on display, while he taps away on his phone. He glances up at the sound of the door opening and smiles at me, the lines of frustration around his mouth softening away.

My heart does a weird thumping action in my chest at the sight of it.

"There aren't many seafood options here yet. I hope you like Italian."

It's a trick question, he already knows that it's a close third option for me. I like seafood *anything*, Mexican, and if those two options aren't available, then I'll go for Italian any day of the week. I still have no clue how he found this out about me, how he knows every little preference, and even my ridiculous order for Starbucks. When I narrow my eyes in his direction, he gives me what can only be described as a shit-eating grin.

He's so fucking smug about knowing my every whim.

I sit cross-legged on the bed and dig into the giant bowl of pasta, my hunger finally hitting me full force. I'd probably feel self-conscious or embarrassed if North wasn't watching me with pure, unadulterated satisfaction. He always was the provider out of my Bonds, the one who wanted to prove himself to my bond with all of the things he could give us both. Even now that we've found ourselves on the same side of everything, he's the first person to sort out every little problem that might pop up.

I give him a saucy grin, literally, because there's definitely some splattered on my chin right now, and he finally seems satisfied that I'm taken care of appropriately, grabbing his own bowl and digging in.

Shockingly, I managed to eat the entire bowl. When I put the bowl back down and stretch out, I don't even feel bloated or overly full. It's as though my body was processing the carbs as quickly as they were going in, thanks to how much of my gift I'd been using.

A handy little trait to have.

My eyes drift shut, my hands clasped over my stomach, and I let myself work through the plans for tomorrow to prove Sage's innocence.

I can't think about any other option here.

I hear North collect my plate when he's finished eating, pressing a kiss to my forehead, but I keep my eyes shut with a quietly murmured, *Thank you.* I could fall asleep here, just slip away into blissful nothingness and forget about everything that is hanging over my head... except the moment I think that, I'm ravaged by guilt and my eyes flutter back open.

What else can I be doing right now for Sage?

Nothing. There's nothing you can do for her, just get some rest, Bonded, Gryphon sends straight into my brain, always meddling in my goddamn head, and I ignore him entirely.

If someone doesn't tell me how to block him soon, I'm going to fling myself directly into the sun. It's too freaking embarrassing to go on like this forever.

North ignores the crisis I'm so very clearly having when he comes back into the room, instead making a beeline for the bathroom and leaving the door open as he turns the shower on. I don't know if it's an invitation to join him or not but, hell, is it tempting.

Except the guilt starts up again, and I find myself glued to the bed, listening to him thoroughly clean away the horrors of the day as the scents of his signature soaps and hair care products waft through to me like a siren's call.

When he slips out of the bathroom wearing nothing but one of his giant, luxurious towels wrapped around his waist, I swallow roughly at the sight of him, my throat drying up and the guilt tripling because of my insanely lust-filled reaction to him.

His hair is still wet, dripping just a little, and the easy curls make him look even more like Nox than he usually does. I mean, they're similar at the best of times, very clearly brothers, but the curls just make it more of a slap in the face.

He watches me as my eyes practically assault his body, every inch of him a pathway paved directly to hell for me because I would give up anything for this man. I would give up anything for any of my Bonds.

"Come here, Oleander," he says, his voice a low and dark demand, and my body complies without any sort of direction from me.

When I get to him, instead of pulling me into his arms like I assume he's going to, North grabs my arm to pull me in front of him. I finally notice the mirror he's got hanging on the back of the open bathroom door, a full length one that is taller than he is. He waits until I'm settled there with my eyes on him before he drops his towel and kicks it away. I can't see him, my back is to him and my body is in the way of his reflection, but I can feel the heat of his erection against my back.

I want to drop to my knees and suck him off here but when I make as if I'm going to move, his grip on my arm tightens.

Instead, he tugs on the edges of the tank top I'm wearing, pulling at it and feeling how much give the fabric has before he finally grabs my hips to move me closer to the mirror. He's so much taller than me that I can watch his facial expressions as he fusses with me, positioning me exactly where he wants me, and then he's back to messing around with my tank top. I'm expecting him to just pull it off and be done with it, but he doesn't.

The armholes are big enough that he can pull them until the edges meet at the center of my chest, my tits popping out and my nipples pulling in tight as the cool air of the room hits them directly. His eyes lap the sight up, darkening with need as he fists the fabric and pulls it tighter, dragging me back until I'm pressed firmly against him.

"I'm going to fuck you here, and you're going to watch me take you. You're going to watch every last thing I do to you."

I let my head drop back a little, my eyes staying obediently on his as I swallow roughly with a little nod. I want nothing more than to just... let him. To be used by him, to stand here and comply with his every whim, knowing that he's going to take care of me while he does it.

And he does.

My shorts are slipped down my legs and his fingers are teasing my pussy, all the while his eyes stay hot and dark on mine. With his other hand, he tweaks at my nipples, tugging and pinching as I ride that line between pleasure and pain beautifully under his intensely watchful eye. He knows my every tell, all of the little reactions I give him as he plays me perfectly, and within a few minutes, I'm begging him for more, more, *more*.

The stretch as he pushes his cock inside of me is everything, *everything*, and sparks of pleasure start at my pussy and work their way over my entire body. My eyes roll up into my head and his hips immediately stop moving, his voice a rough demand when he snaps, "Eyes on me, Bonded."

A whine slips past my lips before I can bite it back, a pure and needy sound. When I try to shove my own hips back for some friction, his fingers bite into my skin, his grip tightening until I'm sure I'll be covered in bruises.

It feels like a heavy task, like moving through honey or tar, but I force my eyes open to meet North's eyes in the mirror again. His hips start moving again immediately, driving into me at a fierce pace, giving me everything he has all at once. He's determined that I'll take every inch of him as hard as he can give it, I'm sure.

I want to move, to change positions so that I can writhe back against him, to do something. Instead, I stay right where he's placed me and I watch as he owns my body. And, *fuck*, does he know how to give me what I need.

I hear the muffled sounds of the others arriving home, the loud noises of Gabe throwing his tools around and Gryphon's heavy-soled boots as he stomps through the house. My pussy clenches around North's cock as my bond reaches out to them without my permission with the yearning to have them all and to have them now. Why can't I be writhing in the middle of them as they worship me in the ways I deserve and—

Bonded, you better get a hold of your bond before we ruin North's night by coming in there after you.

I gasp and groan at Gryphon's voice in my head, the sultry and sex-drenched tones pushing me over the edge until I'm biting down hard on my lip to muffle the sounds, the taste of blood flooding my mouth.

I meet North's eyes in the mirror again. His irises are ringed with black, the last thread of his control pulled taut as he lifts a hand up to smear the blood from my lip with his thumb. I watch in rapt fascination as his eyes flash to fully black and his bond brings the thumb to his lips to lick the blood away.

My own bond pushes at my mind and floods me, clawing its way to the surface, and there's a short moment that I lose all sense of time and where I am, only the immense sense of pleasure and gratification filling me. Whatever the bonds are doing, my body is enjoying it. When I creep back into my mind I find myself on my knees, a hand on the back of my neck holding my face down into the carpet as North's bond fucks me as though I'm nothing but a vessel for his pleasure.

I come again, my mind splintering apart at his rough treatment because I know that sometimes worship looks like degradation and, fuck, I crave it.

My bond craves it.

When his hips slam into me one last time, his bond coming with a roar, I shatter into a million pieces right there with him, a breathless gasp falling from my lips as my pussy gushes and drips with his cum. He makes a growling noise as he recovers and pulls out, something definitely not human, and then I feel his fingers on my legs, scooping up his seed and then pushing it back into my body.

My bond preens at the action.

Me? I'm mildly horrified and also very glad we finally

got my birth control situation sorted out, because this is a very telling action. North might be all about keeping me happy and child-free, but his bond has other plans.

Note to self: keep North's bond away from my prescription.

His other hand finally releases the back of my neck, and my bond slips away from me slowly, satisfied with how well I've been claimed here. I'm slow to sit up, careful with the tense and tight muscles all over my body. By the time I'm sitting on my heels, North's eyes have changed back to their usual deep blue hue. His mouth is downturned and his eyes dart over me like he's looking for some mortal wound he's sure I have.

"Oleander—"

I hate the guilt in his voice and I cut him off, pleading, "Don't ruin it. I'm more than fine, and the bonds are both fucking thrilled, so just... let us all have the afterglow, okay?"

He huffs and then stands, unabashedly naked, and pulls me up into his arms to carry me over to the bed. I let him fuss with me until he's gotten me cleaned up, both of us wrapped up in each other and under the thick duvet that still smells like his manor. He waits until my eyes fall shut before he flicks the lights off and we lie there in the dark together.

It's quiet for a minute, but even with the decadent

thrum of the post-orgasm high still running through my veins, I can't let myself drift off to sleep.

I clear my throat and croak out, "It feels wrong to be lying here with you, feeling like I'm going to die of pleasure, when Sage is sitting in a cell."

North is quiet for a moment, thinking about why exactly he's going to convince me that it's okay and, honestly, I'm not expecting him to be able to come up with anything.

I should already know by now not to underestimate North Draven.

His voice is rough and low as he murmurs back to me, "What do you think she did while you were stuck in that torture camp? She crawled into bed with Felix every night and found solace with him. You're going out tomorrow to find Giovanna and Riley for her. You were just working hard with Sawyer looking for leads. And we both already know that you're no good to her without taking care of yourself as well. Your bond needs this. *I* need this."

FORCED BONDS

I wake at three-thirty the next morning to take another shower and get ready for today, for leaving the Sanctuary and clearing my best friend's name.

There's a lot here that I need to prove, to myself and to Gryphon and my other Bonds, and I refuse to be the liability within the Bond Group. So I'm up, dressed, with my bag packed and my boots laced tightly by the time North's alarm sounds at four. He groans like he's being murdered, shoving a pillow over his face and grumbling under his breath dramatically like he's plotting out a murder for this early wake up. Once he's moved through the entire list of people he wants his shadows to devour for this insult, he reaches out with one arm like he's trying to find me. When he comes up empty, he flings the pillow away from his face and sits up with a scowl.

I smirk and wave at him, just a little sarcastically, but it's a good feeling to see him so off-kilter. I'm so used to being the mess out of the two of us, it's cute to see him sleep rumpled and grumpy as hell.

"Stop that. Stop looking smug and get over here. Gryphon will be here any minute and I need another moment with you before you go." His voice is a rough rasp, one that sounds a lot like his sex-drenched whisper, and my thighs clench together at the sound. It doesn't matter that I'd spent the night with him and his bond fucking the life right out of me. It still feels as though it's been too long since I've felt his hands over my body, his tongue working its way across my skin, and his cock driving into my drenched pussy.

His head drops back on his shoulders and his pupils blow out wide, almost looking like his bond's void eyes. "Whatever you're thinking about, yes. I'll give it all to you, just get over here."

I giggle and shake a finger at him. "I have plans, remember? No matter how much I want you."

He frowns and moves to stand up, throwing a wrench into the mix because his chest is freaking magnificent. When he bends down to pull on his boxer shorts, I get the full view of his perfectly biteable ass.

I should have woken him up earlier.

"You should have, you're out of time now."

I startle at the sound of Gryphon's voice, spinning on my heel to find him standing in the doorway with a smirk, fully dressed in his Tac gear and ready to move out. His eyes drag over me and I can see how impressed he is that I'm ready to go.

I curse under my breath that I was so distracted by North's general hotness that I didn't notice the door opening and Gryphon sneaking up behind me.

He smirks at me and shrugs. "He's not coming with us, so I'm not worried about it affecting you on the mission."

Mission.

Even something as small as that word makes excited butterflies burst into life in my stomach.

I grumble back, "You better keep yourself covered as well. We both know your ass is just as good."

I smile at Gryphon softly and we both turn to watch North's frenetic movements as he gets dressed in a rush. I'm not sure why he's bothering and is so intent on seeing us off. It's just Gryphon and I going, and we could easily say goodbye to him right here.

Nonetheless, he pulls on a pair of sweatpants and shoves one of the very few casual-looking sweaters that he owns over his head, as though it's vital that he puts that delicious chest of his away.

"When is the Transporter arriving?" he snaps at Gryphon, who merely raises an eyebrow in his direction.

It takes another huff from North before he finally replies, "He's already here. He's waiting outside for us. I knew that you would wake up with a shitty attitude, and I thought I'd spare him from this… undignified sight of our fearless leader."

I smother a giggle and when North shoots me a look, I force my face to show none of the sadistic glee I'm finding in his distress. I must say, this version of North might be my favorite yet.

"Is Nox up yet?" he grumbles, and my heart sinks a little.

I glance up at Gryphon, who pointedly does not look at me in return as he says, "Yes, he's up and ready. You're, as always, the last person to be awake. Gabe and Atlas are already up and waiting to see Oli off."

I glance back down at my boots and try to take a deep breath without looking too obvious with it. I should have known that North wouldn't allow me to leave the sanctuary with only one of my Bonds. My reaction isn't because I don't want to be around Nox. It's that this is my first real opportunity to prove myself to Gryphon and to prove that I can be an asset in this Bond Group, whether North likes it or not. I already know that Nox will do everything in his power to undermine that. He's always so ready to point out all of my flaws and failings, every little thing that I do wrong or the little missteps I might have out of inexperience or ignorance. So now I'm not just going to have to be on my best behavior.

I'm going to have to move the mountains and the stars themselves to attempt to impress that man... or at least give him nothing to complain about. I still have his scathing critique ringing in my ears even though it feels as though the Resistance attacked us a lifetime ago.

"I've already packed everything that we need and distributed the supplies between the three of us," Gryphon says, lifting a bag that is easily half my size up in offering to me.

I take it without a word, even though I probably would have grunted and complained in any other circumstances at the sheer weight of it. The bag strapped to his back is even bigger still, and there's a weird sort of stubbornness in my very bones pushing me to just keep my mouth shut and take everything that is thrown at me right now.

Except, I'm not sure how far I'm really going to be able to go with this thing on, and it's only just hitting me that maybe I should have been pushing myself a little bit more in our training sessions at the gym. I can run on a treadmill now for an hour straight, but with this weight on my back?

I'm screwed.

North finally gets his feet shoved into an old pair of sneakers that I'm sure are not his, because I *cannot* imagine Councilman North Draven wearing such things, and he walks back over to me to tug on the straps on the bag. I attempt to look steady on my feet and completely unfazed by the extra weight, but he's too goddamn perceptive and I'm sure he sees through it.

He's good about not completely calling me out about it though, thank God.

"Are you sure this isn't too much?"

When I shake my head back, he frowns at me, probably at my silence. I can tell he wants to prod at me some more, but Gryphon answers for me, "It's not the bag. She's coming to terms with the fact that your brother is coming as well. I told you we should have warned her earlier, but you insisted."

I don't want to have to explain all of the complicated emotions running through me about Nox to North right now, or ever, really, so I give him what I hope is a reassuring smile and turn on my heel to walk out of the bedroom.

I hear him begin to argue with Gryphon behind me, but before I can feel any sort of way about that, I find myself face-to-face with Atlas and Gabe. They both look incredibly exhausted and amazingly sleep rumpled as they wait to say goodbye to me in the living room, their hair sticking up everywhere and the imprint of their pillows still on their cheeks.

Atlas approaches me first, a low-slung pair of sweats on his hips and nothing much else on. It seems like the universe has ordered an early morning of torture for me.

He pulls me into his arms, wrapping me up tightly and kissing the top of my head. "Are you sure that we can't convince Gryphon to let me come as well?"

I shake my head, rubbing my nose against his pecs and reply, "I need to do this. I need to get out of here and prove that there's something I can do here other than waiting tables and washing dishes."

I pull away from Atlas and move over to Gabe, who's standing there wearing basketball shorts and another one of the tank tops with the exaggerated arm holes, which now makes me blush wildly thinking about last night. He gives me a questioning look that I avoid entirely.

When it's clear I'm not going to say a word about the color on my cheeks, he drawls to Atlas, "She's got to be able to live. I would go crazy with the amount of rules that she's living under. To be honest, the fact that she keeps her bond stable around all of our bullshit is more than any of us really give her credit for."

He tugs me into his arms and murmurs quietly in my ear, just between us, "You're also pretty good with a nail gun, for the record."

I snort at his joke and hug him back just as tightly. My

bond reaches out to him in a way that it hasn't reached out to any of the rest of them, and I know it's because he is the only one I haven't bonded with so far.

Other than Nox, of course, but that's a given.

There's still a bleak sort of emptiness inside of me where he belongs, a space carved out in exactly his shape that aches for him. I really need to do something about it… soon.

I look up at him and he gives me that same soft smile that I've come to know. He reserves it just for me, and my insides liquify at the mere sight of it.

"Don't do anything stupid," he murmurs to me. When I raise an eyebrow at him, he continues, his voice quieter even than before, "Bond, we both know that with Nox there, you'll be tempted to scorch the earth at his attitude."

I shake my head at him and murmur back quietly, "No promises," before stretching up on my tiptoes to give him a quick peck on the lips. I'm still not completely comfortable with a lot of PDA around them all, but it feels wrong to leave him without a kiss.

Gryphon and North stomp their way out of North's bedroom, sour looks on both of their faces, and then Gryphon snaps, "We're already running late, thanks to North. Let's get a move on."

I follow him out the front door without another word, determined to be the perfectly obedient soldier, for now.

Nox is waiting on the front step, already dressed in his Tac gear with a large bag on his back. There's a man standing with him who I don't recognize, wearing full Tac gear as well. It still feels weird to use a Transporter that isn't Kieran, and there's a pain in my chest at thinking about my friend.

"We're late," Nox snaps, and Gryphon throws a hand out in North's direction.

"Blame your brother, not us. Oli's been up for hours already."

We jog down the stairs together to join them and I roll my shoulders into the weight of the bag a little, letting my body adjust to it. It's not so bad right now, and I'm sure I can ignore the pain of it for a few hours, at least.

I give my Bonds a quick glance over my shoulder and North gives me a possessive, angry sort of look, one that says he's regretting all of this already. We haven't even left yet.

I kind of wanted more of a goodbye with him than this, but with everyone standing around, I feel awkward going back for one last hug.

"Enough with this shit, we're leaving," Nox snaps, and I turn back to the Transporter, placing my hand on his arm and clenching my teeth in preparation for the travel sickness that always overtakes me.

Deep breath, Oleander. You can do this.

The woodland area that surrounds the lake is creepy as hell.

North had enough intel to find the whereabouts of the security cameras and other forms of surveillance around the lake house Giovanna and Riley are holed up in, so we already knew how far away we would have to transport in order to remain undetected. There's a long hike ahead of us today, but with a deep breath of the clean and crisp air, I'm already feeling more comfortable in my own skin.

As soon as our feet hit the ground, the Transporter gives Gryphon a questioning look and then *pops* back out of existence the moment he gets the go-ahead. My head is spinning and my stomach roils but I swallow against the bile creeping up my throat. Sadly, I don't think my travel sickness is ever going to ease up. Even after this many instances of travel, I still feel fucking horrendous.

Gryphon doesn't even have to look at me to know how terribly I'm doing and, without a word, one of his hands wraps around the side of my neck, his gift flowing into me and easing away the sickness.

I murmur a quiet *thank you* and pull away the moment that I can. He gives me a questioning look, but it should already be obvious to him why I'm pulling away.

I risk a glance in Nox's direction

He's already ignoring us both, his shadows streaming out of his body and taking different forms of various canine-like creatures. Some of them look so much like Brutus that I find myself instantly drawn towards them, wanting to pet them and love on them, but I already know that that would be a bad idea.

There's a small puff of air behind my ear and I reach up to grab Brutus, letting him down to join his siblings. He bounds off and snaps at a few of them playfully, the picture of a content puppy amongst grumpy and brooding shadows. I bite my lip to stop myself from giggling at him.

North had offered to give me August as well, but I could tell from the strain in his voice that he was unsure of how he would manage having his shadow that far away from him. I already know that he doesn't have the same sort of control over them as his brother does, and I didn't want anything to happen to him or August, and I *definitely* didn't want him pulling the pin on the mission just because his connection with August was broken.

"It's a three-hour hike from here if we're making good time," Gryphon says and I nod, adjusting the backpack a little and tightening the straps until it feels more secure on my back.

I am nothing if not excellent at ignoring pain and suffering. Now that my body has taken a moment to adjust to the weight, I'm not so concerned about how heavy it really is. I'll take it, and I'll do it without complaint.

Nox looks around the wooded area as his shadows begin to move ahead of us, scouting and being an extra set of eyes. Gryphon can sense people and hear their thoughts from a few miles away as well, so I don't feel the need to call on my bond yet.

"With any luck, you won't have to call on your bond at all," Gryphon mutters softly, taking the lead and moving remarkably quietly through the underbrush. I try to mimic his movements, but I sound as though an elephant is stomping through by comparison.

Nox takes up the rear without a word.

It makes me a little bit uncomfortable how quiet he's being, but his bad attitude earlier was mostly directed at North and not us, so I let it go. We spend the first hour in relative silence, mostly just the sound of my breathing and stomping to be heard, but I'm also not sure if it's just extra loud to me because I'm trying so hard to be silent.

Brutus bounds around next to me, happy and sweet in his puppy way, and I find that the other shadows are happy to ignore us both entirely. There are two shadow creatures that walk beside Nox the entire time, both of them looking fully grown. Even though they're shadow creatures and don't actually use any energy to hike along with us, their tongues loll out of their heads as they pant, showing off jaws filled with razor-sharp teeth that I know for a fact can consume fully grown men without concern. It would be threatening if it wasn't so damn cute.

Another creature walks beside Gryphon, but it acts as though he doesn't exist, sniffing at the ground with its ears pricked up as though it's chasing some mesmerizing scent.

Naturally, it's only after I become super focused on my breathing and making sure that I am pacing myself nicely against Gryphon's much longer stride and just generally kicking ass on this hike, that Nox decides to mess with my peace.

"What exactly are you gonna do if the girl is a spy? She should really get the same treatment as any other member of the Resistance, once we confirm she killed the Shield."

I stumble over my feet a little bit, mostly startled at his voice cutting through the quiet of the woodlands, but he takes it as a small sign of weakness and doubles down. "Is there a reason your bond didn't notice? Or has it been speaking to you about her this entire time and you've been ignoring it?"

I hear Gryphon sigh, but he doesn't attempt to intervene, which I can appreciate. I have spoken to North a few times about leaving the two of us alone and letting us work on our issues ourselves, but I'm sure that Nox's shitty attitude has come from his brother meddling.

I take a deep breath, that I'm proud to say is only a

little unsteady, before I reply with pure honesty bleeding right out of me, which I'm sure he won't even notice or appreciate. "You've heard my bond speak about her before, and you know it likes her. It likes Kieran, and it likes Felix. I genuinely don't think that she is a member of the Resistance... And the thing I've struggled with most over the last couple of days is the thought of what I will have to do if it is proved that she's a spy. I *don't* think anyone should get special treatment in that situation, and it kills me to think that way when it comes to my best friend. But I have also seen the Resistance torture and kill children. I have seen Silas Davies carve people up, and *everyone* in that camp knew what he was doing. Every single one of them were complicit in his actions. There is no such thing as an innocent member of the Resistance."

I swallow down the emotion that comes with admitting any of that, and Gryphon floods my mind with warmth and comfort. Thankfully, nothing was obvious to Nox, but it gets my knees steadying back up, thank God.

I hear Nox snort behind me and then he snaps, "Bassinger was born into the Resistance. I don't see you feeling the same way about him."

I should have known that this argument was coming, but I already have an answer to it, thanks to the questioning I have had from North and Gryphon.

My voice is strong as I snap back, "He was born

into a family of the Resistance. He was born into their indoctrination and *still* chose not to go along with what they believe in. While he might say that he has only switched sides because of me, I saw the look of horror on his face when he saw the children that his father had killed on that screen. He's not a member of the Resistance, and he does not agree with what they do. He helped us take down his own sister! I don't have any doubts about him. If you do, then that's your own issue, because logic says that he's on the right side of this."

I watch as Gryphon nods his head in front of me, and his presence slips slowly away from my mind now that I've found my fire again. Whatever happened between him and Atlas while I was in North's office, it's helped his perception of my other Bonded. I know that they went to see Aurelia, and I feel bad that I haven't had the chance to speak with Atlas about it yet. I'm sure that that was an incredibly difficult thing to do, no matter what I just said to Nox. I know that it was incredibly difficult for Atlas to not only see his sister in those camps where they had kept and tortured me, but to watch them take her in as well? It wasn't easy for him.

We fall back into an easy silence, Nox's attitude still pouring off of him, but I'm an expert at ignoring him altogether.

After another mile or so, I get a creeping feeling down

my spine that we're being watched.

My bond perks up but doesn't react as though we are in danger, more out of curiosity and reaction to my unease. Neither Gryphon nor Nox react in any way, and the shadow creatures continue on their usual path, so I try to push the feeling out of my head as a small sign of paranoia rather than anything to be concerned about.

If my bond is fine with it, then I have to be as well.

NOX

We stop about a quarter mile away from the lake houses to drop off the majority of our packs. There's a lot of supplies that have been packed in case we get stuck here for a few days, and there's no point in dragging them around while we are busy capturing our targets and bringing them in without any casualties.

Gryph makes a makeshift hole to hide them in and covers it with tree bark and leaves until there's no real way of telling that the area has been disturbed at all. There's a reason he's the head Tactical Leader and it has absolutely nothing to do with his social standing or his place in the Draven Bond Group.

The girl watches his every move as though she is taking

a class in tactical training. When he straightens again, she gives him a small nod. There's nothing of the mouthy college student left standing before me, just a well trained soldier, and I could almost commend Gryph on his work.

Almost, but not quite.

She's never going to lull me into the same state of complacency that she has the rest of them. I can see through it. I know exactly how Bonds operate.

I cast out my Gift again to check in with each of my shadows, but there's still no one anywhere near where we are. This area is frequented by Top Tier families and most of the houses built around the lake are owned by Gifted community members. There are even a few that have full-time staff of lower Gifted families who live here year round to maintain and take care of the property.

North and I have been to a few Council parties and functions out here. There was even a Bond ceremony that he'd dragged me to years ago, back before I was old enough to say no to that sort of thing.

I don't have any bad memories of this place, but I'm not exactly excited to be back either. The fact that Giovanna and her family are, at the very least, Resistance sympathizers and own property out here makes me suspicious of the rest of the family. It's not too much of a reach to think that maybe the time that they spend out here all together has more to do with strategizing and fundraising for the cause than it does about rest and relaxation.

Gryph looks out past the thickest section of trees and then says, "We need to move out. There is going to be nonverbal communication from here on out. The O'Neill family has extensive security around their property, including microphones and heat detectors. Their property borders where Giovanna and Riley are staying, so we will be circling around it just to be sure. Oli can speak to me, and I will relate anything I need to Nox. We will also use the usual tactical hand signaling should we need to."

There's no need to acknowledge his words but the girl nods, rolling her shoulders back, which is the only sign she gives that maybe she was struggling with the pack on her back. I have to admit, I was not expecting her to make it the entire way with the weight of it, and I already know that it was a small test from Gryph just to see what her boundaries were.

He would have made it slightly heavier than he thought she could handle, which is an old tactic of his with his team members. I doubt he would change much just for her. He always will be the tactical group leader, and that'll bleed through to how he goes about his relationship with her, even if he is blind to her manipulative ways.

As we begin to move, I cast the shadows out to a wider perimeter around us. They won't show up on heat cameras, microphones, or even on video footage. If someone has had any experience with them before, they may notice the distortion of video images trying to capture them and possibly figure out that we're here, but there's no way to get a shadow creature on film. North and I have tested it out on every product available and each time, the images come up white.

I do one last check through all of the weapons and ammunition strapped to my body to make sure that I'm fully armed and everything is where it should be before we move off together. Gryph does the same, though he's faster and does it mostly by touch, then he moves over to do the same with our little poisonous Bond. Again, she watches his every move as if there's going to be a test on it later.

Strange behavior, I take note of it for later.

I don't believe that she's actually going to accept it if we have to deal with her little friend and that Bond Group. I doubt Gryph is going to take it well either, if we're being honest about it. Aside from North and I, Kieran is his oldest and most trusted friend. They went through training together and served on TacTeams together for years, witnessing the worst of what the Resistance can do to innocent lives.

There's a connection there that isn't going to just disappear because of the Benson girl's treachery.

I move off and take the lead, leaving the Bonded pair behind as I work my way towards the lake houses. Rahab and Procel stay close to my side, while the rest of the shadows form a perimeter around us. When Gryph and his Bonded start moving behind me, the shadow creatures have the three of us completely covered.

I've trained them well over the years, a desolate and disturbing childhood has channeled that need, and it's like second nature for them all to follow my every command. Azrael, even with his recent rebellion of fawning all over the girl, will jump at any direction he's given.

I will never be helpless again.

We walk in silence until we reach the area where the trees begin to thin out, my feet slowing down as I begin to focus on staying undetected. There's a different feeling here, the sounds of small animals disappearing and the wildness melting away as we reach the area of *human life*.

I'd rather stay amongst the trees and leave the bullshit toxicity of the Gifted community behind, but, alas, I promised my brother I would help defend the smaller and innocent people who live below our own standing.

Once we make it through to the edge of the tree line, I can see through to the water and have to change the way that I'm moving forward once again to make sure I'm still covered. The lines of houses along the waterline runs along the entire circumference of the lake, spaced out and each of them with private decks and piers with boats and watercraft on them.

I shouldn't call them houses. They're mansions built by the richest families in the Gifted community of the West Coast to come out and relax away from their pathetically sheltered lives. I'd always assumed that they were just typical Top Tier cliques, too elite and rich to mingle with those 'beneath' them but our community is in a time of crisis right now. Definitely not the time for a holiday..

There are a lot of people here.

A lot more than you would expect during such a volatile time of conflict, and instantly, I know that North's assumptions about this area being a Resistance sympathizer hotspot is correct.

Nobody takes a holiday within driving distance of their house while members of their community are being gunned down by the Resistance unless they have a reason to believe that they are safe. Nobody.

I make note of which houses are lit up. When I glance back at Gryphon, mostly to see if he agrees with me, he's doing the same, his eyes shrewd as he clocks every single one of the traitors who are here. I'll assume all of the Gifted who have property here are traitors, but the ones actually staying here right now are further up the 'take-down' list.

When we reach the O'Neills' property boundary, we have no choice but to give the perimeter a wide berth to avoid detection. Harriet, Langton, and Grant O'Neill had always been fairly high up on my list of potential Resistance sympathizers, and the smoke coming out of their chimney only confirms for me that they are.

If this wasn't a quiet mission of getting in and out without detection, I would happily send my shadows in to dispose of them all right now. Top Tier families with more money than is good for them, happy to sacrifice the lower families in their never-ending pursuit of power and recognition; it's sickening. It also says a lot to me about their Gifts and what they're able to do if they feel this way.

I have never once felt the need to exert my power over those underneath me.

Only when someone has been unnecessarily flexing have I used my Gift against them to prove a point. I would bet that every last one of them are compensating for what they are lacking, and I can't wait to wipe them all from the face of the earth the moment the girl is no longer with us. If she weren't here right now, Gryphon would have changed the plan. I've worked with him for long enough to have no doubt. He would have taken one look at the frivolity and carefree disposition of these people and he would have gone in, guns blazing. But because we have his Bonded with us, we'll have to stick to the quiet mission North set out for us.

When we finally make it to the edge of the O'Neill property and onto the land behind the lake house Giovanna and Riley are staying in, I send one of the shadows out in front of us to figure out where exactly in the house they are for extraction. I choose Mephis, and he shrinks down to barely more than a palmful of smoke, moving faster than my eyes can properly track. He's the most persistent of my creatures, like a bloodhound when he's given a task, and I have no doubt this will all be over in under a half hour.

Gryphon catches my attention and shakes his head, sending a message directly into my head, thanks to his Gift. *They're not in there. The house is empty.*

For fuck's sake.

The girl is infuriating. "Let your bond out."

She looks at me as though I have suggested she slit her wrists in front of me just for my enjoyment. Gryphon gives me a stern glare as well, as though he believes the same of me.

He's gotten a lot more vocal about my supposed poor treatment of his precious little Bonded, and I don't have the heart to tell him that this? This is nothing. This is me on my best behavior.

It could get so much worse.

After three hours of watching the lake house in silence, waiting for some sign of either of the targets and coming up with nothing, we'd moved back to where we'd stashed away the packs to regroup. I was perfectly happy standing in silence, but Gryph had made the order and he is the lead here. I've been on enough of these missions to know that there's no scenario where you don't follow your lead, that's how you end up with pointless deaths and people being captured by the enemy.

She takes a deep breath and works at keeping her voice steady, though she's not quite successful at it. "There's no need for me to let my bond out. None of us are in danger. Whatever it is that you need me to do, I can do it myself."

The height difference between us means that I can stand over her and really stare her down, but there's a fire behind her eyes as she glares back up in return that says I'm pretty close to waking her bond up anyway, which is the entire point of this endeavor. "I don't need anything from you. I need your bond."

She huffs with the same ferocity as a toddler, and I'm surprised that she doesn't just stamp her foot in a full tantrum. "I can do anything that my bond can do, and I think it's more of a risk to have my bond out right now than it's worth. We're not being attacked. We're not in danger. There are no warning signs of the Resistance lying in wait. There's no reason for it to be at the surface."

She just keeps repeating that, as though she will somehow be able to talk sense into me. "This isn't about me wanting something from your bond, this is about the work that I need to do, and I would rather have your bond here for it than you."

There's a small shocked silence and then she makes a sputtering noise of outrage, glancing over at Gryph as though she's asking him to intervene. She's been so adamant about 'dealing' with me on her own lately that it feels like a win.

She's very obviously whining about me directly to him, but his face gives nothing away, which is a tell of its own, and he holds out an arm to beckon her over into his arms.

This is getting old; you need to grow the fuck up.

Rahab snaps at Gryph's ankles and he shoots me a look, which I ignore. Either they accept my attempts at civility or they deal with me treating their Bonded the way she deserves.

That's all I have to offer.

He simpers away to her, "He needs quiet to work with the shadows for a while. Of course he can't just say this to you, that would be the reasonable thing to do. Instead, he's baiting you. Let's go eat something for lunch and leave him to work."

I turn my back on them and walk away, done with having pointless and fucking stupid conversations. There's an itch that works its way down my spine that isn't exactly mine.

My bond wants hers.

The Bond, of course, that'll never change, but it also just wants to see it. To know that it's still in there, that it still belongs to it, and that they're here on this earthly plane together.

I want to take a knife to my skin to hack away until I can get the being living inside of me out, to carve any link to that girl out of me so that she can never wield her manipulation and sadistic plans against me. I have lived with this other being inside of me in relative harmony my entire life, but the moment she had been dragged back to Draven, it started. The war waged beneath my own skin.

I loathe her for it.

More than I already did.

I walk over to a fallen tree and sit down on the rough trunk, rolling my shoulders back as I let my eyes slip shut. I reach out to each of my shadows and check in with them, seeing through their eyes and taking in the full perimeter of the small community we're monitoring. Procel is inside the house with Mephis, both of them trawling through paperwork and anything else they might come across that could help us with this extraction.

They're both safe and somewhere that they're not going to be spotted, so I leave them and move on, one by one, until I've been through the entire town. I hear a lot of damning things, a lot of pro-Resistance chatter. This community thinks they're safe here, and I'm thankful for all of the training I've done to sharpen my memory.

I'll never forget the Gifted or the evil they're talking about.

When I've gone through each of my creatures, I go through them again.

And then once more, just to be sure.

When I come back into myself, darkness has fallen around me. My muscles are all stiff and sore, my fingers are numb and a little blue in the cold night air, and my stomach is growling viciously.

I've been in the shadows for hours without noticing.

There's a small, wrapped bundle sitting next to me on the tree, simple rations that I inhale without much thought and barely taste any of it. There's not really enough there to fill me up, just ease away the edge of my ravenous hunger instead. Rahab is still sitting at my feet, his void eyes watching out over the trees protectively as he stands guard.

The girl must have brought me the food.

The shadows aren't usually combative against North, Gryph, or Gabe, thanks to the years of trust I've built with them, but the recent issues I've been having with them all have meant that they've been more reactive, even to them.

Never with the girl though.

It's just another thing I loathe about her.

When I stand up, my body cracking and stiff at the

action, I make my way over to the small camp that Gryph has put together. It's standard procedure to have the small camouflage tent set up on the ground and two more of my shadows keeping watch a few feet away. There's silence inside, but they're both awake. They'll be communicating through the mind link they share, partially so they don't disturb my work, but also so that we remain undetected out here.

I don't want to sleep in the tent.

I'll speak to Gryph and then take up watch for the night. There's plenty of trees I can lean against and with my shadows out, I could sleep there without being any risk to us at all. Gryph's Gift would also wake him if someone got close enough for him to hear their thoughts and… the girl's bond has always been good about keeping her alive. I'm sure it'll wake her if needed.

I lift open the flap and hunch over to duck into the tent. I have to almost immediately find a spot to sit down. This thing is only made to keep us dry and unseen, not at all to keep us comfortable.

What did you find? Gryph says before I have the chance to address either of them.

He's stripped off his jacket but he's still fully armed. He'll sleep that way too, always ready to wake with a gun in his hands. It's saved our asses more than a few times. There's a weariness etched into his face that comes with him using so much of his Gift, even with the extra boost he has thanks to his Bonding.

I push the answer to the surface of my mind, the area that we had learned years ago that he'll find without having to pry, and the only acceptable way I'll allow him to use his Gift on me. He knows that boundary and has always respected it.

A lot of Resistance support and treachery, but not the targets. There are signs of them in the house though. I doubt they'll be gone for longer than a day. His contact lenses are in the bathroom, and there's a bag with her ID in one of the closets that I doubt she'll just leave behind.

He nods firmly and sips at the bottle of water in his hands. When he sees me look at it, he leans over to grab another one out of his bag, tossing it over to me.

I down it in one go, and then finally, I look over at his Bonded.

Her hair sticks up in a fuzzy little halo of silver around her head, the cost of her Gift that no one has really commented on yet. The photo we'd originally been given of her showed a dark-haired little girl. Whatever experiments the Resistance had done to her, the testing of her abilities and the limits of what a Render like her could do, had leached all of the color away from her hair, and sometimes I wonder if it's done it to her skin as well. She's unnaturally pale, a stark comparison to the olive tones of North and I, but even Bassinger's Eastern European lineage skin has more tone than she does.

The effects of a Render's Gift is something I've been researching from the moment I'd found out that she was lying about being Gift-less. I'd known from the beginning that she was lying, everything I'd done was to bait the Gift out of her. Having her here was already a threat, but having her here with no idea of what she was truly capable of?

Unacceptable.

If she'd also had the shadows or something like them, there was a chance she could get the better of me, and there was no way I was sticking around for that. No way. North knew it too, he'd spent weeks telling me there was no way she could ever have a curse like ours.

Then her eyes turned black.

Then her bond had a voice of its own, a sentient being lives inside of her that makes its own decisions the way that mine can, if it so chooses. Every little mutter of reassurance my brother had given me was proven wrong. His little Bonded was exactly the threat I knew she would be.

Rahab sets a paw on my leg, sensing the dark recesses that my mind has wandered into, and I reach down with one hand to stroke at his head, ruffling his ears a little. I feel a wave of calm settle over me for a brief moment, and then the panic starts.

Panic because it's time to get up and walk out of here, but my bond refuses to let me leave.

It doesn't take over my body, not fully, but if I think about moving to get my body out of this tent, I can't. When I shift my weight to get comfortable, I can, and when I move to take my jacket off, I can also do that.

Standing? Nope.

Oli and I are going to sleep. We'll be up at first light. I didn't set up your bedroll because I assumed you'd throw a bitch fit about being in here, but it's over there if you want to grab it.

There is no form of torture of this earth that would make me admit to him that I can't leave this tent right now. Absolutely no fucking way.

Except that is a problem in itself, because if I fall asleep, my bond will come out and go looking for hers. Then this whole mission will go to hell in a fucking hand-basket, because he'll slit my throat for daring to breathe near his precious little Bonded.

So I roll out the bedding on the far side of the tent, as far away from them as I can get, and lie down on top of it while avoiding his eyes. He knows something is up, he knows too damn well, but I just lie down and let Rahab curl up over my chest instead.

They both tuck themselves in together, their bedding mixing up as the girl curls into Gryph's body. He does what he needs to do to keep her glued to his side while also keeping all of his weapons attached to himself, and then he kills the lamp.

It's fine.

Until it's fucking not.

After an hour, the girl is sound asleep. Gryph is finally starting to wind down a little. The tension is still in his body but his breathing is evening out some. I'm still staring at the camo fabric above my head as I force myself to stay awake. If I can just stay awake until he's out completely, we should be okay here.

Except then, the girl's bond wakes up.

Gryph goes on immediate high alert, assuming there's a danger here that we're not picking up on, shifting her away from his chest as he sits up and reaches for a gun.

I stay exactly where I am and hope that I'm wrong.

I'm not.

From the corner of my eye, I see the bond move fluidly away from him, crawling over to me on her hands and knees like some sort of feline predator in the night. I sigh and push back at my own bond which begins to flood my mind, pushing and fussing at me to take control and get what it wants.

When she gets to the very edge of my bedroll, right down at my feet, she stops short of touching me. I glance down and am struck by the void stare, my bond shoving at me desperately, but I fight it a little longer. Mostly because I'm stubborn, but also because I can feel the growing horror coming from Gryph.

What the fuck is going on, Nox?

I meet his eye across the tent, which is the worst fucking thing to do because the shock and alarm there is exactly what I knew would happen if he or my brother found out.

We're talking about this, right the fuck now.

No, the fuck we're not. I leave the words at the surface of my mind, but my bond takes over before I'm sure he's had a chance to hear them, my own consciousness slipping away like the tide. Then I know nothing for the rest of the night.

OLI

I wake up to a completely different feel in the air than when I had gone to sleep.

Nox is already out of the tent and his shadow creatures are gone with him. Gryphon is sitting cross-legged with some of the food packages he'd called MREs in front of him. There's a pissed-off look on his face, one that's usually there because something big has gone down with the Resistance, but we have no way of contacting the others… not unless they reach out to me, and I would've woken up if that had happened, so I have no freaking clue what's happened.

He's already packed up and cleared away his bedroll and pulled his jacket back on. I instantly feel lazy for having slept in, and I hope to God that's not why he's sitting there looking around like he's plotting out murder and assassination plots.

I'm sorry. How long have you guys been awake? You should have woken me up when you got up.

He glances over at me and his eyes soften the tiniest fraction, shaking his head as he replies, *I didn't sleep much last night. Nox got up before sunrise and disappeared with his creatures. There's no reason for you to feel guilty about not waking up with the sun, Bonded.*

I shake my head dismissively. It sure feels as though I've been lazing around while the two of them have been working hard. It's frustrating that the two of them have Gifts that can be used at a distance and I don't, at least nothing that isn't lethal. I know these people are traitors, but I'm also not sure that we can just kill them all without some sort of legal proceeding. Not without them attacking first… right?

What exactly are the rules in this sort of war?

That's too much for my brain this early on, so I move as quietly as I can to pack away my own bedroll and slip my jacket back on, attempting to move quickly.

I *desperately* need to pee, but the thought of Nox being outside of the tent and one of his shadow creatures potentially finding me squatting behind a tree is not exactly how I want to continue with the day.

Gryphon smirks and shakes his head at me, my thoughts clearly being 'too loud' again and shouting in his direction. He speaks directly into my mind, *Just let Brutus down, and take him with you. He'll keep everyone away from you while you take care of business.*

I blush, stupidly, and grab out the tiny, rationed roll of toilet paper that I had insisted on bringing and head out of the tent. The sun is barely peeking through the trees, only just breaking into the sky, and the air is cold on my cheeks. It's quiet enough that I can hear the rustling sounds of little creatures going about their lives, the calls of birds above me, and the leaves rustling in the faint breeze.

It's peaceful, and I hope it's a good omen for the day.

I don't actually see Nox or any of his shadow creatures as I walk through the trees, thank God. When I do find a good, sheltered spot, it takes me a second to psych myself up to actually be able to relieve myself. I am very firm with Brutus that he has to turn his back on me while I do, and by the time I get back to where the tent was, Gryphon has it packed away already.

The food that he had gotten out is sitting on a tree stump, waiting for me, along with a bottle of water. I still don't actually feel hungry or thirsty, but I know that I'm going to need my energy, especially if Giovanna and Riley come back from wherever it is that they've disappeared to. I'm hoping I will be of some use today, or at least, more than I was standing around yesterday, and I'll need the energy for that.

I'm tired as hell for some stupid reason.

I'd slept soundly, far more soundly than I thought I would out here in a tiny tent with Nox only an arm's reach away from Gryphon and I. Yet my body doesn't feel as though I had gotten a full eight hours. It sort of feels as though I'd been out to a rave and danced the night away.

Gryphon's eyes flash up to mine and his mouth hardens a little. That makes me blush harder than talking about peeing behind trees because I don't want him to trip over my thoughts and think that I am complaining about being out here or whining about how tired I am. I'm here to prove myself, dammit!

For a second, I forget myself and open my mouth to make an excuse. Then I snap it shut again when I remember that we're radio silent at the moment... or whatever you call this whole not-talking-out-loud thing that we're doing. I should probably ask Gryphon what the official name for it is.

Before I can figure out what the hell to say to him, his words filter into my head. *We'll talk about why you're tired when we get home, Bonded. It's not your fault that you're feeling tired.*

What the hell is that supposed to mean?

I frown, but he turns away from me to pull another

bottle of water out of his pack and downs half of it in one go. There's that same weird energy around him, as though there's something wrong that I've missed that happened overnight. Now there's warning bells going off in my head with what he said.

Sleepwalking? Sleep *talking*? Hell, what else could I be doing while unconscious?

Calm down. It's nothing you've done. We have a job to do today, get your head back into it.

I duck my face back down to stare down at my boots and nod, shaking myself off mentally to get rid of all of the bad feelings. He's right. If I go into today off-kilter, then my bond is more likely to come out at the smallest provocation. Gryphon had relayed a lot of what Nox had been telling him about the people here, so it wouldn't be, like, catastrophic. But the potential for the Resistance to retaliate and come after more innocent Gifted, just because I couldn't control myself is high.

I can't let that happen. Not now. Not ever.

Nox is silent and broody as we move through the trees towards the line of perfect houses on the lake. It's a different sort of silence than yesterday, and I catch Gryphon watching him with a calculating intensity more often than

127

not. I'm very aware that my most vicious and private Bond is probably gearing up to start a riot over the scrutiny and whatever the hell sparked it. I hope like hell that it has nothing to do with me.

The sinking feeling in my gut is a definite warning that it is.

Brutus walks by my side, snapping and snarling soundlessly if any of the other shadow pups get close to us. I don't think any of them mean us any harm, it's more like they're curious about me and want to see what all of the fuss is about, but Brutus is *very* territorial.

It's so freaking cute.

All of the practice and observation I got in yesterday means that my feet are much quieter on the ground than they were at the beginning of the mission. Don't get me wrong, I still sound like a herd of elephants compared to either of my Bonds, but it's a major improvement.

Nox is going to send the shadow creatures in their smallest forms first, and once we have confirmation that they're back in there, then we'll move in.

I don't usually startle at the sound of Gryphon's voice in my head anymore, but I was so far into my own head that it has me tripping over my feet a little. Not enough that Nox hears it and turns around to see me being incompetent, thank God, but Gryphon gets a hand under my elbow to catch me, pulling me to a stop as we reach the area where the trees begin to thin out.

Gryphon's hand drops away from me as he takes a half step towards Nox, watching him closely as he widens his stance a little and rolls his shoulders back, preparing himself for the work he's about to do.

Watching Nox's eyes void out completely is way more unsettling than it had been with North, mostly because I don't know if his bond loathes me as much as Nox himself does… or if he even has another entire *being* living within him. I'm only assuming that he does because his eyes turn black the same way ours do, and I've only ever shared that experience with North before.

The shadow creatures around us all immediately start to mobilize until there is a circle of protection around us once again. Then two of his bigger and fiercer looking creations, both of them in the forms of snarling Dobermans, begin to shrink down until they are barely visible streams of dark smoke wisps that are little more than air as they move, and I watch as they disappear into the trees in front of us.

Gryphon shifts on his feet, crossing his arms as his eyes narrow. A white ring of light circles his irises as he calls on his own Gift to listen in on what's happening around us. It's incredibly frustrating to not be able to do the same. All that I can say for sure is that my bond doesn't feel any danger aimed in my direction that it's concerned enough about to want to take over. It's awake and taking up space in my chest at the moment, but it's mostly content that we're here doing something with two of my Bonds.

There's the ever-present longing for Nox in my chest as well, but it's strangely quieter than it was yesterday.

I find myself side-eyeing Gryphon once again, but he is completely focused on the mission.

They're back, he says directly into my mind, and Nox turns to face us, his lip curled a little in my direction.

Well, that answers that question. There's too much humanity on his face right now, so I know that his bond is not actually in control at the moment, if it ever could be. I don't know if I should be upset about it or relieved.

Something to think about later when we're not about to abduct two full-grown, fully powered Gifted.

We need to move; they're packing to leave. We're following Nox's lead. You go in after him, and I'll take up the rear. Just follow Nox and try not to make any unnecessary noises.

I give Gryphon a curt nod and move in towards my other Bond, careful to keep my feet quiet and a reasonable distance between the two of us still.

I want to show that I am following Gryphon's orders but also respecting the fact that Nox would rather crawl on his belly across glass than to ever be near me. It's a delicate balance to get right, dammit.

We move out as one.

It's harder to keep up with Nox than I would like to admit. His legs are easily twice as long as mine, and he doesn't really seem too concerned about making sure that I'm keeping up. Brutus stays at my side the entire time, and the stealthy way that we all have to move takes up most of my concentration.

It's early enough in the morning that there aren't many people out, thankfully, and we only have to take cover once on our way to avoid being detected. Surprisingly, we don't skirt around the O'Neill property this time. As we get close to the boundary of it, Brutus grows a little bigger at my side, and another shadow creature of the same size flanks my other side as we move through the property.

I glance around and find that the other shadow creatures are doing the same with Nox and Gryphon. It takes a second for it to click in my mind, but then I remember all of the photos that I have attempted to take of Brutus and August over the last couple of weeks. Every last one of them turned out to have light flares or some other sort of lighting problem, so I assume that they are messing with the cameras for us as we move. Since we are moving in on the targets, we no longer have to worry about being seen.

When we get to the lake house, Nox heads straight for the back door. One of the shadow creatures jumps up to slither straight into the keyhole, unlocking it instantly for us.

That's freaking handy.

It only takes me half a breath to start feeling the flushes of nervousness in my gut, but I push it away as Nox looks over my head to meet Gryphon's eyes, one last check that we're ready to go before he gives him a decisive nod.

Nox reaches forward to push the door open and enters the lake house with his gun drawn, his eyes still that same eerie black color that's so unsettling to the other Gifted, and he's moving with the rapid, practiced ease of a professional who has done this a thousand times.

I have no real concerns that anything is going to happen to him, even as he takes the lead, because his shadow creatures all move as one to follow him in, streaming into the house like a swarm from the deepest pits of hell. They're all snarling and snapping silently, as though they're eager to find a throat to rip out. I hope the maid hasn't arrived since we started moving in, although these shadow creatures are not like North's at all. There is no part of me that is worried about them attacking us, or anyone else, unprovoked, because Nox has such a firm control of them all.

I move in after him just as quickly, proud when my feet are still silent as I work my way up the steps, even though it no longer matters. Brutus is quick to stay at my side. I can hear Gryphon moving behind me, but we have done training for this enough times that I know not to slow down or turn back for him. I'm here to protect Nox's back and to help sweep the house until we are sure that we have both Giovanna and Riley captured.

With Gryphon and Nox's abilities, I'm almost completely sure that there's only the two of them in the house. If there was someone else, Gryphon should be able to hear them or the shadows would have sniffed them out, but it's still part of Tac procedure for us to do this, so we're sticking to it.

The lake house is luxurious, and it's very clear that Giovanna's family doesn't just have money, but that they're the deep-pockets sort of old wealth that the Dravens and the Bensons are also a part of. Everything is perfectly designed, and even though there isn't anything particularly flashy or extravagant, it all still oozes money. There's something about scattered decorative pillows in neutral, coastal colors and cashmere lap blankets that really screams money.

The shadow creatures don't seem to notice it the way I do though.

Nox moves through the house with the type of precision that can only come from knowing the layout intimately; the hours and hours that he had spent yesterday seeing through his shadow creatures' eyes have given him an edge by mapping this place out. In under a minute, we are staring Giovanna and Riley down in one of the many parlor rooms on the first floor.

I haven't seen Riley since the football game that Sage and I had run into him at and then promptly left, but he is almost unrecognizable now.

His skin looks tight over his bones, and he's lost so much weight that he's practically a walking skeleton. His eyes are sunken into his skull, and the sallow pallor of his face makes him look at least thirty years older than he actually is. There's a small smear of dried blood under his nose and a frantic look in his eyes as they dart between us all that's almost animalistic.

The horror at what he's gone through without anyone knowing he's a victim is, well, *horrifying*.

Giovanna, on the other hand, looks like the picture of good health, which instantly has me ready to rip her soul out my-damn-self, no vengeful bond required.

Her long, perfectly bronzed legs are exposed, thanks to the teeny tiny mini skirt she's wearing, and her halter top barely contains her tits. She stares Nox down with a look of contempt for a second, which also gets me fired up, but then her eyes flash white as her Gift kicks into gear.

"Give it up, Jordan," Gryphon snaps from behind me. "We already know that you're using so much power on Riley that you don't have any left for us."

A smirk slowly stretches over her mouth and her hand rises to tap one very manicured fingernail against her chin.

"That might have been true a few weeks ago, but I'm fully bonded now," she gloats, and without another word, Riley's eyes also shift to white.

My bond moves my body before I have the chance to move myself, flinging me from where I'm standing and into Nox's side, taking him to the ground until I'm splayed out on top of him. For a second, I think that maybe Giovanna has taken control of me somehow before I see the fire poker lodged in the wall behind us both.

It would have gone straight through Nox's chest.

I stare at that iron bar for a second before my bond flares to life and I'm pushing up off of the ground, brushing myself off and raising a hand of my own to the manipulative bitch. She's ready for me though, as ready as you can be when facing someone who can literally rip your freaking soul out, and furniture starts floating all around us.

She's trying to get me to focus on Riley and kill him first. Now that she's been outed and she has no use for him, he's nothing but cannon fodder in her plans.

Even my bond has some rage feelings about that, and it never really gives two fucks about anyone outside of our Bond Group.

An arm chair comes flying at me but Brutus bats it away like it's nothing, and I keep my eyes on Giovanna, absolutely confident in his ability to keep me safe. "Bad move. You could've been taken in nicely, now you're going to be dragged back, braindead."

She laughs at me, stupidly, and when Riley's eyes flash, I don't need my bond or Brutus to protect me, side-stepping the couch that gets flung my way. I feel Nox step in closer to my side, his eyes still voided out, but there's a blankness over his features now that sends a thrill up my spine.

My bond stretches inside of me, spreading through my limbs as it reacts to seeing his.

My transfixion on Nox is broken by the sound of Gryphon firing at Riley, shooting him in the leg and taking him down to the ground with a scream. His eyes flash back to their usual honey color, and the coffee table that was hovering in the air drops back down to the ground.

What the hell was that for?! He's not the danger here! I snap and Gryphon doesn't hesitate to reply.

You got distracted and were about to be taken out. Besides, he's the one throwing shit at my Bonded, and I'm not going to stand around watching that shit happen. We can heal him when we get them back.

I huff but Nox steps forward and takes over the situation again, directing his shadow creatures. Now that Riley is out of commission, thanks to a freaking bullet, his focus is entirely on Giovanna.

Her eyes flash a brighter white as she focuses on him, but his face remains that same blank slate, nothing there but a cold, emotionless being.

It has to be his Bond.

Three of the shadow creatures jump on Giovanna at once, their forms shifting and morphing until she's cloaked in darkness, writhing and screaming in frustration as she tries to fight them off. It's no use, she's trying to struggle against sentient smoke that can change its own density at will.

I feel her Gift skit across my mind, bouncing away uselessly. Even after being bonded, she's *nothing* compared to me and my power. There's something very satisfying about that.

I smirk down at her, not that she can see it underneath all of the dark smoke covering her, but she can hear me well enough as I drawl, "Honestly, I was expecting more out of you. After so long of worming your way into a high profile Bond Group and messing around with them... I was expecting you to give us more trouble than this. Pathetic, really."

She lets out a strangled scream and then snarls at me, "I might not be able to get into your head, but Silas will. There's nothing you'll be able to do to stop him. You or your cursed Bond Group. It's only a matter of time, *monster*."

My blood runs cold in my veins.

I already know she's right. I've spent more than

enough time being tortured by Davies to know just how much power he has, but the idea of him getting into Nox's head? Or any of my Bonds and Bonded?

I'd rather die.

We get transported back to the Sanctuary in two blocks, the guys take Giovanna and Riley back first before coming back for Gryphon, Nox, and me. We have to go back for the rest of our gear and it's while we were hiking back through the trees that I felt it.

Eyes on us.

Neither Gryphon or Nox seem to notice it, both of them staying focused as we make our way back to the camping spot, and my bond doesn't take over completely, but it takes notice.

It stills in my chest and just… waits. For what, I have no freaking clue, but it waits and watches and is poised, ready to take over if anything happens.

Except it doesn't.

We get the extra packs right before the Transporter arrives again to take us back. I'm about ready to climb out of my skin with nerves, so freaking ready to be out of the woods. The moment our feet hit the ground, Gryphon wraps a hand around one side of my neck to stop me from puking, but when his Gift finishes up and he moves away from me, probably to find North and debrief with him about the mission, the feeling of unease is still lingering inside me. It's definitely not the motion sickness. Nope, it's something else entirely.

Nox stares at me.

Directly at me, no sneering or snarling insults at me for once, and it *also* makes me want to climb out of my skin. He does everything he can to avoid looking at me or being near me, so to have him just standing there and taking me in is just… so deeply unsettling.

I swallow roughly and just stare back at him like an idiot until his eyes narrow. He steps forward, towards me, and then glances back over my shoulder as though he's going to see anything but TacTeam personnel buzzing around. "What is it? What's happened?"

I think it's the carefully considering tone he's using, but I don't just brush it off for once. I could, and I probably should, but I feel as though he's actually seeing me for the first time as his eyes still roam over my face.

I step in closer to him, still careful about leaving a gap between our bodies but ensuring that none of the personnel around us will overhear. "Do you feel like we're being watched? Like there's... something keeping tabs? I can't shake it, and while we were out, I felt it again."

He looks back up and scowls around at everyone surrounding me. "Why the hell didn't you say something sooner? Riordan could have been with us and followed us back with the jump."

My stomach drops.

The sneer he always wears just for me settles back over his face and he snaps, "I need to find Benson. Come with me now."

He pushes past me, not waiting for me to agree, and I follow him because I'd once again forgotten about the Resistance's invisible, virtually undetectable man. Fuck. I *should* have spoken sooner.

I also should know better than to mention that to Nox though, because when I do, his reply is scathing. "Yes, you should have. Your bond is more experienced and more keenly aware than anyone else's, and if you're not going to actually listen to it, then you're a liability and as good as a spy yourself. Stop hoarding information and start talking, Poison, before you get us all killed."

I let him berate me.

We pass Gryphon at the edge of the group though,

and he isn't so keen to let the scolding go on for long. "Hoarding information? You'd know nothing about that, would you, Draven?"

There it is again.

I can't stop myself from asking him, *Are we going to talk about it now?*

He glances over at me and shakes his head a fraction, before eyeing Nox's retreating back like he's thinking about stabbing him. *I need to speak to North about it as well, preferably together. Don't worry about it, Bonded.*

Nox's savage mood doesn't ease up, not even when we get to Sawyer and he can't find any evidence of Riordan being with us, no matter how he heat maps the video footage. The guilt is still eating me alive because deep down, I know Nox is right.

I could've led the Resistance back here, given them the keys to get a spy in here, and that does make me just as bad as the rest of them.

Can you come with us? If you're not busy. It's a cop-out, but I don't want to know what Nox's sneering will turn into if we do find Riordan in any of the footage from our return. I've been so adamant about dealing with Nox on my own, but I was also so goddamn sure I could get through this mission without fucking up.

And here I am, fucking it up.

You didn't. You should remember that you saved his life

back there, you reacted before even his shadow creatures could, and you've done nothing wrong. Even if Riordan came back with us, that's not on you. I didn't even notice the bad feeling you felt, that's on me. Neither did Nox, that's on him. Ease up on yourself, Bonded.

I can't though.

I can't because... fuck, because it would've been so damn easy to just say something, and I didn't. There's a whole heap of reasons they might have missed the eerie feeling, but I felt it, and I should have said something about it.

Gryphon plants one of his big hands on the base of my spine and directs me out of the room, getting us on the path towards the security room after Nox. Instead of letting it drop away, when the mid-morning sun hits us both as we get out into the fresh air, he slides his palm around my hip to pull me into his side. He's not usually this hands-on in public, especially not with his TacTeam around, so I must look freaking miserable right now.

I need a goddamn distraction.

"How did you know shooting Riley would work to get Giovanna out of his head?"

Gryphon shrugs. "A lucky guess. He was already almost tapped out, thanks to Giovanna's fucking around in his head. I didn't think his body could handle the pain and the power use. I've dealt with another situation that was pretty similar, so it was more of a calculated guess, really."

I nod and try not to cringe as Nox barges his way into the security office to harass Sawyer because of me. "And if it hadn't worked?"

Gryphon scowls at Nox but answers me all the same. "I'd have aimed for his chest next. The mission is never going to be more important than you. Remember that, Bonded."

Sawyer can't find any evidence of anyone following us back.

Even when he checks up on the body cam that the Transporter was wearing, he can't find any evidence of anyone else being in the woods with us. Nox doesn't believe him and Gryphon has to intervene to get him to back down, and I can't meet Sawyer's eyes while they stand off against each other. I'm sure he just wants to make some joke about it, something awkward or sexual, but I just don't have that in me right now.

Or he's going to berate me for not having found *something* yet to get Sage out of the confinement she's currently in.

Gryphon gets called away to deal with something big within his TacTeam. He drags Nox out with him, leaving me alone with Sawyer. Well, he leaves me, but only after he makes me swear on our Bond that I won't move from here until Gabe comes to get me. It doesn't matter that I still have weapons strapped to me or, you know, a killer bond lurking inside me with a Gift that never freaking runs out.

I still need a Bond guard, apparently.

But I do as he says and slump into a chair next to Sawyer, the night of subpar sleep catching up to me. It takes exactly the amount of time required for Gryphon and Nox to leave the security office and get out of earshot before Sawyer turns to me with a stink eye.

"Why are you looking at me like you've killed my mom?"

I snort at him and shrug, rubbing both of my eyes so I still don't have to look his way. "I still have nothing. I got Giovanna and Riley back here, but there was nothing else there, no signs of anything other than that bitch being a traitor. I feel fucking useless and guilty over the whole thing."

Sawyer scoffs and I listen to the sound of his fingers flying over the keys as though it's a freaking lullaby. "I wasn't expecting you to find a giant billboard with an explanation out there in the woods, Oli. Were you?"

I kick my feet out a little wider. "I mean… it would've been nice. I need her out of there. I need something to explain this shit. Have you been to see her yet?"

"North won't let me. I was pissed at first, but Gray pointed out that I'm of more use to her up here at my computer, and she's with her Bonds. I made him go down there though, and he said she was a mess. Absolutely fucking devastated that she might've killed someone, even though she knows she didn't actually do it… like, mentally. Physically, she for sure did. I know she did because I've tracked her every movement and there's no manipulation on the video. I've been so freaking thorough with it all."

I nod and finally look at him.

He looks like shit.

The same as I feel, really.

There's dark circles under his eyes and the pile of empty energy drinks around his desk tells a pretty clear story of how hard he's working to get his sister cleared of this shit. There's a fine dusting of fair stubble on his cheeks too, which seems far too 'grown up' for the sarcastic, cheeky asshole that I know. When he catches me looking, he snaps, "I'm aware I need a shower, Fallows. Thanks for pointing it out."

I scoff and throw a dismissive hand in his direction. "I was imagining you with a beard, if this keeps up for much longer, and I just can't cope with that. I need to find something and get you the fuck out of here."

My bond warms in my chest right as there's a knock

at the door. Sawyer presses a button under the table to let Gabe in. My Bond looks as though he's come straight from one of the building sites, his work clothes still covered in a fine layer of dust, and a good, clean sweat still shining on his skin.

It makes my bond perk right the hell up.

"Gross, stop giving him those eyes in front of me. I don't have time for all of the pent-up sexual frustration you two give off."

I roll my eyes at Sawyer's sass. "Usually, you're signing up for front row tickets."

He points at the door and snaps back, "Not when I'm trying to work. Go be young and horny and in love somewhere else."

Gabe scoffs at him even as he holds out a hand for me to take, helping me out of my seat and tugging me into his side securely. "Good to see you too, Benson. Found anything yet?"

I shake my head for the both of us, my mouth tightening up as my throat closes over. Gabe frowns down at me, leaning down to give me a quick peck on the lips. His skin is warm and inviting, the empty space in my chest that belongs to him aches, and I lean more fully into his strength.

He smiles down at me, his eyes soft as he traces over my face. I hope I'm not covered in dirt or something from the trip. "Let's leave Sawyer to his creeper ways, Bond. I have something I want to show you."

We leave together to the sound of Sawyer calling out, "Spoiler alert! It's his dick!"

I roll my eyes and Gabe flips him off behind our backs as we get out of there, the fresh air a relief even as the midday sun is warm against my cheeks. I take a second to actually look around a bit and find that the town center has been cleaned up a lot in the last day or so while we were out on the recovery mission.

There's still a lot of damage, dozens of destroyed roads and buildings can't be fixed overnight, but the rubble and debris has been cleared away and patches have been put in over what could be shored up. We don't have enough finished houses to just move people out of buildings if there's a few broken windows, but the fix up is well underway.

There are groups of men and women everywhere with building supplies and good attitudes as they get to work on it all, and the sense of community has my chest tightening up.

This is what we're really fighting for.

We're fighting for these people, even if they're wary of my bond. I mean, that just says they're smart enough to know when there's a predator living among them. I'd never put someone down for that.

"Here, we're taking the ATV over," Gabe says, pulling me over to the vehicle he'd driven over here for us both. The last time I was in one was with Atlas, the two of us heading out to the perfect night in a cave by ourselves and then the harried trip back the next morning while everything turned to shit, but it still brings a blush to my cheeks.

"Where are we going? Should I get changed first?" I say as he helps me in, my legs still a little sore from the hiking, not that I'll ever admit it.

"You'll see, Bond. Just let me surprise you, for once."

I huff at the smug tone he's throwing at me and cross my arms over my chest, a joking sort of tantrum that he sees through immediately. He grabs one of my hands and tugs at it to link our fingers together, resting them on his thigh.

I settle back into the seat and look out at the houses and buildings we pass, taking in just how big the Sanctuary actually is. North and his family have put in so much money and time here, completely altruistically. They could have just built themselves a bomb-proof bunker, but instead they've created something that really earns the name it was given.

The Sanctuary.

At the outskirts of the town, up a small incline and surrounded by piled-up building supplies, is a mansion. Gabe pulls up and parks the ATV in front of it, killing the engine and gesturing at the palace in front of us.

Okay, it's probably classified as just a big house, but it's at least four times bigger than the house we're currently hunkering down together in.

"Welcome home, Bond," Gabe murmurs, kissing the back of my hand.

My mouth drops open and I give him a shocked look, probably looking like a complete idiot. He grins back at me, sliding out and walking around to help me out, and slings an arm around my shoulders as we pick our way through the piles of supplies and walk up the steps together.

"This is ours? Well, North's, I guess."

Gabe shakes his head at me. "No, you were right the first time. It's ours. North and Gryphon picked the spot together so that we're somewhere a little further away from everyone else and easier to keep secure. I've built it, and Atlas has been helping since he's learned how to put his strength to good use. Nox… has mostly made demands about how he wants his office and library done, but I guess that's still input. North picked out most of the details. I told him he should get your opinion on it too, but… again, he's a Draven. There's only so much I can get out of him."

I grin, because that's true and something I now appreciate about him. There's something really fucking hot about a man who takes control, leaving none of the weight of decision-making on me. Now that I have some autonomy back, I have more than enough decisions to make in a day. I really wouldn't want to be arguing with anyone about paint chips or tile choices right now.

Gabe walks me right up to the front door, stopping there as I peek into the window. "Can we go in? Is there enough done to go in?"

He grins and takes my hand gently to lead me through the house, dodging the tools and piles of flooring that is still waiting to go down. It's all in beautiful earthy tones; the colors go with the dusty, remote desert that we're now living in. Although the house is, at most, a fifth of the size of the Draven mansion, it still feels huge compared to the little temporary house we're currently holed up in.

It feels like *home* already.

"I've been camping out here. I spoke to North about making this place a priority for us. I was focusing on the housing for the other families because there's so many that are sharing but… after everything that happened, it's a security issue to get you into this place. Our other house isn't as secure and… you're always going to take priority."

I open my mouth to answer him, though I'm not really sure what I'd say, when he stops and pushes open one of the doors, tugging me into a huge bedroom and closing the door firmly behind us.

It's stunning.

The room is huge, bigger even than my room back at

North's mansion, and not only is it completely finished, it's also furnished. There's a giant bed, easily the size of two Cal Kings pushed together, with a TV on the wall and a desk in the corner with a laptop sitting on top. There are curtains and plush carpets on the floor and... it's perfectly finished.

"How did you do this? How did you get it all done... just for me?"

He grins sheepishly. "I told you; I've been camping out here. North picked most of the colors and furniture. I'm just the one putting it all together. I wanted to get you out of that house."

I scoff a little and roll my eyes, self-deprecatingly. "I don't think there's anything 'just' about building a whole freaking house, Gabe. Thank you. I feel guilty as hell about this being a priority when there are people who need it more, especially when you see the damage in the town, but... I've been feeling burnt out. I needed this."

He nods and tugs me into his chest again, kissing the top of my head as though I'm some deeply precious thing to him. I know that, of course, I am precious to him, his Central Bond, but it still feels like an honor.

"I wasn't going to let you waste away in that house. Plus, some soundproofing will be nice too. If I had to keep hearing you coming, I might've gone insane."

I blush and duck my head, ignoring him when he bursts

into laughter at my embarrassment, because I don't feel all that bad about it either. If I shut my eyes, I can still feel North's hand closing around my neck and holding me down as his bond fucked me raw. I'll never be able to feel bad about that.

"Look around, Bond, get yourself comfortable."

I walk through to the en-suite bathroom to check it out, practically drooling over the huge bathtub and the shower with the built-in bench seat and *four* massaging shower heads. It's like the upgraded version of North's shower back at his mansion, and I'm eager to climb into it.

There's a door at the other end of the ensuite. When I open it, I not only find my closet, I also find my bags sitting in there with all of my clothes and shoes packed up, everything I'd come here with.

I'm already moved in.

I turn back to Gabe and whisper in disbelief, "We're staying here tonight? It's done enough for that?"

He grins and nods back. "Your room, your bathroom, and the kitchen are done. My room just needs the lights to be wired. North's room is waiting on flooring. Gryphon's is being painted today, and Atlas has been working on his bathroom. Nox's is done, he likes everything to be simple and plain. But, yeah, we're here tonight, Bond."

It's the most romantic thing any man has ever said to me, I swear to God.

GABE

The joy on my Bond's face makes the long hours working on this place worth every exhausting and frustrating second.

She heads straight into the bathroom to wash up, and I go down to the kitchen to fix us both some lunch. When North had called to say that Oli and the guys were on their way back, I'd gone down to the dining hall to shop through the kitchen there, grabbing whatever supplies I could get away with, thanks to the chef following me around and grumbling the whole time. Not that he cared about the actual food leaving his kitchen, he's just pissed that he's not cooking for the Dravens as much.

The man has a lot of pride tied up in his work for North.

I already know that my Bond is easy to please when it comes to meals though, thank God. A loaded sandwich with all of the trimmings has her beaming at me as I kick her bedroom door shut behind me. She looks fucking adorable sitting in the middle of the giant bed in one of my old football jerseys from high school and an old pair of sweatpants that she'd squirreled away from Gryphon.

My voice dries up in my throat.

"Oh, I freaking love bacon in a sandwich! I could smell it cooking when I got out of the bathroom, and I've been drooling ever since."

I smirk at her and walk over to hand her the plate, careful not to brush up against the clean linens. I'm still covered in dust and God knows what else, and I'm not going to disrespect her space like that.

The whole point of getting her in here is so she feels respected and more in control of what her life looks like. There's not much I can do to help with that, especially when I agree with all of the extra security North and Gryphon are putting on her, but I can give her this little haven. I know how badly she needs her own space, even when she's craving her Bonds.

"Are you going to sit with me or just stare at me while I make a pig of myself?" Oli drawls, her sass a little muted now that shit has hit the fan with Sage, but it's still there.

I grab the chair from behind her desk and drag it over to

sit beside her. "I'm covered in dust. I'll grab a shower after I've finished eating. I didn't have time before Gryphon called."

She nods and takes another huge bite of her sandwich, a little of the sauce dripping out of the corner of her mouth, and I grin at her. This version of my Bond, the one who has let down all of her barriers and walls, is my favorite one. I've never been happier in my life.

"You should've just jumped in with me. We could've made the food together afterwards."

I almost choke.

I put a lot of time and effort into not making a complete dick of myself around her, thanks to the small fact that there are four other Bonds in my Bonded Group to compete with. I manage to keep my shit together, though I swallow too soon and it's a little dry going down my throat.

"I didn't know that was on the table. You definitely haven't said that it's an option."

She tilts her head to the side as though she's thinking and nods slowly. "That's true."

We fall back into silence, only the sounds of us both tearing into our food to be heard, and when I set my plate down on her side table to go grab that shower, she clears her throat. I stop and look over at her, raising an eyebrow at her, but she just shakes her head back at me like she's changed her mind.

I'm not pushing her.

I never have and I never will. I don't think that I'm a fucking saint or anything, but I want to know for sure that when I complete my bond with her, it's because she wanted to, not because of some other stupid reason. I never want to have a doubt in my mind that she was just as desperate for me as I am for her.

So I head to the bathroom, rolling my shoulders back and groaning a little under my breath as the bones there crack. I'd gotten up before the sun this morning to lay the carpets in Oli's closet, the last thing that was needed for it to be done, and hauling the rolls into the house by myself wasn't the easiest thing to be doing. I've been slacking on my workouts and, man, does my body feel it.

I get the door open before Oli calls out, "Gabe? It's on the table."

I turn back and find her staring over at me, no signs of her bond taking over and forcing decisions onto her, just those crystal clear blue eyes looking back at me, as sure at the sunrise in the morning.

Well, fuck.

It's impossible to shower without a rock-hard dick now. The scents of her soaps and lotions and girl shit just makes it worse, like I'm marinating in all things Oleander Fallows, until I'm about ready to nut myself.

Would jerking off right now be taking things too

far? Fuck, here I was thinking how fucking good I am at respecting her shit for not getting dust on her sheets and ten minutes later, I'm thinking about spraying her shower screen with my cum because she said four little words to me. Four words that in any other situation are not a fucking turn on.

Jesus Christ.

I get the fuck out of there before I disgrace my family name, grabbing a towel and quickly drying myself off. My bond pulls and tugs at my chest to get back to Oli, but I force my body to just stand there and get a hold of myself. I'm not about to make a dick of myself. I'm not about to freak her the hell out by charging in there and... fuck, okay, I can't think about the shit I want to do to her right now while I'm trying to calm down.

I wrap the towel around my waist and walk back into the bedroom, planning on grabbing clothes from my bag that's waiting for me there, but as soon as I lay eyes on my Bond, I'm done for. She's sitting on the bed, her knees pulled up to her chest, and the ravenous look in her eyes as she takes me in stops me short.

I wonder how she tastes.

I want to know what her thighs feel like around my head or how her face looks when she comes or, fuck, what happens when her bond comes out to join in.

Weeks of living in close quarters with her mean I

already know what she sounds like when she comes. I want to know if she'll make those same noises or if I can draw some new ones out of her. I want to know what edges I can push her to and which ones are worth tipping her over into a pool of writhing bliss.

My bond rages inside my chest for her, pushing and snarling like a rabid beast, and I can feel the urge to shift beating down on me. I need to be the predator, to wear the skin of what hides inside me, because she's always been the ultimate prey for me.

I make it to the bed in three steps and Oli rises to her knees to meet me, her hands sliding into my wet hair without hesitation as she drags my lips to hers. I've kissed her a hundred times before, every make out session I could possibly fit in around the chaos of our lives while she was getting her feet here, but this feels different.

There's nothing to stop us from being together.

I feel like I should say something, ask her one last time if she's sure, but when she breaks away from my lips, it's only for as long as it takes her to tug my jersey off, all of her perfect skin on display, and then she's kissing me again as she shoves the sweatpants down her legs, moving awkwardly to let them fall away.

I unhook my towel with a rough tug, glad that I don't need to think about buttons or zippers right now because they're beyond my capabilities.

Fuck, she feels so good.

I push her back and climb onto the bed, right on top of her, without breaking the kiss. Even with the frenzied motions of her hands as she maps out my back, she's not in a rush to break that connection between us, and I use it to my advantage.

Mostly by telling my dick *and* my bond to calm the fuck down.

It takes me a minute, but once I've wrestled my bond back into submission, I move to kiss down her neck to the delicate skin of her shoulder, sucking and biting as I listen to her breath hitch in her throat. The more slow and careful attention I give her, the more languid but pent-up her body becomes.

It's fucking addicting.

I work my way down her chest, fighting with myself over whether to savor the moment or just rush to get to where I really want to be. Which, for the record, is between those perfectly creamy thighs of hers, with her ankles locked somewhere around my ears.

When I get to her hips, nipping at the bones there and licking the little indentations I'm leaving behind to soothe the ache, she stills for a second, her legs tensing up. I stop, glancing up to see what's spooked her so I can murder it because I do not want to be stopped right now. Not when I'm this goddamned close to finally tasting this pussy I've dreamed of.

She gives me a rueful grin and shrugs. "I'm just telling my bond to go to hell. It wants out to play with you, but I want this first."

Oh, fuck yeah.

I like that a hell of a lot.

"Tell it 'maybe next time'. Like, about ten minutes after this time is over."

Her laugh is like music to my ears, all breathless and excited, and I wait until she relaxes back down against the pillows before I duck back down to finally get what I want, to eat her out the way I'd promised her months ago when I'd first shown her my shift. Fuck, and it's everything I always wanted.

I don't know if it's because she's my Bond, but I can read her like a book, testing out every little movement and swirl of my tongue against her clit until she's writhing and moaning loudly enough that I'm glad we're here alone.

I don't want anyone else hearing this moment between us—it belongs to me.

My own groans of pleasure vibrate through the very center of her body and she begins to pant, her hands rough as she fists my hair and tugs at me like she's trying to get my face even closer to her core.

As her body begins to shake, I feel her bond come to the surface and coax mine out. Our Bond isn't complete yet, but the process is starting. I can feel it come alive in every inch of my body. I have to bite the inside of my cheek until I taste blood so I don't ruin everything right now. The sensations are almost too much, like I should have waited to make her come until I was inside of her first, but the sounds she makes and the way she moves her hips against my face is fucking addicting.

I want to die like this.

"Gabe, please, I need more. I can't... my bond needs *more*," she gasps, and I pull away from the soaking mess I've made of her pussy to look at her again. Her hair is spread out over the pillows like a silky, silver fan, and her cheeks are flushed beautifully. Her lips are red from where she's been biting them, pouty and abused in the best way. I want to remember this moment for the rest of my goddamned life.

I aim for a confident tone, but the dry rasp of it probably gives my own desperation away as I reply, "I can give you what you want, Bond."

And that's how I find myself living out my second biggest fantasy with my Bond as she straddles my thighs and rides my dick like a fucking pro. Fuck, she feels like a dream as she takes every inch of me and her nails dig into my chest as she gets a good rhythm going.

I might've been talking myself up, but with Oli's ass bouncing against my thighs as she slides that perfect pussy up and down my cock, it takes a lot of concentration to not just blow my load. She's fucking perfect, *perfect*, and my bond is glowing under my skin at finally having her.

It was worth every second of the wait.

Just when I'm sure I'm going to come, too soon because I never want this to end, I get a handful of each of her thighs, lifting her up off of my dick and dragging her back up my body until she's straddling my face.

She makes a gasping sort of noise, a mournful and shocked sound, and when I speak, my words are right at her core. "One more time. Come on my lips one more time, Bond."

She hovers there for a second until I tug her back down, seating her sweet pussy against my mouth properly, and then I eat until she's screaming my name, thighs trembling and hips grinding out her orgasm.

I drink down every drop of her cum and groan at the taste of her honey.

She waits as long as it takes for her thighs to stop shaking, and then she crawls back down my body, turning to kiss me and lick away her wetness from my tongue.

I can't lie there anymore, as much as I love her taking control.

I flip us both over and push back into her, my dick still achingly hard and ready to blow. She makes the most incredible sound, a gasping sort of squeal, and then a string of curses and praises fall from her lips.

"Yes, fuck, *please*… God, more, I need more, Gabe, fuck!"

The Bonding feels like finally, *finally*, coming home.

There's no other way to describe the flood of euphoria that spreads through me as my own orgasm nails me in the back of the head and renders me fucking useless. It's as though I've been wandering the plains of the earth on my own for a thousand years, but now I've finally found where I belong.

Oli's eyes shift to black underneath me, but only for a second before those beautiful baby blues are blinking back at me again. It was just a small moment, her bond checking in with the connection we've just made.

When I finally roll off of her, conscious of my weight, I drag her along with me so we're not actually separated. I want her skin against mine for at least the next week, bare minimum.

My chest is still heaving, but I have to say something to fill in the silence now that there's no longer the sounds of our skin slapping together as I'd pounded into her. "That was definitely what I dreamed it would be."

She snorts and buries her head in my shoulder, hiding her face as though she's shy about it now that she's not actually on top of my dick.

"The Bonding, sex in general, the whole nine yards."

She freezes for a second and then rears her head back. "What do you mean 'sex in general'? It hasn't been that long for you."

I grin at her, smug as hell to hear that. "You didn't guess? Clearly the years of porn under my belt have done the job."

She blinks up at me and my grin widens. "You're not the only one who decided to wait. I didn't— I couldn't stand the idea of touching anyone else. I'm not saying that to throw all the others under the bus, it just wasn't for me. When North raged about Gracie and what she did, that you'd been a virgin and your bond had acted without your consent in retaliation, I couldn't believe you'd waited as well. It made me even happier with my decision."

She swallows and glances down, looking unsure for a moment, and her voice is thready when she says, "All of the girls at Draven were acting like you'd slept with half the campus."

My grin shifts into a smirk as I shrug. "Yeah, they all thought that once I met you and you hated us, I'd change my mind. I couldn't, even if I wanted to. My bond got one look at you and I was done for, even if I wasn't already sold on you. Which I was, by the way. I think the reason I was so fucking angry and spiteful toward you was because I knew that I'd never want anyone the way I wanted you. I never have and I never will."

She looks at me like I hung the goddamn moon for her, and I'm so completely in love with this girl, no truer words have ever been uttered.

J BREE

OLI

I wake up in the giant bed in our new home feeling well-rested and a lot more calm and settled than I have been since the attack. I don't know if that is my bond being pleased to have bonded with four of my Bonds or if it's just a mental thing now that I've finally gotten some decent rest, but I'm so freaking relieved.

Gabe is still asleep beside me, the blankets pushed down to barely cover the curve of his ass. I let myself just enjoy the view because he's freaking gorgeous. He's snoring lightly, barely more than heavy breathing, and one small lock of hair falls over his forehead, making him look like a golden prince sleeping there.

We'd spent the rest of the day wrapped up in each

other, utterly obsessed with mapping out the miles of skin between us and finding every little point of pleasure until I think I've become a master at making Gabriel Ardern come.

I'm more than happy for that to be my greatest accomplishment.

The curtains are thick enough that no sunlight reaches us, but I can tell with how good I'm feeling that it's definitely morning and that I've slept a good twelve hours.

After a little while of resting there and enjoying the peace, I notice the tugging in my chest, the feeling that another of my Bonded is close by. I can already feel that it's Atlas, thanks to our own connection, and I stumble out of the bed to find something to pull on.

Gabe makes a grumbling noise under his breath and, after I've pulled on one of Gryphon's shirts and a pair of old shorts, I head back to him to smooth that golden lock back and murmur into his ear quietly, "I'll be back in a minute. I'm just going to see what Atlas is doing."

He huffs quietly and gives a nod without opening his eyes, rolling a little more onto his stomach, and the sheet slips down to uncover his ass. It is absolutely tempting me to give up on my search and climb back into the bed with him instead.

Priorities, Oli.

I'm thankful that this house is smaller than the Draven

mansion, there are a lot less rooms to have to go searching through to find Atlas. I mostly follow the feeling in my chest, my bond leading me like a compass until I end up in one of the ensuite bathrooms staring at a very sweaty, shirtless Atlas as he installs a bathtub that could easily fit three people inside it.

He's moving with ease, but without air conditioning, it's like a boiler room in here. I find myself with a flush across my cheeks pretty quickly.

It's definitely got nothing to do with how freaking hot he looks right now.

Nope.

"Did you have a good night, Bonded?" he drawls, and I raise an eyebrow at him.

"Really? We're not going to have *any* boundaries here?" He grins and shifts the bathtub again until it slides into place, dropping a half inch with a satisfying *thud* sound that echoes around the unfinished room.

He turns back to me and says in a cautious tone, "How're you feeling?"

That's a much more appropriate, but difficult, question to answer. "I don't think I feel any different, but until I let my bond out in a threatening situation, I won't really know."

He nods and shrugs at me. "Well, the world didn't end. We'll take it as a win, so far. And you've bonded with all of your Bonds now.

I pull a face back. "Not quite."

He gives me a stern look back. "You're not actually going to bond with Nox though, are you? All he wants is his power. He doesn't give a shit about you, and you owe him nothing."

I know that from the outside looking in, that's how it looks. For all I know, Atlas is right, but there's something about Nox that I can't quite figure out, something about the way that he words things to me that sets off alarm bells, even when he's being a complete asshole.

"He's still one of my Bonds, and the Bond Group isn't complete until I've bonded with you all. I'll figure out the hows and the whys of it later."

Atlas' mouth tightens a little but he nods, accepting, as always, that it *is* my decision and he has no real power to change whatever it is that I decide to do with my asshole Bond.

He might be the first person ready to murder Nox if he tries to force me into something, but that doesn't mean that he would try to take the choice away from me either.

I try to change the subject away from this because I don't have any real answers for him. Plus, I don't want to waste my morning-after glow arguing with one of my Bonded about Nox. "Are you enjoying working on this place? I can't believe how much of it is already done and that I can move in already."

He smirks at me and gestures around the room. "I don't think I'm cut out to be a builder, and I'm nowhere near as good as Gabe is, but I'm finding myself very motivated to get this done."

I grin back at him and shrug. "It looks pretty good to me."

He steps away from the bathtub and dusts his hands off on his jeans. "That's because you haven't seen my tiling efforts yet. I'm gonna have to try to convince Gabe to help out. Otherwise, it'll be the only bathroom in the place with tiles that are off-kilter."

I roll my eyes and giggle at him, enjoying the early morning banter, even if I'm standing here in this hot-as-hellfire room without any damn underwear on. "I did some tiling work when I was with Gabe the other week. I'm sure between the three of us, we could knock it out today if you want?"

He stalks over to me and cups both of my cheeks in his big hands, swooping down to kiss me thoroughly. I'm reminded once again that we had our own morning-after stolen from us by the Resistance attack. Even though I'm feeling an itch across my skin to get back to Gabe, I'm glad that Atlas is here and that I'm getting to see him again.

"Are you hungry, Sweetness? I checked the fridge this morning to make sure that Gabe had thought far enough ahead to bring over supplies. I can whip you up something to eat, if you are."

I nod back, my stomach rumbling at the mere mention of food, and rise back up onto my tiptoes to kiss him again. "I'm starving, actually. Is it okay if I grab a shower before I head down though?"

He nods and lets me go, bending down to grab his shirt from where he'd discarded it on the floor, and then he pulls it back over his head as he steers me out of the room.

His bedroom doesn't have carpet yet, but the walls are painted and there's already curtains up on both of the huge windows. When I duck my head into his closet to have a look in there, the shelving is already up as well, so it's just the bathroom and some flooring left before he will be moved in as well.

He walks me back past all of the other rooms, dropping me off at my bedroom door before heading back down to the kitchen by himself. I watch him walk away for a moment, enjoying the tight stretch of his shirt over his shoulders, but the itching across my skin to get back to Gabe doesn't ease up.

The post-bonding nesting is in full effect.

When I get back into the room, I find Gabe is stepping out of the bathroom, a towel wrapped around his hips and his magnificent chest on display. It's as though the both of them are trying to kill me this morning with their nakedness.

"Was Atlas working already?" Gabe says, and I nod.

"He's gotten the bathtub in, but he'll need some help with tiling. I offered our expertise. I hope you don't have other plans for today."

He scoffs and steps back into the bathroom to head towards the closet to get dressed. "He certainly needs it. I wouldn't let him tile anything by himself. It's not fucking rocket science, but he can't figure it out, no matter what I try.

I follow him through to the bathroom and strip to climb into the shower, soaping myself up and trying not to get emotional at the scents of him washing away from my skin. I already know that it is a nesting instinct to want that sort of marking, having experienced it three times over, but it doesn't make it any easier.

When I turn to duck my head under the spray to wash out the shampoo, I find Gabe leaning against the door, completely unabashed as he watches me with hooded eyes. I might arch my back just a little more than necessary in a teasing motion and enjoy the groan that rumbles out of his chest as his eyes latch on to my nipples.

"I didn't think you would want to go for another round while Atlas was here, but I'd never say no to you, Bonded," he says with such male satisfaction that it sends tingles down to my toes.

I smile like the Cheshire Cat and shrug with a flirty smirk. "Who said anything about going again? I'm just trying to wash my hair out. You're the one with all the dirty thoughts."

Then I hear him chuckle, except it's not out loud, but in my mind. He's also ended up with that connection and a grin bursts across my cheeks.

I can't believe I was so upset about having my Bonds in my mind.

The fear in me was so strong that I didn't have that connection with him as well. The teasing that they all do when no one else can hear has become vital to me and my happiness. The feeling of belonging and love and companionship, all of those things make being a monster a little easier to deal with.

"Come on then, Bonded. Let's go eat something and get Atlas' room finished so that I don't have to share with him anymore."

I roll my eyes and cut the water off, grabbing a towel and wrapping it around myself as I step out of the perfectly luxurious shower stall. "You guys are surprisingly good at sharing. I was *not* expecting the two of you to last in that room a whole day, let alone the weeks that you have."

Gabe shrugs again, and his eyes roam over my body as I dry myself off, fixating on all of his favorite parts. I know this because he gets a very animalistic look in his eyes when he sees something that he wants to taste again and, *God*, do I want him to taste it all again.

"Stop it. If you're insisting on helping Atlas, then you need to stop thinking that shit."

Getting dressed has never been so freaking hard.

"I went to visit Sage yesterday while you were gone."

At Atlas' words, my head snaps up from where I was completely focused on the tiles in front of me.

He'd cooked us a full breakfast with all of the trimmings and made some awful jokes about being a morning-after chef, but Gabe had just laughed along with him, happily grinning and kissing me at every opportunity as the three of us ate together. Surprisingly, having the two of them together and Atlas making those jokes didn't bother me. It felt more like the dynamic between Gryphon, North, and me than an awkward, kill-me-now sort of thing.

As soon as we had cleaned up the dishes, we went back up to Atlas' room together to get to work. The bathroom isn't small, none of them in the house are, and the tiling job could easily take all three of us the entire day to get through.

Gabe had checked out Atlas' work anchoring the bathtub and measured up all of the points where the faucets were going to go before we rushed into the work. Then the two of them had gone downstairs to carry up giant boxes of tiles, tile glue, and grout.

I'd offered to help, but both of them had shot me down very quickly. As though I am some delicate flower who can't carry a box. Once we had everything we needed, Gabe and I had gotten to work laying the tile while Atlas was mostly lifting heavy things for us and doing most of the manual grunt work.

"How did she look? Did you get to speak to her or just see her? Did you see Kieran or Felix? How did they look?" I fire off questions at Atlas, and he doesn't react to any of them until the stream of words has tumbled out of me. Gabe's movements stay steady and sure from where he's working, but a small wrinkle forms over his brow.

"Sage looks devastated. She looks like a fucking *mess,* to be honest. She was in a room by herself, but Felix and Kieran are close by. Gryphon had originally instructed for the three of them to be roomed together, but Sage requested to be left by herself."

I sit back on my heels, careful not to freak out and ruin any of the very careful positioning that Gabe and I have done around us. Atlas was not exaggerating when he said that he was terrible at doing this, and he has been relegated to mixing the tile glue for us instead of helping.

"Why would she ask to be alone and away from her

Bonds? No wonder she looks like a mess."

Gabe clears his throat, careful to keep his eyes on what he's doing as he lays another tile and levels it off. "She's afraid that she'll hurt them, that's why. She has no recollection of killing Dara, no clue how someone manipulated her into doing it, and she's terrified that there's some sort of 'kill switch' inside of her waiting to be flipped that could be used against either of her Bonded."

My heart drops down to my feet.

I want to burst into tears for her. I know exactly what it feels like to be terrified of something inside of you that you have no control over. The thought that she is now going through this, and going through it by herself, locked in a cell so close to the people who love her the most but completely terrified to even seek comfort from them... I just want to scream.

I swallow my tears back. "I need to go see her. I need to do more to figure out what the hell is going on and get her the fuck out of there."

Gabe nods, and I hand him another tile as he moves our positions further towards the open doorway where Atlas is waiting for us to finish up. We only have a few left to place before we need to leave the room to let everything dry, and I'm proud of how amazing they look.

"Sawyer has been obsessive about finding whoever has done this, and Gryphon went straight back to the cells when you guys got home to continue working through the prisoners there to figure out what happened. Now that we have Giovanna, we should hopefully get some answers."

I make a disgruntled sound at the mention of that bitch's name, and Gabe looks over his shoulder at me. "Did she say anything to you guys when you picked her up? Is there anything at all that we can go on?"

I hand him another tile and huff in frustration. "Not really. Only that she's fully bonded now, which means that she knows who her real Bond Group is and that she had more power this time. Riley looked absolutely horrendous, like he was dying a slow death. She's definitely done a number on him."

Gabe winces and nods. "I still feel guilty that none of us realized what the hell was going on. We all just hated him for what he was doing to Sage, when really he was being assaulted by that woman for years."

A shiver runs down my spine, a warning that my bond does not like the sound of that.

I'm careful as I stand back up to step out of the room, through the open doorway to Atlas. We both stand there and watch as Gabe places the last three tiles on the floor, lining them up perfectly and leveling them off as though he was born to do this.

Atlas takes a sip of his water before handing the bottle over to me. "We can take you down there once we've eaten dinner, if you like. I'm sure North and Gryphon won't mind."

I nod and smile, taking a long sip. The room had been horrendously hot, and even after Gabe had found a couple of box fans for us to use, it still was not the most enjoyable experience being in there. I have sweated more than the last workout session that I had with Gryphon and I probably smell horrendous right now, but neither of my Bonded seem to notice or care.

I hear the front door unlock and feel the tingling sensation of more of my Bonded arriving as North and Gryphon walk into the house together. I can't hear what they are talking about from Atlas' room but neither of them rush to find us, so there's nothing urgent going on.

I glance at Atlas and Gabe before smiling sheepishly. "I'm going to grab a shower before I head down to see them. There's no need for all of you to be forced to smell my stench."

Atlas smirks at me and drawls back, "Yours is the only one that is working, so you might want to share."

I plant a hand on his chest and shove at him playfully, though I might as well shove at a brick wall for how far he moves."

"If I wasn't allowed to get in with her this morning when it was just you here, there's no chance you're getting in there now with the rest of us here," Gabe jokes, and I turn on my heel and scurry away from both of them before they can give me too much shit.

By the time I'm done cleaning myself up and pulling on a set of the silky pajamas that North insists on buying for me, Nox has arrived as well, and my entire Bond Group is sitting around the kitchen island breakfast nook with plates of dinner in front of them.

There are takeout containers at the counter, so one of them has grabbed food from the dining hall before coming over. I almost start drooling at the delicious smell of the burgers and fries. North's chef had moved to the Sanctuary with us but had taken up work in the dining hall to feed the masses while we sort out the food supply and, boy, have I missed his cooking.

I might have to beg North for the lobster and fish sliders.

I also wasn't expecting a family dinner. I'm a little shocked that Nox is here, especially given the sour mood he is so clearly in, but I smile and take my plate from North without another word. He gives me a stern once-over as though he's checking me for mortal wounds, and I smile sweetly back at him.

Gabe and Atlas flank me at the table, and I tuck into my food without another word. The chef is freaking amazing at cooking huge quantities of food to feed the entire community and yet still making it delicious, so there's nothing I want more than to just inhale this plate full of burgers. I'm happy to soak up the company of all of my Bonds together and just enjoy the peaceful moment with all of the people who mean the world to me.

It doesn't last long.

"So, when exactly were the two of you going to tell us all that you have living bond beings inside of you the same way that Oli does?"

My fork stops midway to my mouth and I glance between Gryphon, Nox, and North. Atlas and Gabe both freeze on either side of me, and the silence in the room changes from comfortable to charged.

No one wants to speak first and I find myself desperate to defuse the situation. I answer Gryphon, even though he definitely wasn't aiming his accusations at me. "I thought you already knew. You had mentioned something to me before about their abilities."

Gryphon shakes his head. "No, I knew that they had extra. I knew that they had stronger gifts than anyone else. But while we were away, your bond came out while you were sleeping, approached Nox, and *his* bond came out as well. There was nothing left of him. Your bonds have been moonlighting while you're sleeping."

If I had thought the silence was deafening before, it had nothing on the deafening void now.

North doesn't attempt to speak but he stares daggers into the side of Nox's head, as though he's planning on dragging him out of this room and beating him to death. If you had told me he was capable of giving that sort of look to his brother a few months ago, I would have laughed you out of the room.

Gryphon can't stop staring between the two brothers, his eyes darting between them as he assesses what's going on. I'm sure there's a level of mental communication going on that I can't hear, but whatever it is, he doesn't look happy about it.

I don't need to look to know that both Atlas and Gabe are staring at me. I feel their eyes on me well enough.

I guess this explains why I've been waking up tired.

Gryphon's eyes flick back to me and he says out loud, "Yes, that would explain why you wake up tired, Bonded. When did you find out that their bonds were separate beings inside them like yours is?"

I shrug and reply, "I kind of assumed, the same way I assumed that everybody knew. I've spoken to North's bond before. I'm not scared of it, if that's what you're worried about."

Gryphon's head tilts to the side a little. "I wasn't expecting you to be scared of it. His bond belongs to you. Just because it's a living thing inside of him doesn't mean that there's something to be afraid of."

Atlas chips in, "Oli just thinks that way because her bond has such a vicious demeanor most of the time."

Gabe reaches behind me to punch Atlas in the shoulder, as though I'm going to be insulted that he's pointed out that my bond is a cantankerous murderous bitch. But there isn't really any arguing with that point.

"Did you know?" North finally speaks, ignoring the rest of us and staying transfixed completely on his brother.

Nox doesn't say a word, just brings his burger up to his mouth and takes another bite as though none of the outrage is happening around him.

"Answer me, Nox. Did you know?"

I don't feel as though I should be here for this. It very much feels like a conversation between two brothers that I shouldn't be present for, but when I flick my eyes back to Gryphon, he shakes his head at me.

"No, we are absolutely going to sit here as a group and have this discussion. Because this is big. The fact that these two have been lying to us about their bonds is a *very* big deal, and the fact that Nox has been a threat to you from the moment you have returned to us and then risked your life with his bond—"

Nox finally speaks, cutting Gryphon off. "If North's bond isn't a threat, then why is mine?"

He might as well have placed a grenade on the table and pulled the pin.

"Because you're a fucking psychopath," snaps Atlas at the same time as Gabe drawls, "Well, if you're not happy about Oli being your Bond, then what's to say your bond feels any fucking different?"

North loses his cool and snaps, "We know better than to trust them! We have experienced what happens when you trust them, Nox. Don't pretend this isn't an issue."

What the fuck does that mean?

Gabe tenses a little and puts his hand on my knee underneath the table, squeezing it gently in a silent show of support. Atlas is practically vibrating with his own pent-up anger at what's happening here, but he keeps his mouth pressed firmly shut, which is progress.

A lot of progress.

Nox takes another bite out of his burger, the picture of nonchalance, and then picks up the small whiskey glass from in front of him as though all of this is incredibly boring. "You experienced it, brother. I have not experienced anything of the sort. My shadow creatures listen to my every command."

North squints at him and then a slow smirk stretches over his lips. Again, it's another action I do not ever see him directing towards his brother. "Do they, though? Because I'm pretty sure Brutus wouldn't still be with Oleander if you had complete control over him. You would *never* give one of your shadows away. Especially not to the Bond that you are so certain is a threat to you."

This feels dangerous to me. It feels as though we're standing on the edge of Nox's issues, and any little movement is going to set him off again, the way that my snide comments had unintentionally triggered him at dinner weeks ago.

"My bond gave her the shadow. If you're so concerned that my bond is going to attack her or hurt her in any way, then know that it gave her the creature. When she comes to sleep in my room at night, which all of you insisted on, even though I'd rather not have her there and I have fought from word go, my bond is the one who stays with her. My bond does not wish her any harm. I might, but the bond doesn't. If you have concerns, it should be about me, not it."

Is it weird that those words all seem like a romantic gesture to me?

I've always found North's bond alluring, like a beacon calling out to me, and the thought that Nox's bond might treat me the same way is incredibly tempting.

Gryphon gives me a very stern look, and my cheeks flush.

Don't you dare rat me out right now, I send directly to him and pray that no one else in my mind link can hear it. He flexes his jaw as though he's grinding his teeth, but he gives me the slightest nod.

He's telling the truth though, isn't he?

Gryphon sends straight back to me, no hesitation, *The only thing he has any sort of a lie flagging for is that he might want to hurt you, and I think that that is the use of the word might, Bonded, so I think I will be chaperoning the two of you a little more.*

I shrug, because I already knew that Nox has the capability to hurt me, he has in so many ways already, but I'm not scared of him, and I'm *especially* not scared of him now that I know his bond is in there and wants me.

I'm not particularly arrogant about the men that I have

in my Bond Group. I don't feel as though they owe me anything or that they are tied to me without their own consent, but there has been a small part of me that feels as though I deserve the vitriol that Nox slings at me at every opportunity.

They all deserve to have a Bonded that is not a danger to them and society. They deserve to not be tied to a freaking monster. I still can't walk down the street in the Sanctuary, a place that I protected and saved from the Resistance without a second thought, without attracting the terrified looks and constant whispers of the people who live here.

I will always be on the outskirts of society because even though I may choose to use my Gift for good, I'm still a threat because people change. We know this from how many people have chosen to defect to the Resistance over the years, even after being brought up in good families and knowing better than to believe their rhetoric. I don't blame them for being scared of me.

I'm scared of me.

North gets up from the table, leaving his half eaten burger behind, and stalks through the house until he gets to my room, pushing the door open and walking straight in as though it's his own. I think it's weird for about two seconds before I remember I'm the only one with working plumbing and assume that he's gone either to pee or splash water on his face to calm himself down so that he doesn't murder his brother.

Gryphon tucks back into his own dinner, chewing slowly and scowling around at random points in the room. I already feel sorry for any of his operatives who have to train with him tomorrow. He is not going to be a pleasant person to be around.

Nox finishes off the last of his burger and then pours himself another whiskey. For once, he doesn't seem in a rush to leave, and I don't know whether it's the alcohol dulling his sharp edges or if he is doing it out of spite because he wants to stay in everyone's faces while they digest the news of his bond.

"What did you say to North's bond when you spoke to it?" Atlas says, and Gabe gives him another stern look over my head.

"It's none of your business. That's between the two of them."

I shrug and dip one of my fries in ketchup before taking a bite. "North has always been really worried about his shadows. I wasn't worried, but I wanted to be able to give him a reason to not be as well, so I spoke to his bond before we... completed our bond. It told me that it belonged to me and it couldn't hurt me, that it was impossible for bonds to hurt each other."

"Well, that's not true," Gabe says, shoving the last quarter of his burger into his mouth all in one go. When

I roll my eyes at him, he squeezes my leg under the table again.

"What do you mean?"

"North's dad—" Gabe says before realizing that Nox is still sitting at the table and that it was his dad as well, giving him a sheepish side glance, but Nox is happily drinking the whiskey and acting as though none of us are even sitting at the table with him.

North's dad.

I glanced at Gryphon. He still has that thunderous look on his face, but he's staring at me now as the pieces start to click together in my brain

"North's bond told me that North believes the lie, and that's why he thinks that the bond and the shadow creatures can hurt me."

Gryphon's brows furrow and he reaches out to North through our communal mind connection so that everybody at the table except Nox can hear it. *You need to come back here. Something big is happening.*

In a matter of seconds, North is striding back into the room, his jacket off and the top buttons of his shirt undone.

"Your bond said that you believed 'the lie' and that's why you think that it can hurt Oli."

"It's clearly making shit up to get to her," North snaps, running a hand through his hair and messing it up a little until I can see some of the curls break free.

I tilt my head at him, thinking it all over, but there's too many questions here.

"How sure are we that your dad... hurt your mom?" I say very hesitantly, and North's eyes snap back to me.

"I saw him kill her. I saw his shadows come out of him, and I saw them tear her apart, so I'm *very* sure."

Nox pours another whiskey, and Gryphon takes the bottle out of his hands and sets it across the table where he can't reach it anymore.

Gabe groans under his breath at the power play, but Atlas ignores them and says, "Well, what else could the lie be? I'm not going to just ignore what a void-eyed bond says. I know enough about them to know you don't just write it off."

I need to ask him about his research later, but there's bigger things for us to be focused on.

Except then it falls into place in my head. Of course I already know what the fucking lie would be, because I've just watched my best friend have her entire life get turned upside down because of the Resistance messing with the blood work.

"They weren't Bonds," I murmur, and Gryphon's head snaps towards me.

I swallow roughly, but the words tumble out of me, "If they weren't really Bonds, then the shadow creatures wouldn't know to not hurt her."

North starts shaking his head, but Nox rolls very liquid eyes in his direction. "Would you look at that? The little poison girl figured it out."

Gryphon snaps at him, "You knew." Nox shakes his head back.

"No. But it makes sense. A lot of things in that household growing up make sense, if that's the truth."

I wake up before the sun and have to climb over Gabe and Atlas to make my way over to the bathroom.

After dinner last night, there had been a huge argument between Gryphon and North that eventually I'd had to walk away from. It was incredibly distressing to see the two men who had always been a united front leading the rest of us get into it in such a vicious manner.

Because my bedroom and bathroom are the only two rooms other than the kitchen that are finished, I had no choice but to hide away in there. Gabe and Atlas had both followed me straight in there when I'd left. Once I had thrown some pajamas on, Gabe had set a movie up on the TV to try and drown out some of the sounds of the intense argument.

I realized as soon as I'd seen the bed that it was made to comfortably fit six people if required, but I didn't think that we would be testing it out quite so quickly.

Or in such a sedate way, if I'm honest.

I fell asleep between Gabe and Atlas only to wake up with both of them on one side of me and North still quietly snoring on the other side. I have no recollection of him coming in to join us last night, but my bond feels incredibly settled in my chest.

Bonding with Gabe has gotten me that much closer to completely level.

When I get into the bathroom, I find Gryphon standing in front of the mirror with a towel wrapped around his waist, so he must've stayed last night as well.

I still feel unsettled from the night before, and he's still in a vicious mood about it, but when he opens his arms to me, I still find myself gravitating towards him. I tuck myself into his chest and listen to the steady beat of his heart to calm my nerves.

I'm sorry that we upset you. I'm not sorry for calling him out on his shit though.

I nod and speak directly back to him, conscious that the other three are still sleeping. *I understand that it's about trust, not the actual bond issue, but if it's tied up with his parents and whatever happened to Nox, then I think you need to give him a break. I'm not ever going to be a person to throw stones over keeping secrets about things that are traumatic. I haven't been the one to tell you guys most of my stuff... because it's all just too much. If it wasn't for Atlas, and the fact that my time in the Resistance camps was recorded so heavily, there's a lot you guys still wouldn't know because I just can't talk about it.*

Gryphon's hands cradle the back of my head, his thumbs stroking over the soft tendrils of my hair, and it feels like being sheltered to be held by such a strong and deadly man with such care.

I know. I'm trying not to be an asshole about it, but when it comes to your safety, I have every right to hold them accountable. There is every chance that their bonds could hurt you and that we're wrong about what the lie is. I'm going to get Sawyer to rerun the Dravens' blood tests through the system so that we can see if you're right. If it does come back that they're Bonds, then we need to have a serious conversation about what we're going to do now that we know that they have beings inside them too.

I pull back from him and stare up at him with a stern look on my face, my bond pushing to the surface a little in irritation at his words. *I'm not going to be kept away from my Bonded. My bond is not going to be kept away from either of them.*

Gryphon nods, but he also doesn't back down. *I know that. But you have to realize that we all take precautions because of your bond. There are certain things that all of us have agreed to, even Nox, and we do it because we know what your bond is capable of. It is our responsibility as your Bond Group to help keep your bond happy, safe, and out of the murderous zone, unless your life is in danger.*

I nod and step away from him, happy enough to accept what he's saying but needing a bit of space for a second to wrap my head around it. Why does everything have to be so freaking complicated?

I strip and climb into the shower, mostly to have something to do, not that I actually need it, and I let the hot water fall over my body and soak into my skin as I watch Gryphon get dressed for the day. He has early morning training sessions with his personnel and then a long list of security measures to go through. I already know that he has so much on his plate, and to add any of my shit on top of it just seems completely unreasonable to me.

When he's strapping on his weapons, all of them pulled out from a safe underneath the bathroom sink that I was completely unaware was even there, I send through to him directly again, *What does Nox do? You said even Nox has agreed to certain things about my bond. What has he agreed to?*

Gryphon takes a deep breath, and I can tell that he is hesitant about my interest in the last of my Bonds. I think that even a week ago, if I'd shown this interest, he would have encouraged it and been happy about it because he wants the Bond Group complete and for all of us to have that extra security. But what was said last night at dinner, and whatever he saw in that tent between our bonds, has rattled him, and now he's not so sure.

He agreed to sleeping in his room. He has agreed to give you any of his clothing that you might require to keep your bond calm and centered, and when you were rescued from the Resistance and needed skin contact, he agreed to that too.

Holy shit.

He agreed to the skin-to-skin contact.

My shock must be palpable because Gryphon nods, even with his back turned to me. *North was with him the entire time. He wouldn't let anyone else anywhere near him while he held you, but I wasn't expecting anything different, to be honest.*

You know what his reason is, don't you?

Gryphon glances over his shoulder at me and keeps eye contact with me as he replies, *I do. I can't tell you what it is. No one can tell you except him. Even though I am furious at the two of them, I'm not going to break that. Because like you said, trauma is hard, and you don't get much more traumatized than Nox Draven.*

I nod and duck my head back under the water, mostly to get away from the intensity of the moment. Gryphon finishes up and then comes back over to the stall, opening the door and catching my lips in a quick kiss as he stalks out to start his day.

A few moments later, the door opens again and Gabe stumbles through, making a beeline for the toilet. Something I will *never* get used to, even with having five male Bonds, is the ease with which men happily wander into an occupied bathroom and pee in front of an audience. I can't even comfortably pee with them in the next room over, half the time, without psyching myself up for it.

How did you sleep, Bonded? he sends through the mind connection to me in a soft and sleepy voice that comes through loud and clear. There's a cheeky grin on his face as he revels in the perks of our completed Bond. I can't help but give him one back, even with all of the chaos in my head.

Like a baby. The bed is perfect.

He moves over to the sink to wash up and he sends through to me, *That's good, because we are going to spend the day visiting with Sage and trying to figure that situation out now that we have some more information from Giovanna. Hopefully we can get her outta there.*

My eyes snap over to him and I cut the water off, jumping out of the shower like my ass is on fire. "Why didn't you say anything earlier?"

He shrugs at me and says out loud, "Gryphon just smacked me in the face to wake me up and told me that's what we were doing, so you knew the moment I knew,

Bonded. Now I'm gonna go wake Atlas up the same way, because I'm sure he'll want to come too."

Then he leaves the bathroom with a cackle that's just a little too close to evil.

NORTH

I don't like leaving the Sanctuary.

I don't have anything against traveling or any concerns about my own security or ability to handle any threats that might come my way for being a prominent council member, but the Sanctuary is still in its infancy and far too green to be able to run without someone in charge there at all times. Leaving Gryphon behind is a good start, because everybody there knows that he is able to speak on my behalf, but there's something about a consistent figurehead at the helm that is so desperately needed right now.

Unfortunately, the non-Gifted community has given me no choice.

I arrive at the Council offices and find Penelope waiting there for me. She's dressed to the nines, skirt suit and pumps with a red slash of lipstick across her lips, and the flirty grin that she gives me sets my teeth on edge.

She is fully aware that I am Bonded, and that I have never shown her any interest beyond a working relationship anyway, but she still insists on trying to cultivate something of an affair. It had always annoyed me, but now that I know it is such a sore spot for my Bonded, it's no longer something that I can ignore.

I would never allow Oli to be in the presence of that sort of person, so I will hold myself to the same standard. I might be a controlling asshole, but fair's fair.

"Give me my paperwork, and then go to your desk and do not interrupt me unless there's someone here to see me."

Her face falls at the harsh tone of my voice, but only for a second before she's smiling again and nodding, following my instructions without another word. To be honest, that's the only reason she's lasted in the position, because she never questions anything. Also, I don't think she has the cunning or intelligence to attempt to use her position to further her career at my expense.

Even that won't be enough to save her if she doesn't quit this shit.

I take the paperwork from her and then stalk to my desk, shutting the door firmly behind me so I can go through the paperwork quickly before I have to leave. It's mostly notes from other council members, their own opinions and wishes on today's meeting, and all of it is predictable bullshit that I am not going to take into account.

The only two council members who have been cleared fully by Gryphon are Rockelle and Hannity, the two that live in the Sanctuary alongside us, and I've already spoken to both of them and come to an agreement. I've also spoken to Vivian and Unser about their opinions on the matter and, as high level TacTeam leaders, their opinions matter to me. I would trust my Bond's life with either of them, as well as my own, and if they have something to say about how our community is being governed, then I want to know about it.

I have, of course spoken, to Gryphon and Nox as well.

It's not something that Oleander, Gabe, or Atlas have been involved in before, otherwise I would have spoken to them all at dinner about it. With everything else that went on last night, I didn't want to distress my Bonded with anything else because there was more than enough of a clusterfuck of information for one evening.

I don't know whether I desperately want Oleander to be right about my parents or if I want her to be wrong. The thought that the Resistance might have taken a real Bonded connection away from the people who brought me into this world and loved me so much fills me with a violent rage, but there's also a relief there. The potential that my bond and the shadow creatures are incapable of hurting Oleander is intoxicating and... maybe the poison that broke my brother was not something that had gone wrong in a happily Bonded Group.

Maybe what happened to him is the Resistance's fault as well.

I shake my head to clear the monsters out of it, because there's no denying that following that path is strong enough to drown me.

I've lost more days than I want to admit to at the bottom of a bottle trying to drink away those memories. I will never begrudge Nox for wanting to do the same because while I might live with the knowledge, he lives with the experience.

Neither of us shoulders that very well.

An alarm sounds on my phone to remind me to leave on time to get to the summit, and I quickly check in mentally with my Bonded, mostly to reassure myself and remind myself of why I'm doing this.

She answers straight away. *I'm just going to spend the day with Sage and Sawyer going through everything until we figure it out. Can we let her out if we get enough proof of her innocence together?*

Irritation rolls down my spine, not at Oli, but at the terrible situation that her friend has ended up in, thanks again to the Resistance. I'm confident now that Sage did not intentionally kill Dara and that something else has happened.

I have known her family for too long and am now watching her father almost kill himself in the Sanctuary, going through blood types and trying to fix the mess that has been made of his family's legacy. There's also no way that the sweet, broken little girl who befriended my Bond, even when her own Bonds couldn't see past our own shit to do so, could ever be a member of the Resistance.

I realize this might sound naive, but when you have been dealing with those people for as long as I have, you start to see patterns and similarities in things. I was surprised when I heard that the blood groups had been messed with, but I also wasn't shocked into disbelief over it. Knowing their tactics, it made complete sense that they would go after Bonded Groups in hopes to weaken the bloodlines.

I find myself chuckling quietly to an empty room at the thought that maybe they had planted my mother with my father in the hopes that it would thin out the shadow creatures and instead, they had ended up with two more shadow manipulators in the world, both of us more powerful than our father, thanks to the extra abilities our mothers had given us.

Serves the sadistic assholes right.

I tuck the paperwork under my arm and stalk back

out of my office without another word, ignoring Penelope when she tries to smile at me again. The fact that she has removed her work jacket and is wearing nothing but a lacy camisole underneath is all I need to see to know that she is going to be fired and I will have to find someone else to fill the role. Preferably someone male, competent, and uninterested in social climbing; so basically a fucking unicorn.

Rafe meets me at the elevator, once having been Transported in, and I enjoy the trip down to our car together catching up with him. He and his family had lived in our mansion for more than two decades, and I had watched his children grow up, move out to go to college, and travel the world. Neither he nor his wife are Gifted, but they are some of the most loyal and kind people I have ever met. When everything had happened with the Resistance, I knew there was no way I could leave them behind. Even if we weren't close, they would be targets for what they might have seen from being in our household for so long.

"Two new grandchildren, congratulations! You must be so eager to visit them."

Rafe grins and shrugs. "We're hoping that things will settle down soon and we can go see the twins, but we're not going to rush there and potentially put targets on our family."

I frown and nod, stepping out of the elevator with him

and walking over to the car together. "I'm sorry it's come to that, Rafe. I would never ask this of you, and it kills me that you have to stay with us and miss out on this moment."

Rafe opens the back door for me and as I slide in, he smiles his same warm smile at me. "This is what family does. We don't just stick together when things are happy and fruitful. You have always taken care of us, and we will stick by you now for as long as we need to. My Maria and I are safe with you. And we're more than happy to video chat with the babies until it is safe."

I nod, still not happy about it, and let him shut the door behind me, pulling my phone out again as it buzzes in my pocket. There's a stream of news articles and questions from reporters about today's summit waiting there for me, and I have to take a deep breath before I open any of it.

It's going to be a long day.

"We cannot ignore the significant threat that the Gifted have become to this country. For too long, we have stood by and allowed this portion of the population to govern itself, but time and time again, we have been shown that they are unable to live harmoniously as a community without being a threat to themselves and to others. We *cannot* allow this to continue. There needs to be heavier regulation, more policing of those people of interest who have abilities beyond the norm, and there needs to be a register of some kind to keep tabs, the same way that many other countries have implemented."

Senator Oldham dips her head as if she is bowing to the table of non-Gifted community members and the crowd before turning her back on the Gifted representatives and stalking back over to take her seat.

It's very clear what her dismissal means, but I clap along with everybody else in the room as though she hasn't just dribbled a load of bullshit and prejudice for the last half an hour against my community in an obvious power play to win over her more trigger-happy constituents.

I have been in her presence a few times already, and every inch of my being loathes being close to this woman. Even my bond is repulsed by her and, naturally, she just keeps winning favor with those around her, putting her in my path more and more often.

Lucky fucking me.

I have already spoken here at the summit, discussing the ways in which we are trying to neutralize the Resistance and fight back against everything that they're doing, as well as pointing out how many non-Gifted charities we support. I also made a point to speak about our efforts to purchase at least fifty percent of all of the Sanctuary supplies, both for building it and for our resources that we consume each and every day, from non-Gifted businesses so as to spread the wealth around.

While that may have gotten us some brownie points with some of the people here today, especially those with businesses themselves who just see dollar signs above my head, Oldham had sat there with a sneer on her face.

She is the bane of my existence.

Enemy Number Two immediately after Silas fucking Davies, and he tops the list for daring to physically torture, as well as mentally torment, my Bonded.

Though, to be honest, I wouldn't put those tactics past Oldham either.

There's only one more person to speak after her, and I mostly drown out the sounds of Senator Lilliman droning on and on about the fear that he has for his state.

He lives in New York, which is one of the areas that is least populated by the Gifted in the country, thanks to the population density of non-Gifted and the inability to go undetected there for very long. Most non-Gifted people will stigmatize and ostracize anybody who they know has a Gift because of the fear they have of those abilities. Anybody who is Gifted that moves into such a densely populated area generally doesn't last that long.

Of all of the states, that's not the one to be concerned about.

Now the Wasteland that has opened up in Missouri?

That's something that we should all be concerned about.

The last time the Resistance had made their move with such a massive power play was during the riots in the seventies. They had opened up what were dubbed Wastelands, which was an appropriate name for the front lines of war between the Gifted and the Resistance.

Most of the time, these Wastelands are protected by Shields that the Resistance place around the borders of such areas so that any Gifted that they Transport in or that choose to go there in an attempt to rescue others or take to the fight themselves, or even those who stumble into it unintentionally, are unable to get out again.

The fact that they have resorted to these old barbaric traditions again is unsettling, but unsurprising. Having it confirmed just means that now I need to spend some time with Gryphon to figure out what resources we need to keep at the Sanctuary, and what we can send there to attempt to shut them down before the situation gets way worse. It's not going to be easy; we're already stretched thin. Our best chance would be to send Oli in to wipe them all out.

That is, and will always be, a last resort.

When the senator finishes up his droning bullshit, the entire room politely claps for him before we all begin packing up to get the hell out of here. The crowd moves as one towards the door, and I find my skin prickling with even more irritation at the situation.

Fucking useless, the lot of them.

There are a few Gifted community members making their way towards me that I ignore completely as I make a beeline for the door. I have no interest in speaking to them, having already denied them access to the Sanctuary because they were unwilling to go through the vetting process, but I'm sure they have now seen the errors in their way. The problem there is that we have no ability to take more people in, thanks to the attacks by the Resistance putting us behind schedule by four months on getting more houses completed.

They had their chance and blew it.

I make it three more steps towards the door before Senator Oldham slides in front of me, blocking my path with that genteel smile of hers. My bond recoils inside of me, unhappy for her to be this close to us, but I force a neutral expression to fall over my features.

"Councilman Draven, I wasn't expecting you to show up. Rumor has it, you have found your little *girlfriend* and are ignoring your responsibilities now that you're shacked up with her."

I do not like this woman talking about Oleander.

I don't like the way she is using a dismissive tone, and I hate the language that the non-Gifted use when speaking about something so revered by the Gifted community, but I paste a sedate smile on my face.

"If these are your congratulations, I must admit I find them lacking. I have been busy dealing with the issues with the Resistance and keeping as many of my community members alive as possible while dealing with the worst that humanity has dredged up."

I also include her in this statement, but from the way she gives me a very political smile back, she misses that fact. "Yes, well, it can be difficult dealing with members of our community who are thugs and criminals, though we find that a good police force and a rigid law system has worked for the non-Gifted communities. Maybe you should consider the same for the Gifted."

She has no idea of the policies that we have in place, or the ruthlessness that we employ when dealing with the Resistance. I doubt that her community would happily set Dobermans on criminals and watch them tear them limb from limb the way that we do with the shadow creatures. I *very highly* doubt that they would comfortably watch a nineteen-year-old girl commit mass murder against their enemies, so I find her condescending tone just a little off base.

It's hard to keep my tone from being scathing but I think I manage it. "Is there something that you would like to speak to me about? Because I have other places to be today that will be more productive than this little chat we have been forced to have as a group."

She holds a hand up to her chest as if scandalized and simpers, "How can we live in harmony if we are not all keeping open lines of communication, Councilman Draven? Maybe this is why your entire community has been displaced. Maybe you should hand over their safety and security to somebody who is more capable at providing for them."

I nod slowly at her as if I'm considering her words, rage filling my gut and my shadows writhing inside of me to be let out to just eat the bitch alive, and then I reply, "And how much money does your family have, Senator Oldham?"

She frowns at me for a moment. "I don't see how that's any of your business... but it is all on public record that we've been very fortunate since coming to this country all those years ago."

I nod slowly again, and then say, "And how much of that wealth have you personally used to house and feed and clothe and protect and teach members of your community? How much of that money have you given to the Gifted community? People that are completely separate and different to your own, but who may have requirements that are not being met?"

She frowns deeper at me and blusters, "We live in a society in which people are responsible for taking care of themselves. I owe them nothing."

I nod slowly to her. "Yes, and my community is at war with itself, as well as members of your own community who have chosen to pick a side. So, instead of running away with my money to somewhere safer, I have chosen to stay and protect as many people as I can. I've put my money where my mouth is. I will not be told by some half-bred hick that I am incapable of doing my job. Someday, when you choose a cause that actually means something to you, and you do put your money behind it, then maybe I'll listen. But I don't foresee that day coming anytime soon, do you?"

Her mouth opens and shuts a few times as she gapes at me like a fish, and I give her one last decisive nod as I skirt around her and out of the building, taking a deep breath of the fresh air before walking over to find Rafe and get into my vehicle.

"Everything okay, Mr. Draven?" Rafe asks and I nod, sliding my sunglasses on against the glare of the day as he pulls out into traffic.

"Same shit, different day, but I already knew that there was no real point in attending."

OLI

I had assumed that they were keeping Sage at the council building in the cells in the basement, the same as they were keeping Atlas' sister.

I'm not sure why. Everyone had told me that she was being treated differently, better than those that we know are Resistance members, but it hadn't occurred to me that there would be anywhere else for them to keep her that was as secure.

Gabe and Atlas walk me over to the Tac training building, somewhere I haven't actually been yet. The only time I had spent with Tac personnel was when we were heading out on a mission, and everything for that is kept at North's offices at the center of the Sanctuary.

I only knew this place existed because Gryphon spends so much of his time down here, and I'm starting to begrudge it for stealing him away from me.

When we walk through the door, I find a large training center with a smaller, indoor obstacle course through a set of large glass doors that are smaller than the ones at Draven, but still deadly-looking nonetheless. A small cafeteria with dozens of tables and chairs has a cluster of Tac personnel already sitting there, and there are a hell of a lot of security cameras covering every inch of the place.

I feel a little nervous as we step into the building, but only because there are so many eyes on me the moment we get in there. It feels so much more intense than the wary looks and outright staring that I get from people out on the streets of the Sanctuary.

I have to force myself to stand still and not tuck myself in behind Atlas or Gabe.

"It's okay, they're all just trying to get a look at Gryphon's Bonded. The woman that changed everything when the Resistance showed up. They're all used to having a lot more casualties and facing the disappointment of not bringing people home, but every time you've been involved, the survival rates have skyrocketed. You're sort of a celebrity around here."

I give Gabe a dark look because I don't think it's funny to joke about that sort of thing, but he holds a finger up to cross over his heart as if he's swearing that he's telling the truth.

I still think he's full of shit.

"Lord, help us all. What are you doing in my training center?" booms a loud voice, and I find myself grinning, even though I'm still freaked out by all of the attention.

"Vivian! How did I not know that you were here? I would have come out to harass you so much sooner."

The scarred, surly-looking man stalks over to us and looks down at me as he crosses his arms over his wide chest, squinting at me as though he is dealing with an unruly child.

It gives me the warm fuzzies because I know that despite anything he might say, this man has a soft spot for me that's a mile wide. It was one of the few silver linings to attending Draven.

He scoffs. "Well, I'll be sure to speak to Shore about sending you over here, because if you start hanging around and being a distraction, I'm sure I'll have to find something for you to do."

I grin and give him a little bow, full of sass and bordering on mocking, and there are some shocked exclamations around us from the Tac guys as they watch me shoot shit with their infamous trainer. Not that I'm being disrespectful, I would *never* disrespect this man, but sometimes it's fun to be able to play around.

"I guess you're here to see Benson, your gal pal," he says in a sarcastic tone, and I nod with a small smile.

"She's gotten herself into some trouble, and we're here to dig her out of it. There's absolutely nothing to be concerned about because she is one hundred percent not evil. I know it."

He gives me a sardonic look and nods slowly. "You just know these things, do you? Because she took out the strongest Shield that we've ever had and somebody who was very important to our community."

I swallow as the smile slides off my face a little bit. I don't really want to make light of someone's death. "I know, and I know that that fact will be tearing her up inside. I'm not trying to say that Dara didn't matter, or that someone shouldn't be held responsible for her death. But I think that the *right* person should be held responsible, and that person is not Sage."

Vivian looks at me for a second longer and then nods. "Well, we'll just have to see what you guys come up with because you're right about one thing... She hasn't stopped crying since she was brought in, and even when she has been offered her Bonds to try and help her get through it, she's refused. That doesn't seem like something that a guilty person trying to kill us all in our sleep would do."

I swallow against the tears that form a lump in my throat.

Gabe respectfully nods at Vivian and then plants a hand at the base of my spine to direct me through the building. I'm surprised that he didn't join in on our banter at all. It's not until we get into the elevator that he breaks down and lets out his secret.

"Vivian scares the shit out of me. I once saw him get on the mats with Gryphon, North, *and* Nox. He beat the shit out of them, one by one. That memory has stuck with me, and I don't think I will ever be able to look at that man without shaking in my boots."

I scowl at the security screen in the elevator that shows our images just in case Vivian is watching us in here. I do not like the sound of him raising his hand against any of my Bonded, let alone three of them at once.

"This was early on in their training and they were all still pretty green. I'm not sure he could take them these days, Bonded. But I was young when I saw it go down, and it stuck with me."

There's a swirling, violent sort of feeling building up in me and I take a deep, deep breath.

"Yeah, maybe telling my bond about this isn't a great idea. I'm now feeling as though I should maybe go back up there and pull his soul out through his nostril, and Vivian is one of my favorite people on this earth. So, like, let's just leave this conversation where it is."

Atlas scoffs and laughs at me. "How is Vivian one of

your favorite people? Didn't he torture you in your training sessions?"

That's a simple question to answer. "Because he believed me when no one else did. He didn't let anyone treat me like shit in his presence, and he didn't try to coddle me when I started at Tac training. He just let me fall on my face over and over and over again until I figured out how to work the system myself. I think that makes him a great teacher."

The elevator doors make a chiming noise and open up to show us a long hallway with a set of cells down either side, much like the cellblock under the council building.

I guess if something works, you don't mess with it. The design sure is creepy, if nothing else.

Sawyer is already in Sage's cell with her, right at the very end of the hallway. His laptop is waiting on a table outside as he tries to coax her out of her bed, but it's no use. She's curled up in a ball with silent tears tracking down her cheeks. It makes my heart drop down to my feet to see because I've been there so many times before.

I might seem strong and put together now, but that's only because I'd spent years on the run having breakdowns in coffee shops, bathrooms, empty gas stations, and in the dirty kitchens of highway diners as I had done whatever odd jobs I could to survive. Yes, I was strong enough to eventually pick myself up, but there's a process to it. I hate that my friend is learning that and experiencing it firsthand.

I find Felix in the first cell, sitting with his own laptop in front of him and a stack of medical books as he studies, a reminder that he is still technically a student, even though he has become my Bonded Group's preferred physician.

I stop to speak to him for a moment and, predictably, all he can talk about is our girl. "Please, just help Sage, whatever you need to do to get her out of here. Please, Oli. I can't take much more of this for her."

"I know, I'm working on it, I swear," I reply. "I helped find Giovanna and Riley. Apparently, they've both already given information that might help, and I'm here to help Sawyer go through some things and try and present a case to Gryphon and North to get her out. Please don't be pissed at them for what they're doing. They just can't put the safety of the entire community in the hands of somebody who has been caught on camera—" I falter to a stop because I don't want to say it again out loud, and certainly not here in front of Sage, but Felix nods without another word.

"I get that, and I understand that it takes time. I just need to be with my Bonded again, and she refuses to be anywhere near us."

I nod and move to the next cell where Kieran is doing push ups like the good little TacTeam leader he is. I scoff at him and revert back to our usual sarcastic friendship. "Really? You're spending the time trying to buff yourself up? Are you hoping to impress your Bonded with your big, strong muscles when you get out of here? Or are you just trying to get to the point where you can throw her over your shoulder and keep her away from anything that might blink in her direction?"

He huffs as he stands back up, tugging at his shirt as he grabs a bottle of water and downs half of it in one go. "It's very easy to get complacent if you're not on top of your training. I asked Shore for a set of dumbbells, but the asshole refused."

I quirk an eyebrow at him and point a finger. "Watch it, buddy. I might be on Team 'Get Sage the Fuck Out of Here' but you're also not going to bad mouth my Bonded in front of me without hearing from my bond."

He runs a hand through his hair and mutters under his breath, "Maybe we need your fucking bond to come out to sort this bullshit out."

His frustration is palpable, and I don't blame him at all for it. I also feel incredibly frustrated at how little we've managed to figure out so far.

He turns back to me and says, oddly sincerely, "Thanks for going to get Riley and that treacherous bitch for us."

I shrug. "It's got nothing on snapping your own ankle to rescue your best friend's Bonded, so don't go too far out of your way to thank me. I still owe you, big time."

He smirks at me and I turn away from him to walk

over to Sage's cell at the end of the row, Gabe and Atlas following me without a word between them. I guess they've both spent time down here, so there's not a whole lot for them to say.

Sawyer is already at the door, unlocking it and letting himself out. When he gives me a tight smile, I murmur back, "Why is she so far away from them both? That seems shitty."

He sighs and rubs a hand over his eyes like he's just as close to a breakdown as she is. "Because she can't stop crying. It was driving Felix and Kieran insane. They can still hear and feel it, but their bonds are coping with it better having a little bit of distance from her, and she isn't putting up so much of a fight about every little thing now that she's down here. Breathing room or some shit."

I swallow roughly and nod. "Let me in with her."

He hesitates and looks over my shoulder at Gabe and Atlas and I huff at him in frustration, my temper flaring to life. "We all know that my bond will not let anything happen to me, and I know that Sage wasn't responsible for anything. If there is a kill switch inside of her, my bond will intervene. And I've had enough Tac training that if she rushes me, I can get her on the ground until one of you guys can come in and defuse it, so you will let me in to see my best friend, and you will never *ever* look at my Bonded for permission ever again, Sawyer Benson. Or else I will reach inside of your chest and pull your heart out."

The last few words come directly from my bond and not from me. The change in my voice has Sawyer gulping a little, but it also gets him moving, unlocking the door and letting me in with Sage. I wait until he's got it locked again behind me before I turn to properly look at my girl.

She doesn't acknowledge me or look up and when I move straight over to her, I ignore the commentary behind me of intense disapproval as I climb onto her small, uncomfortable bed with her. The second I'm secure there, I wrap my arms around her, pressing her face into my shoulder as her silent tears turn into body-racking sobs.

"I killed her, Oli. I don't know how or why or anything at all, but I killed her."

It takes an hour before Sage is able to calm down enough to speak to me properly.

I don't begrudge the time lying there with my best friend and holding her while she breaks apart though. I know that we can piece her back together and that the Sage Benson who walks out of these cells might be fragile for a little while, but she will be stronger and more resilient than the Sage who woke up the morning of the attacks. I feel a whole lot of sadness about that fact and want to mourn the happy girl that there was before, the same way that I mourned the happy girl that I was before.

Now isn't the time for that.

Now is the time to hold space for her until we can get her the hell out of here, hopefully today. Once her breathing evens out a little and the tears stop soaking through my shirt, I pull back and rest my head more fully on the pillow beside her. I glance over my shoulder and find Sawyer sitting at the desk with his laptop, tapping away furiously as he works tirelessly to get his sister out of this.

Gabe and Atlas are both staring through the glass at the two of us, ever watchful in case there's some chance that Sage might attack me. I take a moment to think about whether or not Atlas could actually break one of these walls down to get to me if he needed to and he grins at me as he holds up the key. Apparently my thoughts are way too loud again today if even my non-Neuro Bonded can figure out what I'm thinking.

Gabe is sitting on the floor with one of his knees pulled up, resting his cheek on it as he watches us both. I think he's slightly more relaxed than Atlas because he truly believes that Sage is innocent and that the only threat is from a foreign force inside of her or a kill switch of some sort that Giovanna might have implanted in some way.

I turn back to Sage and find her staring at me through bloodshot eyes, but the tears have dried up, so now is the time for answers.

My voice is barely more than a whisper, like this is just pillow talk at a slumber party and not a complete freaking nightmare situation, as I say, "Tell me everything. I know you've already told everyone else, but tell me exactly what happened and how you were feeling and all of the stuff that you can only tell your best friend. Maybe there's something in that story that's missing that can help us. I'm willing to try anything at this point, Sage."

She nods slowly, but hesitates. "It doesn't matter though, Oli. Even if we find out that someone has done something to me to make this happen, I still killed someone. Dara's parents and her Bonds deserve the justice of someone being held responsible for that."

I nod. "I agree completely, and when I find out who did that to you, I will hold them responsible. *Personally*. I will set my bond on them gladly, with absolute joy, and we can all watch it tear that person to pieces."

Sage swallows and shakes her head. "Do you think that's enough? Would *you* think that's enough if this happened to one of your Bonded? It just keeps going through my head over and over again. What would I do if it were Felix or Kieran or even Riley that this had happened to? I would want everyone held responsible, *including* the person holding the knife."

I reach out and tuck an errant curl behind her ear.

"That's because you are being harsh on yourself. I know you better than that. There is no way that you would want innocent lives to be taken. The problem is that you don't see yourself as innocent right now because it was your hand that did it. Sage, if anyone is going to know how that feels, it's me. I have been used so many times to take lives. I've had to learn how to live with that fact. It's not easy, and a lot of the time I still believe that I deserve to be put to death for what I did, but what it comes down to is that I would never willingly take an innocent person's life. I know that about myself, and I'm confident in that. I know that about you too, and so I will fight anyone, including you, to get you out of here."

Sage swallows again and nods, still not looking as though she believes me, but it's a start, and it's something to build on. I settle back against the pillow and shut my eyes as she starts working her way through her day.

There's still nothing there.

That is a warning sign for us. She wakes up in her bed. Kieran and Felix have already gotten up to head out to work for the day. She gets dressed in her running clothes and heads off for her usual morning run, then the Resistance arrives. Kieran finds her and protects her with his TacTeam, including Gryphon. She speaks to Felix, but he's safe enough treating injuries in the Medical Center.

She has no recollection of anything before then.

We already know from the video footage that she had killed Dara and it must have been sometime during her morning run, but no matter how I poke at her story, she has no memory of it at all.

"There should be something there. I've had my mind manipulated before, there's always a blank spot. There *should* be a blank spot," Atlas says, and Sage shakes her head.

"There isn't any. I've spent days going over it all in my mind, but there's nothing. *Nothing*, Oli. I swear."

"No. There's definitely *something*," Sawyer snaps from the table and shifts his laptop around.

I can't see the screen from where I am, but Atlas and Gabe can, and both of them start cursing viciously. Kieran calls out from his cell, desperate to know what's going on, and I dive off of the bed to get an eyeful of whichever motherfucker has framed my bestie for goddamned murder because my bond is so fucking ready to go hunting. Lord, I'm ready for it too, none of my usual squeamishness to be found now that it's Sage's life on the line here.

I find myself staring at Dara's murder again, only this time, it's from another angle. This time, I can see Sage's eyes.

Sage's black, empty, void eyes.

FORCED BONDS

J BREE

"I am going to murder Nox Draven."

The words light a fire in my gut and I have to grip the edge of the table to stop myself from flying off the handle. Atlas had let me out of Sage's cell to come and rewatch the footage on repeat until we're absolutely sure we've seen everything there is and pulled it all apart. There's not really anything new to take from it.

Oh, except for the void eyes that Sage absolutely, without a doubt shouldn't be rocking.

My bond presses at my mind, trying to take over and get control of my body, but it doesn't take a genius to figure out that's a terrible idea. I'm fully aware that Sawyer isn't going to even attempt to follow through with his words and this is all just an expression of how pissed off he is, that he's slinging shit at the most likely target, but my bond is not one to mess around with.

"I am going to—"

I cut him off before we hit the danger zone for real. "Yeah, let's not continue to threaten my Bonds, because there's only so much that I can do to stop my bond from coming out and dealing with you personally."

Sawyer glances over at me and throws his hands up in the air in frustration. "You don't even like Nox! He's an asshole, we all know it. We've all watched everything that he has done to you since you got back, so you can't fucking deny it. He's clearly the one who has done this, Oli!"

Gabe scratches the back of his neck like he is incredibly uncomfortable with this conversation, but Atlas crosses his arms over his chest and nods along like he agrees completely with Sawyer's delusional assessment of the footage.

I aim for rational, because clearly the entire goddamned room needs it. "Okay, well, first, I just found out that my bond and Nox's bond have been meeting up in the late hours of the night together. It doesn't matter which human is wearing that casing, my bond is not going to let you take him away from her. Also, how the hell do you think he is capable of this sort of manipulation? His gift is his shadow creatures and the dread."

Gabe groans and swipes a hand over his face like he is desperate to get out of here and doesn't want to be found guilty by association. I, on the other hand, need to convince Sawyer not to do anything stupid before we call North and Gryphon in.

After dinner last night and everything that is already in question with Nox… he doesn't need any more questions about his loyalty right now.

"Nox has a third gift."

I glance over my shoulder at Kieran, glaring at him for his betrayal, but he just shrugs back.

"We're supposed to be looking into every option possible, right? He has a third gift. North too, but we know what all three of his are. As far as I'm aware, your bonding with North has just made them stronger and hasn't given him anything extra."

My cheeks stupidly flush at the thought of them all discussing my sex life again, but there's more important shit to think about. "I haven't bonded with Nox, so unless you know for sure that the third gift is his ability to use *mind control* to betray his entire family, his community, everything he has ever stood for and believed in, so much so that he has chosen to fight for us all, even when he's so disconnected from us, I think that running out of here to *murder him* probably isn't the best idea."

Gabe nods and points at me. "She's talking sense here, folks. The rest of you are the ones who have jumped off the fucking deep end. Even if there was the slightest of chances that this was Nox, which there's definitely not, if you walk out of here, his shadow creatures will consume you."

Sawyer shakes his head at Gabe and takes a step towards him in an angry sort of motion, like he's about to get in his face to argue with him a whole lot more. It's not a threat, exactly, but my bond feels as though it is, and I find Brutus coming down from behind my ear in response to my own reaction to it.

He isn't the docile puppy that everybody is used to seeing though.

His head reaches my chest as he takes full form, and his ears prick all the way up as his jaws open and his teeth are revealed in a snarl. He looks like the terrifying hellhound that they're all so sure my sweet boy is, but all I can see is a protective pup who would do anything for me.

I've never loved him more than I do at this moment.

"Oh my God, he's sitting here listening to us all figure it out!" Sawyer snaps as he turns on his heel and stalks back around the table to his laptop.

"Sawyer, you need to listen to Oli."

Everybody freezes and turns towards the cell to where Sage has finally gotten out of her bed, standing at the glass with her hands pressed against it and her eyes on her brother. She still looks as though she has spent the last week sobbing herself to insanity, but there's a determined look on her face.

"She's not just saying this because he's her Bond. She's always been the first person to call him out on his bullshit, and you know it. We've spoken about it before! You said that you couldn't believe that she didn't just fall into the Bond haze like everybody else does. If she says that there's no way that he would have done it, then there's no way he would have done it. And to be perfectly honest, I don't think it's him either."

Felix calls out from his own cell, "It would have to be a Neuro. The sort of power to get into someone's mind, wipe any recollection of what they're doing, and force them to take someone's life... that's a Neuro Gift, and it is an incredibly powerful one, at that."

I turn and look at Atlas, who is frowning now. "Do you know of any Neuros in the Resistance whose eyes turn black?"

He lets out a deep sigh and shakes his head. "The strongest Neuro that I know of in the Resistance is Silas Davies, and his eyes turn white, just like everyone else. I don't know anyone else with the voids. I'd heard rumors that the Dravens had void eyes, everyone has, but I didn't really believe it until I saw it myself. I thought it was a bogeyman story told to keep Resistance kids from going to Draven. Even after I saw the footage of you in the camps, I thought you were the only one and that it had something to do with being a Render."

I let out a slow breath of my own and nod. "Is there anything else that anyone needs to say that probably shouldn't be heard by North or Gryphon before I call them in? Because as far as I'm concerned, this is the proof we need to get Sage out of here."

Kieran presses one of his fists against the glass and huffs in frustration. "They're not going to let her out. This is proof that she didn't do it herself, which we already knew. North and Gryphon have already agreed that there's no way that she did it, but if someone's already gotten into her brain before, there's a chance they'll do it again. As much as I need her out of here, I don't want to run the risk of her killing someone else. Beyond the fact that an innocent life would be taken, Sage can't have any more blood on her hands like this."

My eyes flick back to her and I see her staring down at her feet, swallowing roughly as she tries to pull herself together.

All I see there is strength.

"She can handle a lot more than you think she can."

She glances up at me and I nod back at her. "You've survived this, you can survive being out of here as well. So long as we keep someone with you at all times, someone who knows what is going on and can keep an eye on you, then you should be let out of here."

Kieran shakes his head. "It's not that easy, Fallows—"

I cut him off. "If it is a Neuro that is outside of the Sanctuary, and they managed to get to Sage, then they could get to any of us as well. If it's a Neuro that's inside the Sanctuary and has managed to get past Gryphon's security checks and lie detector... *again*, they could do this to anybody. On the off chance it is someone that Sage made contact with before we came to the Sanctuary... Well, that's one out of three options. I'm willing to take the risk as long as there are precautions."

Gabe stares at me for a second and then nods. "It's hard to argue with that kind of logic. She's right though, if someone is strong enough to get through the Shields to get into Sage's brain and commit that sort of act, then we have a lot bigger problems on our hands than worrying about keeping Sage in a cell or not."

I nod, and then I reach out to North and Gryphon through my mind connection.

I need you guys to come down to the cells at the Tac center. We've found it.

Gryphon replies immediately that he's on his way, and North takes a second to get back to me. *I'm still on my way back from the summit. It'll be at least another hour.*

Dammit.

Gryphon speaks to him through the communal mind link so that I hear it as well. *I'll get the information through to you as soon as I'm there. And then we can wait until you're here to proceed with anything.*

There's a flutter in my chest for a second as I prepare myself, but there's no turning back now. *You need to bring Nox as well, and you need to prepare him for answering questions about his Gifts. I've already tried to talk Sawyer out of doing anything stupid, but I might need the backup.*

There's silence for a moment and then North says, *I'll bring Nox with me when I get there. None of you can handle him if things turn ugly.*

"What are the chances it's an evolutionary thing? Like we're somehow evolving from the white eyes to the void eyes?"

Gabe turns from his seat to stare at Felix as though he has lost his mind, but the doctor-in-training doesn't back down. "We have a Soul Render and two Death Dealers with void eyes, and the Dravens have had cases of void eyes over the last few generations, though nothing consistent. Oli, do you know if your family had any history of void eyes?"

I shake my head and try not to look as guilty or as devastated as I usually do when my family is brought up. "I don't think so. My parents were very shocked the first time they changed color... except my mom, but that had more to do with the fact that she had been dreaming of me and my powers for years before I was born."

That catches their attention.

"I've never heard of someone being psychic before, not outside of the phonies in the non-Gifted community who try to claim they can see things, but that's all a ruse for money," North says as he stares at the laptop some more.

As soon as North and Nox had arrived, we let Kieran, Felix, and Sage out of their cells, and now everybody is sitting around the interrogation table together as we try to figure out what the hell could be going on here. Sawyer has managed to contain his accusations and threats so far, but he is eyeing Nox like he's plotting out where he might stab my Bond.

I do my best not to watch him, but I find my eyes continually sliding back to him, and I know it is my bond's interference.

We don't turn our backs on threats.

Ahh perfect, just what I need from my bond right now. There's no real point in attempting to reason with it, but for some stupid reason, I give it a go.

Sawyer is not a threat. He won't be a threat. Is there

anything that you would like to input into today's discussion about void eyes?

My bond's answer is less than helpful. *It's a threat.*

I snap back, irritated, *Perfect! That gives me all of the information that I need right now to figure out how to get through this.*

They're a threat, girl. They're a threat of something coming, something old that we did not want to be dealing with, but soon will have no choice.

A shiver runs down my spine. *We. The collective we? As in, you and me? Or me and my Bonded?*

It doesn't answer me. Instead, it curls up in my chest and goes back to watching Sawyer obsessively, taking Nox's safety to a whole new level of crazy.

I glance over and find Gryphon staring at me as though he's seeing me for the first time. "You're talking to it."

I shrug and roll my shoulders back, uncomfortable now that I have everybody's attention. "Yeah. I told you she's a cantankerous, unhelpful bitch."

He doesn't find that amusing, he just doubles down. "You're asking it questions though."

Why the hell does that even matter? "Yes, well, it *is* an independent thing that lives inside of me and has its own thoughts and opinions and knowledge."

Gryphon leans forward in his seat, planting one hand on the table in front of him as though he's trying to get something through to me that I'm too dense to see for myself. "Where does it get this knowledge from? If it's only ever lived inside of you, how does it know more than you? How does it know anything that you don't?"

I have no answers, but my eyes flick towards North.

His jaw is tight and he looks incredibly irritated that this conversation is even happening, but he speaks for me. "They've been here before. Our bonds are far older than we are, and they aren't joking when they say that they belong to each other. This isn't their first time on this earth, or their first time being bonded to each other."

I don't let the shock that I feel show on my face, because I don't want to call him out like that, so I'm very careful about sending just to him, blocking Gryphon out, *I didn't think you spoke to your bond. I didn't think you guys got along.*

He doesn't look back my way either as he replies, *After I found out that Nox's bond was spending time with yours, I had a conversation with it to assess whether or not it was coming out and speaking to your bond as well. There have been some nights that you've slept in my room where I've woken up tired, and I wanted confirmation and to know what exactly goes on between them.*

Holy shit. *And what did it say?*

It said that it couldn't stay away from your bond any more than I can stay away from you. There is something going on here, Oleander, something bigger than us, bigger than our community, and bigger than the Resistance itself. We need to figure out how to get all of us through it alive and unscathed.

I swallow and glance at Nox, the only other person in this room who might have some input on our bonds, to see how he is taking all of this in, but he is just staring at his hands, stretching his fingers out and then curling them into a fist, over and over again.

Gabe groans and rubs a hand over his eyes like this day has drained his will to live. "Do you think we would know if we came across someone else with these sorts of bonds inside them? Do you think that we could tell? Or is this all just us walking around in the dark until someone comes and attacks us again? Another bond like yours, but one who's aligned to the Resistance... What a fucking nightmare."

"Thank God it isn't another Death Dealer," says Nox, finally breaking his silence. Sawyer snaps back at him, "A Neuro is just as bad."

Nox rolls his eyes back at him, sneering, "It's highly doubtful that a Neuro is worse than somebody who can manipulate shadow creatures to kill indiscriminately, Benson. Just because you are furious that your sister was used as the weapon, doesn't mean that we need to be stupid about this."

I glance over at Sage and her eyes meet mine.

She's sandwiched between Felix and Kieran, both of them glued to her side now that they have been reunited, and there's a little color coming back to her cheeks as she is piecing herself back together. I think the confirmation that it definitely was someone in her head was the news that she'd really needed, but also finding out that it was someone with unimaginable amounts of power has helped as well. There's no way to fight my bond, and I've never seen anyone fight off North or Nox's bonds either, so how could she have possibly fought back against a Neuro like that?

Impossible.

It was never her fault.

Nox says, "We need to go through the history books. If this isn't the first time that they have lived together, then there has to be some records somewhere of it."

Gryphon shrugs. "The last time someone was able to Soul Rend on this earth, they could only kill a handful of people at a time, and their eyes flashed white. When I found out what Oli could do, it was the first thing I looked up. That was all I found."

Nox glances at North and says, "The library at the Hail Mary. There's books there that are under lock and key. If there's anywhere that will be able to tell us about the bonds, it'll be there."

I glanced around the table again, but no one has anything left to say.

"Well, I guess we're going to the Hail Mary."

GRYPHON

There are a lot of rumors about who actually created the Hail Mary, but there's one thing I know for sure; whoever it was, they were fucking crazy.

All of this is vital information for Oli, who doesn't even remember Kieran using the building to get them both out of Davies' hands and Oli's bond out to take out the camp, but it isn't as easy as sitting her down and explaining to her that our community has access to a building that's basically Pandora's box, but on a much bigger scale.

The building itself is made out of six-foot-thick concrete on all sides, with no windows or even a clearly defined door to get in. On the inside, it's a maze of booby traps, sinkholes, holes, and security cameras that cover every inch of the cursed place. It's the safest place on earth, because there's no power in the Gifted or non-Gifted world that can force its way inside.

You *have* to be invited.

"So, what, it's like the rule of vampires or something?" my Bonded snarks out as she dresses in her Tac gear.

I'm glad her snarkiness has come back with a vengeance now that Sage has been let out of the cells and some of the shock of the last few days has worn off a bit. I'm fully aware that the sass is also a coping mechanism for her, a deflection from the way that she truly feels about things, but it still has felt as though we'd lost a piece of her.

"No, not even vampires could get into this place."

She huffs and rolls her eyes at me, pulling her shirt over her head. "Of course not, vampires are notoriously shit at getting in anywhere. Learn your vampire lore, Shore, before you end up as someone's walking blood bag."

I quirk an eyebrow at her and pull my own shirt over my head, enjoying the way her eyes darken as she looks at the wide expanse of my chest. Every second of my time spent in training for my community is worth the effort with the way it makes her weak in the knees.

"And how do you know so much about vampire lore? When exactly did you squeeze in the study time?"

She scoffs. "Romance novels. I read a lot while I was traveling. I know everything there is to know about vampires... and vampire dick."

I turn to face her fully and find her rolling the protective suit up her body to cover the lacy red bra she's wearing. I get distracted before I can tease her or get more details about these books of hers, and my eyes stay glued on her chest, craving the silky smooth skin and the taste of her that echoes in my mind every time I look at my fucking *perfect* Bonded.

When she realizes she has my full attention, she puts a little more effort into her shimmy. Joke's on her; teasing me is just going to get her fucked against the wall here with everyone outside listening. I know that she gets shy about that sort of thing, but only after she's come down from the highs I get her to.

For the record, I'd enjoy every second of it and there'd be nothing but smug satisfaction out of me.

She clears her throat and breaks me out of my fantasies. "I wasn't expecting to be heading out on a mission when I got dressed this morning. I would have found something a little more appropriate if I did."

With all of the sass in the world, her lips quirk up in that way that only hers do, and my dick gets hard at the whole fucking package that is my Bonded.

I reach for her and grab her around the waist, pulling her into my chest and enjoying the feel of that racy, soft lace against my skin. I'm not enjoying it as much as I would enjoy her creamy skin or pert nipples, of course, but it does push the curves of her tits up invitingly until they're begging me to sink my teeth in.

We're leaving in three minutes, stop fucking around.

All I can think as his words ring in my head is how badly I want to murder North Draven.

I'm smart enough to keep it to myself. Oli's bond has probably had enough of that sort of talk for one day, but the guy sure knows how to cockblock.

I'll remember it too.

I press my forehead against hers and murmur to her, "You're going to be a distraction to me because every time I look at you, I'm going to think about this lying underneath, waiting for us to get home."

She grins and shimmies again, this time in my arms so that really all she's doing is grinding against me. "Is it your turn? Or are you going to steal me away from someone else tonight? I've lost track."

I reach down and grab a handful of her ass, hoisting her up into my arms until she squeals and wraps her legs around my waist. "I think we're past the taking turns portion of our bonding, don't you think?"

She makes a squeaking sort of giggle sound, burying her face in my neck and nipping at the skin there until I am having to talk myself out of the plan for the quick fuck against the wall.

My Bonded deserves better but, fuck, is it tempting.

Her voice is all breathy seduction as she says, "I did notice that you're all completely fine with the giant bed situation. Though, I'm not sure how I feel about more than two of you at once. I can't even think about that without feeling... overwhelmed."

I almost feel sorry for my Bonded, knowing that she has five Bonds to keep satisfied. But with one of them almost permanently out of commission, and the others far more than willing to figure out a system, I don't feel bad for long.

"If I drag you into your room by yourself and lock the door, you don't have to worry about sharing with anyone. Promise me that you're mine tonight when we get home."

She licks her lips as she looks up at me, her eyes flicking down to my own as she nods. "I've missed you. You work too much. You work more than North does these days, and that just seems wildly unfair."

I swoop down to kiss her, swiping my tongue over hers to taste her words, but I don't need my ability to know that she's telling the truth. I have had to take over all of Kieran's responsibilities with him locked up, and it's a relief that he has now been let out again, just so that he can help shoulder some of the burdens of our community's safety once again.

Having Vivian in the training center again, now that he

has been able to move his Bonded Group into the Sanctuary, has also lightened some of the load. Unser had been called away with the first wave of Resistance attacks, and Vivian had been unwilling to move Adella, their Central Bonded, into the Sanctuary until Unser had gotten back.

I understand their reasoning completely.

The three of them are some of our greatest allies, the most powerful and trustworthy people that I know, and I, for one, am fucking relieved to have them all home.

I set Oli back down on her feet with one last kiss before turning away from her and pulling the rest of my Tac gear on. It's easier to get it done when I'm not looking at her, and by the time I turn around again, I find her fully clothed and ready to go.

When we step out of the changing room together, we find Kieran already suited up and ready for us, a determined look on his face and a steely set to his jaw.

This is now very personal for him.

They went after his Bonded, and now he has a motivation to get this information that rivals my own. Almost, but not quite, because while he's trying to avenge what happened to Sage and ensure it never happens again, I'm coming to terms with the fact that half of my Bonded Group has beings literally living inside of them that could take over at any time.

I can't believe that there are more of these bonds out

there, that there are more of these *things* that are living inside people that could change the course of the war against the Resistance.

It brings up so many more questions than it answers. How many of them are there? Why are they so powerful? And how do they keep reincarnating into people? How are they different from my own bond and what does this mean for my Bonded, long term? Is she going to end up time-sharing her body with something else? Because that does not sit right with me at all. The thought of anyone *using* her, let alone something that we can't get out of her... it's fucking horrifying.

Would she even want it out of her?

Oli might, but I doubt North or Nox would be willing to give up their Gifts, especially since they have used them to shield our communities and each other so heavily.

We need those books, and we need some answers.

Nox steps out of the elevator followed by North, both of them dressed in Tac gear as we all prepare to head out to the Hail Mary together. I'd tried to talk North into staying home, but he had insisted on coming because of his bond. Apparently, he had made an agreement with it for more 'transparency' once we find these books.

Gabe and Atlas are staying behind to keep an eye on things within the community. With their mind connections now with Oli, it means that we would be notified immediately if something were to happen.

Gabe is focusing on finishing the house and, with enough supervision, Atlas can actually help him with that. They had both railed against the decision, wanting to be helpful in figuring this mess out, but like North had said, there has to always be someone from our Bonded Group in the Sanctuary.

The house is also a priority for us because of Oli's security, nothing about that has changed.

"We're getting in, getting the items, and getting out. This is not a school excursion. We're not going so that you can all say that you have gotten into the Hail Mary and made it out safely. We stick together and get home as fast as possible. I don't like moving resources. If this wasn't urgent, we wouldn't be doing it," Kieran says to the small team of personnel that are traveling with us.

All of them nod decisively and even Rockelle manages to keep his mouth shut. The events of the last few days have worn him out, and the harsh policy of locking up even our most trusted friends has definitely been noticed by the personnel around us.

Some of them have voiced disgust and concern over it, but the majority have only felt respect for the decision. Having leadership that doesn't prioritize their own feelings and friendships over the good of the community is never a bad thing. Dara was important to us all, and North and I had been very careful about what we had done in response to her senseless death.

We'd also been very careful about how we had explained Sage and her Bonded being released. Everybody knew that we were going to get Giovanna and Riley for more information, and they had been made aware of the leak in our security.

Not that we've told anyone about the void eyes yet.

There's no need for mass panic, and North's meeting at the summit with the non-Gifted community has made him even more careful about what information we share with people. We don't want anything getting out to the wrong crowd right now.

Kieran holds out his arm and Oli grabs it without hesitation. I grab his wrist and then wait until North and Nox also have a good grip on him, and then with a *pop,* we disappear, on our way to the most terrifyingly secure place on earth.

We arrive at the Hail Mary and my boots land directly in a giant puddle of water, the rain is pouring down on us, and I slip my hand onto Oli's neck to ease her travel sickness without a word.

I let my Gift out to assess if there's anyone here who

shouldn't be. I'm on high alert just in case Davies left behind some scouts of his own. Shadow creatures stream from Nox like smoke billowing from a chimney, and they spread out around the building to do the same. The TacTeam personnel have been trained not to interfere with the creatures, and they all stand deathly still as the various forms of canines dart around them all, their jaws full of razor-sharp teeth that are desperate to devour fully grown men.

Once I know that Oli is feeling better, I step towards North where everyone can see and signal that we're moving forward. It's easier to just talk to him directly, but we need silent communication, not private communication here.

We had already contacted the keeper to let him know that we were on our way, so it isn't hard to gain access to the building. I can't imagine locking myself in this place willingly for a lifetime as that man has, but after Alistair had lost his entire Bonded Group in the riots back in the seventies, he'd chosen to dedicate his life to protecting this place.

I'd contacted him after Kieran had told us that he sent Silas Davies here, but the sadistic Resistance asshole hadn't made it through the concrete, just as we'd all known he wouldn't.

It had been a very smart move from Kieran.

Oli walks behind me as we move forward, her footsteps

even quieter than the last mission to the lake house as we move through the giant steel and concrete opening that Alistair has unlocked for us.

We end up in the first of four vaults that seal you in one at a time, confirming that there are only friendly faces inside before the next one will open.

The first two chambers are cold, the concrete soaking in the wet and frosty weather from outside, but the deeper into the Hail Mary we get, the warmer it is. The sheer density of the walls is holding in the heat, and I can feel the wariness in my Bonded grow the further into the building we get.

By the time we're stepping out of the fourth vault, her eyes have shifted to black. Her face still has expression though, and I know that she's still in there because I can hear her thoughts. She's called on her bond to see better and to keep it close to the surface because of how nervous this is making her. If we didn't have so many TacTeam personnel around us, I would reach out and hold her hand, but I don't want any of them to question her or her ability right now. Instead, I send directly through to her, *If you need a minute, just tell me, and I'll figure something out.*

She glances over at me and I take a second to marvel at the depths of the black voids of her eyes. It had never really occurred to me that the voids might be a threat to her, but now I see just how naive I was being.

I'm okay. I just didn't realize how different it would feel in here, and it is making me panic a little.

I nod and give her little space, trying not to crowd her and make the claustrophobic feeling any worse. Nox is watching her very carefully now that he's seen that her eyes have shifted, but there's something different about him around her now. It didn't make sense to me before, but I've figured it out.

His bond is getting impatient with the distance between them.

There is no way in hell that Nox would have chosen to stay in the tent with Oli a few months ago. No way in hell. He would have found a tree to sleep under and had his shadow creatures keep watch for us all. But I'd seen the momentary look of panic on his face when he stepped into the tent. His bond wouldn't let him leave.

Then I'd heard the exchange between the two bonds as they had spoken and, though I've chosen not to tell anyone yet, they're both right on the edge of taking matters into their own hands.

I don't want that for Oli.

I don't want the choice to be taken away from her, but I have to admit that the idea of the Bond Group being complete and everyone having that connection is incredibly important to us all. Oli being strong enough to protect herself from Silas Davies when he eventually comes calling for her is also a huge push for me to want them to bond, I just don't know if he's capable of it.

I don't know if she would survive the fallout either.

North turns to face me and uses hand signals to start directing the TacTeam to where they all need to be, taking over because I was too busy fussing over Oli. Rather than calling me out on it, he's done what's best for his Bonded and assumed the leadership position.

Oli swallows as though she's trying not to vomit, and I speak to her directly again, *I'm going with Nox to the library. It's a bigger room, if you'd like to come with the two of us instead of going with North like you were supposed to. It might help you to breathe and get the panic under control.*

North's eyes flick towards her and he replies before she can, *Go with them, Oli. Kieran and I will keep watch here. And I'm more than happy to let my bond assume some control to get a better assessment of the situation.*

She looks surprised that he is willing to do this, and it's pretty obvious that she still hasn't come to terms with just how much North Draven would be willing to sacrifice for his Bonded.

I'm already fully aware, so it's not a shock to me.

We follow Nox down the sloping hallway of old cobblestones and uneven concrete to the library. After the summer he'd spent here with North when things got out of hand back home, he knows the place like the back of his hand.

His shadow creatures walk alongside us, their eyes shining unnaturally in the darkness, an anomaly because they're also voids. Oli is flanked by Brutus and August as she keeps pace with us by breaking into an almost-jog. She's a little taller than the average woman, but we're both tall, and her legs are definitely nowhere near as long as ours. I'd feel bad for her, but I also like being able to pick her up and haul her around with ease.

Mind out of the gutter, Shore.

She'd kept up with our hiking through the woods to the lake house beautifully and without complaint, and she makes me proud to be her Bonded every time we go out on one of these missions.

When we get to the library, Nox heads straight to Alistair, who is waiting with a large ring of keys in his hands, incredibly old-fashioned but exactly what I was expecting for this place, and a stack of books already waiting for us on the desk in front of him.

"It's good to see you again, Mr. Draven," Alistair says, and Nox dips his head a little in greeting.

"Sorry that you had to dig these out for us. I know there are some very unpleasant things up there hidden in the stacks."

Alistair shrugs and waves his hand. "If it helps with

the messy situation, then they're all yours. We appreciate everything that you do for the community."

He keeps saying 'we', which is a little confusing, but then he glances over at me and waves behind his back as though beckoning someone over. A young boy who can't be much older than nine or ten slinks over to us, his eyes a little sunken in his skull, with dark circles underneath them and a sickly look to his skin.

Nox frowns at him, calling his shadow creatures away and to heel so that they don't scare the boy anymore, but his eyes stay glued to the very damaged-looking child.

"This is my nephew, Joseph. His parents were both taken in the last wave, and even though his mother's Bonded moved to the Sanctuary, Joseph chose to move here instead. It's safer for him here."

My eyes flick back to Nox. He is definitely having some feelings about this kid, feelings that he will not want anyone to know about. I need to defuse this situation, and quickly.

I take a step forward, dodging the snarling jaws of the creatures, and reach out to take the stack of books from Alistair's desk with a polite smile. "Thank you again for grabbing these. We will get out of your hair quickly, before we bring any trouble to your doorstep."

Alistair smiles, his eyes crinkling as he pats the bare concrete wall beside him. "Doesn't matter what you bring to my door. No one's getting through it."

And then we hear the explosion.

J BREE

OLI

I already feel as though the walls are closing in on me, and the sound of the explosion just has my heart trying to beat out of my chest in a panic.

I'd never realized that I had any issues with small spaces.

I definitely have been in smaller enclosures than this before, but the heat of the concrete and the stagnation in the air has me gasping for breath, my lungs screaming in my chest as though I'm not getting enough oxygen, even though I know I am.

I have no freaking clue how North and Nox spent *months* here as children, and I wouldn't be surprised if this was the trauma in Nox's past, because I am feeling particularly traumatized right now.

Where is Oleander?

North's words are stern, bordering on desperate, and even though he's using our joint mind link, he is definitely not speaking to me.

Gryphon gets an arm around my waist and sends back, *We're all still in the library. Oli is safe. Where are you and do you have eyes on what just happened? It feels a lot like Unser.*

I almost want to huff and stamp my foot in frustration.

I still have never gotten a clear answer from anyone over who the hell Unser is and what he's capable of. His name is just dropped into conversation randomly by everyone around me, as if he's some urban legend. When I glance up at Gryphon to demand to know what the hell that means, there's another explosion, this one big enough that I feel a little sick from the motion under my feet.

This time, Nox takes a step towards the little boy.

Gryphon starts shoving the books into his bulletproof vest, which is a smart way to get his hands free and protect the ancient tomes of knowledge that is otherwise lost to time. "We need to figure out if there's any damage to the Hail Mary before we go out and neutralize it—"

"I'm not leaving the kid," Nox says, cutting Gryphon off, and Joseph's eyes flick over to him.

I have to admit, it looks as though the kid has been put

through the wringer, and the softness that Nox is treating him with is a little bit of a surprise. I didn't know he was capable of it. Even North gets treated with a wary sort of disdain by his brother.

Gryphon sends through again, *North, do you have eyes on who is out there and what is going on?*

North finally replies, harried sounding, *We do. It's Silas Davies himself, along with at least eight Shields and a whole group of the Resistance's Top Tier Gifted. I recognize most of them, but I was unaware that they had a Trigger.*

"Fuck," Gryphon says out loud, and I can't contain myself any longer.

"What the hell is a Trigger? And who the fuck is Unser?"

Gryphon stalks towards the opening of the library, still shoving the last of the books into his clothing as he looks down the hallway. I'm not sure if he really thinks he's going to see a giant hole hole in the thick concrete walls, but there's been no change in the air pressure, so I'm not worried about it yet.

Surprisingly, Nox answers me with none of the usual sarcasm or vitriol in his voice. "A Trigger is a living bomb. It's a Gifted whose power is literally an explosive. Usually, it's a one time thing. In teenage years, something will 'trigger' them and when their gift kicks in, the use of it kills them, as well as anyone close by."

My gut sinks, and I'm sure my face is horrified, but Nox just keeps laying out the facts. "Unser was the first Gifted to have two abilities, the Trigger itself, and the Regeneration. He's a living bomb that can go off more than once, though his recovery period is a few weeks, so he has to be used in a very strategic way."

I glance over at Gryphon and then back to Nox. I can't help but state the obvious, terrifying truth. "There were just two explosions."

North is quiet again in my head, which raises the panic in my chest a little more, but I try to focus on what Nox is saying because it's important.

He meets my eyes, and that same worried sort of calm is in him as he nods at me. "Which means that the Resistance has a Trigger who has a Regeneration period that's only a few minutes."

Fuck.

I swallow the bile creeping up my throat. "Do you think I'll be strong enough to take him out?"

Gryphon looks back over his shoulder, glancing at Alistair for a moment before deciding that whatever he's about to say, it's worth saying in front of him so that both Nox and I hear it. "My bet is that if the Bond Group was complete, and you were Bonded to everyone, then yes. Right now? I'm not so sure."

I suddenly want to look anywhere but at Nox. It feels like more of a call out for him than it is for me. I've proven myself to be willing to figure things out between the two of us, whereas he has not been shy about how much he loathes to be around me. What a freaking mess.

There's another explosion and my palms begin to sweat.

Outside of these walls is my worst nightmare and a bunch of his friends, who I doubt will be easy for us to deal with. I was hoping to somehow make it through all of this conflict without ever having to see that man again. Naive, I know, but I'd kind of gotten attached to the very secret hope that North or Nox's shadow creatures could somehow devour him for me.

Stupid girl.

They're trying to turn the Hail Mary into a Wasteland. That's why they brought the Shields, they want to take it away from us by having it turn into a battleground.

Gryphon's eyes flick over to Nox, and I know he's sending that information from North through to him as well.

I glance over to Alistair where he's clutching at the wall and looking as though he might vomit. The moment our eyes meet, he blurts out, "You can't take my Joseph with you. They're not going to get through the walls. He's the safest here."

Nox's head whips towards Alistair and he snaps, "He's not staying here."

Jesus Christ, I think we're about to kidnap a kid.

Am I okay with that? Shit. I think I am. The Sanctuary has to be a better option for him, right? Fuck. My morals certainly have shifted lately.

I send through to North and Gryphon, *We're stealing this kid, right? If the guy won't give him to us, then we're taking him. There's no chance that we are going to get out of here without all of our powers. If Nox refuses to move without the kid, then we're stealing a kid.*

Gryphon looks at me and nods, but North is silent in my head. Another trickle of panic runs down my spine and my bond decides that now is *definitely* the time for her to make a permanent sort of appearance.

My eyes shift to black again, and though I can still see what is going on around us and I still have control of my body if I choose to, I let my bond take the reins.

Enough of this childishness. When we get back, we're completing the bond. Whether you do it, or I do it.

Oh God.

She then takes control of the situation, walking past Gryphon and out the doorway until she is stalking back towards where we had left North. I send him one last message before I let go completely and let her keep us all safe.

Help Nox grab the kid. We need to get out of here.

OLEANDER'S BOND

The Neuro man who dared to harm me and the girl has returned for us.

This time, I'm ready for him.

Not only has he come here for us, but he has dared to attack this hell-forsaken place that currently houses our Bonded. There is no part of me, not the god living inside this meat-suit nor the girl who I spend my days with, that is going to allow him near those that belong to us. We just need to get out of this prison first.

We find my Dark Bonded in the large chamber we had first moved through. There's a small group of men with him, all of whom turn and get one look at me before freaking out. I enjoy the look of terror on all of their faces, but their training is such that while they shift on their feet, standing more at attention than they were before, none of them actually flee in terror.

Disappointing.

When the Dark Bonded one sees me, his shoulders roll back and his eyes flicker down to where one of his shadow creatures walks beside me. They're very well trained, both of my little gifts from my Bonds, and as I approach, he says, "We aren't going to open the doors until we have a clear plan. Are you able to work through the solid concrete, or do you need to be outside with them?"

I tilt my head to one side as I consider what he's saying. "The concrete does dull my senses, but I can still feel those outside."

I would be surprised if his shadow creatures couldn't walk through the walls themselves and deal with the people outside as well.

He shakes his head. "I'm not as accurate through the concrete. I can send my shadow creatures out there, but I can't control what they do as well as I can normally. If they have any Gifted hostages, there's every chance that I could accidentally kill them as well."

A minor inconvenience. "I don't care all too much about the casualties."

There's a lot of nervous looks around me as the men all take in that statement, but the Dark Bonded one clicks his tongue at me, shaking his head. "You might not care, but the girl does, and you said that you protect her and keep her safe. Keeping her safe by killing innocent people is not doing a good job, Bonded."

A burning sort of indignation ruffles my feathers, and I find myself pulling at the bond living within him, not wanting to deal with the man anymore. The man with morals and values and a million other useless things.

He gives me a curt shake of his head and turns away from me. "You can't have him, not right now. There's too much at stake."

One of the men murmurs quietly under his breath, "I always knew that Draven had balls of steel, but I didn't know that arguing with *her* was also in his repertoire. You couldn't pay me enough. She's fucking terrifying."

I turn and focus on the man for a second, watching him gulp as he falls fully under my attention. "He's my Bonded. I would rip your heart out of your throat without a second thought, but Bonds cannot hurt one another. He was made for me, perfection incarnate... even when he's being difficult."

There's footsteps behind us, and I glance back to see my Bonded and the Damaged One walking along with the two Gifted that we had been stuck in the library with. The older man is holding the little boy's hand, clutching at it as he sweats profusely.

"Alistair and Joseph are coming back with us. We need to clear a path to get them out."

The Transporter stalks over from the mezzanine floor that he was standing on, startling for a second as he sees my eyes, but dipping his head respectfully in my direction. "I can't get us out of here unless we're outside, so we need to figure out what the fuck we're doing, and fast, because that Trigger is not letting up out there."

I shrug and step towards my Dark Bonded, placing my hands on his chest, irritated that there is a bulletproof vest in the way. "Take me outside. I'll fix it for us all."

He looks down at me, and then his eyes flick over to my Bonded. "What are the chances you can get a gauge of them from here?"

My Bonded steps forward and stares at the TV screen that shows the enemy all outside working towards breaking their way into the building. "I can, a bit. I don't think that she's going to be able to deal with Silas Davies yet… and I don't think she'll be able to sort the Trigger out. The rest of them should be fair game. The Shields are strong, but none of them are even close to what Dara or Franklin were. If we can get rid of everyone else, hopefully that spooks the other two enough that they disappear, for now."

North nods slowly. "That means leaving the Transporter for them alive as well, so they have a way to get out of here."

The Damaged One steps up, still glancing back at the child as though he's ensuring that he isn't going to disappear the moment he looks away. "So, our plan is to scare them away? She isn't the only weapon we have, brother."

The Dark Bonded one nods slowly and raises his palm until more shadows start leaking out of him in various different forms, falling round his body like a cloak of inky night until he really looks like death incarnate.

We were truly made for each other.

I smile as though the sun has come out from behind the clouds and is warming my face. I love them just as much as I love all of my Bonded. I see the serpent fall artfully to the floor, and my smile shifts into a manic grin.

It slithers over to me and wraps around my legs affectionately. I pet its head as it nuzzles my palm, and there is more disbelief and horrified chatter around me at the sight of our affection.

"The snake... she's petting the snake," one of them says and gets shushed by the men around him.

"Bonded, your job will be to take out everyone except Davies, the Trigger, and the Transporter. Do you think you can be that accurate?"

I ripple with frustration at them questioning my abilities and their insistence on keeping the men alive.

I am a god living among them, and they should know better.

I nod. "Of course. I could kill everybody in this room and out of it, if I wanted to. Everybody in this *state,* if I really felt like it."

My Bonded reaches out and takes hold of my wrist as though he is trying to calm me down, but it has little effect on me. They're all being irritating today, and I'd rather we just got to the killing part.

I want to go home to the fucking part too.

The Dark Bonded One looks to his brother. "We leave everyone else to our Bond and we focus on the other two. Everyone else is just there as a backup in case they have snipers or something hiding from the cameras."

It's as easy as that. He's given his directives, and all of the men fall into line around us, finding that their backbones are still encased within their bodies after all. It's a surprise, especially since they're surrounded by nightmares and gods who walk amongst them.

We step out into the chamber and I find that a ring of men has formed around the man and the child as they follow along with us. The men give my Bonds and me a wide berth, clearing a path for us to lead the charge.

The Damaged One refuses to leave them in the building while we deal with the situation, insisting that he can keep them both safe and protected for long enough for the Transporter to get them out.

The moment we get to the fourth vault on the way out, I start picking off the Shields. Their souls are weak and unsatisfying to me, but I funnel the power through to the Dark Bonded one anyway, watching as the extra kick of power simmers underneath his skin. His chest expands as he takes it all in, and his eyes darken until, eventually, his bond wins out and takes him over as well.

"Just what we fucking need," my Bonded murmurs

under his breath and glances at me. "If he loses it, you're going to have to talk him down, because none of the rest of us are going to be able to."

I move towards the Dark Bonded one as I work my way through the rest of our enemies outside, one by one feeling their bodies drop to the ground, even though I can't see it. I send back to my Bonded, *Why would I get in the way of greatness? He was put on this earth to wipe it clean of our enemies and those who might try to hurt us. Why would I stop him from doing so?*

There's no answer to that, and I smile up at the Dark Bonded one, happy to see him here with me at last. The man has kept him locked away for too long.

Then we move to the last vault, everyone shifting around us as they move into position. They're nervous but hiding it well enough, none of them sure of what all we're capable of.

There's no need for fear.

Our enemy is *nothing* in the face of my Bonded. Each and every one of them.

The outer doors open with a grinding sound, and the gloomy day is blinding after an hour in the building, but only for a moment before the shadow creatures consume the light as they move forward, working their way towards their targets.

Our Transporter immediately pops out of existence,

taking the man and the child with him, and the Damaged One steps forward, his mind now fully on the work in front of us. As his shadow creatures fall around us, I fight the urge to reach inside of him and pull his bond out, to have the three of us reunited here together on this battlefield, and watch as our gifts blend together to seek out our victory, but my Bonded is still very nervous about what's going on.

I'll show him that there's nothing to be concerned about.

Instead of worrying about the trivial concerns of mortals, I continue my work of picking out the souls of the lesser Gifted around us, churning up their life essence into pure energy and funneling it through to the Dark Bonded one until I'm sure he's invincible.

There's another explosion to our left, the force of it knocking us all from our feet, and he catches me, one arm banding around my waist like a steel bar as he steadies my feet. His shadow creatures snarl all around us, advancing towards the group a few hundred feet in front of us, and I have to wait for the smoke to clear enough to get a look at them.

Pathetic, the lot of them.

They might be stronger than I am right now, but I have only been in this reincarnation for a fraction of the time that they have walked this earth, all of them fully Bonded and at the peak of their abilities. We still have so much further to go, and I will do everything in my power to make sure that we get there.

Before I can continue working my way through the pathetic Gifted in front of us, the shadow creatures strike, hundreds of them swarming and killing indiscriminately as they work toward the back of the group where the enemy is waiting.

Screams of terror and pain sound around us, the sounds of flesh and bone being torn apart filters through the rain to us, and a shiver of joy and excitement ripples through me.

They're magnificent.

There are *pops* around us as enemy Transporters begin to bring in reinforcements, but I'm picking them off faster than they're arriving, keeping the threat we're facing at a very manageable level. I feel the inkling of a foreign being trying to reach into my mind, his talons digging into my skull, and I change my tactics.

I send power to my Bonded instead.

He glances at me in shock, but he gets my plan instantly, his Gift flooding me and shoving the man out of my head. I might not be strong enough, or practiced enough, to keep him out on my own, but my Bonded is, especially with the kick of power.

We watch as the grass turns red with the blood and gore of those who came here to harm us, and the stacks of bodies begin to pile up. Occasionally, there's the sound of a gun firing, but mostly, the carnage comes from my Bonds and me.

It only lasts for a few minutes, a retreat is called in quickly when it's clear that they've underestimated who they were dealing with and what we're capable of, and then the *pops* become about getting people out of here.

I make eye contact with the man who loves knives, the one who cut and hacked at the girl for years just to get to me, and right before his Transporter helps him escape his death, he smirks at me, dipping his head in acknowledgment.

It's a promise.

A promise that now that the stage has been set, the war is coming together around us, and now that I have my Bonded, we'll face each other until one of us comes out victorious.

J BREE

OLI

My bond doesn't let me take control again until the Transporter gets us back to the Sanctuary.

I don't remember all of what had happened while it was in control, but my body is still thrumming with the power that I now associate with the Soul Rending. It's clear to me that we had killed a lot of Resistance while we were there, and I'm not sure if I should feel horrified at my own lack of concern about that.

I only wish that we had been able to kill Davies or the Trigger.

Gryphon gets his hand on my neck to ease away the churning feeling in my stomach, but North stands stock still next to me without so much as a glance in my direction.

Very weird.

"Are you going to do something to get him back? Or are we going to have to pour a tub of ice water over his head or something?" Gryphon snaps, and I frown at him.

"What are you talking about?"

He leans in a little closer to me so that the TacTeam personnel around us can't hear, but North can, probably why he's doing it instead of just using our mind connection. "Your bond funneled power to us all while we were out there, and it triggered North's bond to take over. It hasn't given him back yet."

Oh, shit.

I wait until Gryphon moves away from me before I reach out gently and take North's hand, trying to get his attention without making a big deal about it in front of everyone. It's unnaturally cold, nothing like it usually is, and I try not to freak out.

The bond notices.

Of course it does, he's devoted to me. His void eyes turn to face me, and I get a good look at him. I love North's bond; I love his bond as much as I love him. That simple but completely sincere declaration that it had given me before we'd Bonded still rings in my ears, and there isn't a lot that I wouldn't do for him.

But Gryphon is really starting to lose his shit about it being here.

"Can I have North back now, please? I'm safe here, you know."

It stares me down, and even though his face still stays completely blank, I can tell that the intensity of his look is making Gryphon nervous. Nox turns around from where he'd had his back to us, and even he doesn't look so sure about the situation. It doesn't matter though. I already know that we're all safe.

I shake our joined hands a little. "Hey, I need North back, please... unless you can sense a danger here that none of the rest of us are feeling. If you're not, then I really do need him back."

The bond lifts our hands up to his face from where I'm still clutching at his, taking in a deep breath of the scent of my skin.

Gryphon gets a hand on the butt of one of his guns, and I scowl in his direction, utterly disapproving of the move. There's also extra shadow creatures around my ankles coming directly from Nox himself.

"Knock it off. It's just saying goodbye to me. You are, right? Because we can hang out a bit later, once we're back at the house and there's less eyes on us."

The bond looks around at the TacTeam personnel who are all shifting on their feet very uneasily. I'd almost forgotten they were all there, and for a second, I can't help but think about what this all must look like to them.

Terrifying, I'm sure.

Gryphon curses under his breath. "Why did you point out the other people, Bonded? He might see them as a threat."

I shake my head at him, and North's bond tugs on my arm again until I'm pressed up against his chest. It's a very impressive chest that I'm well acquainted with, but the way he's standing is so different to North that for a moment, it feels like a whole new being is holding me.

"Mine," he murmurs against my lips before kissing me in full view of everyone around us. I can sense how much it's freaking Gryphon out, but by the time I pull away, the void eyes are gone and North's blue gaze is staring back at me.

"What the fuck was that?" he says, glancing over my shoulder at the other two, but Nox answers before I can find my voice again.

"That was what happens when you trust a Bond. They take whatever the fuck they want, regardless of what you have to say about it."

My cheeks heat, and North's arm around me tightens protectively. Gryphon's eyes flash, but I can't see whatever it is that he's doing.

From the look on Nox's face, it has everything to do with him.

My stomach is doing flips, and when Nox's eyes flick

to mine, I see that same fire in him, the one that burns so hot that makes him hurt me at every opportunity. He's only going to hate me even more if we have to Bond like our bonds have demanded.

I might just hate myself for it too.

I take a long shower.

Showers have always been my safe haven, somewhere I can go to wash away all of my troubles. Honestly, hot water is the answer to everything, but no matter how long I stand under there, there's no getting away from the problems of today.

We need to complete the bond.

Nox would rather die.

He's not exactly my favorite person either, but I can deal with the sex part of it. Actually, the sex part is the least of my problems. I've been lucky enough to enjoy four other amazing men who have shown me exactly how much pleasure is possible between two or more people, how different that pleasure can look, and the limitless possibilities that exist between my Bonded and I.

It's mostly the thought of him being in my head.

Being vulnerable to him, being exposed to his scathing vitriol at all times, the hate that he has for me that I still don't understand. There's too many unknowns in this for me to just... climb into bed with him.

Will he kiss me? He has to make me come to complete the Bond. I know he knows exactly how to make that happen, thanks to the Great Hallway Incident as I'm now calling it in my head, but I'm so in my head about the consequences of this, so it's going to be about a million times harder—

"Move over. How can such a tiny little slip of a woman take up so much room?"

I squeak embarrassingly and clutch at my chest desperately as I slip and almost end up on my ass. Gryphon gets a hand around my arm and manages to keep me from seriously hurting myself, using my distraction to step into the shower with me and shuffle us both under the stream of water. He's gloriously naked, some streaks of mud still on his arms and neck from the attack, and the moment my racing heart settles down, I'm going to do something about his rock-hard dick digging into my back.

Like dropping to my knees and swallowing him whole.

"How the hell did you get in here without my bond warning me? I just lost ten freaking years of my life, and you'll have to be the one explaining that shit to the others!"

He chuckles in my ear, one hand sliding down my stomach and stopping just shy of my pussy. I haven't recovered enough from the shock yet to be mad about that, but in a minute, I'll be sassing him out over it.

He moves his hand away from my stomach to grab the soap, dragging it over my already clean skin like he's obsessed with the feel of me under his fingertips. "You've gotten used to us all. Now that you're happily Bonded and totally satisfied, your bond isn't going to worry about telling you when we're around. Why would it need to?"

"I don't know about *totally satisfied—*"

He grabs my chin and tugs my face up firmly, swooping down to kiss me senseless. I turn in his arms, my legs steady again, and wrap my arms around his neck to anchor myself to him.

This is what I needed.

Kissing Gryphon Shore is like coming home after the hardest, longest day. It's protection from a storm, listening to the rage and destruction of everything while knowing without a doubt that you're safe. If North is my protector and caregiver Bonded, then Gryphon is the surety that nothing is ever going to push these men away from me. Gabe is the one who has proven that he's all in and accepting, as loyal to me from the very first moment as I have been to them, and Atlas is the epitome of dedication to me. They're all variations of the same set of values that I desperately need.

All of them.

Except Nox.

I break away and whisper, "Gryphon—"

But he's already in my head, already knows every last little concern I might have, and murmurs back against my lips, "You said you trusted me. I'm not going to let anything happen to you that you don't want, Bonded. I'm going to make sure… you're taken care of. You deserve to have us without your bond forcing it."

I don't see how that's possible.

Not without Nox giving in to his bond or somehow having a total change of heart and deciding that I'm not actually the root of all evil.

Gryphon growls under his breath at the depressed turn my thoughts have taken. He steps away from me, just long enough to soap himself down and wash away the mud and grime from the day. I watch him with a rapt sort of obsession, enjoying the way that his muscles flex as he moves. He's freaking gorgeous, the type of cut that a man gets from daily training to become a weapon for his people, and I want to taste every inch of his body, to find my own way to worship him.

The moment he's done washing the soap away, he turns the water off, snapping a towel off of the rack and wrapping me up in it. He has to go searching for one for himself, but he barely swipes the droplets away from himself before he's tugging me back into my bedroom.

I tense as we step into the darkness, but there's no one

else there.

"You promised that I'd get you tonight. I'm not going to just forget about that, Bonded. It's been too long."

I nod and throw my towel off, not really caring about where the hell it ends up, and I practically sprint to the bed. It's only a handful of steps, but Gryphon moves faster than I do, catching me and throwing me back against the pillows until I'm grinning like a madwoman.

"Spread that pretty pussy open for me, Bonded. It's been too long. I need to remind it of who it belongs to."

I do exactly that, splaying my legs out and reaching down to hold my pussy open just the way he likes, and I'm rewarded with long swipes of his tongue against my clit as he wastes no time in eating me the hell out. I'm in awe of this man and his lips. He does it like this is his favorite meal and he's been starving himself for a week in anticipation.

He doesn't let me come though, he just gets me right to the edge, my juices dripping all over his face, before he pulls himself back up to kiss me, sharing the taste between us. I could get angry about it, demand that he finish the job, but he's taught me that he'll never leave me wanting, and the fun of drawing this out is everything to me.

I push him onto his back and then crawl down his chest until I get a fistful of his cock, enjoying the groan he gives me as I slide my lips down the hot length. He's always been determined to be in control; it's something else to have him at my mercy for a little while. I moan around him, the vibrations causing him to grit his teeth, and I feel as he lengthens even more in my mouth. I find myself having to focus on relaxing my throat to get him far enough down.

I don't want him to come yet though. Call me selfish, but I want him fucking my pussy before either of us reach our peak, so I pull away. Before he has the chance to flip us over and rail me into the mattress, I climb up and sit on his dick.

The stretch is something else.

"That fucking pussy, that tight and wet fucking hole was made for me. Fuck me, Bonded. Take what you need and give me what I want. More, Bonded. Bounce harder. More!"

The words and praise fall away from his lips as I do exactly what he says, taking control but being obedient all at once. His hands cover my tits and squeeze, toying with my nipples and slapping at the sensitive flesh there until I'm crying out at the overstimulation. My hips slow to a grind as I come, rubbing my clit against his pubic bone as I drag it out for as long as I can.

I want to stay in this bed with him forever.

When he comes with a low groan, he grabs at my arm and pulls me back down onto his chest.

I hear the door open and feel one of my Bonds walk

into the room. It's obvious to me who it is, I only have one Unbonded now, but a shiver runs down my spine when I hear the door click shut again behind him.

My naked ass is still up in the air, all of my most sensitive flesh exposed to Nox's all-seeing eyes in the inky darkness of the room. I tense and move to look over at him, to see whether the loathing and disgust is still etched into every fiber of his being, but Gryphon's fingers curl around my chin to stop me.

Even when I try to pull away from him, his grip tightens, his fingers biting into my skin and his eyes narrowing at me through the darkness.

I frown back at him, but he tugs my face down to his, sealing his lips over mine and sweeping me up into a devouring kiss. It's a distraction, or an attempt at one, because there's no part of me that could possibly have my attention diverted away from the other man in the room.

Goosebumps burst out over my skin at the feel of his eyes on me, a searing brand of heat, and my back arches involuntarily. My bond reaches out to his in the darkness of the room and tugs him over to the bed; a siren's call he cannot resist.

I wonder how much he can see in the darkness without his eyes shifted, if he can actually see my pussy spread open wide for him, glistening with the evidence of the intoxicating sex I'd just had with his best friend. I groan and bury my face in Gryphon's chest, my back arching even more, and one of Gryphon's hands fists in my hair to keep me there.

I feel like an offering, a sacrifice. If I'd thought being used by North's bond was hot, then it has nothing on this. My Bonded offering me up to my damaged Bond. Carefully drawn lines and silent negotiations where the commodity is me, my bond, and my pussy.

It's silent for a minute as he stands there and stares into the darkness.

Then I hear the sounds of him unbuckling his belt, his pants sliding to the ground and the soft rustling sounds of his shirt being discarded. I want to turn to look at him. I want to see whether he's turned on or if he's staring at me like he wants to destroy me.

I almost come just from thinking about it, the anticipation is enough to have me groaning into Gryphon's kiss, and my hips begin to move by themselves.

He takes a second to kneel on the bed, one leg on either side of mine, and there's no mistaking the heat of his erection as it slides against my ass, dipping down to drag over my pussy until he's coated in the wetness there. I push back against him with a gasp, but he shifts away from me, totally in control of this moment and not willing to let me take anything right now.

Not even the pleasure that both our bonds are so

desperate for.

So I hold myself still like a good little Bonded, waiting not so patiently until he decides to give in. God, I hope he'll give in and fuck me, propped up over another of my Bonded like a spectacle.

After what feels like an age, he slides into my pussy, Gryphon's cum spilling out of me a little and dripping down my legs. I whimper at the loss of it, my bond writhing in my chest for more, *more*, everything. Give it all to me.

His fingers bite into my hips as he holds me there for a minute, impaled on the impressive length of him, until I think I'm going to have to beg him to move. Then, finally, his hips get to work. He's brutal, nothing about this is a loving Bonding, but I'm moaning like a wanton. Gryphon's hand flexes in my hair, his body reacting to mine. It's too dark for him to be able to see much, but the sounds that we're making are enough to have him ready for round two.

If I wasn't so terrified of interrupting Nox and losing this moment, I'd demand they both fuck me together, fill me up with their cocks at the same time until I was ready to burst. Fuck, I want to feel them both moving inside of me and drawing me closer and closer to oblivion until I'm nothing but a writhing mess between their bodies.

I want *more*.

I feel Nox shift, the moment that his bond takes over, and he bends over my back until he can get a hand around my throat and pull me back up against his chest, away from my Bonded, in a clear act of possession. I catch the look of concern on Gryphon's face as my eyes slip shut, my pussy clenching around Nox's cock as his hips still drive into me at a brutal pace.

His lips touch mine.

I sometimes forget that he was the first of my Bonds that I ever tasted. He was the very first of them all to kiss me, by force, but my bond had pushed towards him as desperately that day as it pushes against my skin now. I want the bond… I want him as well. Nox and his bond, I want them both, and it kills me to think that way. What has he done to deserve that sort of longing from me?

More than I'd like to admit.

More than most of my Bonded would admit as well, since everyone but maybe North is completely over his attitude, but the more that he says to me, the more that I feel like I can see behind the curtain.

The fingers around my throat flex again, drawing me back into the moment and away from all of my thoughts of my dark and broken Bond. I kiss him back with the same fire that he kisses me with, my tongue stroking over his as I claim him as one of my Bonded, the man and the god that lives inside him. Even if it's paving my path to hell, then I guess I'm on my way down there with a smile and a fucking amazing orgasm.

One of his hands slips down to my throbbing clit, circling it with the sort of practiced ease that comes from lifetimes of us worshiping each other, our bonds two halves of the same whole. He's come back to me after a lifetime away, and I whimper desperately.

He pulls back just far enough that I can see his void eyes again, his face still that blank slate that says Nox isn't in control right now at all, and then he breathes against my lips, "*Mine.*"

I come again, gushing down my thighs and his until the sounds our bodies make as we move together becomes obscene. He tumbles over the edge after me, coming with a roar that doesn't sound human at all, that same otherworldly voice that his brother's bond has.

I'm a gasping mess as my bond curls itself around his, binding us together, and everything feels right.

Perfection.

A void I didn't know existed inside of me knits itself back together until I'm whole. For the first time in my existence I can breathe properly, my lungs at full capacity after a lifetime of just scraping by.

I'm vaguely aware of Gryphon pulling me back down into his arms, cradling me against his chest as he soothes away the trembling that overtakes me with his big, calloused hands. Every inch of my body is hypersensitive, my thighs clenching together as my pussy throbs with the aftershocks of the Bonding.

I could die happy now.

I could walk into any Resistance camp and destroy them all; a weapon that's been forged in fire and come out deadlier than ever.

I feel it the moment Nox takes control of his body again, his eyes shifting back to the same deep blue hue as North's, and I want to whimper as he sits up, flinging his legs off the side of the bed as he gets up. I start to rationalize that of course that's what's going to happen, and I'm absolutely fine right now, but Gryphon has other plans.

"Lie down. You're not going anywhere until her nesting is done. If you can't hack it, then let your bond out again."

Nox opens his mouth, but Gryphon cuts him off without letting him utter a word. "It's not up for discussion. If you step away from this bed, I will drag you back."

I barely breathe, so sure that I'm about to watch the two of them fight to the death right here in front of me, and I'm suddenly glad that my other Bonded are close by.

I'll need the backup.

It takes a full minute, but Nox's eyes shift back to black, then he climbs back onto the bed, facing me without touching me at all. He stares at me, his face blank and his eyes unblinking as his bond takes up watch.

It's a start.

Not a great one, but it's something.

ATLAS

I feel it the moment our Bonded Group is complete.

I'm sure everyone does.

It's as though a piece I didn't know was missing slides into place in my chest. Suddenly I can breathe at full capacity, having no idea that for so long it had only been at eighty percent. I should feel relieved, grateful, *ecstatic*, every good emotion you can possibly think of, that we're now protected by having a closed circuit between the six of us, but there's a part of me that desperately wants to stalk through this house, break down Oli's bedroom door, and kill Nox for touching my Bonded.

Our Bonded.

I don't need to reach out to Oli to know that she's okay.

I can feel her there in my chest, and she's also content with the completed Bond. I'd only been able to stay calm about the whole fucking mess because Gryphon was in there as well. He was acting as a sort of 'chaperone' to make sure that Nox didn't hurt her in any way while she was so vulnerable to him, but I can't shake the feeling that I need to go and see it with my own two eyes.

I don't understand why he hates her so much.

I don't understand how her running away could've hurt him so deeply that he still couldn't see sense once the truth of it all was presented to him.

I get the feeling that the guy has some deep-seated mental issues or something from the way that everyone treats him. I have to admit that the idea of him being in our Bonded Group still pisses me off. He's a liability and a danger to Oli. I'll never take that shit lightly.

We've almost lost her too many times already.

I'm still sleeping on a mattress on the floor of my newly finished room, but I couldn't care less about it. I'm hoping to only have to sleep in here a few nights a week when Oli wants time alone with her other Bonded, so the idea of picking out anything and being fussy with it just doesn't interest me. Gabe had been a good sport about helping me get it done, as well as his room, while everybody else was away. There's still so much to be done around here before the house is actually finished, he easily could've told me to fuck off.

He's also a surprisingly patient teacher, and his dedication to getting this place finished, and getting Oli away from the rest of the community, is definitely something that I can get behind.

He's someone I don't mind sharing her with.

Once we'd finished grouting my bathroom and laying the carpets, we had moved on to North's room, which needed the most work. The guy is fussy as fuck when it comes to interiors, which means more work for us. I would point it out to him, loudly and often, just to be an asshole, except that the guy also built an entire town for his community without once asking *anything* of them beyond their loyalty to each other and to help where they can.

I might cut him some slack for insisting on incredibly fussy tile work.

Gabe hadn't let me touch a single thing in North's room, not trusting me to not fuck it up, and I don't blame him. The only good perk there was that during the day, we had figured out how my power had grown.

Gabe had been working underneath a Jacuzzi large enough to fit eight fully grown men in it that North was having installed in his bathroom, when one of the temporary supports had given out and the whole thing had plummeted towards Gabe's head and chest area.

It probably wouldn't have killed him, especially if

we'd gotten him to Felix fast enough, but he definitely would have been seriously injured had it actually managed to land on him.

The moment I heard the wood cracking, my Gift had burst out of my chest, completely involuntarily and in a way that I had never felt before. I could see it though. I could see the protection that it had placed on Gabe. When the Jacuzzi bounced off his chest and back into place, he'd caught it and held it up with ease, as though he had all of the strength in my body.

He'd glanced over to me in complete and utter shock. "What the fuck was that?!"

I shook my head, but a small bead of sweat formed on my forehead as I snapped back, "Get out from under there! I don't know whether or not I can hold this."

He scurried out and placed the tub back onto the ground, changing out the support and checking to make sure that it was secure this time with the practiced ease that he does everything. "Could you do that before? Is that something that you've always had up your sleeve and just forgot to mention to me or…?"

He let the sentence trail off and I took a second before I answered, staring down at my hands where they were glowing and then back over to him, that same glow over his skin. "I've never done that before. I don't really feel my Gift the way that you guys do. It's just a part of me. I can't manipulate it… or, at least, I couldn't before. *Fuck.* I don't even know how I did it now!"

Gabe cackled and pushed a hand through his hair, covered in sweat and dust from all of his work. "Well, I guess we can say now that we are definitely friends if your bond is deciding to protect me from shit. I wonder if it would do that for the rest of the guys too?"

I shook my head. "Fuck knows, but I doubt it'll do it for every one of the other Bonds."

Gabe gave me a side-eye and slumped against the bathroom countertop. "You know you're gonna have to let that go, right? Oli is Bonded with the rest of them as well… or she will be soon. You're only gonna hurt Oli if you keep kicking up a stink about him."

He didn't say exactly who he was talking about, but it didn't take a genius to figure it out. "I know, and I'm careful not to put that sort of pressure on her. Doesn't mean I have to like him, and it also doesn't mean I have to use my Gift to stop bathtubs from falling on his head. Natural selection isn't always a bad thing."

Gabe scoffed and shook his head, moving back through the bathroom to collect his tools so we could head off to have something to eat before moving on to another room. We'd eaten breakfast early, and I was fucking famished.

I should've just let it go, but I couldn't. "Why are you fine with him? You know what he did to her."

He grimaced and pulled a face as he snapped his toolbox shut and lifted it into his arms, stalking out of the bathroom. "I do know, and I know how Oli feels about it, which is enough for me. I'm not going to tell her how to feel about something, and she told me that it was between the two of them.

I shook my head at him, but I kept my thoughts on that to myself. I don't want to tell my Bond how to feel about something, especially something like *that*, but I also am not going to stand around and let him hurt her, to have her just accept it because he's her Bond.

When we got to the kitchen, Gabe placed his toolbox down on the floor gently, careful with the hardwood floors he'd spent so long installing, before opening up the fridge and grabbing out the take-away lunches that we had ordered from the dining hall. Neither of us had wanted to stop to make lunch, and the chef was always thrilled to know that he was cooking for us.

Another perk of being in the Draven Bonded Group.

Gabe waited until we're both eating before he spoke again. "I think maybe that you are seeing things that you want to see because of your sister and that whole fucked-up situation."

I gave him a hard look and he shrugged back. "I'm not saying that Nox did nothing. I'm saying that Oli is not your sister, and her bond *definitely* is not your sister's bond. I think at any point, if it was what you think it was, her bond would have done something to protect her. It's wiped out entire camps for her. Fuck, we've both seen the destruction it's wrought. I'm not saying it would have killed them, especially now that we know that it probably can't kill him, but killing isn't the only thing that she can do. I'm pretty sure the bond would have, at the very least, punched him in the mouth. If it was what you thought it was."

He couldn't even say the word, but that conversation rings in my head, even as I lie on the mattress hours later and sink into the feeling of *completeness* in my chest. I'm also feeling more than a little guilty at how much I enjoy it, because even though the other Bonded might feel a different way than me, I'm enjoying the feeling of my Bonded sacrificing something vital and important right now just so that we can feel this, and that will never sit right with me.

Gabe lets slip to North and Gryphon about the boost in my power, and the next morning, I find myself being shaken awake before the sun has even risen to head down to the training center to test out these new limits. I would say that I have fucking amazing restraint, because I stop myself from yanking Gryphon's arm straight out of its socket the moment I'm conscious enough to realize what the asshole is even doing in my room.

"We're in the middle of a war, Atlas. That is a *very* handy gift for you to have, especially now that we know the Resistance has an unlimited Trigger, and there's no time like the present, so get your ass moving."

I throw my pillow at him as he retreats, but he bats it away as if it is nothing, stalking back out the door as he calls out, "Five minutes, that's all you get."

I'm out in three, dressed in my training gear with my shoes already on and laced up. It's too early to grab breakfast or even a protein shake, but I grab a bottle of water out of the fridge and stretch out. I already know we will be jogging down to the Tac Training Center as a warmup. Gryphon is a sadist, there's no doubt about it, but there's no denying that his methods work.

I feel the warmth in my chest before Oli walks out of her bedroom, quietly shutting the door behind her as though she's trying not to wake someone up. A ripple of irritation works its way down my spine at the thought of Nox sleeping in there.

Get a hold of yourself. Don't let her know how badly this is killing you. It's not her responsibility to shoulder it. I have to keep that mantra in my head and also make sure that my own mind barriers are up enough that Gryphon won't be able to trip over any of these thoughts.

I have no doubt that he could probably pry his way into my brain and find out anything that he wanted to know but, since I've proved myself, he hasn't shown any interest in doing so, respectful of the boundaries within the Bonded Group. He doesn't have the same respect for Oli though, still not teaching her how to put up barriers herself that could keep him out.

I could teach her.

It's a skill that was taught to me by my parents when I was barely out of diapers, because there are a lot of Resistance sympathizers who are Neuros, and even the most devout followers don't want their family secrets to be outed by a child's errant thoughts.

There were a lot of secrets in my house that would have brought my father to his knees.

"How did Gryphon talk you into volunteering for one of these training sessions?" Oli murmurs as she slides into my open arms without hesitation.

I can't see any injuries on her, and the only emotion I'm getting out of her at the moment is a sort of bone-deep weariness.

"He didn't give me much choice, but it's probably a good thing for us to explore it."

She nods, her face still pressed against my chest, and Gabe finally comes stumbling out of his room, bleary-eyed and yawning so wide that I can see his tonsils.

"Did you have a power surge too?" Oli says quietly, only shifting away from me far enough so she can get an arm around him as well, bundling herself up in the two of us and making happy sounds under her breath.

He kisses the top of her head and says through another yawn, "No, but Gryphon wants to see if he can force anything out of me as well. Then he figured out that Atlas' only made an appearance because I was about to be squashed, so you're probably about to watch Gryphon beat the shit out of me to try and test that working theory."

Oli frowns and makes a grumbling noise, turning around to send a glare Gryphon's way as he opens the front door, jerking his head at us all.

"We're losing daylight. Let's go."

"There isn't any fucking daylight. The sun isn't up yet," I mutter under my breath, and Oli giggles as she sets off down the front steps at a slow jog.

Her pace picks up quickly, and she breaks into a proper sprint as she catches up to Gryphon and keeps pace with him.

"It's disgusting that he's turned her into a workout person," I gripe, and Gabe laughs at me, as if he thought it would go any differently.

"Then you're an idiot. Gryphon was never going to let his Bonded slack on this front. He knows what happens to defenseless Gifted."

I want to reply, to point out all of the ways that our Bonded will *never* be defenseless, but the pace is brutal, and cardio has never been my strong point. We make it down to the Tac Training Center in decent time. When we stop in front of the building, I take the time to stretch out my legs a little more, easing the cramp that is trying to take hold in my calf.

Fuck cardio, and fuck Gryphon Shore.

"I can't believe I outpaced you guys! Do either of you ever run, or do you just lift heavy things?" Oli says in the most cheerful and sassy tone.

I flip her the bird, because I know it'll just make her laugh even harder at my expense, and Gabe grabs his chest like he's hurt by her words, but he's panting as badly as I am.

"I will have you know that I can shift into animals that can run for literally days on end, if I need to," he says, but his argument is kind of ruined by how much he's gasping.

She cocks her head at him like she's assessing his words and then snarks back, "Prove it, because from that performance, I highly doubt it."

Gryphon ducks his head so that she doesn't see him grinning at her sass. He's always pretty careful about trying not to let her see how much he enjoys her inner brat, but I feel no shame in beaming at her. I'm fully aware that encouraging it only makes it worse, but there is nothing about my Bonded that I would change.

Especially not her bratty ways.

"Oh, look. Unser's here. You might actually get to meet him, Bonded," Gryphon says in an attempt to divert her attention that actually works.

She stumbles dramatically, as though she is shocked off of her feet, and the other two both get a hold of each of her arms, because there's every chance she could still end up flat on her face.

"Unser? *The* Unser is here? The man who has been dangled over my head like a threat the entire time I have been back with you guys? I'm going to get to meet him. How exciting! I wonder if I can convince him to blow something up?"

Gryphon rolls his eyes at her and pushes his way into the building. Even at this early hour, it's bustling with bodies, personnel everywhere, and they all stare at him with hero worship in their eyes, open and plain for all to see. They also all gulp at the mere presence of my Bonded, and I enjoy the feeling of superiority that that gives us.

All these highly trained men who deal with the worst of what our kind have to offer and they stare at my Bonded as though she is a walking nightmare.

That no longer irritates me.

I have fully come to accept that it's better for her to be a nightmare to these men than to try and make friends with them, to play the docile and neutered monster who wouldn't hurt a fly. Besides, we've got more than enough friends, and those we do have are proving to be a handful.

"Good lord, not this early in the morning! I can't deal with that smart mouth."

I glance over to see Vivian walking towards us, his mouth downturned as he greets us, although there's a twinkle in his eyes as he stares Oli down. She grins back up at him, truly happy, and then, of course, she opens that smart mouth of hers and starts in on him.

"You should be happy with my dedication. I'm no longer a college student bound by unfair rules. I could choose to walk home at any time, and yet here I am, learning restraint and the proper way to kill our enemies. *You're welcome.*"

He rolls his eyes and another man approaches us. He's tall and wider than Vivian, and he is easily more muscular than even I am. He has a stern look on his face, but he looks at Oli with interest.

"An honest-to-God Soul Render. I never thought I'd see it."

"I go by she/her, not it, but lovely to meet you. I'm assuming you're Unser. I've heard a lot about you," Oli says, tuning her sass down just a little at the end as the much larger man looms over her. He's not trying to intimidate her or threaten her in any way, he's just looking over every inch of her, like he's trying to see some sign of her Gift etched into her skin.

Gryphon looks between them and then back to Unser. "This is Oleander Fallows, our Central Bonded. And, yes, she is a Soul Render. She's the reason that the Sanctuary was cleared of the Resistance last week."

Jesus Christ was it only last week that I'd had the greatest night of my life followed by one of the worst mornings in existence?

I share a look with Oli and see the same disbelief in her face that so much could have possibly happened in such a short amount of time. Yet, we're still no closer to getting rid of Davies and the rest of his band of sadistic followers.

Unser holds out a hand and starts ticking off fingers. "A Soul Render, two Death Dealers, a Neuro with unmatched powers, an unlimited Shifter, and… what exactly are you?"

Oli's hand slips into mine as I answer, "Strong enough to move a semi, and completely indestructible."

He looks me up and down slowly and then says, "I guess we'll see about that, won't we? War is good at testing limits, kid."

OLI

I wake up safe and sound in my bed between Gabe and North, the nightmare still clinging to my mind, a cold sweat drenching my body and my heart beating so hard that I feel as though it's trying to crack my ribs open and escape my chest.

"I'm gonna puke," I say out loud as I scramble over bodies, not really caring where my limbs are ending up, and lurching towards the bathroom.

I don't bother shutting the door, mostly because I know I'm not going to be alone for long. Even though it's incredibly shameful to be puking my guts up in front of them all, I know it's inevitable. As I vomit uncontrollably, a cold, wet washcloth presses over my forehead and my hair is twisted away from my face. Another set of strong hands strokes down my back in a comforting gesture, soothing me as the retching continues until I'm a shaking and miserable mess.

I don't know what the nightmare was about.

I don't have any clear memories of any of it, only the fear clinging to my bones and the way that my stomach revolts against it all. My bond doesn't register that I'm in any danger, but it's quiet in my chest, a grave, solemn sort of quiet.

It knows what the nightmare was about.

"What happened, my Bonded?" North murmurs to me as the retching finally stops, and he reaches over to pull me into his chest.

Gabe flushes the toilet and grabs the washcloth again to wipe my face down before moving away. Atlas stands by the door, clutching the frame and staring at me as though he's seen a ghost, but I tuck my head under North's chin and cling to him as the panic slowly recedes out of my veins.

"It was a nightmare. I don't know. I don't know—" I stop as my voice cracks, and I press my face into his neck again, tucking myself into him even more.

I'm probably hurting him, clinging so hard, but his arms are like bands of steel around me as he pulls me in closer, as though he would happily tuck me inside of his skin if he could.

I try to take in his strength, but all I feel is hollow… and terrified.

"Gryphon's already gone down to the Tac Training Center. Do you need me to call him back?"

I shake my head. "I don't want to go back to sleep, but I'm okay now."

"You're definitely not okay," Atlas grumbles, but North stands up with me still in his arms as though I weigh nothing and carries me back to the bed.

When he realizes there is a wet spot where I had been lying, my sweat soaking through my clothes and drenching the sheets underneath me, he makes an unhappy noise and hands me off to Atlas with directions to sit down while he fixes the situation. I don't really care about some sweaty sheets, but North has always been very particular about the ways that he fusses over me. I already know that if I don't get up and change my pajamas myself, he's just going to do it for me once he's done with the linen.

Atlas follows me into the closet and helps me into some dry, clean clothes when it's clear that my limbs are shaking too much still to be of much use. Then he holds me up as I brush my teeth in the bathroom. Gabe comes in with a bottle of water from the kitchen and hands it to me as soon as I'm done with my teeth.

It's the first time I've really seen them all working

together on something solely for me, something that makes me feel as though I'm the center of their worlds the same way that they're all the center of mine.

I start to tremble all over again.

When I hand the water back to Gabe with a shaky smile, he cups my cheeks with one of his big hands, a frown over his face. "You don't remember any of it at all?"

I shake my head, and the two of them share a look in the mirror.

My stomach drops. "What? You both think I'm going crazy, don't you?"

Gabe frowns at me and cups my cheek again, pulling me back into his chest for a hug as his thumb traces my cheek.

I feel a little better having had a physical connection with all three of them, and I know that if I could touch Gryphon and Nox as well, I would probably be fine to go back to sleep again.

Not that Nox would let me.

My heart does a weird thump in my chest before it races again, the panic coming back. I purposefully direct my thoughts away from my Bonded who still would rather not be near me, not needing anything else to upset me right now while I'm so fragile, for no apparent reason.

"Do you know what your third Gift is?" Gabe murmurs out of nowhere, and I glance back up at him.

"Yes. Why?"

He looks a little rueful, but Atlas answers me nonetheless. "Your mom dreamt of things to come. We were both worried that you were going to say no, and we were about to be forced into a whole new search for information about what that Gift could possibly be. You have to agree that we're kind of at our max for that sort of shit at the moment, Sweetness."

I don't want to talk about my third Gift.

I shake my head. "I've never had a dream like that before. I've had nightmares, plenty after I left the Resistance, but I always knew what I dreamt of. It's like there's nothing in my head."

They share another look, and I try not to feel irritated at either of them, I've clearly rattled them both this morning. I can't blame them for the friendship that they've struck up. "Just say it, whatever it is. I don't need the two of you tiptoeing around me."

Gabe pulls away from me and looks down at me. "Well, Sage couldn't remember a single thing about the asshole who got into her head and forced her to kill Dara. What if someone was trying to get into your head? Maybe your bond got them out, and it woke you up."

Shit.

Well, Goddamn.

I sigh and walk back into the bedroom right as North is

bundling up the dirty linens and heading into the bathroom to leave them in the laundry hamper in there. We must have some sort of cleaning service that I'm blissfully unaware of, because the hamper is always magically empty in the afternoon when I get back here, but I've yet to see any of the guys point out where the laundry is.

I sit down on the edge of the bed and shut my eyes to check in with my bond, hopeful, but not really expecting any clear answers.

Did someone try to get into our head last night?

It takes a second to answer me. *No.*

Do you know what I dreamt about?

Yes.

I want to scream. *Is there any chance of you being even slightly helpful to me right now and telling me what is going on so that we don't end up on some useless mission for no reason?*

You ventured into one of your Bonded's heads… the 'astral projection' as the Dark Bonded One called it. You ventured into his head, and I'm making sure that you don't remember what you saw there. I'm respecting a Bonded's wishes.

Jesus fucking Christ.

I know *exactly* what happened, and there's no way I can tell Atlas or Gabe about it, not without a whole lot of fallout and arguing.

I keep my eyes closed so that neither of them realize what I'm doing, but I reach out to North by myself. *My bond said I projected into Nox's head accidentally while I was sleeping. I saw something there, and she is keeping it from me so that he doesn't get upset about it.*

North walks back into the bedroom with a furious look on his face, but it isn't directed at me. I already know without a word between us that it's more about whatever it is that happened to his brother than it is about me overstepping.

He directs a stern look at Gabe and Atlas. "You two can go down to the Tac Training Center. Gryphon was going to let you sleep in, but if you're awake, you might as well get back to training."

Both of them look as if they might argue with him, but I climb back into the middle of the bed without a word and they both seem to realize that I need some space and that North is just slipping back into his usual bossy demeanor to get it for me.

Once they're both out of the house fully, North climbs onto the bed after me. He's wearing nothing but a silky pair of boxer shorts and that same frown on his face.

I feel guilty as hell.

"I'm sorry. I didn't mean to."

He answers without hesitation, "I know, Bonded. I know that the girl who wouldn't look into Atlas' memories because you were respecting his boundaries, even when there was a chance he was betraying us all, would never cross that line. I just don't know how Nox is going to take this… if he already knows about it. If he doesn't, then we can never tell him."

I don't like the idea of lying like that to him about something so important, but North has a much better view of the situation, and I trust his opinion.

I nod and then duck my head back into his chest, lying down fully with him and letting the steady beat of his heart underneath my ear lull me back into a sense of peace.

North is silent for a long time but then when he speaks, his voice is a low rumble beneath my cheek. "His nightmare would have pulled you in. If we're going to stop this from happening again, we need to make sure that he's not sleeping at the same time as you are, because the only way to get him to sleep without dreaming is for him to go to sleep intoxicated. I can't have him turning into an alcoholic again. None of us can live through that again."

I didn't know it was that bad.

Trauma? Absolutely, I knew he had trauma. Like Atlas has said before, you only need to look at him to know that something happened to him, but I didn't realize he was still facing it daily like that.

All of my trauma is packed up neatly into little boxes in my head, marked clearly with red tape and labels that read 'warning: do not open'.

I can't imagine living it over and over again like that.

I swallow roughly and nod. "I can switch to sleeping during the day. Take up a night shift somewhere. Maybe I'll head down to the Tac Training center and start training there as much as possible."

North's hand buries itself into the long tresses of my hair where it's spilling down my back. "Nice try, Bonded, but no one is going to accept you not being in this bed every night. Nox has been going through the books that we got from the Hail Mary, so there's no reason that I can't convince him to take up a night security position somewhere while he's researching. I'm used to him sleeping on my couch during the day with his hangovers. It won't be any different.

The Hail Mary.

My mind drifts to Joseph and the surety that Nox had about bringing the little boy back to the Sanctuary with us. "Do you think the boy was the thing that triggered the nightmare? I've never seen Nox like that before."

North sighs and rubs a hand down my back. "I can say with almost certainty that that's what it was, Bonded. I'm sorry that it's affected you. I'll do what I can to fix it, I promise."

Such a heavy weight that North carries for his entire Bonded Group, his community, and his beloved brother, so broken inside.

North attempts to coax me into staying in bed for the day, worried about the shakes that take over an hour to dissipate, but there's no way I can just sit around.

I already know that things are only getting worse for everybody in the Sanctuary. Gryphon has been recruiting more members for the TacTeams, but without letting new people in in our safe little haven, that's a fairly impossible feat. We're already using up all of the resources that we have on the repairs to the town. Everything is moving along slowly, and even with Gabe and Atlas going back to working on other people's houses during the day and finishing off the last of our rooms at night, it still is going slowly.

No one really kicked up a fuss about their rooms being done last. Nox is the only one of my Bonded who even sleeps elsewhere, the rest of them are happy enough to take turns sleeping next to me in my giant bed.

With the kitchen being complete and a few of the bathrooms, we're at a functional level. It doesn't matter that they still don't have a lounge room or any other communal rooms done, because no one really has time at the moment for sitting back and relaxing together.

I get dressed and follow North to his offices to spend the day helping him with paperwork. There's only a few jobs that I can do without having to be around a lot of people, and I like being around North, keeping him company while he sifts through the bullshit that the council and outer world has to throw at us.

I'd asked if I could read the books that we'd brought back from the Hail Mary after Nox was done with them, mostly for my own knowledge, but also because I wanted to see if there was anything in them that he might have missed about our situation. He's a professor with a doctorate in literary studies, so I know the chances of him missing *anything* is highly unlikely, but it's another way for me to feel useful.

My bond also might decide to be useful, for once.

When we arrive at the offices, there are a lot of people waiting around in the foyer area. I dodge them all as best I can, but we find a small and quiet-looking man waiting at the elevator for North, a nervous look on his face as he dips his head at the two of us respectfully.

"Councilman Draven, I have spoken to the other council members about today's meeting, and it has been moved to a video chat instead of in person, as per your request."

North nods and takes a pile of files from the man, thanking him politely as we step into the elevator. When the doors shut firmly behind us, I turn to give him a questioning look.

He fusses with the cuff of his jacket, looking as though he'd like to climb out of his skin rather than deal with being here and the genteel councilman today. "His name is Tamir, and he's my new secretary."

I raise an eyebrow at him, a little shocked, but he just shrugs back. "You didn't like Penelope, and I could no longer look past all of the lines that she was intentionally crossing, so I had her moved elsewhere to be someone else's problem. Tamir comes from a good family, and Gryphon has already vetted him and his Bonded Group."

I try not to let my indescribable joy show all over my face, but I'm sure I fail miserably.

His eyebrows creep up. "You didn't think I'd fire her?"

I shrug back. "I'm still learning to trust this. I might trust you implicitly, but there's been a lot of changes in our relationship and the Bonded Group in such a short amount of time. It's taking me a little while to catch up with it all."

I don't mention that having a complete bond hasn't magically solved all of our problems, there's still a whole load of bullshit that we're still trying to figure out between us all. I have no idea how we're going to manage it while also dealing with the Resistance and, you know, the end of the world.

There go my dramatics again.

North nods slowly and the elevator doors open back up to his office. There's a desk for a secretary in the room, but with a palm against the base of my spine, North directs me over to it and gets me settled there instead.

"If you don't like Tamir, I will find someone else. If he upsets you or your bond reacts to him in any way, that's what we'll do. That's what we'll do about anyone in the future, Bonded, and not just me. If there's someone on Gryphon's TacTeam who upsets you or your bond doesn't like, then they're gone. I know Rockelle can't keep his mouth shut around you. I'm happy to move him somewhere else if you don't want to see him anymore."

I smile and duck my head, opening up the laptop that he places in front of me. I log on to see that scans of the books that we had brought home from the Hail Mary are already waiting for me in my inbox from Nox.

He doesn't leave a note or anything, but it still somehow feels like progress to me.

Slow and steady, right?

"We don't have enough TacTeam personnel for me to start having opinions about them... and Rockelle is fine enough. It's mostly just soldier banter. I think that he relishes having something to rally against Gryphon with, but we both know that my Bonded can take care of himself."

North nods and gets to his own work, spreading open

the file in front of him and scowling at the information there. "Rockelle's father is not only another councilman, but somebody very respected within our community. It's sometimes hard for kids to grow up with that sort of pressure on their shoulders. I know that Councilman Rockelle did not want his son to be a TacTeam grunt. His words, not mine. Top Tier families don't usually like letting their kids serve. They think that labor is beneath them. But Rockelle idolized Gryphon from a very young age and could not be persuaded from joining the TacTeams after him. I think he pokes at you to get more of Gryphon's attention. Don't take it personally, Bonded."

I giggle. "So… he's a superfan and just wants Gryphon to love him? That's kind of cute."

North smiles and shakes his head at me. "He's a good fighter and has worked his way to being third in the chain of command. I'm relieved that your bond doesn't oppose him being around Gryphon, because there isn't an obvious choice to take his place."

I open up the files on the computer and take a sip of the bottle of water that North had left behind for me. "I would put up with a lot if it meant keeping you guys safe. Even if Rockelle did bother me, if he's the best choice for Gryphon and his team, then I would have sucked it up and let it go."

North nods and the frown slips back over his face as he gets sucked back into whatever is on his screen.

We fall into a calm silence as we both work, but I can tell that North is frustrated. Whatever is going on within the council is incredibly taxing for him. I stay quiet so that I don't disturb him and pretty soon, I lose myself in the document about the void eyes and just what they mean.

We've definitely been here before.

I don't know if I can really say *we* because I don't feel as though I have been reincarnated, but my bond has definitely been around a few times.

The book I'm reading is about myths and legends of the Gifted community, spanning back hundreds and hundreds of years. The void eyes just keep cropping up in it. The ability to manipulate the shadows, the ability to kill people, the ability to mess with people's minds in such a way that they don't even know what's happening; all of it is there.

It's a little terrifying.

I read it all, nonetheless. I read it until I think my eyes are going to bleed, and then I read it some more. At some point, North accepts an invitation into a video conferencing call and signals to me to stay quiet, and I nod.

He gets onto the video call with the other council members, and I'm sure I'm not supposed to be in the room listening to any of it, but he doesn't seem too concerned.

At first, I'm so engrossed in the text in front of me that I don't take much notice of what's being said. But as

North's temper gets shorter and shorter, I find myself being dragged out of my own work to sit there and listen in.

A snide voice comes through the speakers, "There are *five* Wastelands in the country now. Why are we not doing more to prevent this from happening?"

North cocks his head at the screen, as though the speaker is incredibly dense. "And what manpower are you handing over to assist with that, Williams? At no point have you attempted to take security into account, and it's only now that you're on the run and your Bonded Group has been targeted that you suddenly have an interest. Are you missing your pool back home or something?"

There's an indignant noise through the speakers and then someone else, a woman this time, speaks, "Councilman Draven, you can't speak like that! You've been responsible for security since you took the seat at the council. It's your responsibility."

"I took over security because no one else was doing it. If I wasn't doing it, there would be nothing standing between us and the Resistance. If you want to know why we aren't doing more for the Wastelands opening up, then perhaps you should assess why we have such a lack of TacTeam numbers. Those we do have are highly trained and ready to move out at a second's notice, but we do not have the numbers that the Resistance have. I'm not going to risk the lives of good men on a whim because you think that we are not doing enough, even while we are keeping thousands of members of our community alive and safe at the moment. Which is something that the council didn't even deem important a few months ago. There are women and children living here. I can't leave them unguarded."

He sounds pissed off, and I think the other council members are glad that he's here and nowhere near them.

Absolutely gutless, the lot of them.

An hour of useless whining and moaning later, he finishes up with the meeting and snaps the laptop shut, fuming as he cracks his knuckles and looks around the room until his eyes meet mine.

"They're all a bunch of fucking idiots," he snaps, and I nod.

"They're the type of people to sit around talking about a problem and never actually do anything about fixing it. They're the type of people who send others in to fight their wars for them. That's not who we are, and I'll never be able to respect them, North. You're a better person than I am for not having killed them years ago."

OLI

As much as I would like to continue to hide away in North's office with him and make myself useful, I know that I need to get back into training to make sure that I don't lose all of the hard work I've already put in.

I'd been so proud of my efforts during the recovery mission and proud of not being overpowered by the heavy gear or the long hike, so I find myself incredibly motivated to be able to pull my weight even more.

I *refuse* to be the liability.

Gabe and Atlas are both still going to their training sessions at the Tac Training Center each morning before they head off to help in the rebuilding efforts, and I force myself out of the incredibly comfortable bed to go with them. I need to be ready for the next time we get called away from the Sanctuary, and I don't want to rely on my bond to do the heavy lifting for me.

A few days after the council had threatened North during the meeting, I wake up to the sounds of Gryphon getting up to head off for the day. When I move to head into the bathroom to get myself ready to go with him, North grumbles in his sleep, his arms tightening around me, making it even more difficult to get out. I've come to learn that he's the worst of all of my Bonded when it comes to waking up.

You'd never guess it from all of the suits.

Once I'm dressed and ready, I meet Gryphon, Gabe, and Atlas on the front steps of the house to head down to the Tac Training Center together. The jog down there has become one of my favorite parts of the day.

Gabe and Atlas start to get *very* competitive with Gryphon and me, and it's not long before our slow warm-up run turns into an all-out sprinting war over who is going to get down to the center first.

It's childish and stupid and the perfect distraction that I need so desperately these days.

I arrive at the Tac Training Center with the taste of blood in my mouth, my lungs screaming, but, to my great joy, the three fully grown men running with me arrive seconds later.

I beat them all, finally.

As I catch my breath, I find Kieran and Sage waiting for us outside. I almost burst into tears at the sight of my best friend, my eyes watering the second I realize it's her standing there, and when she gets a good look at me, she does the same.

She hesitates for a second, as though she's not sure how I'm going to react to her, but I fling my arms around her neck and cling to her desperately.

I'd spent the last few days messaging her constantly, trying to get her to agree to meet up, but every time she'd answer that she was spending time with her Bonded and getting her feet back underneath herself.

I wanted to be very respectful of her Bonded Group and give her what she needed, instead of just taking what I wanted from her, but it's been the hardest few days. Almost as hard as the admittedly few days her loyalty had been in question.

"Thank God, I honestly thought I was going to have to come and fight Kieran for your honor."

She snorts into my shoulder, a very wet sound that I will not judge her for, and mumbles, "Sawyer beat you to it. We tried to keep him out, but he just used his Gift to unlock the doors and bitch me out for the state of myself. He's dragging me to dinner tonight with our parents. It'll be the first time that Kieran is coming to see them in a formally Bonded capacity, so feel free to snatch my soul right out and get me the hell out of that situation."

I bite my lip and glance at Keiran, ignoring the way that he glowers down at me, as if daring me to say something.

Joke's on him, I give zero fucks about his feelings on the matter.

"Meeting the parents! Do you feel nervous? I should probably let you know that their opinions on their daughter's Bonds have always been pretty weird, so you're gonna have your work cut out for you. I can totally give you some tips though. I won them over pretty damn quick. How do you feel about walking into burning buildings?"

Sage grimaces and buries her face in her hands. "Don't remind me! My dad is still falling over himself trying to get my forgiveness. Even after this whole 'Neuro hacking into my brain' debacle, he's been even more protective about it. He's trying to convince us to move into the same house as him, my mom, and Maria, but I honestly can't think of anything worse."

Gryphon greets Kieran with a clap on the shoulder and then reaches past us all to scan his card to get access to the building. Gabe and Atlas are squabbling over who beat who in the running race, and I throw an arm over Sage's shoulder to tuck her into my side tightly, already feeling like today is going to be a million times better than yesterday, thanks to Sage's appearance.

We step into the center together and out of reflex, I duck my head so I don't have to see any of the curious and wary looks that I know will be slung my way.

I distract myself with my bestie. "So, are you here to see me to do training or because Kieran refuses to let you out of his sight, because he's a typical boorish Bonded man?"

Sage scoffs and kicks her feet against the concrete. "A mix of all three I suppose. I heard about Atlas' power surge, and I'm interested to see if Gabe has one too. I hope you guys don't mind having an audience. I can go back home, if you want some privacy."

I glance back at Gabe, just to check in, but I'm also desperate to hang out with her, so I'm sure all he's seeing on my face is that.

He shrugs and replies to her, "There's still no sign of my power surge, which I'm taking as a sign that I was already the most powerful shifter on record and there's no upgrading what's already perfect."

I smile back at him, and Atlas makes a gagging sound of annoyance. Their friendship is mostly a competition of who can be the most childish. "You're so full of shit, Ardern. You just need to have a bit more patience, or maybe we need to drop a bathtub on your head again without me saving your ass and see if it finally draws something out of you."

Gabe clutches a hand to his chest. "I would, but your Gift got in the way last time without you even trying, so I doubt it will work."

Sage turns her head until her lips are close enough to my ear that they won't hear her and whispers, "Since when have these two been best friends? It's weird."

I giggle and pull her with me towards the training room. "It's freaking bizarre, and they figured it out all on their own. We're very proud."

When we get into the training area, I immediately move over to the mats to start stretching out, something that is even more important than it was before, thanks to our competitiveness running down here. Sage drops to the mats next to me and follows through my stretching routine with me. She's a little more subdued than what I'm used to, more like the shy girl that I had first met when I got to Draven, but I'm not surprised at the change in her at all.

There are a lot of TacTeam personnel eyes on us.

It doesn't take a genius to figure out that they're all put off by Sage and I being here. I'm used to them all looking at me, but today I'm hyperaware of it because I don't want anyone making her uncomfortable now that she's finally ready to join us out here again.

Kieran and Gryphon both notice it too, and while my Bonded is good about ignoring it most of the time, his second-in-command is not quite so calm. Within the space of the time it takes the two of us to stretch out, every single TacTeam personnel who dared to side-eye us is put on some sort of terrible job, groaning and muttering under their breath as they are sent off in all different directions.

Sage grimaces as though she feels bad for them, and I give her a sardonic look back. "If they were smart enough to keep their opinions to themselves, they wouldn't be in this mess. That hasn't got anything to do with us."

She shrugs. "I don't blame them though. They're all just looking out for Kieran. I can't blame them for that, can I?"

I shrug back. "You can because their superiors have told them to get the fuck over it, so they're not the good little soldiers they should be, are they?"

Gabe scoffs at me from where he is stretching out next to us. He's not usually so enthusiastic about it, but I think that the extra attention has him on edge as well. "Since when have you been a good little soldier, Bonded? You'd have to keep your opinions to yourself for that."

I smack him on the leg gently, hurting my own hand more than him, and shrug. "I haven't heard any complaints yet. I'll have you know that I am *very* good at keeping my head when things go to shit around me, and I'm more than willing to learn new ways to fuck up the Resistance. I think that makes me a fantastic soldier."

Sage leans forward to grab her feet and stretch out her

legs. "I didn't think that I would ever be able to fight or be much help in this, but I think that the option of sitting around and letting everyone else do it for me isn't viable anymore. I only used to show up here to learn defensive techniques, but I think if we find the person who got into my head and made me do those terrible things, I will happily throw a fireball at them."

I give her a gentle pat on the back. "That's the spirit. Looks like you're working your way through the stages of grief really well. Next thing you know, you'll be compartmentalizing like a pro, and we'll be able to swap war stories."

She huffs a small laugh under her breath, and then her eyes flick up as Gryphon and Kieran approach us again. They both look pissed off, but I doubt that it has anything to do with us. Nope, it'll be whatever updates they're getting from the other TacTeams that are currently deployed out in the Wastelands.

I've learned not to ask about it.

Gryphon takes a quick look around at us all before barking out his orders. "Sage, you can work through the last workout that you did under Vivian's tutelage. Gabe and Atlas, you're both working on figuring out your extra powers. Kieran will work with you both. You're with me, Oli."

My eyebrows shoot up my forehead, but I get up and

nod obediently, waiting until the others move off to follow his directions before I murmur, "What are we learning today that's so different? I thought I was going to be doing hand-to-hand combat again."

Gryphon shakes his head and hands me a bottle of water for our session. "No, if our run-in with Davies at the Hail Mary has taught me anything, it's that you really do need to learn how to keep people out of your head. Keeping your mind blank and your thoughts to yourself isn't enough. It's time to learn how to shield yourself."

It's utterly shameful, but no matter what Gryphon does to try to teach me how to keep him out of my head, I can't do it.

We work through the entire training session together, with him explaining in a dozen different ways how to build a wall up in my mind to keep him out, but nothing that I try works. I've never failed so miserably in front of any of my Bonded before. I have to say, I *hate* the experience.

One by one, as each of my Bonded and friends finish off their training circuits, we collect a little crowd of them sitting around, offering advice to me as though there's some small thing I'm missing to be able to make this work. None of their suggestions help, unsurprisingly.

"You have to see him as a foreign being, trying to get in your head," Atlas says, curling himself around me and pulling me against his chest.

Gryphon gives him a stern look, as though he suspects he's trying to distract me, but what he's saying actually makes a bit of sense to me.

It doesn't make it any less impossible though.

"I can't though, can I? We've Bonded. I can't even sense when he is entering a room anymore because my body is so used to him that it doesn't give me warnings like it used to!"

"You used to be able to sense us?" Gabe asks, his chin propped up on one of his knees from where he had just stopped mid-stretch to join the conversation.

I give him a little nod. "Of course. I always knew when one of you was around. Over time, I started to figure out which one of you it was, but now you can all sneak up on me and scare the shit out of me while I'm innocently trying to take a shower."

I shoot a glare at Gryphon, and Atlas scoffs from behind me. "Maybe we need to get a different Neuro in to try and get into your head. You can practice against them."

Gryphon immediately shuts him down. "There isn't anyone strong enough to get into her head that we have access to. It's me, and it's Silas Davies. That's it."

I groan and cover my face with my hands. Sage walks

over and tucks herself in beside Atlas and I, crossing her legs and taking a deep breath. "So you're just going to have to learn how to block people out and hope that you're doing it right when the time comes? That doesn't seem very… safe. Or helpful."

I groan again, the sound muffled, thanks to my hands still being over my face. "This wouldn't be such a big deal if the person trying to get into my head didn't already know how to trigger my power and turn me into a weapon of mass destruction! That kind of raises the stakes."

Sage winces and rubs a hand down her workout leggings, like her palms are sweating just thinking about it. "Is the plan going to be just to keep you as far away from him as possible?"

"Yes," all three of my Bonded say at once, and I roll my eyes.

"I'm not going to sit on the sidelines while my Bonded all have to fight. For one, my bond wouldn't let me, and for another, I'm just not built like that. The problem is that Silas has done it before, and I don't know whether bonding is enough to keep him out."

God, I hope it is.

My bond definitely thinks it is enough, but there's so much I don't know about its limits or the lives it's lived before. Has it ever gone up against someone like Davies before? Did we survive it?

Can I keep my Bonded safe?

It's quiet for a moment, then Gabe says, "What did he do before? If you're trying to figure out if you can keep him out, then that's the part of your head that you need to keep protected."

I don't want to think about that.

I definitely don't want to talk about it, not with anyone, not ever.

"It was twice, right?" Atlas says. "Twice you were taken out of the camps by a Transporter. Both times, I thought you were getting moved somewhere else, but after a couple of hours, you were brought back and you slept for days. I know now that that's part of your recovery pattern from a big power usage."

I nod slowly and I meet Gryphon's eyes as he stares at me for a second before nodding, as if encouraging me to speak.

I *really* don't want to talk about it, but I'm also aware that Sage is with us and that I've been encouraging her to let go of her own stigma around what had happened with Dara.

Maybe this will help her.

It's a little more terrifying than taking out one person, although I didn't have a close relationship with any of the people that Silas had forced me to kill. It doesn't make it feel any less horrifying to me though.

I glance around to make sure that we're alone here only to find all of the TacTeam personnel around us have a white ring around their eyes. None of them move other than breathing, their chests going up and down but their minds just shut off completely.

I glance back at Gryphon, and he shrugs as though the answer is obvious. "I'd rather not have any rumors of what is said here circulating on the street by lunch."

I swallow, grateful that he was thinking that far ahead, and Sage leans over to hold my hand.

I try to lighten the serious mood that's overtaken the room. "That's an awful lot of people. Have you noticed how much your power has grown?"

Gryphon smirks as Atlas and Gabe both roll their eyes. "Oh, he's noticed," Gabe snarks, and I glance between them all, not understanding the joke.

"Like you, I have found no limit to my power yet, Bonded."

No limit.

Is that going to be my legacy to my Bonded, the ability to use their powers with no restrictions or worries about personal consequences?

I clear my throat and find a small scratch on the mats to focus on so that I don't have to look any of them in the eye as I let my terrible legacy tumble out of my mouth. "The first time... I was taken to an underground bunker. It was full of Gifted that the Resistance had taken from the streets and that all had their heads picked apart by Davies. Any useful information that they might have had was already extracted, and none of them had Gifts that the Resistance wanted to 'utilize'… so they were nothing but cannon fodder to him. Most of them were so broken already that they didn't even get up from their small, stinking little cots in their cells. But there were a few who got up to take a look at me. I think about them a lot, the ones who stopped to look."

I take a second to swallow and glance up to see if any of them hate me yet. I trust them. I trust them all, but I also wouldn't blame them for changing their opinions of me after hearing this. Gryphon holds my eye and nods, the white ring around his iris glowing, and I can feel North in my head, reaching out to me to offer what little comfort he can. Nox is there too, the same tiny remnant that I can feel of him now that we've completed the Bond, but he's there and he's listening.

Deep breath. "They wanted to test how far my Soul Rending ability could go. Silas was afraid that I had limits that would take me out. The strongest Soul Render in history… the one that he knew about, died because he pushed his power too far."

Atlas nods behind me and adjusts his hold a little. "He killed twelve men at once. It burned him out, and he dropped dead at the same time as they did. He did it to protect his family, but it killed him all the same."

Davies had talked about it enough that I already knew that little fact, and I clear my throat again. "There were four hundred people in the underground bunkers, and Davies had made a comment about how he didn't want me burning out the same way but... I was already so tired of being stuck in the camps, and I didn't want to be in pain anymore. So I asked my bond to kill them all, and it did."

I swallow and look down at my hands, refusing to make eye contact with anyone. They've all seen my work before, seen me killing huge numbers of people at a time, but it had always been our enemy. There's something particularly shameful about them knowing that I had done this to our own people.

"The second time they took me, I refused. My bond refused as well. It was only after Davies got into my head and manipulated my Gift that my bond took the people out just to get him away from us. That's when he figured out that my bond was a separate being, and he knew that he needed to deal with it more than me. That's when he realized that I could be the weapon in this war that he so desperately wanted."

NORTH

Despite what I've told the other council members, we do have TacTeams out in the Wastelands at the moment, trying to shut them down. There's one in Virginia that's so big it has swallowed up an entire town, and I'm not going to waste resources there.

It's too far gone.

I have no doubt that it will end up being one of the main battlegrounds that we will be forced to fight on, and I've been monitoring the fighting there closely.

However, there are three smaller Wastelands that we have attempted to get to soon enough to shut them down before they get out of hand. Gryphon was the obvious choice, his team being the strongest and most experienced, but with only just completing the Bonded Group, I didn't want to split us up so soon.

The matter might have just been taken out of my hands.

The call comes in that one of our TacTeams has been wiped out, with a handful of prisoners taken, just as I'm about to leave the office for the night. I've had a fucking terrible day between dealing with the non-Gifted community summit fallout and Gryphon sending through the images of Oleander discussing her time at the camps. I'm not really all that interested in dealing with anything else, but to have an entire TacTeam wiped out is catastrophic.

The fact that Unser had gone along with them is an especially devastating blow.

I immediately send a message to Gryphon to come to my office so that we can figure out a plan of action, and then I make the call to Vivian to let him know the situation.

It's bad, but not as bad as having to call Adella to let her know what's happened to her Bonded.

It's always the worst part of losing men out in the field, and losing someone who is a close friend to my Bonded Group makes it even more devastating.

"He's not dead. I can still feel him."

I rub a hand over my face and try to figure out the best way to explain the predicament of that to Adella. I go with just being honest with her. "That means that they have two

Triggers, and that we have none. On a personal level, I am devastated, but it is also my responsibility as Councilman Draven to think about this from a strategic point of view."

Adella is a no-nonsense sort of woman, someone who has dealt with having two TacTeam leaders as her Bonded her entire adult life, raising their children alone most of the time, and still maintaining perfect relationships with them both.

After losing my own parents' Bonded Group at a young age, they were definitely the sort of people that I looked up to, and hoped that my own Bonded Group would look something like. I still have that hope today.

"I understand what you're saying, and so I'm telling you that you need to go and find him. He's alive, and it *is* a threat for him to not be with us. The same way that if the Resistance got their hands on you, or your brother, or your Bonded, it would be a threat to us all. There are certain people that we need to protect. He's one of them, North."

She's got me there, not that I need any encouragement to go after her Bonded... I just don't want her getting her hopes up.

"I will leave Vivian here in charge with my Bonded, but I will personally go and find him. One way or another."

She makes a tutting noise under her breath. "He's not going to like that. You know that he will want to go after Unser himself."

Despite the shitty situation, I find myself grinning at her tone. "Like you said, there's certain people that take precedence. If anyone is going to be able to bring him home, it's me."

The elevator doors open and Gryphon steps into the office, Nox trailing closely behind him with a savage look on his face, a book tucked under his arm, and a bottle of whiskey in his other hand.

He hadn't taken the news of switching his sleeping patterns very well, mostly because I think he saw through my reasoning for it easily. I had been forced to explain it to him in no uncertain terms. If he's not willing to go back to therapy and figure out how to coexist peacefully with our Bonded, then this is the next best choice for him.

I turn my computer screen around so that they can both read it while I finish up the conversation with Adella. "I'll get him back. One way or another. You just need to stay here and take care of Vivian and those kids. You'll have your hands more than full, I'm sure."

She chokes out a tearful sort of chuckle, strong as ever, but still clearly worried about her Bonded. "The youngest one has already asked why the age restrictions on TacTeams haven't been lifted yet. I hope you're ready to face what we have brought into this world, because I'm not sure you're ready for my boys."

The smile stays glued to my face, genuinely happy to

hear it, and I sign off by saying, "They certainly can't be any harder to train than we were, and Vivian did a great job of that."

The moment I hang the phone up, Nox says, "We need to leave now. If they get him back to one of the camps and we can't figure out which one, we're done for. One Trigger is bad enough."

He's not saying anything that I don't already know, but a ripple of irritation runs down my spine.

"We're going to need to take everyone," Gryphon says, and I shake my head.

"We can't take everyone. It's not safe to have all of us in one place at the same time. We need to stick to the rules of one of us being here at all times. Oleander is still resting after the Bond being completed, so we can't take her. Her bond is volatile at the best of times."

We both pointedly don't look at Nox, and I shrug back at Gryphon. "You, Atlas, and I are the only ones who have bonded and found our power increases. Everyone else should stay here."

Nox reacts immediately and exactly the way I know he will. "There's no way I'm staying here. If there's a fight to be had, I'm going."

I shake my head, not entirely sure why I'm fighting him when I know he'll never back down. "You're in the same boat as Oli, you need to let the bond settle."

"Fuck that. Bassinger and the little poison Bonded both fought the Resistance when they came here the day after they had bonded, so don't feed me that bullshit as an attempt to get me to stay behind. I'm going, and I'm finding Unser."

I already know that it's going to be pointless to try and convince him otherwise. He doesn't have any particularly strong ties to the Trigger, but we all understand the significance of the Resistance taking him hostage. They know that Oleander has found her Bonded Group and they are doing what they can to shore up their defenses for when they have to face her. Silas Davies having two Triggers at his disposal, one of them with a huge range and the other able to regenerate at the drop of a hat, it's definitely dangerous for us all.

"Fine. The three of us will go. Oli, Atlas, and Gabe can stay behind."

We make the decision to leave Kieran behind as well, as an extra set of eyes on the Sanctuary. He's still extra jumpy, thanks to Sage's mind abduction, and we're not sure how long we will be gone, as it is a recovery mission.

I find myself as leery about leaving my Bonded as I am about finding Unser dead.

Oli doesn't take the news of us leaving well, not that she shows it, but we can all feel the inner turmoil inside her as she ducks her head and nods. I hate it. I would do anything to fix it for her, but the compulsion to keep her away from Davies for as long as I possibly can is stronger than anything else, especially with the Bond being so newly complete.

Someday soon, she's going to be as close to invincible as any mortal will ever get. Until then, I'll be her first line of defense.

"What if you need a power pick-me-up? What if you run out while you're out there?" she says, and while Nox keeps his back to her as he pulls his Tac gear on, I can see that she has his interest.

I already knew that he'd been interested in the power exchange from a philosophical point of view. I get it, I'd never heard of a Bond being able to do something like that before. I know that he had doubled his research on Soul Renders once I had told him what had happened when the Resistance had shown up here and she had funneled all that power through to me.

"I'm not going to need the power. The Wasteland we're going to is still brand new. Between the three of us, we'll be able to have it dealt with. We have done it before, before you came home to us, and we all know how to do our jobs. Just trust me, Bonded."

She huffs a little under her breath. "It's not about trust. It's about wanting you all to come home."

Gryphon stands in the doorway and checks over his weapons one last time, that same obsessive tic that he has as a ritual each time he goes out on a job, as though touching each of his guns and knives in a certain order will ensure his safety. I can't really give him too much shit about it.

He has always made it back.

We're standing in the supply area sectioned off just for our Bonded Group, mostly so that we can have privacy when conversations like this need to happen, and while I was expecting Nox to get dressed and disappear like he always does, he hasn't made a move yet to leave us. There's something about our conversation that he is particularly interested in. Oli seems to think it's a good sign, but I'm not so sure.

I don't think my brother can be saved.

I feel a little bit of shame in admitting that, especially since I have been the one to rally so hard to keep him alive and with me, but part of that is my own selfishness and not wanting to lose the last member of my family. William's death had rocked me to my core, and I find myself even more desperate to keep Nox alive now because of it.

He has thrown that fact in my face more than once in his drunken ramblings in my office, and I have no choice but to stand there and let him, because it's true.

What could it be about this conversation that has caught his interest so much?

"We'll be back soon, Bonded. Don't worry. I haven't needed to draw on your power yet, and I have still found no limit to what my Neuro powers can do. Let's just trust North and Nox to get the job done."

She nods and glances down at Nox again. "They're not going to know what's hit them, two Death Dealers and the Neuro with powers that rival Davies'. I'm sure it'll be fine."

It's the closest she's come to acknowledging that Nox is in the room, not because she is rude or showing favoritism, but because he's proven that he doesn't want any of her attention. In fact, if she shows him any, then he'll lash out and do everything he can to tear her down.

I hate it.

I understand it.

I hate that I understand it.

He stands and tightens the straps on his vest one last time. "Are we going, or are we going to stand here and talk meaningless shit for a bit longer? Unser's fate isn't going to be secure with us here."

Gryphon's face sets like stone, but Oli nods her head as though it's all fine. "You're all going to go and I'm going to be fine. When you get back, I'm sure Gryphon will have a lot to say to you about your manners when it comes to saying goodbye."

He sends her a dark look back and walks out of the room without another word.

I groan and shove a hand over my face, but Oleander pushes herself against my side to force her way into my arms. Not that she has to, I would rather stay here with her than deal with this mess, and I have no hesitation in telling her so.

"Unser is important to us all. I might not be friends with him the same way that you guys are, but I understand what it means to lose him from a community point of view... Just promise me you guys won't do anything stupid."

She's perfection. "Of course not, Bonded. I don't know the meaning of the word."

She scoffs at me and then reaches up onto her tiptoes to give me a quick peck on the cheek. Not the goodbye that I was hoping for, but I'll take it, nonetheless.

"If I kiss you on the lips, we both know that it will be even harder for you to leave, so come home to me if you want a proper one," she says, her voice full of sass, before she tugs away from me and does the same to Gryphon.

He gets a handful of her ass and pulls her body in closer, stealing a proper kiss from her, even as she squeals and struggles against him playfully. There's a pain in my chest at the sight of them, but we're running on *Unser's* borrowed time here.

We need to get out of here.

I'm not a fan of the Transporter that we have to use, but he does the job well enough, moving our small team to the combat zone in one effective *pop*. The area is only a few miles wide and a few more miles long, but the Shields that surround it are strong, strong enough that there are dozens of people inside that are unable to get out.

They're not strong enough for us though.

As the other TacTeam members spread out, ready to move as one inside the perimeter, Gryphon's eyes flash to white as he hacks into the brains of every last one of the Shields, turning their Gifts off and rendering them immobile.

I let my shadows fall from my body as I move forward, a gun already in my hand because the Wastelands are not a place that you walk into without every possible option of defense, and Nox stays close to my side as we move together.

He's usually happier working alone.

But when I glance at him, there is a ring of darkness around his irises, his bond is sensing *something*. I check in with mine in my chest, but it's just that same nervous adrenaline that I always have when we're about to enter a fight. I'm not sure if it's because he has a better relationship with his bond, or if it's more sensitive, but I slow my pace a little as I scan the area.

There's nothing I can find.

I share a look with Gryphon, but he shrugs, not hearing anything that could tip us off. Whatever it is, Nox is the only one feeling it. We don't have time to just stand around on a whim.

But the moment we breach the perimeter, I finally feel it too.

It's a trap.

OLI

I feel jittery even as I help lift the boxes of tiles into the damaged building that we are working in today.

Gabe and Atlas tried to convince me to stay at home and get some rest, their plan for me to just sleep while my Bonded are away, but there's no possible way I could sit around right now, let alone sleep.

I needed a major distraction from being away from my Bonded, so I had convinced them both to pull a late night at the houses. Gabe is fine with it, because he's desperate to get as much done as possible and move people into the buildings. He's very aware of how much he is capable of helping with this and has taken on the responsibilities of it. I know it's his way of trying to lighten North's workload, and also something that will keep him here in the Sanctuary with me.

He's very concerned about the two of us being split up again, and I don't blame him for that at all.

Atlas, on the other hand, finds the building work deeply frustrating. While he's learning quickly and definitely a huge help to Gabe, he's still inexperienced, and my very alpha male Bonded is struggling with that fact. He would much rather be eating dinner in my giant bed with a movie on right now, and I kind of feel bad for making his long day even longer.

Gabe just gives him shit about it until he huffs and gets back to work.

"You know that they're going to be fine, right? Sending in one Death Dealer is enough to get the job done, but sending in two of them? Fuck, it's almost overkill, Bonded," Gabe says as he takes the boxes from me and stacks them where they need to go.

In the last few days, he's managed to coordinate huge numbers of volunteers to work on the repairs, so now we're back on track to getting more housing ready for people to move into. North has shifted the priority from getting families into their own houses to taking in more displaced and targeted Gifted people from around the country.

So far, there's been two or more families sharing houses so that we can get as many as possible. The few people who'd been vocal about not liking that situation have been thoroughly silenced, thanks to the Sanctuary being breached by the Resistance. Something about finding themselves being rescued and their safety prioritized in a way that they never had been before had shifted their opinions on the matter. Safety, understanding, and their basic needs being met goes a long way to gaining favor with people.

As far as I'm aware, it's only a handful of Top Tier families that still have complaints, and I'm still more than ready to deal with those people myself.

North is starting to get close to that point as well.

I let out a breath, wiping the sweat from my brow with the back of my hand. "It doesn't matter who is out there. I'm always going to feel this way about being separated from you guys. Especially with something as dangerous as this, I don't know how the other TacTeam families cope."

Gabe shrugs as he directs Atlas where to stack boxes. "A lot of the TacTeam personnel on Gryphon's team aren't Bonded yet. Most of them are hoping that Sawyer's work with the blood bank will figure out why they haven't been able to find their Central Bonds yet."

I nod and sigh, it makes sense. My mind is still drifting to all of the terrible things that could be happening to my Bonded right now. It's irrational because there's no way that any of them could hide grievous injuries or anything too dramatic from me, but my brain can't stop going over all of the 'what ifs'.

North had been so adamant that I stay behind because the Bond was so fresh between his brother and I, but Nox had refused to stay as well. And as often happens, North and Gryphon would both rather give in to his demands than argue with him. I don't necessarily disagree with them, but it still grates on me that I've been left behind.

I can't stop thinking about if they need me and my power. North had been handling the situation with the Resistance attack really well before Atlas and I had arrived, but there's no denying that the power boost I gave him meant that he could wipe out much larger numbers at a time. I'd like them to get in and out of that place as quickly as possible. And a power boost would definitely help with that.

If I gave one to Nox as well? Game changer, I'm sure of it.

Gabe nods and sits down on one of the stacks of boxes, unscrewing a bottle of water and offering it to me before draining half of it in one go. "You should know by now that North is all about risks and rewards. Everything that he does is a calculation of what we can afford to risk. It's one of the biggest things that he does as a councilman. The risks of moving to the Sanctuary too soon were too great; it's why we stayed at Draven for so long, even after we did have some livable properties here. He had to get Gryphon to screen as much of the population as possible to ensure we weren't bringing anybody in who was a risk. The same as when it comes to you and Nox." He glances at Atlas for a second, knowing that this is a sensitive topic to him more than anyone else, but I want to hear what he has to say.

When Atlas doesn't immediately kick off, he continues, "He's constantly trying to figure out how to bridge the gap between the two of you, but the risk of setting Nox off again is too great, at the moment."

Atlas scoffs and kicks his toes against the concrete on the ground, a little plume of dust billowing around his shoe. "So he's fine to just sacrifice Oli?"

I shrug. "No, he trusts that I am not lying when I say that I'm fine and I can deal with him… which I am, by the way."

Gabe shrugs. "I think if you were handling Nox differently, North would have stepped in by now. We were all around for the last time that Nox was sent off the deep end and, to be honest, you don't understand, Atlas. You can't understand, because you *weren't* here and you didn't see it. I'm not willing to sacrifice Oli, but if she's fine figuring this stuff out for herself, then I'm happy to leave it up to North. He's never led us astray before. For someone that everybody insists has to be a monster because of his Gift, he is awfully good at doing everything he can to help his community."

There's a warm glow in my chest at hearing one of my Bonded speak so highly of another. Even though I already knew that Gabe had a great relationship with them all, it still brings me comfort to know that they look out for each other in some way.

Knowing that Atlas is also finding his place in the group, even with his incessant questions and picking things apart, is also a huge relief. I know that it's his own response to his childhood and his parents that has him being a pain in the ass to the rest of them. He has to question everything and get to the root of every issue just to make sure that we're both safe.

Maybe someday, if I can convince Nox that I'm not an evil, manipulative Bonded who wants to take over his life and control him, I'll also be able to convince Atlas to give him a break.

Asking for two miracles at once isn't such a big deal, is it?

After an hour or so, we've cracked open all of the boxes that we need to, and Gabe and I have shifted to the tiling work itself. Gabe is good about letting me pull my own weight, and Atlas watches us both for a little while until he is sure that there's nothing left for him to do in the room before he moves on to put up Sheetrock in another room. He's much better at that than the fussy work of tiling, and

I find myself comforted by the repetitive motion of laying the tiles.

Gabe is happy to work in silence, the two of us getting lost in our own heads and the work as we move together across the room. We're almost to the door when I feel it, a sharp pain in my shoulder that can only mean one thing.

One of my Bonded has been injured.

"The last time I let you convince me to take you on a little adventure, Fallows, I almost lost my job, all of my friends, and my life, so no, I don't think I'm going to take you anywhere."

I have to physically hold my bond inside of my chest with every inch of my willpower as I convince it that I can get this situation sorted out and get us to our Bonded.

Both of my Bonded can feel this war happening internally, and Gabe gives Kieran a look. "You're about to get your soul sucked out if you don't do what she asks, because her bond is *not* happy with you right now."

Sage glances between them nervously, her brows dropped down low over her eyes, and she glances up at Kieran. "I mean, this time you're at least taking her *to* North and Gryphon. They can't be that mad about it, right?"

He gives her a very insulted, "Really? You're really

going to side with Oli over your Bonded on this?"

She gives him a sheepish grin back. "I kind of have to. It's part of being besties."

I scoff at their banter, but it's hard to concentrate on what's being said around me when my bond is feeling so vicious. The ache in my shoulder is still there, and it is proof that whoever it is that has been injured has not yet been healed.

My bond is *pissed*.

"So, what are you going to do? Get there, heal him, then just... come straight home? I need to know what your plan is if I'm going along with it this time, Fallows. I also need to know that you're going to stick to it and not just disappear on me the first chance you get."

I take a deep breath, trying to ignore the ghost of my Bonded's pain in my shoulder, and say as calmly as I can, "I'm going to go and find whichever one of them has been injured and heal them. I am then going to kill every Resistance piece of shit I can find to get the job done. I will then help with whatever recovery is required for Unser, and then we will all be returning back here as a group. I know my bond will not let me leave them there, so this is not going to be an in and out thing. This is me joining the mission... and all of you as well."

Gabe nods along with me and then gestures at his chest and Atlas'. "And we'll be going along with her because there is no way in hell that I'm going to be left behind again while my Bonded goes to face the Resistance. Atlas has figured out how to extend his powers onto others in our Bonded Group, and I'll shift into the biggest thing with teeth I can think of and do my part. We both know that I've been on enough of these missions that I will carry my own weight."

Kieran rolls his eyes. "I'm not worried about that, Gabe. I'm worried about taking Shore and Dravens' Bonded into the Wastelands against their wishes and the consequences of that, even if things run completely smoothly and follow all of Fallows' carefully thought-out plans."

I shrug. "Part of being my friend is knowing that I'm always going to be impulsive and run to wherever the conflict is, especially if it involves my Bonded Group or my friends."

Sage nods along. "You can't be mad at her for that, Kieran. She's always running after me to save me from whatever new crisis I've found myself in. Look at how many different shitty situations she's been in just because my life keeps turning into a clusterfuck."

Okay, that's not where I was planning on this conversation going, but it is the first thing that any of us has said that has gotten through to Kieran in any way.

He grits his teeth and lets out the breath he was holding. "Fine. We go there. We stick together. No one is going to act like a cowboy. And until we find Shore, I'm in charge. Look at me, Bassinger. *I* am in charge."

Atlas stares at him blankly, and then a slow smirk stretches across his lips. "Sure you are. You'll be in charge for as long as it takes Oli's bond to just decide that it wants to come out and play. Then we all know she's in charge, because if there is *anyone* that I am going to trust implicitly and follow every order from on a battlefield, it's going to be my Bonded's bond."

Kieran's eyes flick down to mine, and then he shocks me by saying, "Agreed. Get your Tac gear on."

It's a freaking miracle.

We are dressed and ready to go in under ten minutes, everyone moving quickly and efficiently to get us on the road. Sage comes with us all to North's offices to say goodbye, and Felix arrives just as we're about to leave.

He looks at Kieran and gives him a nod, the two of them having formed their own friendship since discovering that they're in the same Bonded Group, and then Felix looks down at me. "If your bond can't heal their injuries all the way, then you need to get bandages and pressure around whatever the injury is. You need to think about blood loss, first and foremost. We'll worry about infection and mobility issues after, okay? Whatever you can't do, I will fix."

This is why Felix is in my top five favorite non-Bonds.

I look at him with a grateful smile. "I will get them back to you, no matter what. Even if my bond does heal them fully, I will still get them to come in and check in with you, but thank you. It's good to know for the other members of the TacTeam that I can't do anything for."

He grimaces a little, his eyes flicking back to Kieran. "Should you be taking me as well, just in case? If someone in the Resistance has managed to injure someone in the Draven Bond Group, then that doesn't bode well for everyone else."

Kieran is shaking his head before Felix even finishes speaking. "You're staying with Sage and making sure that she's safe. We need as many of our people here while we're gone as possible. It's very likely that Oli's Bonds have been made target number one for the Resistance or that Nox has thrown himself in front of something recklessly. I'm hoping we'll get there to find most of our forces unharmed."

My stomach drops.

That seems like wishful thinking. The throbbing in my shoulder is also still consistent, and I don't want to think about how the injury occurred, let alone the thought of any of them doing this to themselves on purpose.

Kieran is right though, it would be a typical Nox response to throw himself head first at something. He always has been both very sure in his Gift and just a little bit reckless with his own wellbeing at the best of times.

Then it's time to leave, everything already either said or hanging in the air between us all, unspoken because it's too terrifying to speak our worries out loud. I give Sage what I hope is a reassuring smile and then turn back to her Bonded.

"Get ready for hell," Kieran says, and we all take a steadying breath as we grab his arm, the *pop* sound of our transporting echoing in my ears as we're thrown into space towards the Wasteland.

It's a bloodbath.

My stomach revolts the same way it always does the moment our feet touch the ground again, but the moment I look around us at the field of dead bodies and debris, I lose my dinner.

Thankfully, I avoid our shoes.

"We're exposed here; we need to move," Kieran says, completely ignoring me emptying my guts up everywhere, and I'm weirdly grateful about that.

Gabe and Atlas are more restrained in their responses than they usually are, but they both get their hands on me the moment I bend at the waist. Atlas gets an arm around my waist as a support and Gabe tucks an errant lock of hair away from my face.

I swipe the back of my hand across my mouth and mumble, "I'm fine, let's move."

I'm not sure where in the country we are at the moment, no one had mentioned where this Wasteland was, but there is a clump of charred oak trees that we move over to for some cover. Kieran looks around as though he's sure we're about to be ambushed, and my eyes can't stop flicking back over to the piles of dead bodies.

There's a lot of them, some in Tac gear, but, thankfully, most of them seem to be Resistance.

"It's not supposed to look like this," Kieran says quietly once he has us tucked away safely behind the trees. "It's a new Wasteland. It's not supposed to look like this yet."

I swallow roughly and nod before giving him a shrug. "Like you said, once North, Nox, and Gryphon arrived, they probably changed their tactics and got more people in. That would be the smart thing to do, if they're on the offensive."

His mouth presses into a firm line as he nods, glancing around at the area, and then he curses under his breath. "We're not going to find them without having to risk ourselves in a big way, and I'm not sure how I feel about that, Fallows. Gabe and I have experience, and Atlas is bulletproof... your bond coming out would be helpful, but it's a risk all on its own. We might have to consider splitting up."

Well, fuck.

I think about it for a second, then the answer to that problem huffs a little puff of air behind my ear.

It's so obvious that I almost feel stupid.

I reach up and grab Brutus, bringing him down to the ground and waiting until he grows to his full size before I give him a quick scratch behind his pointy ear.

"I need you to find Nox for me. North and Gryphon too, but I know that your connection with Nox will get you to him much faster. We need to know who's injured, and we need to get to them as quickly as possible. Can you do that for me, baby?"

He stares at me with his void eyes for a minute, his head tilting as though he's thinking about it, and then he's off, moving faster than my eyes can track.

As he becomes a blur of smoke, I straighten back up. Atlas slips his hand into mine, his eyes glowing with a white ring around them. I'm not used to seeing that on him because his power is usually so intrinsic, but I know that he has been practicing his ability to shift the power on to others, and there's a pretty good chance that I'm bulletproof right now.

Gabe is more serious and solemn than his usual smiling self, looking out at the damage around us with a very critical eye. He's been out in the field before, his

Gift strong enough and his connections within the Bonded Group getting him an early pass, and I find myself intensely curious about what he's seeing and assessing out there that I'm not.

"We're just going to wait until the shadow creature brings them to us? Don't get me wrong, it's a better plan than splitting up, but we're burning valuable time here," Atlas says, watching Kieran carefully. He hasn't attempted to question anything about the plan so far, and I hope we're all about sticking to it.

Gabe shrugs. "It won't take long. Brutus probably already has them alerted that we're here and is bringing them back. The shadow creatures are way more useful than you're giving them credit for."

I'm desperate to reach out to them all and check in.

I can't though. I don't want to distract or startle them by speaking to them with our mind connection just yet. I'm very aware that the slightest distraction could get any of them killed, and it's just not worth the risk.

My bond starts to warm in my chest, flooding down my limbs and getting ready to take over as it senses danger is near, right as I hear the sound of approaching footsteps.

Kieran signals us all to be quiet and palms a gun, moving around us until he's got the rest of us pinned between his body and the tree, effectively shielding me from the danger.

A large group of at least thirty Resistance walk through the Shield boundary in front of us, arriving fresh onto the front lines and making it through the same weak point we had.

They spot us straight away.

"Cowering like fucking children, that's why we'll win the war against the sheep, boys!" one of them calls out, and my bond hammers at my mind to be let out.

I take a deep breath, what I assume will be my last one while in control for the day, before there's a snarling sound and then the darkness rolls in. It's breathtaking.

Literally, I can't breathe as I watch the group get torn apart.

They all attempt to fight it off, but how exactly does one fight off smoke and the dark itself? Their arms flail about even as the creatures' sharp teeth shred them to pieces, a gory death that they all surely deserve.

Through the darkness, Nox appears as if out of thin air, Brutus padding along obediently by his side. He looks like death incarnate, blood spattered all over him, but it only takes a quick glance to know that he's in one piece and the injury I'm feeling isn't his.

The relief and dread mix like an acid cocktail in my gut.

I chuckle nervously. "Just in time, thanks for that. I thought I was going to have to shove Kieran out of the way to deal with this myself."

The last man standing there with pure terror on his face snaps, lurching towards us with a knife in his hand, one last desperate act of a man staring down a blood-soaked death. Nox is quick to act, planting himself between us both and using the butt of his gun to knock the guy out without much effort. He was nothing more than a bag of bones anyway, but the shadow creatures don't seem to mind as they get to work consuming him.

Kieran pulls a face and turns away from the sight of it.

"Are you trying to die here, Poison? Get your bond out and make yourself useful."

I feel like he's obsessed with my bond at this point. I snap back, "Just accept the thanks and move on. It's not that hard."

"How about you do something useful and stop walking around like this is a field trip for your enjoyment? People are dying here."

My bond still doesn't react to his jabs but boy does my temper. When I feel the next group of arriving troops from the Resistance, I let my Gift out to kill them all at once. Fifteen men, gone in the blink of an eye before they even had the chance to spot our little group.

Atlas' hand tenses in mine, but his shoulders roll back a little as he prepares himself for whatever comes next.

"Like that? Should I kill everyone now, regardless of

whether or not they're actually Resistance? Should I let my bond out again to just wipe the area clean and call it a win?"

He leans forward and his eyes flash black, but it's his own voice he speaks in. "Yes. There's no saving them once they're killing their own anyway. Just take them all out."

Kieran is far more confident moving through the Wasteland with Nox at our side.

He'd given a quick and dirty debrief of what had happened when they'd arrived a few hours ago, about the ambush that was waiting for them here, and the massive amount of resources the Resistance were willing to sacrifice to capture one of my Bonded. There's no doubt in anyone's minds about whether or not that was the plan. They had made it very clear that Silas Davies wants my Bonded Group.

He honestly thinks he's strong enough to capture and keep us all.

Stupid, stupid man.

I managed to stay calm for as long as it took to hear Nox out, and the moment he was done, I'd demanded to leave, my eyes still blue but my bond coming out in my voice a little bit, just as impatient as I am, at this point.

I need to find my Bonded.

As we all move out, following Nox as he leads us to where he'd last seen North, we find signs of them everywhere. There are bodies torn apart and the greenish acidic goo stuff that the shadow creatures sometimes leave behind.

The area is full of slopes and dips, which makes it an ambush nightmare. Every time we start on an incline, there's a moment where I know we're exposed, not able to see who might be hiding in the valleys ahead of us, or even beside us, making us a giant moving target.

Except Nox sends out his shadow creatures out all around us to scout, screams and gunshots ringing out around us as they find our enemy lying in wait. My bond is still warm in my chest and limbs, poised at the edge and ready for the moment that I finally let go, but I'm not ready to tap out yet. I'm not ready to miss out on seeing my Bonded and knowing that they're healed up.

My legs speed up all over again.

Atlas moves with me, still intent on staying close to me and using his Gift to protect me fully. Gabe is taking up the rear with Kieran, one eye on me and the other looking around in case the shadow creatures miss someone.

I don't think we're going to miss anyone.

Nox stops abruptly and speaks without turning, "The main fight is happening over that ridge. There's another Shield in place, it's why you can't hear anything. The moment you cross it, it'll feel as though you've stepped through a portal. North is in there. I was as well. Gryphon was pushing the front lines forward to get to Unser, and we were cleaning up everything he sent our way. He had a small team with him. I'd guess it's him who's hurt, but he'll still be pushing forward. We made the call not to withdraw until we got Unser."

A shiver runs down my spine.

I haven't said it to any of them yet, but my plan isn't just to find whoever is hurt and heal them. I'm also going to start funneling power to the rest of them. I'm going to use my ability to turn the deaths of our enemies into a weapon to use against the rest of the Resistance until we're all safe.

I don't care if that makes me a monster.

"Bassinger, stay with Fallows, no matter what happens. You can all speak to each other through the mind connection now, right? Use it," Kieran says, and then we move together down the last slope and into the next phase of hell in the Wasteland.

We're immediately split up by a Flame, a wall of fire heads towards us that we all have to dive away from and take cover. Atlas shoves me behind an overturned truck, our feet stumbling over the asphalt that is unexpectedly underneath us as we hit a road of some sort. Visibility is freaking terrible, and I have to duck my head to stop my hair from being set alight.

Brutus trots around the side of the truck, unbothered by the heat of the flames, and he sits obediently the moment he gets eyes on me.

Even if Nox still sees me as poison, his bond wants me safe.

Atlas pushes me further into a crouch, his body covering me more fully. There's the sounds of screaming around us and the smell of burning flesh that's indescribably horrifying wafting over to us.

Atlas makes a sound like he's trying not to puke, and I feel a little better about how my stomach is doing flips like I'm about to puke up whatever is left in my guts.

I glance around until I find a small area to one side of us that we can move to and find a more comfortable position. I squat down fully and shuffle over, following the side of the truck until I squeeze through the gap there. Atlas moves with me. When I stop, worried about whether or not he'll fit through the same gap, because it's pretty clear he won't, he just puts a hand on either side and I watch as the metal crumples like wet paper under his strength.

It's a much hotter act than it should be while we're

about to be turned into freaking barbecued ribs.

Check in, Gabe. Please tell me you still have your eyebrows.

I try to make light of the situation, but I'm anxious as hell about where the hell he is now that I can breathe again.

I got Kieran out of there before he needed a new face. Nox is with us. He's sending his shadow creatures to take the Flame out now. Just sit tight, Bonded.

Easier said than done.

From the corner of my eye, I see a member of the Resistance taking refuge a few feet away from us. Brutus hadn't alerted us to the tiny, huddled form, and my bond doesn't react to her either, but she has a gun strapped over her chest and a vest on that clearly marks her as our enemy.

I can't take the chance.

I make the decision to take her out right as she lifts her head. She's young, around my age, but she doesn't look scared. She looks... ready to die.

Is that comforting?

Should I feel less guilt for doing it if she's miserable?

I lift my hand as though I'm going to take her soul as well, but then our eyes meet across the blood-soaked path, and... I can't.

I can't take her soul.

I mean, I can. My power is sitting there and waiting to rip her soul out for me to consume, but even my bond is pausing, hesitating.

I need her alive.

I drop my hand and swallow, praying that my bond isn't leading me astray. It can't be, not really, because it's always so ready to kill *anyone* outside of our Bonded Group, so it must mean something.

Right?

Fuck.

Why is this so hard?!

Atlas notices her and gives me a look, but I shake my head at him, not ready yet to let the others know about her. Nox will just kill her, I know it, and… I can't figure out why I don't want to do the same.

I wait until the wall of flames finally dies out, more screaming tearing through the air, and then I make my move. I run towards her, still in a crouch, calling for Brutus to follow me. As I awkwardly hop over two bodies on the path, an insurgent Transporter *pops* into reality next to the girl and lifts a gun, aiming right at my chest.

Before my bond has the chance to deal with him, the girl lifts her hand and his eyes roll up into the back of his head, hitting the ground in a faint. She then aims her gun at his head and shuts her eyes as she pulls the trigger, killing him instantly.

Atlas finally catches up to me and curses under his breath as he shoves me behind his body, but I'm already speaking to the girl as he does it. "You just killed a bad guy, but you're also a bad guy."

She swallows and glances around. "I'm a captured girl, actually. I saw someone who might believe me, and I'm taking the chance. Help me. Please. I'm begging you, don't let them take me back there. You're with the Tac guys, right? The clothes kind of give you away."

Atlas stops me from stepping around him and snaps, "We're not a fucking taxi service, and you're holding a Resistance issue weapon. You're saying you're not a sympathizer?"

She frowns and looks down at the gun, clearly detached from the reality that she's found herself in. "You can have it. You can take whatever you want from me. I'll tell you everything I remember. Just, please, take me with you... or kill me. I'd rather be dead than go back there."

Atlas flinches when she says that, and I reach out to him in our mind connection to soothe whatever it is that's upsetting him.

My sister said the same thing. She said she'd rather be dead than go back.

I press a hand against his back, a small reassurance I can give him, and then I see three of Nox's shadow creatures pop between the gap in the truck that we'd squeezed through. The others have found us.

Kieran comes through first, lifting his gun immediately,

and I have to fling out an arm to stop him from shooting the girl. "Hey! We're keeping her, so stop with the murder plans, Black!"

Kieran's eyebrows shoot up his forehead as Gabe pushes his way through the small space, Nox coming right after him. He's the one I'm really worried about taking the girl out before we have a chance to explain... whatever the hell it is that's going on here.

"What's your name?" Atlas asks, and I give him brownie points in my mind. It hadn't even occurred to me to ask her.

"Aro. Aro Han. I'm a student from Austin, and I was taken by the Resistance... maybe three months ago?"

Kieran scowls at her, but I keep her talking. "Three months? And they trust you with a gun here after only that long?"

She shakes her head. "No, I had a handler, but the... dog things ate him. I grabbed the gun, and I've been trying to get out of here since."

Atlas glances over his shoulder to catch Kieran's eye. "A handler means she has a Gift worth keeping. She's a Neuro, must be strong."

Kieran doesn't look happy about that. Then, surprisingly, Nox is the one to make the decision for him.

He stares at her for a second, then his eyes flicker to black. "Take her back to the Sanctuary and lock her up. My bond wants her alive as well. It's probably just pandering, but now isn't the time to stand around chit-chatting."

Kieran doesn't bother asking questions, just grabs a hold of Aro's arm, and then they both disappear with that trademark *pop* sound.

We stand in silence for a moment, and then I feel it.

My Bonded is here.

I'm drawn to him like a moth to a flame, my feet moving without much thought from me. I hear Atlas cursing under his breath as he jogs to catch up with me. Brutus stays at my side, and when I spot August padding towards us both, I almost burst into tears at the sight of him.

"There's my pretty baby! Are you okay? Have you been eating all of the bad men and women for us? Of course you have, you perfect boy!" I gush, falling to my knees to love on him.

I'm probably a little more dramatic than usual, but it's a relief to see him here and to know that North has to be alive and well for his shadow creatures to be happily walking around like this.

I bury my face in August's smokey fur, and I feel North finally reach me at the same time as he says, "What are you doing here?"

I have to take a deep breath and keep my face buried in August's neck. I'm sure it's written clearly all over my face how pissed off I am that he's even asking me this. "I felt one of you getting hurt. If it's not you, then Gryphon is out there injured right now. I had to use every skill and trick in the book to keep my bond from coming out and throwing a full-blown tantrum about it. Then I had to convince everyone around me to let me come so that my bond didn't just walk out of the Sanctuary itself to find you."

I glance up at him to find him grimacing, wiping away sweat on his forehead and leaving a trail of blood from his hand behind. There's none of the sophisticated councilman left on his face at all. Here, he is the Death Dealer, someone who I'm sure is the worst nightmare to the men that we are around.

He glances over at the others and then reaches down to help me to my feet, drawing me away from the shadow pups. "I'm sorry if I sound unreasonable about this, Oleander, but it's a dire distraction to us for you to be here. Things aren't going according to plan."

I shrug. "Not as much of a distraction as a bullet hole in Gryphon's shoulder. At least, I hope it's just a bullet hole and nothing... worse."

I don't mean to be snappy, but my nerves are completely fried from feeling Gryphon and the pain he's in.

Nox looks between the two of us and then gestures behind us to an area I hadn't noticed as I'd raced towards August. There's a shimmer in the air where the Shielding here is different somehow.

"While we're here, you might as well take care of that for us."

I frown, but then I see it.

The shimmering is the spot that the Resistance are using for Transporters to arrive, a small space that they are keeping unshielded to bring in more Resistance.

There's an arrival while we all are standing there, a dozen men who look fresh and ready to fight, appearing out of thin air.

I'm a little leery of just wiping people out, thanks to finding Aro, but without so much as moving a muscle, I wipe out everybody that is standing there. The collective sound of their bodies hitting the grass is loud enough that a shiver runs down my spine.

I don't feel guilty.

North's eyes are hard on me as he watches me struggle with this, but I shrug and attempt to convince us both. "I do not feel guilty, because all of them are a part of the Resistance. All of them. Aro was an exception."

"Who the hell is Aro?" North snaps, and I cringe a little.

His eyebrows creep up his forehead, and I rush to finish speaking before he can freak out about it. "I found a member of the Resistance who was not here willingly, and my bond doesn't want to kill her. You guys have all said that we need to trust my bond because it knows more than the rest of us. Well, the girl is coming home with us, *has* come home with us. Kieran has already taken her to the cells."

North blinks at me as though he has never seen me before. I think my arrival might have broken him a little, and he's not coping with me being here, as well as hearing about Gryphon's injury and our separation from him.

He still has questions, because *of course* he does. "Are you sure that it's coming from your bond? Are you sure that it's not just you seeing a little girl?"

"She's not a little girl. She is at least my age, and I have killed people my own age a million times before. Okay, that's an exaggeration." I feel the need to point that out before anyone freaks out about my death toll.

Nox rolls his eyes at us both. "My bond agreed. Both of them wanted her alive and with us.

That gets North's attention.

He flicks a look his way but, without even acknowledging it, Nox continues, "All of the research says that we need to do better about listening to the things living inside us. I'm listening to mine. Fallows is listening to hers. You need to accept that that bond is a part of you, and listen to it as well, brother."

Oof.

That is a fight I do not want to get into.

I glance at Gabe, and he looks the same way that I'm feeling. Atlas steps over to us all and nods politely at North to indicate that the transporting has stopped. I think they finally figured out that my bond has arrived and anybody else they send is going to be cannon fodder.

We all take a second to breathe, our next big mistake.

There's another explosion on the other side of the Wasteland.

Screams of pain and terror fill the air, and I feel searing burns down my legs. Gryphon was close to the explosion.

The look of horror on my face tells all of my Bonded here everything they need to know. I take off at a run, disregarding my own safety entirely as the pain ripples through my legs. The shadow creatures take the lead, bounding before me as I sprint over the carnage to where the explosion was.

I reach out in my mind to him, but there's a wall there, a blankness that I can't get around, and the panic bubbles in my chest.

I can feel Gryphon's pain, but I also can feel him in my chest still, so I know that he is conscious and alive. I'm pissed that he's blocked me out of our mind connection, but I also understand that he is probably in a lot of pain right now and can't focus enough to speak to me.

I hope that the explosion wasn't Unser, because I think that the TacTeam professional that I had met only a few days ago would be furious to find out that he had been used against his own men in such a way.

My eyes shift to black as we move together through the Wastelands, visibility already an issue, and there's a few times that Brutus or August have to catch me as I stumble a little, but I refuse to slow down.

I don't know what was here before the Resistance turned it into this battleground, but there's a lot of debris on the ground, rubble and charred wood, enough that it's clear that people definitely lived here before all of this chaos and death arrived.

There's a small hill that we have to climb to get to the area that the smoke is billowing from. There are crowds of people streaming down from the top, most of them wearing Tac gear and very clearly ours, but there are some Resistance running along beside them in fear of what is happening down there.

I scan all of their faces just in case I see someone that I recognize from Gryphon's TacTeam, but I don't see anyone or anything else that is of any use to us. We slow down a little as the crowd gets closer to us.

It's harder when they're moving like this, and I have to raise a hand just to steady myself, but I pick them off one by one, until it's only TacTeam personnel making their way down the incline. I can feel the ripple of frustration from North that I've been the one to take them out. I know that this will be something that is brought up later, but I also think that it's better to be safe than sorry. Especially when, in this case, sorry is a knife in the back.

North breaks away from us to start directing the men, issuing a retreat now that we've arrived. Nox continues up the incline and I follow him, desperate to find Gryphon. I'm terrified of what I'm going to see on the other side of this small hill. If I were with any of my other Bonded, I would be reaching out to hold his hand right now for some comfort. Instead, I reach down and place one hand on Brutus' head, a small connection to the man I have tied myself to for all eternity. I'm sure he would rather die than accept that affection.

When we get over the top of the hill, I regret having my eyes shifted as I see the damage wrought beneath us with crystal clarity. There's bodies strewn everywhere, except instead of the clean death of a soul being ripped out of them, or the blood-soaked demise of a shadow creature, these ones are unrecognizable, in pieces around us.

Please, please tell me where you are. We're here. We've come for you. Please, just tell me where you are.

I'm desperate to hear back from Gryphon, but there is still nothing down the line from him, my words bouncing off of the barrier in his mind. There's only the small reassurance that he is still breathing, his heart is still beating somewhere

"Let your bond out," Nox says, his voice grave as he looks over the damage.

If anyone's gonna find him, it'll be the bond. I let my eyes slip shut and then I surrender to the dark god inside of me.

It's not happy.

OLEANDER'S BOND

The Damaged Dark One and I spend over an hour searching for my Bonded One.

My other Bonded all move off to help the survivors of the explosion leave this area and take out any new enemies that arrive while they're doing so. I can feel that my Bonded is alive and in pain, but it's still difficult to pinpoint exactly where he is in the mess and rubble that has been left behind by the Trigger.

He has to be unconscious.

I'm tempted to request that my Dark Bonded One bring me some Resistance to snack on to get a power burst so that I can find my Bonded One a little faster, but I become single-minded in this search.

The girl is terrified inside of me, fretting about our Bonded. No matter how hard I push, she doesn't go to sleep, always aware in the back of my mind as I work. There are a few survivors. My Damaged Dark One mostly directs me to kill them, whether they're ours or not.

"They're too far gone," he says quietly, glancing up at the smoking epicenter on this godforsaken field that we're stuck on. "We don't have any Healers with us, and to Transport them… they wouldn't survive the jump."

I nod and do as he directs, happy for his humanity to direct what is right in this situation.

I'm almost ready to cast my Gift out and tear everyone to shreds, when finally I feel him nearby. The relief from the girl and the echo of the others realizing we've found him is palpable, all of them checking in with the girl while I work.

I go to my knees beside him, looking over the damage and fighting the urge to wipe out every living thing in a ten mile radius.

He's a mess.

A bullet wound in his shoulder, burns up his neck and face. He looks as though he was attempting to get away from the Trigger as it went off. From the position that he's fallen in, he had gotten pretty close, but there's a tree that has fallen over the lower half of his body, knocked down in the explosion, that's pinning him to the ground. The fact that his chest is still steadily moving up and down as he breathes is a miracle of its own.

"Jesus fucking Christ," the Damaged Dark One mutters as he kneels beside him, taking his pulse at his neck.

There's no real need to try and administer any medical assistance. I am his Bonded, and I will fix this. They've only ever seen me heal them in bursts of uncontrolled power being drawn out of me and into them during times of crisis, but this is different. I was hunting for him to find him and heal him. I know exactly what I need to do.

I lean forward and press our foreheads together, conscious that he must be in pain, especially when he grunts under the slightest amount of pressure against his damaged skin. The few souls that I had consumed on the way to finding him have given me more than enough of an extra kick, but I'm careful about how I slowly funnel that energy into him. I need to be careful to make sure that it is the least painful way that I can, not wanting to cause any more harm to one of my own. My skin begins to glow and then, starting from our connection at our foreheads and working its way down, his skin begins to glow with that same light.

Slowly, *gently*, we watch as the bullet hole knits back together. The bullet slowly pops out as my power pushes the foreign object out from where it doesn't belong. The red and damaged skin gradually begins to change and heal, the swelling going down and the skin slowly healing from the red shiny burns until it is once again the perfect tanned skin of my Bonded.

Two shadow creatures approach and work together to remove the tree trunk from my Bonded's legs, and he groans at the pain of it. I send a savage look to my Damaged Dark One, and he murmurs back,

"They're doing it as gently as they can, but his legs are crushed."

I let my eyes slip shut, and then I gently funnel that same healing light down to the shattered bones. Slowly, carefully, gently, we knit him back together, me and the souls that I have consumed for this exact purpose, making sure that I can protect and love my Bonded exactly how they deserve and give them everything they could ever possibly require.

I heal everything that I can find on his body. I heal the blisters on his feet from tracking through the mud when they'd first arrived. I heal the splinters in his hands. I heal anything that might give him any sort of trouble, until he is returned back to the perfectly healthy Bonded that I had said goodbye to as they had left.

When the healing light slowly dissipates away from the two of us, I stay exactly where I am until his eyes blink open. He doesn't look startled to see me in control of the girl's body, and he doesn't look concerned at having me so close to him either. One of his hands comes up to cup my cheek, and he murmurs, "How did I know that you would come looking for me when all of this blew up."

I press forward the few inches it takes to kiss him gently, and then I murmur back, "You're mine. There's no getting away from me, so stop trying to find death by throwing yourself into these dangerous situations just to try and get away from the monster I am."

He frowns and pulls me in for another kiss. "You're not a fucking monster. Even when you're in Oli's head, thinking all of that crazy shit about being a god and ripping people's hearts out, that still doesn't make you a monster."

"No, it makes her right," says my Damaged Dark One, and my Bonded glances over at him.

He doesn't look outright shocked that my Damage Dark One has said that, but he does give him a once over. "Is the Trigger dead yet? This wasn't Unser. This was the other one."

My Damaged Dark One curses under his breath and stands up, pressing the earpiece and muttering, "The bomb is still live. Do you hear me, brother? *The bomb is still live.*"

I glance back to my Bonded One. He props himself up on his elbows slowly, beginning to move as though he's checking that his newly healed muscles will actually hold up underneath his weight.

"Unser can go off once or twice a day, at most. If it were him, we would be safe by now, because he wouldn't be able to go off again. It's the other one. Unless you have taken out someone very strong and not told us, then there is still a bomb somewhere in the Wastelands."

I shake my head, glancing back at my Damaged Dark One as he scans the area around us more critically now that he knows the danger he is looking for. "I haven't consumed anyone of that level of strength, but I would like to."

They both share a look, and then my Bonded One stands up to stretch out. He holds out a hand to help me to my feet. I enjoy the sight of all of my hard work. The smooth skin of his face, healed again, is a glorious sight.

"Glorious, huh?" he says with a grin.

I agree, and then I remember, shoving at his chest a little bit and enjoying that I caught him by surprise, and he rocks on his heels. "Don't you ever ignore me again, Bonded. If I call for you, you *will* answer me."

He smirks and does a full body check of his weapons. More than half of them are missing, and I can tell that he is disheartened by how little ammunition he has left.

The Damaged Dark One hands him a few clips that he secures to his chest immediately. "It's hard to answer someone when you are unconscious, my Bonded, but I will take note and try to do better in the future."

It sounds as though he's teasing, but I nod because whether he's joking or not, that is the correct answer.

Once we know that he is steady on his feet, we move

together towards where we had left the rest of our Bonded Group. The terrain is the only thing that stops us from moving as efficiently as I would like to. The shadow creatures move around us, more thorough in their search of the bodies now that we're looking for some sign of the Trigger.

He's nowhere to be seen.

We find my Shifter Bonded first, standing with a gun in his hands at the edge of the explosion site, the last line of defense before the Resistance could come to find us.

He looks at my Bonded with such relief, clapping him on the back as he joins us. "North and Atlas have gone to escort the last of the TacTeam back to the Transporter zone. Kieran came back for us, but he's been working overtime getting people out. He's the strongest transporter we have."

He directs the last bit at me and I nod because this is information I already know.

We make it a few hundred feet before the next explosion hits.

It comes from further in the Wastelands, right where North and Atlas are escorting TacTeam personnel, and it's clear to us all that they've come across the Trigger.

While I don't feel pain immediately from that, a minute later there's a searing heat in my stomach that says that North has been injured over there. This time, I cannot stop myself from going straight in that direction. My Shifter Bonded looks at me and nods, pulling his shirt over his head. "I'll shift and get to them faster. They'll need backup."

His bones and skin morph and twist into a giant feline predator.

I shake my head at him. "Think bigger."

My Bonded looks at me with a raised eyebrow. "He's a leopard, the biggest Shifter I've ever seen. What could be bigger than that?"

I reach into his chest, bond to his bond, smaller and quieter than I am, but still there and alive and more than anyone elses. As I lean down and look into the perfect, honey-colored eyes of the leopard, I say, "Think. Bigger."

His eyes shift to white, and my other Bonded both falter to a stop to watch as his body writhes and grows, bigger and bigger and bigger, the fur slowly slipping away to reveal shiny black scales. An extra set of limbs burst from his back, shifting and morphing until, slowly, he has a set of wings protruding from his shoulder blades. Bigger, bigger, *bigger*, until suddenly, we're staring at a monstrously large creature. One who has never walked the earth before now.

"What the actual fuck?" my Bonded sputters, and my Damage Bonded nods slowly.

"A fucking *dragon*."

J BREE

GABE

A fucking dragon.

Never in my wildest dreams did I think I would have the ability to shift into a fucking dragon. When I'd first realized I could shift into any living creature, hell, I thought I'd won the jackpot. The possibilities seemed endless, and I'd spent months researching different animals to figure out just which ones were the most useful to me. I loved the wolf and the panther the most, the predator nature of them both had called to me.

Wearing the skin of a dragon is different.

I can't describe it any other way. When I shift into any other predator, it's as though my own mind is blended with the beast. I still have control, but my own thoughts and cravings and impulses become wild.

The dragon is something else.

The dragon wants things for himself. The dragon doesn't want to listen to my directions and impulses. The dragon wants to burn them all alive.

How dare they touch what is mine?

I have no choice but to sit in the back of my own mind as the dragon takes over, taking off in flight and letting out a medieval roar as it rises up and up into the sky, until I can barely see my Bonded and the others I'd just left behind. I've shifted into birds before, flown around Draven just for fun, but this is something else entirely.

We're hunting.

We're going to burn them all.

From up here, I can see the magnitude of the situation we're in. The Wastelands are at least five times the size that North had first told us they were, and I can see the amount of Resistance who are still alive and moving towards my Bonded. They're clearly being used by Davies and the higher-level Resistance leaders as a test of our powers and what we're willing to do, but none of that matters to me or the dragon.

Burn them all.

The panic I felt at hearing that voice in my head disappears, because it's right. My Bonded Group is being targeted, there is evil heading in my Bonded's direction with every intention of hurting her and taking her away from me and using her to hurt others.

All of them must burn.

I have no clue whether or not it's even possible for me to breathe fire. I didn't know I could shift into a fucking dragon an hour ago, but I surrender completely to the dragon. I stop fighting it for control. I stop trying to dampen the thirst in me for death and destruction, and I let the ultimate predator take full control.

It lets out a roar, a booming sound that cracks out across the sky like a physical thing, and then it dives down, the huge jaws opening as we get closer to the men on the ground. It roars again, but this time, acid pours out of my throat. The acid bursts into flames the moment it hits its target, the sounds of screams tearing into the air as I wipe the first group out in one pass.

The dragon is satisfied with the kill, but we want more. All of them, they have to burn.

I soar back up into the sky, circling as I watch the destruction I've wrought, and when I'm sure that they're all dead, I move on to the next group.

One by one, I destroy them all.

One by one, I keep my Bonded safe and secure and by my side.

I find North and Atlas at the Transporter zone, both of them staring up at the sky. Although I can't see them clearly from this distance, I can imagine pretty easily what they're both feeling. The look of shock and disbelief on Gryphon's face is still echoing in my mind. I'll have a great time ribbing him for it later.

Nox had taken it surprisingly well, but I'm not surprised. He has a *living being* inside of him and creatures that have their own personalities that can appear out of his body at any given time.

I'm sure it's hard to be surprised by things when that's your reality.

I swoop down towards the last group of Resistance who are working their way to the Transporter zone. There's an uneasy feeling inside of me about the one whose skin is glowing, a sure sign of a Trigger. I'd seen Unser go off once before in a controlled environment, and he'd done the same thing.

I don't want him dead though. I mean, I *do* want him dead, but not right now.

The dragon is mindful of my directions to aim the acid that comes alight carefully, and before the Trigger has a chance to go off, I swoop down, the flames touching my scales but not harming me in any way, and grab the Trigger in my talons.

It's risky, but I get one of the long claws around his neck, cutting off his airway until he passes out. I can feel that he's moving and struggling, but it feels as though I have a kitten in the palms of my hands, absolutely useless in his fight.

My wings beat quickly against the wind again, taking me back up into the sky, and I let them stretch out more fully as I fly. The cargo in my claws is too important to sit around with. It only takes a matter of minutes before I spot my Bonded again.

They're all moving as quickly as they can towards the rest of the Bonded Group, but on foot, it is still a long way to travel.

I swoop down low and watch as they all look up at me, my Bonded reaching up one hand as though she is beckoning to me, and I circle slowly until I can land once again. I keep one talon off of the ground as it clutches our enemy.

I want to shift straight back, but the Dragon will not let me take hold again. Instead, it moves the Trigger around until it can deposit the man at our Bonded's feet, snuffling out air through the giant nostrils as it takes in a deep breath of the small slip of a woman that belongs to us.

This pattern of thinking is a little bit terrifying.

Gryphon steps forward and nods. "He sounds like the bonds do. Like Oli and the Dravens' bonds. The dragon sounds the same."

Well, *fuck*.

"Did you bring me a gift? I love it. Delicious. Strong

souls are my favorite," my bonded says, and the grin on her face makes it very clear she's not lying.

She lifts both hands over the unconscious body and her eyes take on that otherworldly glow that they do as she works. There's nothing that you can see as she tears the soul out other than the body jerking a little as it releases its last breath, but the euphoria on her face as she takes in that level of strength is a beautiful thing.

My dragon wants to go hunting.

It wants to find more of these beings to bring to her feet as a sacrifice to our love, to bring her everything that she could ever want.

Everything.

Gryphon groans under his breath. "Jesus fucking Christ. If there's going to be more of these for us to have to contain, we're *fucked.*"

J BREE

OLJ

I don't remember much of our trip back to the Sanctuary, only my bond happily munching on a soul inside of me. I know that we're now a hell of a lot safer having dealt with the Trigger. The only bad thing, freaking terrible thing, is that we were unable to recover Unser, the main reason that they'd gone out in the first place.

Everyone feels defeated.

We arrive home right as the sun is coming back up, and I feel that bone weary exhaustion that comes from a lot of hard work all night and after a particularly long day. I need a long soak in the bath and at least three days of sleep. My bond munching means that though I'm sure I'm hungry, there's no way I can stomach food right now.

Bleh.

When we had gotten to North and Atlas, North had some burns on him but was mostly unscathed, thanks to Atlas' Gift covering him. My bond had healed him easily and poured some of the extra power from the souls into him for good measure.

I can tell that Atlas is angry at himself for not being able to fully cover him yet, especially after seeing Gabe's fully formed dragon. Those two have become the sort of friends who are also just a little too competitive with one another. I squeezed his hand, using our mind connection to remind him that North is *alive* and that's what counts.

North had refused to have an immediate debrief, very unusual for him, and had instead found an ATV to load me into to get us back to the house together so I didn't have to walk the distance. I have to admit, I love the man a little more for that move.

Every inch of my legs is sore, a stark reminder of just how many miles I'd covered last night.

I'm tired and a little cranky by the time we pull into the half-finished garage, ready to get clean and pass the fuck out. North swings me up into his arms the moment I step out of the vehicle.

"Aren't you also tired as hell right now? I can totally manage the walk to my room, no need to kill yourself getting me there."

He hitches my ass a little higher and mutters, "You healed me, and now I feel as though I've just woken up from the best rest of my life. Let me take care of you, Bonded."

He does.

He gets me inside and into a bathtub in under three minutes, the water set at the perfect steaming temperature as the bubbles slowly rise around me. I groan as I lean back and immerse myself in it. My arms and legs are pretty gross, caked in mud and God knows what else, but North doesn't care about that as he strips and climbs in.

He slides into the bath behind me, his body taking up more than half of the space, and the water gets dangerously close to overflowing. I'm waiting for him to fuss about it, ever the perfectionist, but he's only focused on one thing, and that is me.

It's a special sort of joy to be the complete focus of North Draven and his obsessive ways.

Nothing about the bath has healed my body or rejuvenated me, but at the feel of North's skin sliding against my own, my bond perks up in my chest. It abandons the rest of the soul, leaving it tucked safely somewhere around my kidneys until it's ready to come back to it, and it floods me until I let it take over again, surrendering to the waves of desire it has. We share the space in my head, though the bond takes over our movements and what we're saying. I can still feel and experience everything alongside it.

"What do you need, Bonded?" North says, and my bond turns in his arms to face him.

He doesn't look worried about the void eyes anymore, no longer concerned about the ramifications of whether or not I'm going to be hurt by what my bond does with him. Honestly, I want the same things as it does.

I want more.

North nods, whether he heard my bond or maybe this is just a part of his knowing ways, but he cups the side of my neck with one one his hands and draws me into a possessive kiss. The type of kiss that leaves no doubt who I belong to, who is kissing me, or who is going to worship me like the god I am.

His free hand slips down my body slowly, stroking and pinching as he teases out the gasps and moans he wants to hear. By the time he reaches my pussy ,I'm rocking against him, desperate for more friction.

His cock is hard and heavy between my legs, the perfect length for some friction as I slide my pussy against it. His hand reaches around to cup my ass and direct my hips, moving me exactly the way he wants me to.

The water splashes over the edge of the tub as I make waves, my bond not caring in the slightest as it kisses North again. It bites his lip until it draws blood, impatient and demanding.

Give me what I want.

"Then tell me what you want, Bonded. You have to say it."

I can feel the bond's frustration, the way it pulls at his bond to get its own way, but North holds strong and refuses to give in to its demanding ways.

"Tell me, Bonded."

I want to whine at the dark, commanding tone he's using. I want to submit to him and find myself being fucked roughly against a hard surface somewhere in the house while he shows us both exactly how in control he really is.

My bond likes the power play.

It leans forward until my lips are brushing against his and whispers, "Fuck me now, or I'll go find one of my other Bonded to have me instead."

He picks me up, standing in one smooth motion and stepping out of the water without any concern that we're dripping everywhere. I wrap my legs around him so that I'm secure in his arms, and the move gets my pussy much closer to being impaled by his hot, throbbing cock.

His eyes flicker under the harsh bathroom lighting, blue, then black, then back to blue again as his bond struggles to the surface. I want to tell him to let it out, to let our bonds be together because they've spent an eternity being together and then torn apart, but my bond won't let me speak.

It's too busy trying to slide down onto North's dick.

He yanks a towel off of the rack and then walks us into the bedroom, the motion of his legs moving drops me down just a little more until the tip of his dick slips into my pussy, more of a tease than a relief.

He throws the towel down on the bed, holding me with one arm and a tendril of shadows as I balance there on the tip of his dick, and then lays me out like a buffet he's planning on gorging himself stupid on, his hands spreading my thighs wide open. He fists himself roughly, sliding his hand up and down his length as he stares down at my wet pussy that's on display for him.

I might fucking die if he doesn't give it to me now.

There's a murmur of voices further down the hallway, the others all in the kitchen eating together and giving North and I space, but I don't want it. My bond doesn't want it.

I want them all.

It's as easy as breathing to beckon them all into my room, to send out a siren's call that their Bonded needs something from them all. They all move together as one to find me.

Well.

Not all of them.

One of them resists me, but I'm too focused on the others right now to put up too much of a fight about it. Someday, he'll come to me when I need him. Someday, he won't resist my call.

Atlas is the first one through the door, his pupils blown wide at my call, and he looks surprised to find North and I still naked here together, but his feet don't stop as he comes to me. Gryphon is next and he's not at all surprised, he merely steps into the bathroom and I hear the water turn on as he moves to clean himself up before joining us.

Gabe stops the moment he sees us, and North finally pushes his hips forward, filling me up to the brim and drawing out a low moan from the deepest depths of my chest.

I reach a hand out to Atlas and murmur, my voice stained by the bond, "More. I need more."

Gabe hesitates on the threshold, one foot still out of the door, and looks at North. "That's not Oli speaking."

He replies even as he fucks me in long strokes, never faltering. "It's not asking for something that Oli wouldn't want herself. We're Bonded to both of them. If you don't want this, then just leave. No one will judge you for going. Especially if you're concerned about Oli."

I want to chip in, to tell him that I'm here and I want this. I want everything that my bond is asking for and maybe even more, but my bond has other plans for my mouth, reaching out to grab at Atlas' pants and help him get them off. He reaches over his head to get his shirt off as well and, being the invincible and untouchable Gifted that he is, there's barely any sign of the work that we'd done tonight on him.

There's no damage, only another cock straining towards me as my mouth waters for him. I want the weight of him against my tongue, the grunts and groans that tell me I'm giving him all of the pleasure that my Bonded deserves. And I want to know that he's eager to give it all back to me.

He looks down at me with hooded eyes, enjoying the sight of my tongue sticking out towards him, lapping against his tip and slowly inching my way down until he's pushing at the very back of my throat. He reaches out to pinch my nipple, groaning when I moan around him, and when North's shadow tendrils start to play with my clit, we're both done for.

I moan and whimper like a harlot, and Atlas really starts fucking my throat, his hips moving faster than North's as he practically rides my face to get off. I want it so badly. I want to swallow down every drop that he wants to give me. When he pinches my nipple one last time, I come with a gasp, my throat opening up a little more, and he slides in all the way to his public bone as he comes as well, grunting as he shoots straight down my throat.

I swallow every last drop, my bond satisfied for as long as it takes for me to come down from the orgasm. When Atlas pulls away from me to grip my chin with one hand, I smile at him, a little dazed in my afterglow.

He grins back and swoops down to kiss me, chasing the taste of himself on my lips, and I let him lap it up, possessive even in a room full of my other Bonded.

He steps away and into the bathroom, leaving me to focus once again on North, who is still staring down at me like I'm the greatest sight he's ever seen. I arch my back a little as I reach out to him, giggling as his tendrils wrap around my arms and pull me back down.

"Give me what I want, Bonded," I whisper, and he leans down to cover me more fully with his body, kissing me with his own dark possession as he takes me higher and higher, his shadows tugging my legs wider and flicking over my clit in the perfect rhythm. Right as he comes, slamming inside of me one last time, I see his eyes shift into the voids, just as my eyes slip shut at my own orgasm.

It's a little sign that his bond gives me so that I know that it wants me just as desperately as North does.

I know it's a struggle for North to get up and leave me, to let my other Bonded be with me the way I need them to, and I make my bond press another kiss to his lips before I reach out to Gabe.

My Shifter is still looking a little unsure about this.

I don't think he's struggling with the group sex or being put on display the way he will be the moment he steps up to me. Nope, it's definitely my void eyes and the way my bond keeps demanding things from them all.

He's loyal to me, to the very end.

I want to take full control of myself again, to reassure him and coax him into giving me what I need, but my bond won't let go.

It's waited long enough for them all.

Instead, it reaches into him and calls out to the shifter inside of him, his bond that takes the form of a dragon, and beckons it out to play with us. His eyes begin to burn brighter, shifting to the amber-gold of the dragon, and I inch my way further back onto the bed as he stalks forward to me.

The dragon kisses me like it wants to eat me, none of the playful fun of the man left behind, and it's not hard to convince the dragon to fuck me.

No, it rears up and away from me for only as long as it takes to tear away the pants and shirt, revealing the body still streaked in blood and dirt.

I want it all.

It fucks me hard and deep, like it wants to tear me in half. I take it all, my body begging for more as my fingernails dig into his back hard enough to draw blood. When his mouth drops down to my shoulder, his teeth pressing into the soft flesh there, I think for a second that he is actually going to take a chunk out of me But as he bites down hard enough to bruise, my pussy clenches around him as I come for him, riding the line between pleasure and pain until I think I might shatter.

He roars as he comes, never breaking the fierce pace his hips have set as he takes his own pleasure in our Bonding. His eyes shift back to the human when he's done, blinking as though he's come into the light and isn't quite sure what's going on.

I smile up at him like he's the sun, letting him curl around me for another, far more sedate, kiss.

When Gabe finally steps away, his cheeks still flush as his eyes drift down to my pussy, cum leaking out of me already from where they've been pumping me full. I can feel it slipping out, and the memory of North's bond scooping it up and shoving it back inside of me pops back into my mind.

If I were capable of blushing right now, I would be.

Gryphon finally comes to me, dropping the towel away and climbing onto my body, ready to fuck me exactly how I need him to. There's still an ache inside of me for him, an ache I know won't ever be fulfilled until I've had them all. The use of my Gift has left me feeling empty and needy, desperate for them to help me balance back out.

Gryphon doesn't waste time, slamming into my abused

pussy in one stroke and setting a fierce pace as he pounds into me.

I writhe underneath him, my nipples so sensitive that even the lightest brush of them against his chest has me wanting to weep, and he leans down to whisper in my ear. "Is this greedy Bonded pussy going to come for me too, Bonded? Are you going to squeeze me so tight as you gush for me, stain these sheets with your cum like the perfect Bonded you are?"

I nod, wrapping my arms around his neck and pulling him in closer as I do exactly as his filthy mouth asks, shaking and sobbing as I come apart.

He murmurs to me, "That's my good girl," as he comes too, his hips stuttering a little as he rides out his own waves of pleasure.

I could die happy.

I think I just might.

Gryphon rolls off of me, pulling me with him so that I can curl up on his chest, but North is quick to see just how close to passing out I really am and bullies me into cleaning up first.

Gabe is already snoring on the far side of the bed when I get back in there, his shifting draining the energy out of him. Atlas looks as though he's minutes away from doing the same. I climb up into the middle and let him pull me into his arms so that we can fall asleep wrapped up in each other.

It's been too long.

North comes to bed last, leaving the bathroom light on as he makes his way over, and once we're all settled down, I let myself finally get some rest.

The girl goes off to sleep in our mind, sated and exhausted from the long day and night we've had, but there's an itch under my skin that hasn't yet been cured.

I need more.

I slip out of the bed, careful not to disturb any of my sleeping Bonded, and step out of the bedroom covered only in one of the robes that my Dark Bonded One had brought here for me, the lapels of it barely covering my chest. I find my Damaged Bonded One stepping out of his room with a book in his hands.

We stare at each other across the hallway.

I want him.

I want his bond to come to my room and fuck me on my bed, to leave his scent behind for me, to use me for his own pleasure until we can fix some of the cracks in the man's soul. I want all of them, every last piece of each of my Bonded.

His eyes flash black as he looks back at me, but the man fights it, furious that we're trying to be together now, in this way.

His eyes flash back to blue as he turns away, walking

down the hallway, and then I hear the front door slam shut behind him as he leaves us entirely.

I understand why.

I do not like it.

My Dark Bonded One steps out of the bedroom, sliding an arm around my waist as he kisses my neck. "Leave him, Bonded. You don't need to chase after someone who can't love you the way you deserve when you have four other Bonded desperate to fulfill your every need."

I wake up the next morning with more than just the happy feeling of the afterglow. Every muscle on my body is tight, and there's an ache in my thighs from clenching so hard, over and over and over again, that I think I'm going to need to start stretching out after sex if it's going to be like that all of the time now.

There's quiet snores and deep breathing around me as the four of my Bonded who slept here last night all stay asleep, worn out enough that even Gryphon, my early riser, is still here.

I wiggle carefully down to the end of the bed until I can get out without disturbing anyone, tiptoeing quietly to the bathroom and taking a quick shower. North had cleaned me up before tucking me in, but there's still a feeling of relief at washing away the sweat and residue of our night.

I throw on a pair of old leggings and one of Nox's jumpers, the only one of my Bonded that had opted out of the sexfest. I'm not surprised at all, but there's still an ache in my chest for him. I know it's my bond being pissy at not getting to have him as well.

The jumper is one that he had left behind for me, part of his agreement with North to supply me clothing on the regular if he was not willing to spend more time with me, and even though that should be an insult, I still find it just a little bit endearing. The more time I spend around him, the more that I see through the things that he is doing. Being cruel and unkind to someone for no reason is one thing, but lashing out because of trauma is another, and my own experiences mean that I have a lot more understanding of that than most people. My bond still feels particularly bloodthirsty about whatever the nightmare had been, and I know that there's a good chance that someday we'll be hunting down some monster for my Bonded.

My bond and I both agree on that fully.

No one harms my Bonded and lives.

I creep out of the bathroom and grab my phone to light the way out to the kitchen. My stomach is both empty and settled now that my bond has finished her meal of the Trigger's soul, and I'm desperate for some food. I know that North will be furious at me for not waking him up so that he can be the one to feed me. His quirk about keeping his Bonded fed and happy was a delightful surprise to me.

Except they're all sleeping so soundly that I can't bear to wake them up, so he'll have to just get over it.

I get out to the kitchen and rummage around in the fridge until I find everything I need to make an omelet and toast. I make the toast first so I can eat it while I'm frying up the omelet, and I'm so hungry that I seriously consider making a fruit salad afterwards as well.

I'm so hyper fixated on eating that it takes me a second to notice that I'm no longer alone in the kitchen.

I curse my bond for not warning me anymore about my Bonded, and then curse it all over again when I realize that Nox is now sitting at the dining table, a coffee in one hand and one of the ancient texts from the Hail Mary in the other.

So much for a peaceful breakfast.

He doesn't say a word to me, just sits there and studies the words in front of him, the ones that speak of the lives that we've lived together many times before.

"Do you… want some breakfast?" I say hesitantly, and he shakes his head.

"The coffee is enough."

I know that he's spoken civilly and even *nicely* to my bond before, but I think it is the first time he's ever uttered words in my direction that weren't laced with acid.

I don't push my luck though. I flip the omelet out onto a plate and dig into it with a fork, still standing at the kitchen counter because there is no way that I'm leaving the kitchen without the fruit salad.

I might even make some more toast.

"Have you found anything in there? I've read the texts that you've sent through so far, and I couldn't spot anything that you hadn't already highlighted." I cringe as soon as the words are out of my mouth, waiting for the rebuttal from him.

But he just takes a sip from his coffee cup and places it back down on the table, the picture of a sedate professor. "Your bond isn't crazy for calling itself a god. They *are* gods. I don't know where they've come from, or anything else about them, but the things that they can do and their genetics… they are higher beings than are found anywhere else."

Jesus Christ.

I shove some more of the eggs into my mouth, chewing happily on the mixture as I try to think of something not irritating to reply back to him.

He speaks before I have to. "Unser is being tortured. They've taken him back to Davies. Adella called last night, I spoke to her. She can feel what they're doing to him, even though he is trying to block her out."

My stomach drops and I pick up the plate of eggs to walk over to sit at the dining room table with him. I don't think I'm going to be able to stomach much more food if this is the way the conversation is going to go, and I try not to mourn the fruit salad too much.

"Is there any indication of which camp they took him to? We're gonna have to go after him."

Nox flips the page, his eyes still roaming over the words as he reads and holds a conversation at the same time. That's a skill that I desperately wish that I had. I imagine studying would be so much easier that way.

"North called in all of the TacTeams before we came back last night. There's going to be a meeting with all of the leaders today, and we'll decide if we will go, and who will be in the teams."

I nod and shift the eggs around a little on my plate, my stomach is still growling with hunger, but it's hard to eat while thinking about such things. "We have to go though, right? We're the best ones for the job. Especially if Gabe's going to be turning into a dragon at the drop of a hat. We need to use that to our advantage."

Shadow creatures, a dragon, complete mind control, super strength that can also shield and keep the rest of us alive, and my bond.

We're a complete arsenal at this point.

I sigh dramatically. "I know North doesn't want us all

going at once—"

Nox shakes his head at me, interrupting me. "He doesn't like the Sanctuary left unguarded. We'll leave enough of the TacTeams here. Then, if anything happens, we can come straight back, as long as Kieran's with us as well. We can't leave Unser with the Resistance any more than we could leave one of our own Bonded Group behind."

My cheeks flush a little as he acknowledges our Bonded Group to me for the first time.

I desperately want to push it and ask him a million questions, pry into him and his reasoning for everything that he's ever done, but I also know that he is speaking civilly to me right now only because we're discussing work. While he might not trust me on any sort of a personal level, I might just have proved myself to him on an operative level, something that I am incredibly proud of myself for.

I didn't want any of them giving me leeway just because I was their Bonded. I want to be able to carry my own weight and be an asset to them, to be more than just the ability to kill people on a whim, and maybe, just maybe, I've done that.

"Unser will get through the torture."

His eyes finally flick up to mine, the deep blue of them so much like North's, but so much colder than his brother's have ever been.

I swallow in case I've pissed him off, but continue

anyway. "It's hard to survive that sort of thing but, if he's strong enough to be in a TacTeam and to lead people, strong enough to be a Trigger and cope with taking that amount of lives at a time, then he's strong enough to push through the pain and get through it. If I can do it, then anyone can."

Nox picks up his coffee cup again and drains the last of the black liquid inside of it. "I don't think there are many fourteen-year-olds who could survive that amount of pain. Some of that was your bond, yes, but it also took a certain amount of strength in you."

Holy shit.

Was that a compliment?

That felt like a compliment.

I nod and duck my head, shoving a spoonful of omelet in my mouth before I say something stupid to him, and he gets back to the book in front of him, flipping the pages slowly.

I hear my bedroom door click open and hurried feet heading in our direction until I find a half naked North Draven standing there with wild eyes as he stares us both down as though he's caught us doing something illicit.

I chew on my mouthful slowly before swallowing, waiting for him to say something, but he is too busy glaring at his brother.

What has he said to you? he sends directly through our mind link, and I get weirdly defensive about it.

Nothing. We've been talking about Unser. Nothing bad. I can be trusted with my own Bonded.

His eyes finally flick my way and he eases up a little bit. *It's not about whether or not I trust you, Bonded. I was making sure that he was behaving himself.*

He's not a child, and I've told you before that I can handle him. Either you trust me with that, or you don't.

Nox flips another page and then says out loud but quietly, "He doesn't trust me. He won't ever trust me with you, and that's not something to blame him for, Bonded."

Gryphon, North, and Nox all leave to go to the meeting with the TacTeams soon after my surprising conversation with Nox. I decide that maybe I can stomach some more food and make myself the fruit salad, carrying the bowl back to bed to climb up between Atlas and Gabe.

Neither of them have any motivation to get up, and I don't particularly blame them.

I have a couple of text messages from Sage and Sawyer, both of them having heard about Gabe shifting into a dragon and desperate for more details. I giggle over Sage's commentary and try not to get jealous or defensive at how much Sawyer wants to know about the anatomy of said dragon.

I will never get comfortable with how many details about my Bondeds' dicks that boy wants.

By the time I finish up with my food, Atlas has gotten up and showered, dragging his feet in a way that I haven't seen out of him before, and he makes himself a protein shake before coming back to bed. He picks up a pillow from where it's fallen onto the carpet and throws it at Gabe to get him moving.

He snarks at him, "If we're going to get dragged out again to go look for Unser, you're going to regret not showering."

Gabe groans as though he's being murdered. "Shifting and flying and breathing fire is hard, okay? You wouldn't understand."

I scoff a little under my breath, but when he looks at me all betrayed, I school my features into something much more contrite. "Of course, it sounds very difficult. So much more difficult than tearing souls out of people left, right, and center."

Gabe glares at me and then pulls himself up, groaning as his back cracks in about four different places. "Why?! Why can't we just stay in bed for one day? This is fucking stupid."

I bite my lip and stop myself from pointing out that we're going on a rescue mission because someone's literally being tortured right now. I'm only glad that it's just the three of us here, because Atlas is good about keeping his mouth shut as well and just letting Gabe have a gripe about it.

He heads off to the bathroom, and I hum happily under my breath at the chunks of watermelon in my bowl, picking out the nicest-looking bits first.

"They're going to be in the meeting for at least a couple of hours first while they hammer things out. There'll be a lot of conversations about whether or not it's smart to have the Draven Bond Group all go together," Atlas murmurs as we listen to the shower turn on.

I nod and offer him a piece of fruit, happy when his hand comes up to cup mine, drawing it to his lips as he bites into the piece of apple directly from my fingers. It's a very flirty move, but there are aches and pains in me that say that sex is definitely *not* on the table for us this morning. Damn, is it tempting though.

I attempt to shift my mind back to the matter at hand. "I want to go and see Aro. I can't shake the feeling that she's important, and the fact that Nox felt it too makes me curious about her."

Atlas nods slowly. "The fact that he felt it definitely says something, Bonded. We can head straight down there once Gabe's done in the shower, if you like."

I nod and finish up the last few pieces, offering him more, but he shakes his head, draining the last of his protein shake.

I get up with a little bit of wincing at the aches and pains, and Atlas' eyebrows shoot up his forehead. "Do you need to see a healer?"

My cheeks flush scarlet. "There is no fucking way I am going to Felix about *this*."

Atlas frowns at me for a second before he smirks. "So... not injuries from last night then? Or not the part of last night that I'm thinking of anyway."

I grab a pillow and shove it at his face, ignoring his laughing at my expense, and I rummage around to find a pair of shoes to pull on.

I head straight to the Tac Training center, bypassing as much of the town as possible. Word has definitely gotten out about Gabe's dragon, beyond just our friends, and the few people we do pass all stare at him with a mixture of awe and distrust that makes me feel a little... violent.

He wraps an arm around my shoulders and presses a kiss onto the top of my head, a total heartthrob move, as though this is all perfectly acceptable behavior from the Gifted in our community.

I'm not feeling so kind about it.

Atlas swipes a card at the Tac Training center to get us in, and Gabe greets a few of the TacTeam personnel in there as we head straight down to the cells. No one attempts to stop us or even escort us down there, and when I raise an eyebrow at Gabe in the elevator over it, he smirks.

"I have clearance. You and Atlas don't yet, but I do."

It makes sense, what with him going on missions with Gryphon in the past, but that doesn't make me any less insulted.

I sputter out, "I listen in on North's council meetings. I'm fucking great at keeping secrets! What do I have to do to get clearance? Clearly sleeping my way to the top isn't working!"

Gabe cackles and kisses the top of my head again, still acting a little too calm and loved up right now for the situation we're in. Am I the only one with the sense of doom and dread hanging over my head?

Maybe.

Atlas is calm as well, totally at ease as the elevator doors open and we find ourselves walking into the cellblock again. It's much nicer this time around without all of our friends in here, much less guilt and terror running through my veins at least, and not hearing my bestie sniffling is nice.

The girl is sitting on the bed at the end, a book in her hands and a pile of snacks sitting there with her as she happily munches away on some corn chips. She glances up as we walk in, putting the book aside and staring at both of my Bonded distrustfully.

I know that look.

My stomach turns at the sight of it, and I step forward to draw her attention back to me, to attempt to look like I'm non-threatening and that both of my Bonded are absolutely not going to... hurt her.

I fucking hate those Resistance camps.

"Hey! Sorry it took us so long to come see you. I see they've brought you food. Is there anything else you need? My Bonded, Gryphon, he'll be down sometime soon to question you. If you pass all of that, we can figure out how to get you... out into the Sanctuary. We can find you a house or something. Lots of female roommates."

I slip that bit in at the end as a reassurance, but she's shaking her head anyway. "I need to speak to someone who is in charge. Like, now. I need to speak to someone about my brother."

Right.

A brother.

"Sure, I can speed things up a bit. Your brother, what's his name and why is it so important you speak to someone about him?"

"Lahn. He's... all I have left now. He's back at the camps and... I need to know if there's a chance you'll be going there. He's only five."

Oh, God.

I could handle just about anything but them having a freaking kid as a hostage. My bond stirs in my chest, taking an interest in the conversation, which is a little weird.

Find the boy.

Ahh, excuse me? *Since when do you care about rescue missions for kids?*

We protect them all, not just the Bonded. Even the mouthy one.

The mouthy one? Sawyer? I poke at my bond a little more, but it just goes back to sleep, still processing the aftereffects of the soul.

Sawyer.

Holy shit.

I grab my phone, ignoring the looks my flailing about is getting from everyone else, and I send a message to Sawyer, and then Gray, for good measure. "No one judge me here if I'm wrong. My bond... said something and I want to test it out."

Gabe nods along happily and questions Aro a little more while we wait, mostly about her brother and where she'd come from originally before the Resistance had grabbed her. She's actually twenty-one, older than she looks, and she'd lost her parents when they'd all been grabbed.

The elevator doors open again and Gray steps out, frowning over at us all like this is particularly weird. I mean, it *definitely* is, but we're on borrowed time right now.

Any minute that meeting is going to end, and we'll be

off to find Unser and bring him home.

I'm not at all subtle. "Gray! Hey! Come over here for a second. I have someone I want you to meet. This is Aro, she was kidnapped by the Resistance, and her brother is being held captive. Any chance that you're... feeling something? About her?"

Gray stares at me like I'm freaking insane, but when he looks at the tiny girl in front of us, he looks so unsure of how the world is still spinning on its axis that I know that my hunch was absolutely correct.

Aro is Gray and Sawyer's Bond.

Their Central Bond.

Ten minutes later, Sawyer finally arrives, only to also stare at Aro like he's about to propose, glancing over at Gray like he's trying not to publicly pinch himself. They both fumble a little over their words with her, and I will absolutely be giving Sawyer shit about it later.

Aro is hesitant, again thanks to the Resistance camps, I'm sure, but it's plain to see that she's having that same pull to them as they're feeling to her.

It makes me wonder how the Resistance ever lied about Bonded Groups and what they make you feel deep in your chest the moment you lay eyes on them. But I guess if you've never felt it before, how do you explain it to someone?

I glance over at Gabe and murmur, "Strongest Bond

Groups, right? We take care of family, that's what makes us different from them. We can't leave a five-year-old behind. Not now, not ever."

NOX

The meeting with the returned TacTeams is less frustrating than sitting in on one of North's council meetings, but it's still an exercise in restraint.

All of the men here deserve my respect.

Every last one of them has chosen a career that involves them risking their lives over and over and over again for members of our community, not all of whom respect and appreciate that. The problem is that all of them think guns first, brains second, which is the entire reason that North, Gryphon, and Vivian are so high up within leadership roles.

They think like tacticians instead of soldier grunts.

"Just go in, set your Bonded off, get her to do whatever it is that she does, sucking souls out of all the men like some sort of—"

"I'm going to stop you right there before you say something that has a shadow creature ripping your head off your fucking shoulders," Vivian says, cutting in.

Marcus stares over at him before flicking his eyes in North and Gryphon's direction, finally sensing that he might have worded things a little bit on the disrespectful side. I'm sure I look nothing but bored, but he still gulps when his eyes land on me as well.

There's nothing quite as terrifying to anyone who has met North and I before than staring down a Draven. Something useful our father had left behind was a legacy of rabid shadow creature beasts, and while that isn't the case, the perception of them being that way sure does come in handy at such meetings.

"Our Bonded Group is newly completed. That means that our powers have not had the chance to settle yet. It was only at the Wasteland yesterday that Gabriel Ardern discovered what his power growth had done for him. It is still a risk to have my Bonded go."

Marcus rubs a hand over his chin and speaks again, reckless as ever. "I have heard rumors that he shifted into something else. I didn't think the boy could give us any more surprises."

The boy.

I reach forward to grab the bottle of water in front of

me, wishing desperately that it was whiskey to take away some of the sharp edges inside of me. There will always be a level of superiority in this man when it comes to anyone that he deems below him, and that grates on my last nerve.

While his Gift isn't at any of our levels, he has years of experience on the TacTeams, and it means that he is quick to lord that over anyone around him. The fact that Gryphon hasn't called him out and thrown his own weight around is a minor miracle, *especially* considering that Marcus is his uncle.

Family reunions are never pleasant.

North clenches his teeth together for a second, visibly calming himself down before speaking again. "I'm not saying we aren't going to go in. I'm merely saying that we need to have a plan before we do."

Vivian rubs a hand over his short, cropped hair, looking a decade older than he had a week ago. Watching his Bonded feel the pain of Unser's torture had clearly been an ordeal for him overnight, and he looks as though he is ready to fight alongside us. I know that North would prefer for him to stay behind at the Sanctuary and keep an eye on things here, but I get the feeling that this time he is going to insist.

One does not merely say *no* to Vivian Wentley.

"It's not that difficult. There's only one Transporter spot to get into any of the Wastelands—"

"The camps are different though," North cuts Marcus off. "They don't have Shields on them in the same way and, though I'm sure there is added security wherever they're keeping Unser, they're not going to waste that many people while they are on the offensive elsewhere."

"Do we know which camp they're keeping him at?"

North's eyes flick over to me at my question and he gives a sharp nod, but it is Vivian who answers for me. "It's the one they kept your Bonded at. That's the one that Davies prefers, where he keeps all of his 'special' and 'important' guests."

My bond does not like that. I can feel the shadows in the room and darkening, and I take a moment to check in with the bond and tell it to calm down.

I've become an expert at reasoning with it.

We will go to this camp, we will set the creatures on everyone. We will torture the man responsible for these things. We will do everything that it wants to do, but we cannot start that here.

There's an audible gulp out of one of the men further down the table, and North and Gryphon both stare at me for a second, subtly enough that no one else can tell that they're both checking in with me in a very shocked manner.

Surprise, my bond is obsessed with the girl and the god living inside her.

Things move quickly as soon as it's been agreed on that our Bond Group will go with a smaller TacTeam to retrieve Unser and take out the Resistance camp. We had lost more than thirty operatives at the Wastelands, a number far too large for how limited we already are, and the decision was made to send in a smaller but more powerful group.

As I suspected, Vivian refuses to be left behind this time.

None of us want to leave Marcus in charge but in the end, it comes down to splitting up the Bonded Group to stop that from happening, or having everyone together.

I know which I would rather, and I have a suspicious feeling that when we arrive at the camp and come face to face with Silas Davies, the man who was responsible for kidnapping and torturing Fallows, it will not be North or I facing him.

Our bonds will insist on taking over.

With such a small group going, it's easy to coordinate and move out. I change into my Tac gear at North's offices before everybody else arrives and triple check that all of my weapons are clean, strapped in correctly, and fully loaded. Then I run through all of my shadow creatures, checking in with each of them and making sure that there aren't any signs of danger or weariness in them. It's a necessity, especially since I've only had a few hours of sleep on the couch at North's office between arriving home and heading off to the TacTeam meeting.

I can't shut my eyes without seeing Fallows' bond standing there in that robe and beckoning me towards her. She looked and smelled as though she had been thoroughly fucked by every last one of her Bonded, all of them except me. It had meant that it was a nightmare trying to go to sleep with my bond warring inside of me to go back to her.

I couldn't though.

I couldn't go back to her any more than I could have stepped into that room.

Azrael lets me know that they are on their way back to me, Fallows bouncing happily between Gabe and Bassinger as she celebrates her victory of being right about the girl we'd brought back from the Wastelands.

Another Bonded Group put back together by her intuition.

She's smarter than I could ever give her credit for. Even without her bond, she pieces things together that other people just can't see.

She is the perfect match for each of her Bonded. For North's desires to love and protect and covet, but also needing someone who can go toe to toe with him. For Gryphon's desires to have someone who can keep up with him and stand with him against anything that might threaten the Bonded Group. For Gabe's need to have companionship and a friend as much as a lover. And for whatever it is that Bassinger requires, she clearly fits that mold perfectly.

There's also a part of me that thinks that maybe if things had gone a little differently in my life, she might have been perfect for me too. Except, the hole in my chest that she should have fit perfectly into was destroyed, blown apart, taken to with a pair of scissors until there was no one on this earth that could take up the space there. Though I've blamed her over and over and over again, because of that stupid word, *Bonded,* I already know who's to blame for it, and it's not the little white-haired girl.

So I'll leave her my shadow creature, the only part of me that can treat her the way she deserves, and I'll stay as far away from her and the Bonded Group as I can. As far away from the people who understand me, love me, and accept me as I possibly can, because I know that my brother's patience is wearing thin, even if he refuses to admit it.

Gryphon arrives first, always eager to get ready and be on the road as swiftly as possible. He ducks into the locker room to grab his gear and then comes back out to stand with me.

As he pulls his uniform off, he glances over his shoulder at me. "Did you hear about the girl we brought back? She's Sawyer and Gray's Central Bond. You guys did good, finding her and spotting what she was."

I shrug and run a hand through my hair. "Your Bonded found her, my bond just backed her up. For all I knew, she could have held information that we needed and that was it."

Gryphon nods slowly and glances out the door quickly to make sure that we're alone and he has time to say this. "She has a brother at those camps. We need to find him and bring him back as well."

I do not like complications, and I definitely don't want to be bringing more potential risks back to the Sanctuary.

Before I can protest, Gryphon mumbles, "He's five, Nox. What do you think they're doing to a five-year-old in that place?"

I don't want to think about what they're doing to a five-year-old. I don't want to admit that I *know* what they're probably doing to a five-year-old, and I know for sure that I will not be returning today without that five-year-old.

There is a burst of noise as Oli, Gabe, and Atlas arrive together, all three of them bouncing off of each other's energies as they stumble into the room.

Gabe grins and waves at both of us before ducking into the changing room with the lockers in it that are set aside purely for us, and Fallows looks slightly awkward as she glances between us with a smile and scurries after him.

Bassinger stares me down like he's thinking about how exactly he'd cover up my murder, but that's run of the mill for him, so I don't give him any of the reaction that I'm sure he's so desperately after.

When the locker room door has been closed and locked behind them, I turn back to Gryphon. "So the targets are Unser and the boy... Do we know if there are any other children there? Any other priorities?"

Gryphon turns back to me as he pulls the bulletproof vest on. He has a different type this time that covers a little more of his shoulders, and I'm sure it comes from knowing just how badly he'd panicked his Bonded, badly enough that she'd found Kieran and dragged everyone to the Wastelands after us.

It's a good thing she did too, because he would be dead otherwise, maybe North and I as well.

"Aro didn't know if there were any more children. They were separated as soon as they were taken to the camps, but he'd been brought in a few times to where they were processing her and used as a threat to get her to comply. The only reason they got her into the Wastelands to begin with was by using him."

I know I don't need to question it, but I do anyway. "And you're sure she's not lying about anything? There was no whiff of deception on her? Being a Central Bond doesn't mean that she's not a sympathizer being sent to feed us false information."

Gryphon looks around again, which piques my interest. "I didn't just use my lie detection on her. I looked into her memories. I filtered through every little part of her life for the last six months, and there is no way that she is lying. I don't think even Davies himself could have planted that sort of complexity into her brain."

I nod, and then a slow smirk stretches over my lips. "But you can."

He looks up at me in shock and I shrug. "I know you think that I haven't noticed any of your boundary-pushing with how far your Gift has grown. But I've definitely noticed some things."

He bites his cheek as though trying to smother the grin, but he can't. "I am going to tear Silas Davies apart, starting with the innermost part of his mind, and then I'll work my way to his limbs."

It sounds like a perfect plan, except...

I reach up a hand and he watches as my palm slowly turns black, spreading down to my fingertips and staining my skin until it slowly creeps up my neck.

"Only if you get to him first."

OLI

North is very clear about what the mission for today is going to entail and what my role is going to be.

I'm once again going to stay with Atlas and Gabe while North, Nox, and Gryphon push forward to deal with as much of the camp as possible. My job initially is to take out all of the Shields and anyone there that my bond senses might be a big player, although North is very clear about what I am to do with Silas Davies if he is actually there.

Absolutely *nothing*.

"Shouldn't I see if my bond is strong enough to take him out? Should I at least test it? I mean, I don't think I'm going to be, but isn't it worth it to try?"

North shakes his head emphatically as he does up the

last of the buckles on his vest. He'd been the last person to arrive at his offices to get changed and ready, even after all of the other TacTeams and Vivian himself.

He'd been stopped by one of the other council members on his way over and had gotten into a heated argument. I already vehemently dislike the other council members, and the savage look on North's face as he'd arrived just makes me feel that little bit more bloodthirsty.

"Nox and I will set our shadow creatures on him. From what we have heard from Atlas, it's our best chance. If he gets too close to us, he can use his Neuro abilities, and that's just not worth the risk. Trust me here, Bonded."

I pull a face and glance over to where the rest of our Bonded Group is standing together. Nox looks strangely calm, the same way he has for the last few days, and it makes me nervous. Part of me wants to believe that it is because we've Bonded now and, though it's coming along slowly, he's finding some sort of healing peace from that.

But I can't shake the bad feeling.

North glances over his shoulder to follow my line of sight and says, "Don't worry about him, Bonded. He's not going to bother you."

I shake my head. "He's not bothering me, North. I know you don't believe me, but I'm worried about him."

He grimaces back to me and presses a hand against the side of my neck, using his thumb to tip my chin back so that I'm looking right at him. "Unfortunately, knowing Nox and being someone he is close to, even unwillingly, means that you're going to worry about him constantly. I'm sorry about that, and I know that if he were capable, he would be sorry about that too."

I reach up on my tippy toes to press my lips against his, ignoring the fact that there are so many people around us and that he usually tries to keep our PDA to a minimum. "Don't get caught up in an explosion this time. I'm still half tempted to insist that Atlas go with you guys. Gabe's dragon and I will be more than fine on our own."

North smirks at my teasing and tugs on the buckles of his vest, the slightly larger one that they have all changed over to after Gryphon's gunshot wound. "You took care of the Trigger, remember? There's nothing for me to be concerned about anymore."

I still have a sinking feeling in my gut that that isn't all true.

Gryphon approaches us, his heavy-soled boots loud on the tiled floor, and he slips an arm around my waist, another public show of affection that they're not usually so open about.

"We need to move out and get this over with."

North nods and his eyes flick back to mine. "We're going in three sets. We'll all go in first and then wait for the next two sets to come through before you cast out your

Gift and get to work. Kieran is going to stay close by to you as well, and there are two other Transporters who will be tasked with bringing home Aro's brother and anyone else we might need to evacuate."

I swallow roughly. "If there are any other children, we'll bring them back here, right? Adults can be taken to the processing area, but the kids can come here… right?"

North grimaces and nods, looking away from me. "We always try to keep the kids with us. There's too many chances of things going wrong otherwise."

My bond coils in my stomach as if she doesn't like the sound of that, and I understand completely. The thought of anything going *wrong* with a child makes me both want to ask a lot of questions but also never have them answered.

"Oleander, just do your best not to let your bond completely take over, unless it's an emergency. We need to go about this in a very careful way, and your bond can sometimes complicate things."

I scoff. "You mean like when it told Gabe that he needed to *think bigger* and he pulled the dragon out of his ass?"

He chuckles under his breath, pressing one last kiss to my cheeks.

"That sounds about right," Gryphon mumbles, and we all move back over to our Bonded Group and the Transporter waiting there with them.

I frown at the man, the one who had been so resistant to taking me to the lake house where Riley and Giovanna were holed up when Kieran had been locked up and out of commission.

Gryphon dismisses him to another group straight away. "Black is around here somewhere. He's just saying goodbye to his own Bonded."

I duck my head and nod. That makes sense.

I'd had the chance to call Sage and tell her about what had happened in the Wastelands, and I think that the reality of how dangerous these missions really are had hit us both pretty hard. I wouldn't want to leave my Bonded without a proper goodbye either.

North looks at Gabe and Atlas and gives them both a firm nod. "Don't go anywhere without her. Use whatever weapons or Gifts that you need to to get her out if things go wrong."

Both of them stare back at him solemnly, Atlas replying with an equally firm, "Of course."

Then North turns to look at Nox and gives him the same nod. "Unser, the boy, and taking out Silas Davies."

Nox nods again, still strangely quiet, and then Kieran approaches us.

North looks around at each of us one more time. "We're ready to head out."

Deep breath.

Here we go.

We leave the Sanctuary as the sun is setting behind us, but when we arrive with that same little *pop* sound that echoes in my nightmares, it's already completely dark wherever we are.

Night has fallen.

I'm thankful when Gryphon takes my sickness away for me, but even when he's done, I take a few slow and even breaths to stop the panic from rising in my chest and triggering my bond.

Everything about this place is familiar.

It's not like going home, that feeling of returning to something so intrinsic to you, but instead like tumbling into the same nightmare you've had for years. The one that never leaves you behind even though you've grown out of it, and the moment it starts again, you find yourself covered in a cold sweat.

Horrifying.

The air still smells the same. The warm sticky night still clings to my skin the same way, and it takes every inch of control I have taught myself over the years to keep myself calm. Thank God they hadn't brought Kyrie back here all those months ago, because I would have been useless to Kieran in this place.

There's that same small *pop* noise next to us as the second set of TacTeam arrives, and I know my time to calm myself is coming to an end. Another deep breath and then another one. Atlas' hand slips into mine, and I have to give myself a second before I stare up at him.

He reaches out to my mind carefully, making sure that no one else can hear him. *Are you okay? If you can't do this, we can go home right now. No one needs to know why.*

I shake my head rather than answering him back, knowing that right now I probably don't have the control to only speak to him and not have the others overhear it. I don't need them all questioning my ability to do this right now.

I *can* get my head together.

The third and final *pop* sounds as the last set of people arrive, and I wait until North meets my eyes and nods at me before I cast my Gift out carefully.

Everything I do here tonight has to be careful.

I see Gryphon's eyes shift to white as he starts to assess the surroundings as well, and I let my own eyes slip shut so that I'm not distracted as I map the area out.

I find Unser very quickly, knowing exactly where to look for him. Finding the children is a little harder because they've moved where the prisoners are kept since I was held here but, sure enough, I find fifteen children amongst another larger group of adults, all of them in cages to the east of the camp.

There's a dining hall that is filled with people eating

their dinner and a small tent filled with Shields. I don't immediately take them out though, wanting to get a full picture of what we're dealing with before I start the killing.

There's every chance that Davies will notice through security cameras or something similar, and I want to know if he's here and where he is, first. It's dangerous though, because I know that he will feel my bond reaching out. Sure enough, in the last tent that I explore, his torture tent that I am so intimately acquainted with, I find Silas Davies and his bonded, Lydia.

Fuck.

I open my eyes and meet North's stare, opening my mind up to the rest of them to send them as much of the mapping as I can. I'm still not very good at this, but I feel Gryphon's Gift flow into me as he helps illuminate it for everyone else to see.

Fuck, Atlas thinks down the mind link ,and everyone turns to look at him.

Lydia is here.

I share a look with him, knowing exactly what that means, but Gryphon and North both frown at us.

Who is Lydia? Gabe asks.

Atlas replies, *Lydia is Silas' Bonded, and she is not someone that we want to be dealing with tonight. If we had the option, I would say we should all go home, but getting Unser back is non-negotiable.*

Gryphon scowls at us. *Lydia has a low-level power.*

Atlas shakes his head. *No, she doesn't. Lydia refuses to use her power in areas that would get her found out by everyone, but she definitely has power, and it is not the sort that we want to be dealing with.*

North glances at Gryphon and then snaps down the mind control, *What is her power? We're running out of time before we're spotted here, Bassinger.*

I answer for him, *compulsion. I don't know what else it's called, only that she's a Neuro and her specialty is compulsion. If she gets close enough to you, she can make you do anything. I have watched her force men and women into killing themselves or their own family members merely at her suggestion. Anything that she wants from you, she's going to get you to do. She's not strong enough for my bond. Not unless Davies gives her a power boost by sharing his strength with her. I've seen him do it before and there's every chance he'll do it again, especially if you actually get close enough to take him out.*

North glances around at all of us and then he says to Atlas, *how far away is her range? Is that the same as Davies? This doesn't change our plan all that much. Just that there will be two moving targets we need to stay away from but send the shadow creatures in to deal with.*

Atlas shrugs. *I don't know exactly but I would say at least the same distance as Davies.*

North nods intensely back to me. *Do it bonded. Take out the shields and anyone else that is a threat that you can. We're moving in.*

It starts off perfectly fine.

I take out the Shields and four other Gifted who are stronger than most others that are here, everyone else is at a level that is completely fine for the TacTeams to deal with themselves. Once we feel the barriers of the Shields fall, North gives the signal for everyone to move in and they disappear into the dark of the night towards the camp.

My skin crawls and I desperately want to go after them.

But I can't. I stay behind with Gabe and Atlas, my own Gift still cast out and monitoring what's going on, keeping a close eye on where Davies is. I keep my mind connection open to my Bonded but I'm careful to keep myself out of their heads. I don't want to be the distraction that gets any of them killed.

Atlas keeps his hand in mine, squeezing tightly as he watches what's going on through my eyes. Gabe, on the other hand, is busy watching around us. His eyes have shifted to the amber color of the dragon and I'm incredibly intrigued to know what he can see using them but it'll have to wait until later.

There's gunshots and screaming around us and I feel *terrified* of what is going on because of the children in the camp. The trauma of what I experienced here is too fresh in my head right now, the box I keep it in is smashed open and dragged to the surface. Every cut into my skin, every bone that was broken and knit back together without pain relief, every questioning session that went on for hours with thousands of cuts and burns.

The screams from the shower blocks.

I don't take a proper deep breath until the Transporters arrive at the prisoner holding tents and start getting them out. Kieran himself takes the kids, all fifteen in one go, and even Atlas lets out a deep sigh when he sees them disappear from the Gifted mapping in my mind.

Gryphon is using his own Neuro abilities to get North and Nox within a perimeter of Davies and it's only when they get within a few hundred feet of the tent that Davies finally calls in for backup. I'd guessed that he would either disappear immediately or come out to face them head on.

The pause is confusing.

A Transporter appears in the tent, and my bond comes alive inside of me.

Stop, I send out to them and thankfully, all three of them listen to me.

I can't fully map out where all of the shadow creatures are, only knowing that they're out and hunting but they move too quickly for me to be sure that they are arriving at the tents. They're not going to be able to be able to kill Davies. Not now.

The problem is that the transporter isn't just there to take Davies and Lydia to safety.

He's brought in someone else, someone I don't know.

I can't *feel* anything about the person.

It's as though there is someone standing with them who is as unknowing as my own void eyes, nothingness, blankness, even when my Gift comes across a Shield I can tell what they are but this person is *nothing*.

My entire body fills with dread.

Come back. Don't go to the tent, you need to come back, I say and there's a moment of quiet but North replies, *this is our best chance. We'll send the shadow creatures in first and if they can't do anything, then we will leave.*

I feel as Kieran gets to Unser, evacuating him with only the help of Vivian as they assess the mass amount of damage that has been done to him by Davies.

The moment he disappears I plead with North again, *we have everything that we need. We don't have to kill Davies now, we can do it later. Come back!*

There's quiet down the mind connection and then pain.

All I can feel is pain, all that I can think of is pain, everyone and everything is pain.

It takes over every fiber of my being and even though

it's not mine, all I can see and think and feel is his pain, pain, *pain*.

I can't even pinpoint what injuries any of them have. There's nothing in the air to say that there's been an explosion or a fire or even gunshots, there's only pain.

I'm taken to my knees, my bond flickering in my chest as it tries to take over, but my mind is flooding with everything that is going wrong right now and Gabe lets out a shout as he goes to his knees next to me desperate to find out what is wrong with me.

Atlas uses his Gift to transfer his strength to me but this is not an injury that is happening to me and so it does nothing to help. This is not something that I need to be shielded from, this is three of my Bonded being tortured in ways that I do not understand but my bond does.

My bond always knows.

It takes over my body, ripping through my mind and flooding me as my eyes shift, the souls of everyone around us that is our enemy being torn from their bodies all at once as my bond takes from them and funnels everything it can to my Bonded, giving them that strength from us to survive whatever it is that's happening to them.

I'm relieved for a split second.

Except Nox refuses the power.

I want to scream inside of my head where I'm stuck but he refuses the power, putting up a wall inside his own mind as he moves it on to his brother, giving everything he has to North to make sure that he survives whatever is happening right now to them.

I fight my bond for control of my limbs, scrambling to my feet and running, running towards them, running towards the pain and the horror of what is happening to them, diving over the bodies of the men I just killed, barely seeing through the darkness of the night as I run towards them.

I run towards them as I feel the life slowly draining out of Nox as he gives everything to North. My bond still funnels energy through to Gryphon and North as fast as it can, desperately beating at the wall that Nox has put up between us. But it's no use. He won't accept it.

Whatever is happening, he wants his brother to make it out alive.

Take it! Take the power, I'm coming but just take it! I scream at the wall in his mind but it's no use, I feel his soul slipping away.

His voice echoes in my head, the last thing I hear as chaos reigns around me and the only time he's ever spoken to me through our connection.

I'll see you in the next life, Bonded. Maybe I can love you right there.

I feel the thud of his lifeless body hit the ground, the echo in my bones as our connection severs and the puppy running at my heels disappears in a gush of warm wind as though he really was nothing but smoke.

My Bonded is dead.

SIGN UP FOR MY NEWSLETTER TO HEAR
ABOUT UPCOMING RELEASES

Also by J Bree

The Bonds That Tie Series

Broken Bonds

Savage Bonds

Blood Bonds

Forced Bonds

Tragic Bonds

Unbroken Bonds

The Mortal Fates Series

Novellas

The Scepter

The Sword

The Helm

The Trilogy

The Crown of Oaths and Curses

The Throne of Blood and Honor

The Mounts Bay Saga

The Butcher Duet
The Butcher of the Bay: Part I
The Butcher of the Bay: Part II

Hannaford Prep
Just Drop Out: Hannaford Prep Year One
Make Your Move: Hannaford Prep Year Two
Play the Game: Hannaford Prep Year Three
To the End: Hannaford Prep Year Four
Make My Move: Alternate POV of Year Two

The Queen Crow Trilogy
All Hail
The Ruthless
Queen Crow

The Unseen MC
Angel Unseen

About J Bree

J Bree is a dreamer, writer, mother, and cat-wrangler. The order of priorities changes daily.

She lives on the coast of Western Australia in a city where it rains too much. She spends her days dreaming about all of her book boyfriends, listening to her partner moan about how the lawns are looking, and being a snack bitch to her three kids.

Visit her website at http://www.jbreeauthor.com to sign up for the newsletter or find her on social media through the links below.

f　　**◎**　　**♪**

Printed in Great Britain
by Amazon

43040627R00280